What People are saying about
End of the Long White Line

"**Raymond Edwards is a true storyteller.** What I especially love about this story is the [trucking] lingo and the speech patterns giving us a real-life feel for the characters."

~Stephanie Bain,
writer, producer, and
Creative Director for
Little Roni Publishers
Alabama | Tennessee

"[*End of the Long White Line*] includes subjects like love, trucking, ranching and country music. Come on. It's for everybody! **And America, keep trucking!**"

~Cylk Cozart,
Actor, filmmaker,
*Conspiracy Theory, White Men Can't
Jump,* & *16 Blocks* with Bruce Willis,
Mos Def & David Morse.

"[The novel] *End of the Long White Line* is an Americana faith-based trucking story, soon to be in film production …**It's gonna be an awesome movie!**"

~ Christopher Hensel,
Producer, Director,
Jeb Stuart Productions

"**5-Huge-Stars. I couldn't put it down.** … now, every time I see a semi, I think about Bobby Ray & Jalynn!"

~ Ellen C. Maze,
Amazon #1 Best-selling author of
Rabbit: Chasing Beth Rider

End
of the
Long White Line

*The Story of a Lifelong Trucker and the Struggles,
Decisions, and Events He Encountered Along the Way*

BY RAYMOND EDWARDS
WITH JAIMIE EDWARDS

END OF THE LONG WHITE LINE
By Raymond Edwards
Copyright ©2024 by Raymond Edwards
All rights reserved.

ISBN: 9798336002775
V09122024SC
Also available in eBook

Front Cover: Josh Rowan, RowanConceptz on Facebook.com
Creative Writing Assistance: Jaimie Edwards
Publishing Assistant: www.TheAuthorsMentor.com
American Veteran Logo © www.vecteezy.com/Veteran Logo Vectors
Disabled American Veteran Logo, public domain
Truckers Against Trafficking Logo © Truckersagainasttrafficking.org

PUBLISHED IN THE UNITED STATES OF AMERICA

I dedicate this book foremost to My Lord and Savior Jesus Christ.

Thank you, Lord, for saving my soul and giving me eternal life. Lord, without you my life would be headed down a long rough road that went nowhere.

And to my wife, Jaimie L. Blake Edwards

Thank you, honey, for supporting me!

Being there for me throughout my Army career and my truck driving endeavors means the world to me.

Please know that you were, and will always be, on my mind and in my heart, every mile I have traveled and each mile I will travel in days to come. I love you!

NOTE TO THE READER: For your enjoyment and edification, various lists of trucker lingo, city nicknames, and trucker 10-codes are listed in the back of this book. Enjoy!

AUTHOR'S DISCLOSURE: *End of the Long White Line* is what we consider to be a Christian Faith book. Brief entries of the content may be found explicit. Please keep an open mind and remember this is a fictional book that is based on real life issues that numerous walks of life face each and every day. We all fall short. It is through this character's experiences of trial and triumph that his faith is tested. In many instances, it is when the most faithful individuals hit rock bottom and are pulled from the rubble that they find God and the warmth of inner peace he instills in us.

This is a story that needs to be shared far and wide. Ask yourself, am I perfect? What would you do differently than Bobby Ray? While following his journey, it is promised you will find something inside this beautiful story that is relatable, whether you are of the Christian faith or not.

ABOUT THE NOVEL: This book is nothing short of action-packed. Once you begin reading, you will become immersed in this phenomenal fictional take that follows the life of Bobby Ray James. You will find yourself anxious to see what happens next with every turn of the page. While the story's baseline is that of an over the road truck driver, it is so much more. You will flash back to Bobby Ray's early days of growing up on his family ranch, playing college football, being drafted to Vietnam and then battling PTSD, searching for his purpose, and finally, finding the love of his life. As he struggles with faith, sobriety, and infidelity, will his marriage survive? Find out with every mile as he searches for answers toward the End of the Long White Line.

TABLE OF CONTENTS

1

THE AWAKENING

Evanston, Wyoming (Bear River)

BRIGHT SUNLIGHT SHINED THROUGH THE DUST COVERED window of my Evanston, Wyoming, farmhouse awakening me from my most recent drunken slumber. *What day is it?* I wandered in a momentary fog, mustering the energy to stumble my way into the bathroom. I relieved myself for ages as *"How much did I drink?"* rolled past my fuzzy memory. As I made my way out, I took a doubletake.

An undeniable swath of dried blood stained the mirror frame, and the reflected face was one I will never forget. Staring back at me in the shattered glass stood a bearded man with bloodshot eyes, a pronounced bruise on the left eye, busted lips swollen with traces of dried blood that matted the hair that hung down in strings.

Then the pain associated with whatever had transpired hours before. My entire body ached and as I sought anyplace uninjured, the most painful thing of all came to mind—I had broken my promise. Once again, the promise I made to my wife, Jalynn, years ago had been broken and my eyes filled with tears.

I made my way through the house, floors littered with broken glass, doors busted and walls sporting fist holes throughout. With a parched throat, I managed to call for Jalynn in a faint and quivering voice.

No reply.

I called again, this time a little louder, and again no answer. I continued to call her name, and each time, nothing.

In the kitchen, I grabbed the water ladle and got me a drink of water to quench my thirst and ease my parched throat. I then opened the fridge, seeking something to feed Cash, who had followed me whimpering as I stumbled through the wreckage left by my drunken rage. Pushing it closed, I noticed a note that sent chills down my spine.

Singled out and held in place by a family photo magnet next to the calendar dated two days prior. With tears streaming down my face, I mumbled the note out loud.

> *Bobby Ray,*
>
> *I have gone to Jamestown to stay with Amberleigh. I refuse to stay with a man that reminds me of the past and this time, I do not recognize. Your drunken rage is too much for me to bear all over again. You seem to have forgotten the most important promise you had made not only to me but to God on the day you were saved, declaring that you would never drink again. And yet after all these years of sobriety, you threw it all away, including us! I will undoubtedly always love you, but I will not stick around with your destructive behavior and broken promises. Please get help and look to God for his forgiveness. As for me, I am not sure I can forgive you, but I will pray for you.*
>
> *Always,*
Jalynn
>
> *And by the way, you need to call and apologize to Ray and Gracie.*

I noticed she didn't say I love you at the end. More pain than I could ever imagine filled my heart and I eased myself to the floor, sobbing in disappointment and regret.

After some time of grieving over what I had done, I was left with the harsh reality that I had screwed up, yet again, and needed to reclaim my life from this devilish behavior. I dried my eyes and gave Cash a quick rub on the head to let him know that I was alright, since he had been by my side the entire time of my mental breakdown. I rummaged through the mess and found my phone; time to try Jalynn. She did not answer my multiple calls, so I searched until I found Amberleigh's number. Reluctantly she answered.

"Amberleigh, can I…?" I began, but she hung up. I called back. "Amberleigh, can you please put Jalynn on the…"

Click.

I knew they were mad, and Jalynn was upset and heartbroken. I thought to myself, *how in the hell am I supposed to say I am sorry if they won't even take my damn call?* In the end, I decided to let it be for now. I'd concentrate on taking care of myself.

First, I made coffee. After finishing a cup and working on my second, I decided to heed Jalynn's suggestion and call Ray and Gracie.

Ray answered the phone.

"Son, I am sorry!" I said.

"I got noth'n to say to ya, Pops," he answered.

"Son, I am sorry!" I repeated.

Amidst the silence, I could tell he was trying to hand the phone to Gracie. I could hear them whispering. He said, "here you talk to 'em." And she said, He is yer daddy, and you need to talk to him. I know ya are upset at 'em, but he needs you right now. This is between yuns two."

Ray said a little louder, "I don't wanna to talk to 'em, Gracie!"

"Please, talk to 'em. If not fer you, do it fer me. I love ya both and I hate to see ya both this way. He really needs a friend and be'n his son, ya know ya are his best friend and probably the only one he's got right now."

Between their conversation, I took the chance to say again, "Look, son, I'm sorry fer what I have done. Can you please talk to me? I called to apologize and see if you could help me figure this mess out and to find out what I have done. I know ya don't want to talk to me, and ya are upset, and I don't blame ya one bit, but ya are all I have. Please talk to me, son! I need ya!"

Seemingly, my pleading worked, because he responded by saying, "Pops, ya made a fool of yerself and completely embarrassed Gracie and me, as everone knows ya are my dad. I kept apologiz'n to everone. Luckly, they were all very forgive'n and generally concerned about ya as well. But ya left a bad impression of yerself.

"I guess I should start from the begin'n, from the time ya came in fer some lunch, and, against my wishes, ya ordered a beer, which led to two and then three and more to follow. Ya got to where I could not even control ya. When ya got irate, I loaded ya up in yer truck and took ya home. Gracie followed to give me a ride back. By the time we got ya in the house, Mama started in on ya and how ya had broken your promise, and she was very disappointed in yer behavior. The more she lit into ya the more ya got irate, until you jumped back in yer truck and took off, sling'n gravel as ya flew out of the drive. I grabbed Gracie, and we took off after ya. But ya had outrun us, so we went back to the bar to get thangs in order. After a few minutes, ya came bust'n in the door demand'n a drink. The bartender came and got me from the back and let me know what shape ya were in, stumble'n around and shout'n, make'n lewd comments, and letting the booze take control over ya. It had been a long time since I seen ya that way. I was embarrassed at the sight of ya. Ya were totally disrespect'n Mama as if ya had forgotten ya were even married to 'er. Hellfar, Pops, ya were flirt'n with every woman in the bar; even Gracie!

"So, to calm yer outbursts, I gave ya one and said this is yer last and then ya gotta go. However, that just added fuel to the far, and ya continued with no signs of stop'n. I had never stood up to ya befer, but I couldn't take it anymore. I tried to stop ya and ya told me to mind my own business, Hell, Pops, ya even took a swing at me, and I knew at that point ya had crossed the line, and some'n had to be done, so I called the sheriff."

Hearing all the stuff that I had done I just hung my head in shame and disappointment in myself and said, "I'm sorry, son."

He continued, "Ever'one was pretty forgiving of yer actions because we were all neighbors, and they knew it was the booze cause'n ya to act in such a manner. That was until ya flirted with the wrong woman who had a husband that wasn't going to take any of yer shit. He stood up and told ya to go home and put his huge hands on yer chest. Ya just shoved it away. You must have felt like a giant to even attempt to face that burly cowboy. And with ya take'n a swing at 'em, it started. Ya were no match for 'em. It was like ya were a punch'n bag, because with every punch of his huge fists, ya would just keep come'n back for more, until he landed the final blow across yer jaw and knocked yer lights out. I am sure yer still feel'n that one! That's when Gracie and me, with the help of that big feller, loaded ya into the bed of yer truck and took ya home."

4

I listened on because he did not pause for even a second.

"As we were bring'n ya into the house, Mama was sob'n and yell'n at ya. As ya were begin'n to come to yerself, she was pack'n her bag to head to Amberleigh's house. That's when ya jumped up and started yell'n back and demand'n 'er to stop. When she didn't, ya started get'n angry and threw an ashtray at 'er. It flew by 'er head and broke against the wall. She started cry'n more and told ya go to hell and ya started punch'n the walls, and ya even kicked in a door, break'n it from its hinges. Ya even threw a lamp out the window, shatter'n 'em both to pieces. Ya stormed into the bedroom, and that's when we took our chance to escape yer wrath and leave."

I hung my head held low and tears were streaming down my face. I repeated, "I am so sorry, son."

He stopped for a moment and his tone changed. "Pops, ya really broke Mama's heart this time. I love ya, but I hate what ya have done to Mama, not to mention the fact that ya disrespected Gracie and me in our bar. Ya really messed thangs up for yerself this time. I ain't sure how ya are gonna make up fer this one."

He took a breath, and I stayed quiet. Then he said that he had talked to my youngest daughter, Faith.

"Ya should call 'er, Pops. She talked to Mama and is really upset. Ya know how she gets, carry'n 'er heart on 'er sleeve and all."

I said, "I've been so depressed lately not be'n able to make ends meet; it's put some strain on our marriage. I just don't know what came o'er me. I can't believe I acted like such an ass. Son, I am so sorry fer all of this, fer hurting ya yung'ns, and especially, yer mama. How can I make it up to ya?"

Ray took a deep breath and said, Ain't sure ya can this time."

I said, "I'm sorry."

He said, "Quit say'n yer sorry and just fix it the best ya can. I'm done talk'n, I gotta get to work."

I said okay and I love ya, and he hung up.

Sitting in my recliner with a fresh cup and a smoke, I pondered the conversation I just had with Ray. I understood why Jalynn left and why everyone was upset, and I don't blame them for being angry. I'm so ashamed of myself. Here I am a grown man and acting so stupid. I know my mama and daddy raised me better than this. If they were here, I

5

would get a good talking to from Mama and probably a house shoe swatting me anywhere she could land a good hit so I would know she meant business. Pops would tear me a new ass. In my mind, I could feel Pop's stare and his huge boot across my backside. But the tears rolled as I could hear Mama's sweet voice saying, *"Son, you know better than this."*

I sat there in silence for what seemed an eternity, searching deep for the will to move. Cash came over and gave me a nudge as if to say, *you got this and* let me know that he loves me. Or maybe he just needed to go outside. Both assumptions were right either way.

We went outside and as I was looking over the damage I had done to my truck and Cash doing his thing, I was gathering my words for what I was going to say to Faith, her being the baby of the three and so tenderhearted. Nervously, I dialed her number and awaited the answer, hoping her husband Landon, who we had nicknamed Hoss, would be the one to answer. No such luck.

Faith answered in a quivering, crying voice, and I could just see in my mind her big tear-filled eyes. In that very instance of her saying *hello, Daddy,* my eyes filled with tears as well.

I forced out, "Hey, baby girl." I wanted to reach through the phone and give her a big hug to comfort her as a father does when their kids are hurting.

With her weeping voice and trying not to break down she asked, "Daddy, what have ya done to make Mama mad and leave ya?"

I took a shot from the hip, hoping she wouldn't enquire anymore and simply said, "Don't ya worry, baby girl. Daddy just made a bad mistake, and I am gonna to make thangs right. I promise I will work on fix'n it here in just a bit, as soon as I get myself together. I love ya. Just hang in there fer yer daddy."

That seemed to calm her for the moment. However, to my surprise, I could hear her sister Lacey, the oldest of the three in the background with her loud voice demanding her sister to give her the phone. They tussled over the phone and Faith yelled at Lacey to hold on a minute.

"I ain't through a talk'n to my daddy!"

This made the situation worse which made Lacey even madder with Faiths multiple rejections, them both being as bullheaded as their daddy. Hoss was in the background trying to referee, but I knew my daughters, and he was getting nowhere. Faith fought her sister off long enough to say, "Ray told us everthang ya have gone and done and how ya were behave'n. Why did ya do this to Mama? To us? To yer grandkids, even? I thought ya loved us!"

I said, "I don't know, baby, I was just in a bad way, and I am so sorry."

"I don't 'er want my kids or the rest of yer grandkids, for that matter, to see ya in that condition!"

As she began to sob, Lacey grabbed the phone and loud and boldly shouted. "What the hell were ya even think'n, Daddy?"

I said, "I'm so sorry, baby."

"Yer damn right yer sorry, sorry of a man! Tell me, after all this time, what made ya go on some drunken stupor? Being stupid is exactly what it is. Ya sure have gone and done it this time. I truly thought those days were over."

I know she was hurt, because being the oldest, she was there in her younger years during my addictions, before I gained my sobriety and made thangs right with God. She remembers the anger, the separations, and the broken promises I made to God, to her mama, and to them.

She started in on me again. "Mama doesn't want anythang to do with ya anymore, and I don't blame 'er. I will support 'er decision, even though I do love ya both. Just know this, if ya don't get forgiveness from Mama, then ya most certainly won't get it from me. If Faith has any sense, she won't forgive ya either. Also, until ya get yerself together, I want ya to stay away from yer grandkids!"

I said, "Wait a minute now, young lady! You can't use my grandkids as a bargain'n chip. That just ain't right."

She bluntly said, "I ain't the one who screwed up. I am done talk'n to ya, Daddy. Pull your shit together and fix it!"

"I know I screwed up," I said, "but please don't deny me my grandkids just because ya are mad at me. They didn't do anythang wrong and don't deserve to be punished."

She said, "Just fix it and we will see about it."

I responded by saying, "I'm gonna go over to Amberleigh's house later to see if yer mom will even talk to me since she will not talk over the phone. I hope ya girls can soon find it in yer hearts to forgive me. I love y'all so much and this is kill'n me know'n I hurt my family so much. One more thang. I know Doc is work'n later, but I wanna ask if you and Hoss could bring Faith over later. I know it is a lot to ask, but she needs a big daddy hug."

Inside, I knew it was I who really needed a hug from them both.

There was a long pause, and she reluctantly said, "We'll see. We love ya, too, Daddy."

"Tell Faith I love 'er," I said. "And please give 'er a hug for me." She said okay and hung up.

Sitting in my old recliner with my life hanging in the balance, I was pondering what to do, feeling more awake than I was earlier. Still in pain, but alive.

I went to the kitchen and grabbed the pain medicine and a ladle of water, hoping it wouldn't take long to work. I decided to clean up and try and make thangs right with Jalynn. I took a shower and shaved and tidied up my beard and mustache. With every stroke of the razor and clippers, the stranger looking back at me faded away and the man that I once was slowly reappeared in the shattered mirror. I gargled a couple of times to rid my mouth of the mixture of beer, coffee, blood, and cigarettes.

Feeling better, as best I could and with a hard mission ahead of me, I made my way to my truck. Cash was right behind me to take his place. With his head out the window, we set out for Jamestown, Wyoming. As we neared Amberleigh's house, I prayed that Jalynn would take pity on this old fool and find it in her heart to forgive me.

I approached the familiar house where she would be and found myself more scared than my tour in Vietnam. My heart was pounding and hurting something fierce. My words raced through my mind, trying to figure out what I would say. As I pulled into the drive, I seen the curtains open, and she was staring out the window.

Before I could even get my truck to stop, Amberleigh came flying out of the house yelling, "She don't wanna to see ya, Bobby Ray!"

Quickly putting my truck in neutral and setting the parking brake, I jumped out and met her in the yard face to face. "I just wanna apologize to er' in person since y'all won't talk on the phone."

"She doesn't wanna see ya, I said, let alone talk to ya. She is mad as hell, upset, and hurt at what ya done."

I lowered my head and started to cry. She was set back a little that a man of my size and roughness was weeping in front of her.

She said, "Hey, Bobby Ray, why don't I grab us a cup of coffee and relax fer a bit and talk."

I said, "I'll take ya up on that, but while ya are in there, can ya please tell Jalynn I love 'er, and I am so sorry. Maybe she will come out in a bit?"

Amberleigh said, "I will, but I doubt she'll come out. I'll be right back; don't ya go anywhere."

I asked if Cash could go in and see his mama and she agreed. The dog was happy to oblige at the offer when Amberleigh said, "Come on, Cash! Wanna see yer mama?"

I told her I wouldn't go anywhere. I lowered the truck's tailgate for a seat and lit a cigarette as I looked toward the window where Jalynn was looking out before, but she was no longer there. After a few minutes, Amberleigh returns with the coffee and Cash, who followed but kept looking back as if he didn't want to leave his mama.

Amberleigh joined me on the tailgate and began the conversation. "Bobby Ray, I am so mad at ya right now fer do'n Jalynn the way ya have done, but I don't want ner bit of trouble. For that reason, I am try'n to be as friendly as I can."

I sipped my coffee and shook my head in agreement. We lit another cigarette and talked about the situation, and I asked her if she told Jalynn what I said.

"She doesn't wanna hear a thang ya gotta say right now. She is in there with er' head buried in er' pillow and cry'n. Heck, she won't even talk to me right now. She just told me to go away. She really needs 'er space to sort thangs out, Bobby Ray."

I agreed and said, "Geez, Amberleigh, what am I gonna do?"

She said that I should try to work on myself and get thangs in order, do some thinking about the future. As for my wife, her plan was to stay with Amberleigh until she could find a place of her own.

I said, "There's no need for that if I can just get 'er to come back home. I will never put 'er in that situation er' again."

"We done heard that befur', Bobby Ray."

As I pleaded my case, our idle chat quickly turned into an argument.

"I never seen 'er this way befur'. I'm not sure she will forgive ya this time."

9

I slipped off the tailgate and shouted, "I will not give up on 'er or us! She's my wife and I love 'er, and I am noth'n without 'er!"

Amberleigh jumped down and walked away fast, shouting, "Ya should have thought about that befur ya went act'n like an ass!"

I shouted, "I love ya, Jalynn, I love ya!"

Amberleigh shouted, "I think ya should leave, right now!"

At that request, I called Cash, and we jumped in the truck. Before I shut the door and knowing Jalynn could hear me, I shouted again, "I love ya, Jalynn! I am sorry!" Then I tore out of the driveway, kicking up gravel and slinging the half empty cup of coffee off the tailgate.

Heading down the road thinking about what had just happened, I needed to calm down and talk to someone who would not judge me. As I was coming back into town, I decided to stop at Chapman's Truck Stop. It is owned by our old family friends the McGomery's. Mr. B (Bear Dog) and Mrs. C (The Chicken Lady) were my parents' old friends from way back before I came along. Mr. B managed the truck shop and Mrs. C ran the restaurant and was a wonderful cook and wise in her years. That's the two things that I need right now: a good meal and some good advice.

As I pulled up, there sat the Saturday crew at the counter. I slowly walked in and took my usual seat. The stares from the others seemed to tear a hole in my heart and Mrs. C came over to take my order.

"Oh, Bobby Ray, honey," she said, "what in the world have ya went and done? Yer face is in such a mess."

I said, "Well, Mrs. C, looks like I really messed up thangs this time with Jalynn. I reckon I am the talk of the town this week."

"I have heard a few thangs from people come'n in and out, but it ain't ner bit of my business. I will have to say we have ya to thank for the gossipers leave'n the rest of us alone," she said with a chuckle and poured my coffee. "Let me come around there and get me a hug and we can chat for a minute."

I said, "That would be nice. I need a good hug." I hung my head in shame as I knew she knew everything that I had gone and done. She said she was shocked at what the folks were saying, but before she would say anything she wanted to hear it straight from the horses' mouth. Or in my case, the jackass. I told her that I don't remember a lot, so whatever she had heard must be true. She pointed her finger scolding

10

me and said I should be ashamed of myself.

I hung my head lower and said, "I am, Mrs. C. I am."

She patted me on the knee and said, "Bobby Ray, I have known ya since ya wer just out of diapers and watched ya grow into a fine young man with a good head on yer shoulders. Going off to that fancy college over yonder in the Great Smokey Mountains of Tennessee to play that football. I remember when we were getting started with the truck stop over there in Evanston years ago, yer daddy would bring ya into town with him and y'all would stop in for lunch 'ever Saturday after y'all finished yer chores on the ranch."

I agreed and said, "Yes, ma'am, I remember 'em, too. I sure do miss those days."

She said with a smile, "Even though yer daddy was fifteen years older than Mr. B, he could outwork most of the men when it came to building the shop over yonder. I remember ya were such a well-mannered boy. Ya were raised right by yer mama and daddy. And in my mind, ya have done right by 'em. Me and Mr. B couldn't be prouder of ya as if ya were our own son. Ya gave up yer dreams and sacrificed such a bright future for the good of yer family. Somewhur along the way, that ole devil snuck in and did a number on ya. Bobby Ray, we all make mistakes. I know ya are still a good man, and ya have been through a heck of a lot over the years. But as I recall, yer mama would say in times like this ya just have to turn to God and pray. Find that good Christian inside ya and face yer demons. Find a way to make amends with God and yer family."

As tears rolled down my face, I said, "Yes, ma'am, yer right. I need to dig deep and find my way."

She gave me another hug and excused herself. After I ate my delicious meal and feeling better about myself after our chat, I decided to grab Cash and go over to Mr. B's shop to chew the fat for a bit. I found Cash by the outside kitchen entrance eating some food that Mrs. C had evidently instructed them to give this beggar of mine. He knew how to work them ladies with his looks.

We walked into the shop and Mr. B was busy giving instructions to a mechanic. He is one of the best diesel mechanics around these here parts. Even in his 80's and with health problems himself, he was always willing to listen to others about their troubles and offer up his advice and years of wisdom.

I walked up and said, "Hello, old-timer."

"Well, heck!" Mr. B said looking at me over his glasses. "Lookie what the cat drug in. I was wonder'n when ya would get around to come'n in for some checkers."

I knew what he meant. It was time to walk away for some man-to-man talk. He said, "Bobby Ray, how the heck are ya, son?"

"Not so good, as I am sure ya have heard by now."

"Well, ya know how folks overreact to gossip round here. But hey, ain't nothin right all the time. Today is a new day to do better!"

I said, "I suppose ya are right, Mr. B. I sure wish I could erase ever' day of the past week. I sure messed it all up."

"What did ya do to make ya regret an entire week? If ya don't mind me askin'?

"I went on a drunken binge and showed my ass. I upset Jalynn, not to mention I broke my promise to her about ner' drinking again. She left me this time for good, I suppose, Mr. B. I am not sure why I did it, but it has been a long time since I had even thought about a drink, let alone lost my temper. I guess I just felt the weight on my shoulders not be'n able to take care of my family, and in oer' my head with the bills pile'n up, and no work for this ole truck driver. I just wanted to have a beer to relax and then I just wanted to drink all my worries away as I had done many times befer my sobriety. I guess I got carried away and snapped."

Mr. B smirked. "I understand all too well about the pressure of be'n the backbone of the family. It certainly can get heavy at times. I have gone and acted out a time or two myself. We are all human and we falter. But son, it is what ya do next that matters the most. Put what happened behind ya and take yer whoop'n. Hit yer knees and pray, and trust in God, and I know things will start to look up for ya, ole buddy. Maybe it would do ya some good to get back out on the big road for a week or two. It might give ya some time to gain clarity and collect yer composure. Plus, it will give Jalynn time to thank with her know'n you are try'n will help 'er decision. I will make sure to get the word to 'er and give ya some help."

I said I may just do that. I told him that the sounds of the air wrenches and the running trucks were hammering my increasingly pounding hangover headache back and I had better head home and figure it all out. As he shook my hand, he pulled out some cash from his bib overalls and slipped me two hundred dollars. He said he hoped it would help and assured me it was not a loan. I tried to give it back and he said, "Yer daddy would have done the same fur me and mine."

I turned and called for Cash as he had been going from truck to truck like a lot-lizard to see what he could get with those big brown eyes. We climbed in the truck, and as I sat a moment thinking about my conversations with a million thoughts running through my pounding head, I hollered out the window and said thanks to Mr. B for the advice.

He yelled back, "Any time, Bobby Ray, just hang in there!"

As I was pulling out, I just happened to notice Mrs. C had snuck a snack sack in my seat for me and Ole Cash. I thought to myself as I rubbed Cash's head, *I love them two! They are very special people.*

With that we were headed back to our empty house to do some thinking and to figure out a way to get my wife back.

All the way home, I was soul searching and it made time fly because, before I knew it, I was pulling off the main road and heading up the driveway. I started to cry as I recalled many times I pulled my Big Rig down this dusty road and my wife and kids would be in the yard waiting with excitement to greet me from my long journey of one, two, three weeks, and if needed, a month. I had always hoped that someday they would understand why their daddy had to be gone so long.

Getting out of my truck and heading towards the house, I hear the faint sound of a big rig's jake break come on as it was gearing down, and I knew someone was pulling in my driveway. Standing in the yard waiting to see who it was, I heard the big diesel engine getting closer to the house down the half-mile stretch. As it neared, I didn't recognize it, a light blue metallic Peterbilt 379. I thought, *"Who the heck…?"*

The big rig came to a stop and the dust cleared, settling to the ground and the air brakes were set. As the driver stepped out, I noticed the Bible in the windshield and then recognized the faded Ford hat of my good friend RJ Harrellson. As usual, he had a bottle of Mt. Dew in his hand. Although he and I were diehard Ford men, we both preferred a Pete as our hauling rig and a Cat engine as the horses pulling our rigs down the highway. He always said that both Fords and Peterbilt's were so good they circled their names as you will notice they are similar.

RJ and I graduated high school together. He started working for my daddy on the ranch right afterwards, as he didn't want to go to college, and I did. So, he kind of took my place.

He said, "Hey, ole buddy, I just stopped by fer a few minutes to see what ya think of Ole Blue Bird, to show 'er off and brag a little."

"Not a bad rig, buddy," I said. "Good to see ya. I heard ya were run'n around these parts." I knew he was there to get the scoop on what the whole town was gossiping about. He said he was in his way to the feed lot, or death row, as we call it. (The feed lot being the last stop for cattle to get fat enough to go to the slaughterhouse.) It is kinda sad but, America loves her meat.

He asked, "What's go'n on, buddy?"

I told him I didn't feel much like talk'n about it.

"Alright," he said. "Ya know whur to find me."

We shifted our conversation gear and started talking trash about each other's truck, as us drivers always do.

To be nice, I said, "Nice truck ya got there, RJ. How does she run?"

He double slaps the side of his truck and exclaims, "There ain't not'n like her. She's a fast one! She's got a Cat 550 and 18 gears on the shifter. She might run faster than yer Reba!"

I quickly responded, "RJ, ya ole slacker, ya know there ain't no trucks yet that she can't keep up with, and even blow right by." I met his double slap on Reba to show my bragging rights. "There ain't none like this ole gal," I added. "She is a 1998 Pete 379, too, and has a Cat 550 bored over with dual turbos, 18 gears, and double train horns to let you know I am come'n through."

Now, she could use a fresh coat of paint, though her original reddish-copper color has faded something fierce. Plus, she's had a good bit of hail damage. Still, she's all chromed out with lots of chicken lights.

He said, "I don't know, Bobby Ray. You haven't seen this ole girl blow black smoke scoot'n down the road in the hammer lane."

"Well, we'll just have to see about that one day. Won't we?"

He said, "Yes, sir! Ya bet!"

I asked if he wanted to kick back around a fire and pick some tunes on the old Gibson guitar. He agreed, saying he wasn't in a hurry.

"Alrighty then!" I said. "Let me go in and grab the gee-tar. You rustle up some wood from the shed and start the fire."

14

When I returned, he had put on a fresh pot of fire-brewed stump water coffee.

We sat there for what seemed to be hours, talking and picking at the guitar, although it was evident he could not carry a tune in a bucket. We discussed trucking, the good ole days of our past, as well as catching up on each other's lives. For some extra entertainment, we took turns throwing Cash's favorite ball to fetch while we talked.

Holding back my tears, I tried to sing a song I had on my mind a while by the great Merle Haggard, entitled, "So Tired of it All." I had never sung it before.

I finished and RJ said, "Wow, buddy, that song… that was something!"

I got up to put some wood on the fire and he asked, "What's really go'n on, buddy? Why are ya the talk of the town?"

I told him I broke my promise to Jalynn and got drunk and made an ass of myself.

He said, "What made ya go and do some'n so stupid? You have been sober fer so long now."

I said, "I didn't intend to, but the bills were pile'n up with no freight to haul in oer' a month because of the slow down. I felt myself sink'n into a deep depression, wonder'n what we were gonna do. With my anxiety and my PTSD at an all-time high, I realized that it had taken a toll on our marriage, and we had become distant. When we tried to talk about things, it would always end up in an argument, me sleep'n on the couch. So, last week while out search'n for local work, I happun to pass by Ray's Tavern (Turbo Jr. is his nickname). I decided to turn around and see what he was up to since it had been a while since I had seen him. He fixed us a sandwich and we talked. It reminded me of times past and gone and I was feel'n sorry for myself and decided I needed a beer to take the edge off. He tried to talk me out of it, but he knew not to argue with me. I felt I needed it. Besides, it had been years, and I thought I could handle it. Well, one turned into two and three and befer I knew it, I was three sheets in the wind."

RJ sat quietly, shaking his head. I continued my story.

"By the time I should have gone home, I couldn't even walk, let alone drive. Ray and his wife Gracie loaded me up and took me home and helped me inside. Seeing the shape that I was in, Jalynn started in on me, and I guess it just hit me the wrong way. I was immediately thrown into a drunken rage. I started throw'n things, punch'n walls, and kick'n down doors. I was so frustrated with life and I didn't need her harp'n on me. Instead of sleep'n it off like I should, I took off out the door and went to satisfy my thirst and keep the drown'n of my sorrows go'n. After that, the last few days have been a blur, until I woke to the harsh reality of my actions this morn'n."

RJ's eyes were as big as saucers as he said, "Man, I hate to hear that but I want ya to know that ya were wrong in treat'n Jalynn that way. She is a good woman, and she has stuck by yer side through thick and thin. Ya know she loves you. I have known 'er for a long time now and I believe all ya had to do is just confide in 'er and tell 'er ya needed help. She would have listened to ya and ya both could have worked out a plan. Ya wouldn't have turned to the alcohol in the first place."

I shamefully agreed. I needed to get the matter at hand off my mind, so I grabbed a few rags and the chrome polish and started polishing ole Reba's chrome grill. And just like that, RJ jumped right in to help me.

We talked more as we polished that old and faded chrome until she was bright and glistening in the moonlight. I needed that time with my dear friend, and what was to be a quick trip, turned into an all-nighter.

When it was time for RJ to leave, he said he was going down to Chapmans to get fuel and a few winks before he headed out. As the sun was dawning a new day, peeking through the fog, and outlining the horizon, he climbed up in the cab of Blue Bird. (I have to say it really was a nice Peterbilt, but I won't ever let him know that.)

He fired the truck up. As he shut the door and held his head out the window, he said, "I wouldn't be the friend I am if I left without do'n my part and telling ya how big of a mistake ya made and what a jack ass ya are fer do'n so!"

I said, "I know. Thanks for remind'n me."

He said, "That's what I am here fer, buddy, and remember if ya need me, I am just a phone call or CB yell away. If you wanna come run with me, ya are more than welcome. It doesn't pay much, but it's work."

I said thanks and I watched him pull away through the fog, quickly grabbing gears and gaining speed as his rig blew black coal smoke, which added to the majestic sight of his chicken lights and chrome fading in the dust. He disappeared in no time flat. I could hear him pull

16

onto the big road and wind it up to top speed. Before he was out of earshot, he gave his train horns a long bellow, just to say goodbye.

I stood there in the early morning dew, lonely once more. I was left with a lifechanging decision to make. If I stayed, what would I do without the woman I loved? With only a few weeks to go until I could retire and hang up my keys forever, should I give it up now, or should I take back out over the road?

I figured I would ponder on it for a day or two. I returned to the house and sat in my old chair to rest and think. I must have dozed off because I was startled by yet another big rig that had pulled up outside. And with the engine still running, there was a pounding on the back door in the kitchen. It sounded like whoever was there was trying to break in.

Then I heard the unmistakable voice of Big Mike hollering, "I know you are in there, Turbo! I just passed by RJ, and he told me o'er the CB that ya were here. Now open this damn door before I break it down."

I was very hesitant as he was demanding I get outside so he could give me the ass whooping I deserved for hitting Jalynn. I tried to reason with him and explain I didn't hit her. But he wasn't having none of it; he just kept on yelling. I got myself together and went to the mudroom. I unlocked and opened the door and was met with the huge fist of this mountain of a man. As I picked myself up from the floor, I asked, "What was that fer?"

"That's for hit'n Jalynn!" he exclaimed.

"Hit'n Jalynn…?" I tried to tell him I didn't lay a hand on her but before I could get her name out of my still-swollen mouth, now bleeding again, he hit me again. That blow sent me stumbling backward, into the kitchen and across the table. I took that time to quickly hide under the table to escape those huge fists, try to plead my case, and plan my next move. Still, he kept coming. I hollered, "Hey, you left yer truck run'n!"

He turned and still yelling, he said, "Shit! I will be right back. Don't you go and hide, you woman-hit'n weasel!"

Don't get me wrong; I ain't no coward. But Big Mike, even at 60 years old, ain't someone to go toe-to-toe with. As the engine went quiet, I could hear more trucks coming up the driveway, some already there and setting their air brakes. I started to pray to God because I couldn't take any more beatings. I heard them talking and yelling at Big Mike to calm down. I could see out the window that they were trying to hold him back. I looked to the heavens and thanked God and RJ for sending my rescuers.

When I decided it was safe to come out from my cover, I wiped the blood bleeding from my mouth and nose, and I walked outside. I was standing on the porch watching as more trucks were pulling in. That is when Big Mike broke loose and came up on the porch with the other drivers running to save me and yelling at him to settle down. He took another swing at me. I barely ducked out of the way and jumped the railing, stumbling and landing on my backside in the yard. The guys grabbed him as he was headed down to get me. He stopped in his tracks as Mr. B got out of his pickup and hollered at him to stop. Mr. B had evidently heard of my emergency over the CB and came to save the day. We all respected him.

He hollered at Big Mike, "Stop that nonsense and leave him alone!"

Big Mike said, "I will kill the coward, wife-hitting, piece of cow-dung, no-good bum!"

Another driver spoke up and said, "Turbo never hit Jalynn, Big Mike. The gossip was all half lies. The stories got turned around. You know how stories get turned around. He punched the walls instead of hit'n her."

It took several tries as Big Mike slowed down, trying to comprehend all the information being yelled at him. With his anger now eased off, he stops and looks straight at me and sees what he has done to my face. He asks, "Is that true, Turbo?"

"Yes, Big Mike, ya know deep down I would never hit Jalynn."

He shook his head and softly said, "I am so sorry brother."

The others let him loose and he starts to shed a tear at his actions. A bit shaken, I move over and give him a hug.

"It's okay. I am just glad you didn't kill me befer you found out the truth. My face feels like I've been hit by an anvil."

Everyone breathes a sigh of relief and chuckles at my comment. Big Mike says, "You know that doesn't make it right what ya did to Jalynn! Men ought not treat their woman that way! Do ya hear me, Turbo?"

I said, "Yeah, I hear ya. I know I did wrong and believe me, I am ashamed of myself and intend on make'n it right by Jalynn."

I invited them into my shambled house for a fresh cup of coffee and offered up the truth of what happened, so everyone would know the details. After the story, with each one of them offering their disapproval and well-deserved harsh comments, they pitched in where they could and helped me for a better part of the day to put what we could of my house back in order. As we finished and they each said their goodbyes, they filled the sky with black smoke, and the convoy of trucks made their way out to the big road. Then they were gone, and I was left with my thoughts once more.

After the sound of engines and air horns filtered away, I went back into the house, left with the rest of the evening. I decided to take a shower and try to ease my pains and try to call Jalynn before I went off to bed. The shower and pain meds helped to ease the pain some and after my attempt to call Jalynn was rejected, I went to prepare the bed. Low and behold, just like clockwork, here came my faithful friend Cash to comfort me and hear my troubles.

Truth be known, he hates his own bed and prefers to sleep with me as he has done in the truck for so many years now. I settled in under the covers and gave him an earful of my drama. He just yawned, telling me he was tired, so I just rubbed his head, and we faded off to sleep.

After a few hours, I awoke in a sweat from a nightmare, which was not uncommon. The jingle of Cash's dog tags let me know he was awake and by my side to check my situation. I got up and went and made a pot of coffee. Since it was not that late, I decided to call Jalynn again in hopes she would answer my call. But I was rejected yet another time. I sat in my chair for a better part of the night pondering and dozing in and out of sleep. Before I knew it, the sun was peeking through the window letting me know it was time to get up.

I fixed me another cup of coffee, the old one now as thick as tar being on the burner all night. It was doing its job, giving me a little bit of energy. I sat at the kitchen table and lit a cigarette. I figured I would make another attempt to talk to Jalynn. Nope, she wasn't having it this time either, or the next four times I tried.

It was time to go to the barn and get to cleaning Reba and get this off my mind.

Working on my truck, I listened to an old gospel tape my Mama and Daddy recorded years ago. As the tape switched sides, I heard my mama's sweet voice singing a song she had written at a time when she was at a low point in her life and turned everything over to God. As she sang, "Jesus is the Answer," I started to cry and recall the memories of my childhood.

She and Daddy were good Christians and tried to raise us right and keep us in church. Daddy would always say, "Raise 'um up right, teach them about God, and to have good manners, and a good work ethic."

I remembered Daddy telling me the story of old Job from the Bible. Of his struggles, and no matter what he was faced with, he endured. From losing his sight, to losing his family, and everything he had, I thought to myself, *"I wish I endured like ole Job."*

I recall my mama telling us when we had a problem, just pray about it. With tears on my cheeks, I hit my knees and started to pray. I poured out my heart to God and He filled it with inner peace and joy. As I finished praying, I remembered the love my daddy had for my mama and how he would always say, "Your mama is something special. A gift God gave me to keep me straight."

At that point I realized that I had taken Jalynn's love for granted all these years. They had their little arguments just as we did, but I guess because they were so close to God and had His love, they kept the love for one another. I had forgotten that. They always seemed to pull themselves back together and at the end of the day. I could hear them through the walls as they lay in bed telling each other, "I love you."

After my plea with God and my memories, I wiped the tears from my face and regained my composure, with a new peace inside. I started cleaning my truck again and I remembered how being on the road helped me think. It was at that point I decided it was best hit the road and search for the end of the long white line.

I finished my task, wrapped everything up, put stuff away, and headed into the house to search for loads. After a few phone calls, including one to Ray to see if he would take care of everything whilst I was gone, I made a call to Angie Baxter (The Drifter Queen) to see if she knew of any loads.

She said, "Hello, Turbo, how the heck are ya?"

I said, "I am alive and on the greener side of grass, thank God. But I am in dire need of work."

She said, "You're in luck. My husband Jason (Lunatic) has a load we can't cover, going from Orin, Wyoming, to Sacramento, California. You interested."

I said, "Set it up, ma'am, I need to get the heck outta here fer a while and put the hammer down."

"You bet, Turbo," she said. "Be here by six in the morning and you can hook up to one of the trailers in the yard."

I hung up the phone and told Cash we had us a load. He sprang up excited because he loved to go on trips with me. I told him we need to pack a bag and get a good night's sleep, because we were gonna hit the road and search for the end of the long white line.

And that is just what we did.

2

THE SEARCH FOR ANSWERS

Evanston, WY – Orin, WY

I WAS UP EARLY THE NEXT MORNING WITH TWO CUPS OF coffee down and several cigarettes burned as I filled my daddy's faded green Stanley thermos. I locked up the house and headed to the barn to warm ole Reba up. With a quick inspection, I climbed up in the cab. With the turning of the key and a push of the start button, with a couple or three puffs of black smoke from her chrome stacks, Reba came to life after sitting for what seemed to be an eternity.

While she was warming up, I fed and watered the horses and cows. Ray promised he would take care of them while I was on the road as he had always done. As the tone of Reba's engine changed, I knew she was ready for the road.

I hollered for Cash who was out chasing something, as I could hear him barking. He came a running, and we climbed in. I sat preparing myself. I looked around the cab at the half-faded pictures of my family taped all over my visor as I had done so many times, telling each one I loved them, not knowing if I would make it home to see them ever again. I always made sure I told them when I was home and with every hug and at the end of every call, because a truck driver never knows what might lie ahead of them down the road.

After my usual prayer, I turned on my CB and Channel 19 came to life. I did a radio check. As soon as I said, "Breaker-breaker, one-nine, can I get a radio check?" multiple voices replied saying, "Loud and clear, buddy." There was even a Lima-Charlie (loud and clear), and I knew right away that it was my old army buddy (Odie) from his home base station.

After a few howdies, Odie said, "Glad to hear my old battle buddy is out here truck'n again. Stop by and see me if ya get a chance. I am sure the misses and the kids would love to see ya and we can catch up on each other's go'ns on."

"You bet!" I responded. "I am headed over yer way right now and will be there befer night fall."

He said, "Okay, buddy, I will see ya then."

I put ole Reba in gear and we were off. I headed to Chapman's for fuel and a few snacks. After fueling, I was waiting for biscuits and gravy for Cash and me. I walked over to the bank to get some traveling money and to make sure Jalynn had enough to get by. The looks and the whispered comments from the ladies in the bank gave me reassurance of my decision to head out of town for a while. I returned and got our breakfast and Mrs. C hugged me as I tried to pay our bill.

"Your money ain't no good here, son. Mr. B said yer fuel was taken care of, too. Our gift to ya."

I thanked her and gave her another hug. She said, "Be careful out there on that old road and come home safely and know that God loves you."

Cash and I sat in the truck and ate our meal and then it was time to leave. As I passed the shop, I gave the horns a quick two bursts and waved at Mr. B. Within a minute, I hit the road to search for the end of the long white line.

The early morning fog was heavy as we headed towards Orin, Wyoming. It was a six-hour dead head from Orin to Evanston, and I knew I would be there overnight for the loadout the next day. I didn't mind the drive; I was happy to be rolling again. It was lonesome though, with all decisions filling my head. I thought of how many times I had driven this road over the years.

I crossed The Three Sisters (The Highway to Heaven, as it is referred to) heading east, and as I topped the next hill and looked in my mirrors, it was showing in all its glory the view as if it disappeared into heaven. I wondered if one day I would ever drive into heaven and see my mama and daddy. What a reunion that it would be. I missed them so much even though I talked to them often.

While I rolled down the road chasing the white line, I was thinking of how many miles I had driven over the years. It was probably in the millions-range. I started to recall all the things I had missed as well as the stuff I had seen and encountered along my life's journey. I thought, *"How in the world have I made it this far with all that goes on while over the road?"* Then I thought to myself I probably wouldn't be alive if it wasn't for God protecting me and the prayers from mama and Jalynn ensuring God knew to watch over me. And my faithful friend Cash for having his German Shepherd sense to let me know when things didn't seem quite right. He would always jump up and check things out and his dog tags would rattle to let me know he was on the job of looking out for me. If something wasn't right, he would let out a woof and if I didn't respond, he would let out a big bark to wake me to check it out myself. We are a good match for each other.

We pulled into Odie's place just before dusk, and as he had mentioned, the kids came running and jumped up in the truck when I set the air brakes. They were all over the cab and in the sleeper, they gave me hugs and said we love you, Uncle Turbo. After the excitement of me showing up wore off, they went off to play with Cash who loved the attention.

We adults finally had some time to ourselves. Odie asked me about how I got the markings on my face, and I told them both the story. His wife Alice gave me the same look that I had been getting from all the other women who knew the story. But I guess she figured I had been told enough that I screwed up and she didn't say a word about it. She just went in and started cleaning the kitchen.

Odie just said, "Man, I can't believe you did that. I wouldn't expect that behavior out of you in a million years."

I agreed and said, "I know, buddy. I am sore at myself fer it, and I will not do it again."

We sat there for some time, and they caught me up on the family and how the kids were doing in school and that he had gotten a job at the local Veterans Clinic and was doing pretty good helping the servicemen and women. He said it helped him cope with his own issues from the war. He asked me how I was doing on that end of things, and I told him about the nightmares and the night sweats. He said if I ever get a chance to come to the clinic that there were people there to help us with things like that. I agreed and said I would try sometime after I get my life back on track.

When I finished my third glass of sweet tea, I figured it was time to go. I called for Cash, and we said goodbye. We continued on. When we made it to the old truck stop that was once owned by Mr. B. and Mrs. C., I topped off my fuel tanks and found a spot to park for the night. Then went in the diner and grabbed Cash and I a bite to eat. This place had changed over the years. While I ate my dinner, I was taken back to my childhood days when I would ride into town with Daddy on Saturdays. He would stop for lunch and would always say, "Don't tell your mama we stopped and ate, she will be sad." He would buy me a BLT with no Mayo. Then we would walk over to the shop and talk with Mr. B. While they were catching up on the weekly goings on around town, I would climb in his wrecker and act like I was driving. Then we would go and get supplies, and he would buy me some hard tack candy for doing a good job of my chores. Then we would head back to the ranch where I would spend the rest of the day playing until mama would call me in for supper.

My daydreaming was interrupted when the waitress came over and asked if I needed anything else. I told her I was good. Then she asked if I was Bobby Ray that used to own the big ranch out by the Blake ranch. I said I was. She told me that it wasn't long after I sold the ranch that the big corporation came in and started clearing it off, building a housing subdivision. Her news made me tear up because I remembered the handshake and promise that was made to me from the feller from the city about how he would keep it as a ranch. I asked if they bothered the family cemetery. She said they left it alone, and in fact put a bigger fence around it, and they pay someone to take care of its upkeep. I thought how stupid I was for even being in the situation that I was in and having to let it go. I just knew Mama and Daddy were ashamed of me for what I had done and for letting things get in the shape they were in, especially after all I had done to keep it running for all those years.

I ordered Cash some food, paid my bill, and left the diner. After returning to the truck, I gave Cash his food which didn't last but a minute and the plate was clean. We went out for a smoke and for him to do his business. I decided to try and call Jalynn and let her know I loved her, and I was sorry, and to let her know that I had decided to take a load from The Drifter Queen and Lunatic. Even though it didn't pay as much as I wanted, it would help on the bills and give her some running money as soon as it was deposited. I still had some of the money that Mr. B had given me, and I could run on that. I just wanted her to know that I still care about her well-being. However, my efforts were all declined. Cash and I made our way back and climbed up in the truck. We settled in the bunk to get some sleep for the busy day ahead.

The next morning, I grabbed a cup of coffee and looked over my truck and beat the tires with my old thumper to see if any sounded low on air. I started ole Reba up and puffs of black smoke filled the air. After a few minutes, she was warmed up. I turned the lights on, and her chicken lights gave off a glow that could be seen through the fog of the early morning.

We left the truck stop and headed down the big road towards the Blake Ranch, which was about twenty miles outside of Orin on the other side of the town settled between my old family home place and The Garrett Ranch. We creeped through town so as not to wake anyone from their slumber in the early morning. Afterall, the roosters haven't even started to crow yet. Reba's lights were like Christmas tree lights shining off the storefronts. It was truly a sight to see, and I was glad to be back in my hometown.

We rolled out of town. I hammered down the road faster now that there was just farmland as far as one could see. As I passed my old home place, I seen what the waitress had told me about. There were houses where once there were rich pastures filled with the best livestock and great crops. I had a sad moment of memories and deep regret, but a smile came over me as I passed the family cemetery where Mama and Daddy were buried. And there was the old tree where I carved Jalynn's and my name when I first brought her out here. I said hello to Mama and Daddy in heaven and asked them to watch over me as I was trying my best. As

26

the tears filled my eyes, I could hear Mama say, "Just trust in God, son." And Daddy would say he was proud of me for what I did many years ago, and ashamed of me for what I had done recently.

I know it was my conscience making me hear these words, but it was a welcome reminder that I knew they were watching over me.

We went over the iron bridge and turned onto the old farm road and headed to the corral. That is when Cash's head perked up, for he knew the route all too well. He started jumping from his seat in the front and to the bunk area back and forth. He was so excited and acting like a fool. Knowing that he would soon see his little girlfriend, Bella, and get another delicious meal from Mrs. Blake.

Bella was Mrs. Blake's black and white Peek-a-poo, and they had known each other for five years now. I don't think they realized the size difference or the fact that they were different breeds. I think Bella thought she was as big as Cash was and gave him good run for his money. All they knew was that they were in love. It really did him good to get out and run around since he would be in the truck for a long haul later.

We made it to the corral, and I barely got the truck stopped in time before Cash opened his door using the rope I had tied to the handle for his convenience and had taught him to open and close the door by himself. He could come and go as he needed to while we were parked. In a flash, he was running all over the yard looking for her. When he didn't see her, he made a beeline for the old farmhouse where he was certain she would be.

I climbed out of the truck and walked over and met Mr. Blake, who was pushing 90 years old but was still able to get around on his good leg, with help from his cane and his fake leg. He also had a wheelchair and his four wheeled buggy. His sons had taken over the ranch, but he still felt that he had to be part of it as he would always be the boss. We shook hands.

He said, "We have missed ya, son. Do you want a cup of coffee before we head to the load-out area?"

Of course, I accepted. While he poured, he asked me how Jalynn and the rest of the family were faring. I bluntly replied, "Probably better now that I am headed back over the road for a while."

He said, "Why don't we take a ride over to the others so I can show you around a bit and show you what this ole buggy can do?"

As we made our way to the load-out area, there were already thirteen or fourteen trucks ahead of me. I saw familiar faces of drivers that I had not seen in years. There was RJ, Slow-Go, Half-pint (who was showing off her new rig), Flip, Huggy Bear, Lil Bo Peep, Sassy Pants, then there was Tony Justice in his truck (Purgatory), John Jaikes in his purple Kenworth (ONLY CLASS), and his wife Kim in her purple Peterbilt. Bill Stoneking, who was a legend in his own right, with his wife Angie and his daughter Teresa in her truck (she also rodeos), and his son Travis in his truck; it was a family business. There was even Goat, who had gone and gotten himself a truck and was out here pounding the pavement.

I knew this was going to be a very long day with that amount of cattle to load out. Heck, I figured I might even half to wait until the next morning. As we neared the corral, I could see some familiar faces that used to work for me and some that looked just like their daddy's that once worked for me and followed in their footsteps and was now ranching.

Knowing he had already heard the gossip, he said, "Why do ya say it like that? Everthang okay, Bobby Ray?"

I said, "It will be, as soon as I get myself straightened out and back on track with God. That is why I am here getting back on the road. That is where I do my best thanking."

He nodded in agreement and said, "Yeah, I know. I heard lots of talk about yer situation, and I figured ya would get by here at some point and I would hear the story from ya." I reassured him that whatever he had heard was probably true, except for the one about me hitting Jalynn. He didn't fuss at me. He just patted me on the shoulder and said, "Well, ya know what ya did was wrong, and ya know what to do to make it right by Jalynn and the kids. Don't you worry about the town folk. They just need something or someone to talk about."

The other drivers, of course, started talking shit, as usual, and laughed at my black eye and still swollen lips. I told 'em I would give them the same treatment I got. And we jokingly laughed it off, because it was evident that I was in no shape to hand out such punishments. After a short prayer from Mr. Blake, Billy Jo, Mr. Blake's oldest son, handed out the job assignments and the truck order. We were ready to begin as the sun was making its way above the mountains. His other son Ryan was there guiding and letting us know when it was our time to grab our truck to keep the process rolling.

It was a long hard day since I was not used to the labor and still sore from my beating. However, it was always fun to do what we loved to do. We weighed and loaded 600 head of cows, and while we were taking turns, another 15 trucks rolled in earlier than they were supposed to with some calves. So, we all pitched in and helped brand them and put them out to pasture in the back 40 acres of the ranch.

The sun had made its way to the other side of the sky to make room for the moon. As it was setting, we had just finished loading my trailer when we heard the familiar voice of Mr. Blake's grand-daughter Missy. We called her Moonshine Missy, the nickname the folks gave her many years ago and it just stuck. She was yelling at us to hold up a minute; she had something for us.

Missy came walking over from the barn with a couple of mason jars full of her latest concoction for us to sample. She held up her newly decorated jars with "Moonshine Missy" labeled across them.

The other drivers took their turns sipping from the jar and she asked, "Well, what y'all think?" They offered up their approval of the fresh batch from her still, not to hurt her feelings. She said, "Well, hey there, Bobby Ray! I sure have missed you round here. How have ya been, darlin?" She gave me a big hug and a kiss on the cheek. "Why didn't ya have a taste?"

I said, "I will pass," as I knew I probably shouldn't have any alcohol since it was what got me in this shape in the first place. Then I thought I didn't want to break this pretty lady's heart. I knew how hard she had worked to perfect her family's generational recipe. She had even put her own special spin on it to make it even smoother and more tasteful as it went down. I told her I would have one sip. I took the jar and with a little guilt I took a swallow and gave her my own approval which put a huge smile on her face. We passed the jar for a couple more sips. Of course, I pretended the next few times.

Missy said, "Now, tell me what y'all really think, since y'all only took little sips. I know y'all drink more than that, I have seen it myself." The other drivers and Mr. Blake scattered then at the ringing of Mrs. Blake's dinner bell, leaving me with Missy wanting the truth. She said,

"What about ya, Bobby Ray? Did ya not like my new blend?"

I said softly, "Oh, sweetie, I assure ya, it is good. My mind is just elsewhere."

"Well, Granny and Mama are finish'n up supper. It should be ready by the time we walk up to the house." As we walked, she grabs my hand and says, "How about after supper, we build us a fire and you can tell me what is on your mind." I told her I recon' that would be fine, and she gripped my hand even tighter.

In the mudroom, Mr. Blake was washing up. He said, "Come have ya a good home-cooked meal, Bobby Ray! You know Mrs. Blake is a good cook and fixes enough for an army. Besides, she won't let you bed down for the night without get'n your belly full and send'n ya fellers with a doggy bag."

We walk into the kitchen and Mrs. Blake says hello and gives me a hug and a kiss on the cheek. I said, "I know where Missy gets her looks and affectionate nature from."

She said, "Bobby Ray, ya are just the dearest boy!"

Even though I'm in my 60's, she's 30 years older and has known me since I was a little boy.

As she set the fresh pan of biscuits on the table she said, "Now, ya boys know no hats on at the table."

We all obliged and put them in our laps.

"Wow, Mrs. Blake," I said, "everything looks so good."

She said she hoped that we enjoy and eat as much as we like.

"There's plenty to go round," she added, "but don't nobody touch a thang until it has been blessed."

I responded by telling her that she sure knew the way to a trucker's heart.

She said, "Befer we dig in, Missy, would you please say grace?"

"Sure, Granny" she said. "Thank you, Lord, for this food that Granny and Mama prepared for us to eat, and thank you for my good moonshine and my still and…"

She was interrupted by Mrs. Blake as we snickered at her prayer. "Okay, little Missy, that's enough of your shenanigans."

"Sorry, Granny, I got carried away. Amen, let's eat."

Mrs. Blake sat a plate down beside her on the floor and said, "Come on over here, Cash, you get a plate, too." He jumped to his feet and was happy at the offering.

We continued with idle chat while we ate. Afterwards, Mrs. Blake, her daughter Elaine, and Missy cleared the table and then made plates for each of us to take.

Mr. Blake said, "Whoo-wee! I'm fuller than a tick on a bloodhound's ass!"

Mrs. Blake said, "Now, Daddy, you ought not talk like that. You know cussing aint very Christian-like."

"I am sorry, Mama," he said. "It's only words, and I tell you what, you let any Godly man hit his thumb with an Estwing hammer or let one of those bulls step on his foot and see what words come out of his mouth!"

I laughed because Daddy used to say the same thing. But Daddy said that Jesus was a carpenter, and he knows how it is, and he understands. He would always laugh and say, "Can you imagine Jesus hitting his thumb and yelling, 'Forgive me, me.'"

Mr. Blake walked into the mud room to put his boots on and said he was going out yonder to the corral to finish up and then retire for the evening. This meant he was going out to supervise the others and get him a lip full of Bruton snuff.

Mrs. Blake scolded him as he was walking out and said, "Don't you be talking like that at my table anymore, mister, and especially in front of these young'ns."

I slid my chair back and told Mrs. Blake that it was delicious as always. Missy said she was going down to the barn to check on the still, and Mrs. Blake rolled her eyes.

Missy looked at me and said, "Hey, Bobby Ray, you and Cash want to walk me down to the barn to check on the brew?"

I took Missy's words as my cue to join her for our quiet time by the fire."

Mrs. Blake abruptly said, "Missy, ya mind your rais'n now. Bobby Ray is still a married man."

"I will, Granny," she said.

I told her sure I would love to go out to the barn with her and that it would give us a chance to walk off some of this food we ate. I looked down at Cash who was snuggled up by Miss Bella and said, "Come on, ole boy. Let's walk out here with Lil Missy," as I laughed.

31

On the walk to the barn, Missy puts her arm around me and says, "Don't mind Granny; she is from a different time." Then she added, "Ya know, we have been friends fer a good spell now and back in the day, as I recall, we were sweet on one another a time or two in the barn, even though we never made not'n of it. Do you remember when ya would come over with yer daddy and we would go play in the barn? We would say we were married and try to kiss like our mamas and daddys."

I said, "Ya were a very good kisser back then and I really liked ya." She exclaimed that she remembered thinking that one day we would get married. I said, "Me, too, but our friendship was more important. I remember we would meet at the creek on the property lines of our ranches and go fishing and skinny dipping."

She laughed and said, "We were so foolish back then, but we were still friends either way. So, I know when something is really bother'n, ya. I want ya to know that I am here and want to help."

I said, "Thanks, but it's a long story."

She said, "That's what Lil Missy's here fer, honey."

"Sounds good, sweetie," I said. "It may do me good to get a woman's perspective on the matter and ya can give me some of yer womanly advice on how to fix it."

"You betcha!" she said, as we entered the barn.

After a quick overlook of the still, I was impressed with her set up and how she had it hidden so well; nobody would ever think to look under a cow's stall camouflaged with hay and fake cow patties. You would have never guessed it was underground. I thought to myself, if it ever blew up, Mr. Blake would not have a barn left.

I chuckled at my thought and Missy said, "Don't laugh; this is the best set up in six counties. I have several police officers and sheriff deputies that come by fer their rations. Heck, I even have the mayor over in Chug Water as one of my repeat customers."

I was sure surprised how the moonshine making has come over the years. I remembered my granddad's set up back in the days of my youth. Missy had this moonshine making process down to an art. It was no wonder she was doing right for herself.

We decided to go up and add some wood to the fire that had been kept going during the loadout. While the coffee was brewing, she said, "Okay, mister! Spill the beans and tell me every detail."

I told her everything and she offered an occasional, "oh, my goodness," or, "my gracious honey." She agreed with my comment about how I screwed everything up with Jalynn. I told her of my addictions and my incarcerations, accidents, and hospital stays. I told her of the broken promises I had made to Jalynn, even the last one I broke, that I would never drink or do drugs again.

After what seemed like hours sitting there drinking coffee, recalling my rough past, and shedding a few tears with Missy, I finished. She sat quiet a couple of minutes with tears in her eyes, processing what I confessed.

I got up and put a couple of logs on the fire to keep the warmth going. The fire started popping and crackling again and I poured the last of the coffee in my cup. I patted Cash on the head as he lay by the fire with Bella, his belly still full of supper and probably wondering when we were going to bed.

I sat back down beside Missy and saw the sorrow and disappointment in her eyes. I said, "Well, lil' lady, that's my life in a nutshell."

She took a very deep breath and as she exhaled, she hit me on the arm. "Bobby Ray, what the hell were ya thinking? A promise is a promise not to er' be broken. And shame on ya fer doing drugs; ya know better than that. Yer mama and daddy would rollover in their graves if they knew. Ya did mess up! And bad, too. Ya should be ashamed of yerself. We would spend the day girl-talk'n while ya fellers were loading up. She is a good woman, and she loves ya very much, and whole heartedly, too, and would do anything for ya, this I know. I can't see now how ya could ever break her sweet and caring heart. I can see why she left ya and does not trust ya anymore. I don't blame her fer leave'n your ass. If I were her, I would have whooped the T-total shit out of ya and then left. I am really disappointed in ya. Women ought not be treated that way. We are stronger than ya fellers give us the credit fer. We endure a lot taking care of y'all and the babies and the house and go from day to day without complaining. But we are sensitive and have special needs of our own. Some of them y'all can't give us, but there are some important ones that we need. Especially, the longing and need for the true love and compassion of a man. And to know that y'all are faithful to us. Ya just totally disrespected her. I know ya love her with all yer heart, and I believe ya are truly sorry. And now ya need to fix what ya have broken. Go fix her broken heart."

I hung my head and admitted my guilt by saying, "I know, Missy, I am sorry for treating 'er that way and doing the thangs I done. I do love 'er with my whole heart, and I know she loves me. Well, at least I hope she still does. I have tried to talk to 'er, but with every effort I give, she refuses to talk to me, let alone see me. I do wanna to fix what I have done, but I thank I took it too fer this time. I just want to get my wife back so we can work through this. I want my kids and grandkids to forgive me and be a happy family once again. But I ain't sure she is will'n to accept my apology and come back home. That is why I decided to get back out here on this road and do some thanking and figure out a way to fix it."

Missy took a sip of coffee, sighed, and took my hand and held it tight. "Well, now that I have given you what fer, I will offer my advice. Give 'er time, Bobby Ray, and don't give up on 'er love fer ya. It is stronger than ya might thank right now. She is hurt'n, and with all them wounds, it will take time to heal. Just take yer whoop'n like a man and do what is right. I feel in my heart that with a little time and lots of prayers, with the love that ya two have for each other, God will work his miracle, and thangs will work out. Be patient, but persistent. Don't go and give'n up just yet. I will tell ya that it will take time to gain 'er trust back. Just be the man I know ya are and if she does end up coming home, be the husband I know you have been and can be again. Remember, be compassionate; she ain't the one who screwed up. And don't go break'n any more promises! I mean it, mister, under any circumstances, do ya hear me? And no more drink'n, even if a beautiful woman like me offers it to ya, not one little sip, mister."

I said, "Thank you for yer advice, and as fer yer moonshine, I didn't wanna to hurt yer feel'ns. Ya know it is always tasty and goes down so smoothly, and ya know we always love come'n here to see ya and catch'n up on the good ole days and leaving with a quart or two."

With that she caught me off guard when she leaned over and laid a friendly smacker right on my lips and said, "Now then, young man, that is the last kiss from another woman that ya get from now on. Do you understand me, mister? No more of those shenanigans."

I didn't know what to say but yes ma'am.

She said, "I guess we both need to get our rest." As she was walking away and I was climbing up into the truck, she turned around and said, "Be careful out there, darlin, and don't be a stranger."

I nodded and waved as I climbed into the bunk area where Cash had already put himself to bed and was taking up most of the small mattress. I lay there, running things through my head and trying to wind them down. I said a little prayer and tried to call Jalynn one more time, just in case, but I already knew the outcome. I took heed to Missy's words and was patient. I rolled over to get some sleep for the next day's journey chasing the long white line down the big road.

Early the next morning, I woke up and started Reba to warm up before I headed out. Hoping not to wake anyone up with the sound rumbling from the exhaust stacks, I stepped out to do a quick inspection to get rolling as soon as I could without disturbing anybody's sleep. But as early as it was, I did not beat Mr. Blake up. I thought to myself, *he must signal the roosters to alarm everyone else to wake up.*

Mr. Blake was on the front porch enjoying his morning coffee. He caught a glimpse of me and waved as to say good morning, goodbye, and be safe. I waved back to let him know that I appreciated everything. I knew with a heavy heart that at his age, his life was nearing its end, and I probably would never see my old friend again. But I knew that he and the missus had lived a full and happy life. In the truck, I found a note that read,

> *"Bobby Ray, here is my number and the number of a veteran friend of mine, Hank. He also suffers from PTSD. I think you two could find help in each other. Feel free to call us anytime. Love, Lil Missy."*

Cash was still sleeping as I settled in my seat. I turned on the lights, put her in gear, and started rolling out to the big road. I pulled onto the road heading west, grabbing gears and gaining speed as fast as I could. Then I put the center of Reba's long nose on the white line and began my search for the end of it.

3

THE REMINISCENCE

Orin, WY – Winnemucca, NV

THE SUNRISE BROUGHT LIGHT TO THE NEW DAY AS I ROLLED along, pondering the night before. I made my way to Rawlins, Wyoming, before I stopped for an overdue cup of coffee. I filled my thermos, fueled up, and got us some breakfast. We ate in the truck to save time and afterwards, Cash and I used the restroom (or grass, in his case). It was time to hit the road once again.

I made my way onto I-80 west and put the wind to my back. I could see the sun silhouetting the mountain range way in the distance behind me in my mirrors; I had to make up for lost time. I poured the coal to Reba and hammered down. As I made my way, the CB awoke with radio checks. I turned it down to avoid the nonsense chatter that followed but left it just loud enough to keep myself informed of goings on in my path. I was listening to country music and making my way to my destination one mile at a time. I had a good pace on this long stretch of highway to make up the time.

I made it through to the west side of Salt Lake City, Utah, the sun now in my rearview mirrors, seemingly hanging like a fireball in the sky. I was squinting for some time until it rose higher out of my rearview mirrors. Now it cast its light on the mountains ahead, which were mesmerizing and

36

tranquil. I held the wheel and stared out the windshield at this beautiful landscape that God created. It set my mind at ease, and I started to think about my career coming to an end with retirement around the corner. I began to reminisce how it all started years ago in the winter of 1966.

My mind drifted back to my yester-years at the beginning of this journey. It all started in December of that year, when I was just a young man of eighteen attending the University of Tennessee in Knoxville, Tennessee. I had been going there on a football scholarship and was studying to be a sportswriter. I chose to attend college so I could get out of my small hometown; I didn't want anything to do with the ranch life. Raising livestock and hauling them to the auctions, feed lots, markets, and slaughterhouses was not for me. I needed a life as far away as I could get.

It was on a Saturday night after our last football game of the season when a few friends and I were crossing the field to our cars for a night out in the town to celebrate our victory. We were discussing our plans for Christmas break since our championship game was after the new year. I asked everyone what their plans were.

Bubba said he had thought about going home for a minute and then changed his mind at the fact that he had heard that some sorority girls were staying behind and he was going to stay behind too in case he needed to show any of 'em some love and comfort over the holidays. He said, "I will be their Santa Claus for Christmas."

We laughed, and I said, "Bubba, yer really something else, ya know."

Clem said he was driving down to Huntsville, Alabama, to be with his folks. He let us know that his Nana wasn't doing so good, and this might be her last Christmas. I felt bad and said, "Sorry, man, hope ya have a memorable holiday with 'er."

He thanked me and then Harvey said, "Well, I ain't go'n too fer since I am from Sevierville. So, Bubba, if those ladies get too much fer ya to handle, give me a shout and I can come help ya out. If you want, ya can have Christmas dinner with my family."

Bubba said, "Thanks, man! How lucky am I? Lonely ladies and Christmas dinner, too! Yee haw! Merry Christmas to this ole boy!"

Bud, being in love with Suzie, a cheerleader from the squad, said they were going to drive down to be with her and her crazy folks.

Earnest, in a low deep voice said, "Well, y'all, it's just me, Mama, and my brothers and sisters now since Dad passed this summer. I saved up my earn'ns and I am gonna surprise her. I rented her a cabin over there in Gatlinburg. She has always talked about want'n to see the Smoky Mountains and she doesn't get to do much of nut'n but take care of my sibl'ns. So, when she comes to pick me up, I am gonna drive 'er up there."

I told him that was mighty nice of him to do that for his mama. He said that after all the sacrifices and the hell she'd been through, she deserved it.

Harv' said, "Wow! That is awesome! You'll be the son of the century." Everyone laughed to lift the conversation up. Bubba asked what I was gonna do – stay or go home. I told 'em I had planned on staying to study the playbook for the championship game, but I did miss home, and I figured I should go since it was the holidays. I told them I'd gotten a flight out to go home to be with my folks.

Clem asked, "Are ya excited about go'n home, BR?"

I said, "Heck, yeah! Since I decided to go, it can't get here fast enough. I sure am miss'n my mama and her home cook'n. I can just taste them homemade biscuits and nanner pudd'n. Supposed to fly out in the morn'n."

Bubba kidded me by saying, "Look, fellas, our star quarterback is a mama's boy." They all started making fun of me for it. I jokingly started a scuffle with 'em and told them I would meet them at Smokies Bar as I climbed into my old orange 1960 Ford F-100 step-side truck. I nicknamed her Blossom after the Orange Blossom Special, and because she was Volunteer orange.

I drove to the bar where we were meeting and had a root beer or two. I wasn't a beer drinker even though I had my share of 'shine. Then I asked Becky if she wanted to go with me and help me pack for my trip and keep me company. She said yes, if I would walk her home afterwards.

We had a good time packing, talking, and joking around and then it was time for me to walk her home. While we were walking to her dorm, she grabbed my hand and said, "Bobby Ray, I really like you."

I said, "I really like ya, too, Becky."

She said, "When you get back, I would like for us to go off by ourselves for the weekend." I agreed and we continued our walk. When we reached her dorm, I gave her a goodnight kiss on her cheek and said I'd see her in a few weeks. But that was to be the last time I would see her ever again.

I thought of her request most of the night until I dozed off, which caused me to oversleep. Bubba must have stayed out until early morning 'cause he didn't get up either to take me to the airport. I busted through his door and said, "Hey, Bubba, get yer lazy butt in gear and drive me to the airport! We are running late! I will let you drive. That way, I can hop out and ya can drive Blossom while I am gone. I really don't wanna leave her at the airport. Just don't ya go and forget to come and pick me up in three weeks."

He jumped to his feet and got dressed, and we were out the door in a flash. We made it to the airport in record time. I got out and grabbed my bags and told him to take it easy with my truck.

Bubba said, "Don't worry, BR. I will treat 'er as if she were my own." Wouldn't you know; it as soon as he finished talking, he took off squealing the tires as smoke rolled from the exhaust. I shook my head and rushed in to find my gate.

I boarded the plane and settled into my seat, nervous as we took off because I had never flown before. All I could think about was giving my mama a big hug and eating a good homecooked meal. I was more relaxed once we were in the air, and I faded off to sleep. Before I knew it, the captain came over the intercom and said that we were fixing to make our descent. When we finally landed, I was so relieved. At the gate, I hurried and made my way off the plane. I scrambled to the baggage claim and then went outside in anticipation of my daddy arriving and picking me up. I wondered what it would be like on the ride back to the ranch.

Within a few minutes I recognized the ranch truck coming down the passenger pickup lane. It looked as if it had seen better days, but, "looks ain't everything," my daddy always said. It still ran like a top. But it wasn't Daddy driving; it was Slim, one of my dad's ranch hands. I guess Daddy was either too busy to come and get me or he was still upset at me for pursuing my dream. Every time I called home over the past few months, he would not speak to me; I always talked to Mama. As he pulled up, disgusted, I threw my bags in the back and climbed in.

Slim offered a handshake and then asked how I been. "Ya been hitting the weights, or what? Man! Ya buffed up since I last saw ya. I bet the girls are all over ya. How is school go'n? How is football?"

I gave him a look that told him I was angry that my dad sent him instead of coming himself, even though it was not his fault. I said, "Slow down on the questions, buddy. There is plenty of time fer that. Just get me home."

The ride to the ranch took almost two hours so I decided to close my eyes and take a little nap. That was until Slim asked, "Hey, Bobby Ray, ya gonna help us loadout the cattle tomorrow or ya just gonna lay around all day?"

With a disgusted look at him with one eye open I said, "Do ya honestly think Daddy is gonna let me sleep past the roosters' crow'n? He will make me help regardless of what I wanna do. Ya know that is the way he is. He is a stubborn ole man and set in his ways. Which is why I went off to college in the first place." After that, I turned back to the window and nodded off to sleep.

When we went across the old iron bridge, I awoke, and I knew we were almost home. As we turned down the driveway and drove by the pasture leading to the house, I could see everyone gathered at the corral. I noticed Daddy driving that beat-up 1958 B-model Mack down the long-haul road to meet them. We walked to meet them and say hello. Everyone greeted me with a handshake or a pat on the back. The lady ranch hands gave me a hug and a kiss on the cheek. Then Mama gave me my much needed and overdue hug and told me she loved me. They all asked some of the questions that Slim had asked and commented on my build. The ladies asked me if I had found a girlfriend. I told them that I had a girl, but I didn't say she was mine for sure. I just mentioned we had gone out a few times. The guys started pulling money from their pockets and exchanging it and I knew right away that some bets had been made on my success in the mission.

Dad, of course, was still too busy fooling with that old truck to welcome me home. We chatted a little bit, catching up. I was wondering in my head, had my leaving upset my daddy so bad that he was rejecting me?

I told Mama I wanted to relax from my trip. She said, "As soon as yer daddy gets the rig and trailer set up for tomorrow, we can go in and catch up with ya."

With his strategic placement of the rig, he shut it down, climbed out and walked over. To my surprise he reached out and grabbed me into a big dad hug and said, "Welcome home, son."

He made it known that he was shutting everything down for the day so we could celebrate my homecoming. It shocked us all, because he never

40

stopped work except on Sunday to observe The Lord's Day and attend church services. He always ate and slept the ranch life, saying that hard work will make a man out of me.

We strolled on to the house and as we walked, he put his arm around Mama's shoulders to escort her on the way. I couldn't help but notice his huge, callused hands, scarred and weathered from the work he did to keep the ranch running like clockwork. It was a wonderful sight to see their love in motion as she accepted his offering. She looked up at him as she put her loving arm, not without its own markings of arthritis and hard work, around his waist and said, "I love ya so much, Hubert James." He met her eye and replied, "I love ya, too, Ann James."

As we continued into the house, there was a nice fire going and a wonderful smell came from the kitchen. It felt good to be home again. I settled on the couch and with the aromas of fried chicken, pinto beans, and cornbread filling the house. I must have dozed off for a bit because before I knew it, Mama was calling us to wash up for supper.

During supper, as usual, some of the ranch hands and their families or significant others joined us. Most of them lived on the ranch in the bunk house attached to our house with a porch and a breezeway. It was two stories. The women folk lived upstairs and the men downstairs. Two of the hands and their families lived in houses that daddy built for them, and would do the same for the rest, as they were all considered family. Mama cooked three meals every day, including supper, except on weekends when most of them would go out on the town. Some had worked for Daddy for as long as I could remember. As we sat around the supper table, we talked about how the ranch was doing, how my sister Jackie was doing at school over in Paris, and how my big brothers Peanut and Dimples were doing down in Georgia with the truck stop. We didn't discuss my current situation. I guessed it was because it was a sore subject to be talked about in front of Daddy. My decision to leave had left him a might upset at me, since I was the only one left, and he really had it in his head that I would stay and help run the ranch and someday, take over.

After supper, the men went into the den while the women offered to help Mama with the kitchen. In the big den, there was a fire going strong in the fireplace. Daddy grabbed the shine jug and poured him a glass and lit a cigarette as he passed the jug around for us to have a swig as he usually did. By this time, the ladies were joining us.

41

Daddy with his back to us, his foot up on the rock and staring at the glimmering fire, he took a deep breath as if he was dreading what he was about to say. Then he asked, "How is school going fer ya, son? Are ya stay'n outta trouble?"

"Yes, sir," I replied. "It's noth'n like ranch life. The city of Knoxville sure is different, but everyone is nice. There is a lot go'n on but, I have enough to keep me too busy fer the trouble to find me."

Daddy took a sip of shine and looked me in the eye and said, "Ya know, son, I wouldn't thank any less of a man of ya if ya find yerself in a situation and need'n to just load up and brang yer tail home."

I said, "I know, Daddy, but I'm do'n what I have always dreamed of. Football is my life and I have worked so hard to get where I am. Besides, my team needs me. As fer the ranch, if my dream doesn't work out, I will be home in a flash. I know ya had different dreams fer me. Can I please try this fer myself? I want to prove that I can do some'n with my life instead of have'n it handed oer to me."

Still staring at the fire, he spoke. I knew from the sound of his voice he had tears in his eyes as he said, "Son, ya know that ya are a man in my eyes, and I trust ya. Just know that yer mama and I support ya as long as it's honest and good. But no matter the situation, know that we love ya and ya are always welcome home."

I knew at that point that he was proud of me, even if not fully in agreement with me for not wanting to carry out his plans for me on the ranch. The fact of the matter is that it had caused us to butt heads from time to time up until now. I knew he needed my help, and before I had left home for college, I had told him that I would help him out anytime I was home from school in the summer and during any of the holidays I was able to make the trip, though I don't think he believed me at the time. I reconfirmed it after he had spoken his peace.

I said with a sigh, "I know, Daddy. I have always known the love and support that y'all have shown to all of us, even for everyone in this room." He continued to look deep into the fire to avoid us seeing his disappointment and at the fact that more tears were streaming down his rugged aged face from my comment. He took the last sip from his glass and sat it on the mantle. Without turning around he said, "Guess I'm gonna head off to bed. We have an early and hard day ahead of us. I suggest y'all do the same. I need y'all to be rested and ready. I need to get our cattle loaded and down yonder to death row and do the other hauls so I can get back home to load out at The Blake Ranch for their haul next week." And with that, he retired to his bedroom.

A few of us stayed for a little bit catching up and me answering all their earlier questions. When they were satisfied, we all went to bed.

Early the next morning, I had planned on sleeping in a little. After all, they had managed without me for the last few months. But Daddy had a different plan. I was startled from my sleep at 4 a.m. when he forcefully knocked on my bedroom door and with a stern voice said, "Hey, boy, time to get up and get this day started. Don't think fer one minute yer gonna lay around here all day and do nuth'n."

Not wanting the repercussions of disobeying, I quickly responded by saying, "Yes, sir! I'll be right there."

I jumped up and quickly got dressed. Still half asleep, I stumbled down the stairs to have some of the breakfast mama had fixed for Daddy's small army of ranch hands. They had already got their fill and left. Mama was cleaning up when I entered and greeted me with a hug and kiss.

"Good morn'n, son! Did ya sleep alright?"

I drowsily said, "I would still be asleep if it wasn't for Daddy wake'n me."

She chuckled and said, "Well, ya know, son, yer daddy has missed ya and he does love ya. He just has a funny way of show'n it."

I said, "Yes, ma'am, he does."

She said, "Son, while ya were away, he told me how proud he is of ya for go'n off and getting a good education. How ya are go'n to make a good writer, knowing the ends and outs of the sport. He even thanks ya could be a professional quarterback. He just wishes ya weren't so fer away and could help around here more. Since ya are the only one to follow in his footsteps. This is just his way of get'n to spend time with ya without have'n to say it because ya know he is a bull-headed ole man and doesn't show his feel'ns." She chuckled again and said, "Now get ya some breakfast and get down to the barn."

I said, "Thank ya, Mama, I never thought of it that way. I too wish I had more time to spend with him and I will one day."

At this point I had no time left to sit down at the table and eat, plus there was only a biscuit and a few pieces of bacon left. I grabbed them and put them inside the biscuit and poured a glass of fresh milk as I headed to the mud room to put on my boots and hurry out back door. I shoved my food in my mouth and washed it down with the milk and as I ran down the steps, I sat the half empty glass on the railing and headed to the barn.

No one was there, so I ran to the corral where everyone was standing around the fire pit, drinking coffee and either smoking a cigarette or cigar. As usual, Tank and Slim had a big chaw of backer in their jaw, and even though Dinky was a young woman, she too had a chew in. They were chatting and discussing the plan Daddy had and throwing in an occasional cuss word here and there.

"Bout damn time ya got yer tail end down here!" Daddy hollered.

I said, "Sorry, I must still be on Tennessee time."

Daddy said, out loud to make sure I heard him and with a little bit of laughter, "Well, I will just have to fix your clock then, won't I?"

A few of the cowboys that were not at dinner chimed in with questions to change the subject.

Dinky said, "Hello there, Bobby Ray, welcome home."

Duke hollered, "Lookie there, the college boy is back home."

I gave him a firm handshake and said, "In the flesh, ya ole slacker."

Scooter said, "See, I told ya he would come back, Duke! Ya owe me five bucks!"

"Oh, dang it," Duke responded. "I thought fer sure ya would have gotten yerself a pretty young thang and didn't know if we would see the likes of ya again."

Dinky spoke up and said, "Are we gonna get this show on the road or what?"

Daddy was coming from the bull barn where he put George in the pin where he would be out of the way, as he gets mean when you mess with his ladies. Daddy is the only one on the place that can handle that ole beast. He said, "Dinky, ya are right we need to get go'n," as he poured a fresh cup of coffee that was warming over the fire. He took a couple of sips and lit a cigarette before he started assigning jobs. After a few more sips, he finished his smoke and summoned everyone over for morning prayer.

We held hands in a circle. As he said the prayer, I was holding his hand and I could feel the age and roughness of his palms with the calluses and permanently oversized knuckles, evidence that they had been broken several times, and I couldn't even imagine what they had been through to get in that shape. I thought that with all that hurt in his hands, he still held mama like a precious fragile rose and comforted us children with tender loving care when we were hurting.

After the prayer, he directed everyone to their positions and each person began his or her task. Dinky walked over to the rear of the cattle trailer and hooked up the shoot. Dad yelled out to everyone to be on their toes and pay attention. The first few head were tagged and loaded, and everything seemed to be going like clockwork until Sissy, who had her mind on other things and wasn't paying attention, let one of the cows slip out of the corral. It wandered over to the bull pen and hit the gate, which had not latched good when Daddy closed it.

This immediately set George off. No one noticed her mistake until it was too late. George had already gotten loose and was now in a fierce rampage. Best I could figure, he was looking for his latest mate who we had already loaded up. Daddy was trying to get him under control by waving and hollering at him, trying to chase him back into the pen. But ole George, mean as he was, was not having any of it, and was getting angrier at our efforts. He was after one thing and one thing only, and we were all in his way.

All of us besides Daddy were running scared as we had never seen this happen before. Daddy was far off from the pen when he started yelling at George, and as he ran the distance, Old George was just a little quicker than he was, charging at Daddy with all his might and anger.

We all yelled at Daddy to run, but he wasn't fast enough. They were going to meet just short of the pen, and I yelled at Daddy to jump in the back of the truck. Daddy, who remained calm as he knew his plan was not working, yelled at us to stay back. He stopped in his tracks and got stern with George, which seemed to settle him down, knowing that Daddy was in charge.

Scooter yelled, "Jump the fence, Hubert!"

Sissy yelled, "Lasso him, Tiny!"

45

Tiny had tied one end of a rope to the hitch of one of the trucks and made a lasso in the other in hopes of getting it around him to hold him back, but George was too clever and dodged his effort. This set him in motion again. George gave a few loud blows from his nostrils and dug his hooves in the ground. Then in a flash, he darted towards Daddy, and when he did, I thought if I ran interference, Dad could escape.

Daddy saw me jump from my cover and started yelling for me to stay back. I never felt so much fear as Daddy, seeing that there was no stopping this raging beast, took charge and started running away from us all so we would be safe. Before we knew it, and right before our gazing eyes, the unimaginable happened. Daddy, being the hero, we perceived him to be, just couldn't run fast enough, and with one swoop, Goerge tilted his head. When he raised, it one of his horns pierced Daddy's side and he sent him head over heels into the air. Daddy landed hard and lifeless on the ground, but George was not satisfied. He bucked and turned around and with his huge hooves, trampled Daddy several times.

It all happened so fast yet seemed to last an eternity. As the bull landed deadly blows all over Daddy's motionless body, everyone stood in disbelief, living a nightmare as George continued his rampage.

RJ, who had made it to Daddy's truck during all the commotion, grabbed the 30/06 rifle and got off a couple of rounds into the head of that beast of a bull and sent him backwards. He fell almost immediately after the second shot. We all ran over to Daddy fearing the worst, as blood was coming from his head and several other places on his body, soaking his clothes. I thought for sure he was dead. With tears in my eyes and full of anger myself, I took the rifle from RJ and put two more rounds in that bull's head, just to make sure. I looked at him and said, "Rot in hell, you S.O.B!!!"

Knowing the bull was dead, Daddy lay lifeless before us. Tiny knelt beside Daddy to check his breathing and pulse. "He has a weak pulse, and his breath'n is shallow and raspy." Tiny said. "We need to get him to the hospital quickly!" Slim said he would go to the house and call an ambulance, and Tiny shook his head. "We have no time for that! We need to load him up and get gone now!"

Everything seemed to be going in slow motion in my mind, but the chance of Daddy's survival was a race against time to make it to the closest hospital two towns over. Duke told Sisco and Bucky to grab some fence boards from the barn and he would get some horse blankets and rope to make a back board. I remained by Daddy's side, holding his head and telling him he would be okay, and to just hang in there, not knowing if he could even hear me. Within a minute or two, they were ready to load him up. Once we had him secured in the back of the truck, I told Slim to go to the house and get Mama and follow us to the hospital.

Sissy said, "I will go with ya, Slim."

I yelled at her to go to hell because she was the reason my daddy was almost dead. I told her to gather her belongings because she was fired, and I would make sure she never worked on any ranch again. She was crying her eyes out as we pulled off, but I didn't care. She screwed up and hurt my Daddy; I would never forgive her for it.

As we pulled up on the driveway from the haul road, I saw Slim meeting my mama on the back porch. She was waiting there because she must have heard the rifle shots. I saw her bury her head in her hands as she ran back into the house. We hit the main road and quickly gained speed to get to the hospital.

It seemed like it was taking forever. Sisco and I were freezing in the back of the truck, but I just kept talking to Daddy, telling him I loved him, and I was sorry for all the pain I had caused him for leaving. I wasn't sure if he would make it or not, but I wanted him to know. I started praying that God would save him. Pleading that I would stay and take care of him, Mama, and the ranch. After my prayer, it was just a few minutes until we arrived at the hospital and Tiny ran into the Emergency Room yelling, "We need help here!"

The staff came rushing out with a gurney and we all helped load Daddy onto it. They took off, leaving us outside. It was only about fifteen minutes until Slim and Mama pulled up with RJ who had jumped in. Mama ran over to us, and I hugged her while trying to hold back the tears. While we were hugging, she asked what they were saying about daddy. I told her they said to stay in the waiting room and when they had news, they would come out and give it to us.

The small waiting room was quickly overcrowded due to all the people waiting to hear news of Daddy's condition. There was so much support as we are country folk and stick together in times of trouble.

It was about three hours before the doctor came out and said that

47

they had done all they could do, and that Daddy's injuries were very extensive. He was stable but in critical condition. They said they put him in a medically induced coma and would need to be taken by helicopter to the city hospital Cheyenne, Wyoming, two hours away. Upon arrival, he would go straight into surgery.

As we left the hospital, the helicopter with Daddy on board was lifting off. We lost them as they flew off in the distance. We loaded up this time with Mama and I, along with RJ. A few others joined behind us in a convoy for the trip.

It was a sad drive as Mama said, "I just knew some'n like this would happen someday. I never liked that old bull. Yer daddy always praised him and said he was a good stud bull." Then she started crying and prayed out loud, "Lord, please, let my Huey be okay and come home to me. Lord, ya know I love him, and I need him."

As I drove, I looked out the driver's window and cried, not only for my daddy, but for my mama's sorrow and her broken heart.

We finally made it to the hospital and Daddy was still in surgery. We were again instructed to stay in the waiting room, and when they had news, they would let us know. Hours went by with no news, and we were on pins and needles waiting to hear from the doctor. Finally, he came out to make us aware of Daddy's condition.

Mama sobbed as the doctor began.

"Mr. James is in recovery in the ICU. He has a brain injury with fluid around it causing it to swell, a collapsed lung, a ruptured spleen, and several broken bones." He explained to us that Daddy was still in a coma and there was nothing more he could do at this point. There was nothing we could do either; the doctor told us we should go home and wait by the phone for an update.

After a long sorrowful debate, with tears in her eyes and a heavy heart, Mama agreed that it was best that we head home and finish the load out. As we left that little room and went outside and headed towards our truck, Mama broke down and collapsed to the ground. She cried out, saying, "Lord, what am I gonna do? I don't want to leave him. He needs me and I need him to be alright."

I immediately grabbed her and held her tight as Scooter grabbed a blanket from the truck to keep her warm while she sat there on the freezing cold asphalt. She cried out in prayer again, questioning what she would do if he died. How was she going to make it without him? She said she wished Sherman (Peanut) and Jackie Lee were there. She questioned how God could let this happen to such a good man.

We sat there for about an hour until she felt like getting in the truck to head home. On the way, she softly cried and stared out the window.

We got home around the crack of dawn. Once in the door, she asked if we had talked to my brother and sister.

I said softly, "Yes, ma'am. Peanut is on his way and Jackie is try'n to get a flight out."

Satisfied with my answer, Mama put on her apron and put on a pot of coffee and started making breakfast. We all knew not to say anything to her because she would raise her voice and get whatever she had in her hands thrown at us. We knew she was just doing something to deal with the events that had happened and to ease her mind a little.

With tired eyes, we sat in silence around the table waiting for Mama to bring the food. Slim, being the lead ranch hand said, "Listen, I know that Mr. James's rule is no talk'n work at the table, but we got a problem."

Everyone turned to him waiting on the explanation as he continued.

"We need to figure out who is gonna get this load down to the death row and do the other run'n so we can load out the Blakes' stock next week. With the market be'n down, if these loads don't make it there on time to Winslow, Arizona, the ranch will suffer, and so will our pockets."

Daddy had made it known that the mortgage was past due, and everyone had hung in and worked for a month with little pay. There was no one around that could drive because everyone was just as busy as we were. My brother who was coming from Fairmount, Georgia, was a disabled veteran, and couldn't drive. And my sister? I wouldn't trust her with my old truck let alone a rig and trailer loaded with cattle. That left me. I didn't know how to drive that old Mack truck, and I didn't have a license for it. The ranch hands had to stay to take care of branding the new cattle and run the ranch. There had to be someone who could or would do the haul for us.

Mama came in and set the food down and said, "Y'all get the trailer loaded and God will supply us with a driver."

We ate our breakfast, and with Slim's instruction, we got the rest of the cattle loaded and fed them, since they might be in there for a spell. I was in solemn thought all day, wishing Daddy was here to haul this load. I prayed for his guidance and for God to help with the situation.

As we were finishing up, it was looking like the decision was coming down to either the haul not making, it or me taking on the huge task and filling in my daddy's shoes. I climbed up in the old Mack to be alone and to check it out. After a few minutes, the hands noticed and began to crowd around.

As I looked at the complexity of the machine, Duke said, "It's easier than it looks. Don't let it scare ya. We can help ya learn quickly."

I was sitting there contemplating the idea in my head when Mama came walking up with tears in her eyes. She said to me, "Ya look just like yer daddy sit'n up there in that driver's seat."

With all eyes looking at me for an answer, with all odds stacked against me, and against my will, the decision was made. I simply said, "Well, looks like I got some big boots to fill."

With that, Mama shouted, "Thank ya, Lord!" Knowing her prayers were answered, she turned back to the house. I sat there wondering how I was going to even begin filling my daddy's big boots.

My thoughts were interrupted by Cash letting out a huge bark, telling me either something was wrong, he was hungry, or had to go. Not realizing that my daydreaming had consumed me for a long time, I had covered a lot of miles. I had almost reached my planned stopping point in Winnemucca, Nevada.

We pulled into the truck stop, and since it was not yet crowded, I fueled up so we could get an early start. After I parked, Cash and I went in, since he was always welcome to come inside and eat his supper and get his fair share of attention.

As we sat there, a young gal came over and introduced herself as Starlette. I said that is a unique name and she explained how her parents had come up with it, and then she began to take our order. Playfully she asked Cash what he wanted, and he gave out three barks as an answer. She rubbed his head and said, "Okay, darlin, coming right up."

Since the place was a little empty, when she brought our food, she sat down at the trucker's seating, reserved for us hungry drivers coming off the road. We chatted about goings on and such to pass the time while I ate. She asked me about my black eye and the other cuts on my lips and I told her it was from a grown man acting foolish and stupid.

She laughed and said, "I bet there was a woman involved somewhere."

I looked down at my left hand and rubbed my wedding band from underneath. "Yep," I said, "little lady, ya are right. I have done wrong by 'er, and now I am try'n to figure thangs out."

She asked in a bossy manner, "Ya ain't running from your troubles, are you, mister?"

I said, "No, honey. I just do my best thank'n out here on this ole road. I am try'n to figure it all out and how to fix what I have done."

She responded, "Good! You can't fix things by leaving them behind." I nodded agreement and she added, "Remember, you can't get rid of your temper by losing it."

"Ya are right, little lady. I will remember," that I responded.

We finished our conversation as I finished my meal. Starlette brought my thermos back from a cleaning and a refill for the morning cups. I thanked her and gave her a tip as I summoned Cash busy making his rounds for scraps and attention.

We left the café, and I lit a cigarette. Cash went off roaming so he could find the right spot to mark his territory. When we finally made it out to the truck to settle in, I lit another cigarette and figured I would call Jalynn to see if there was any change. The line rang and rang but still again no answer. I didn't bother calling Amberleigh because I wanted to keep her out of it for the time being. I settled in to get some shuteye for my early morning start of my long white line adventure.

4

THE JOURNEY BEGINS

Winnemucca, NV – Sacramento, CA

THE MORNING CAME TOO QUICKLY, REVEALING I'M NOT AS young as I once was; it's getting harder and harder to get these old bones started. I lit a cigarette, poured a cup of coffee, and lay there a while, feeling my age. On the radio played a song Jalynn loved by Kathy Mattea, "Eighteen Wheels and a Dozen Roses." I recall every time I would come home, I would stop and grab her a dozen and tell her that she was my Rose, filled with beauty and always smelling so good. She would embrace me and say, "Aww, honey, you are the most romantic man in the world. I love you!" I thought to myself, how I longed to have those moments back. As I wiped the tears from my eyes, I climbed out of the bunk to get my day started.

It was still dark outside. Cash had already climbed out to do his own thing. I started the truck to warm it up and to let him know it was about time to head out. I went in and grabbed us a biscuit or two, and when I returned, he had returned and settled in the bunk. We ate our breakfast and after I filled my travel mug with coffee and lit another cigarette, we started rolling.

It would take us 5 hours to get to Sacramento, California, and I had hoped that I would be able to get another load out of there as soon as possible. We were heading towards Reno, Nevada, when a familiar female voice came over the CB saying, "Break 19, break 19. Turbo, is that you and Cash up there?"

I grabbed the CB mic and hollered back, "10-4, pretty lady."

The voice came on again and said, "Hey, I am try'n to catch up with ya. Slow'er down and we can run together."

Cash's ears perked as he knew this time for sure that it was Strawberry Short Cake, as clear as a bell, and she was close by. He got all excited again as he knew Dolly Jean, her little ankle biter of a dog would be with her.

We traveled together for a while chatting until she said, "Hey, I gotta jump off the road for a minute in Reno. Ya want to stop for a few?"

I said, "Sure. I think Cash wants to ride with ya for a bit and since we are go'n the same way he can hitch a ride."

We pulled into the rest area, and she came running and gave me a hug and a kiss on the cheek. Cash and Dolly Jean were doing the usual butt-sniff greeting and then they were both running around and rolling in the grass while we visited at the picnic table. We talked there for a while and then climbed back into our trucks. This time, Cash climbed up into her truck for the rest of the ride.

Once we were on the road, we put the hammer down. I started thinking about everything again. I guess I held my foot to the throttle enough to outrun the capabilities of our CB's, because I couldn't hear her anymore nor see her in my mirrors. I figured I would see her at our destination, and I just kept rolling along. The scenery went quickly by and I focused on the road and the long white line that lay ahead of me.

As I was hammering down the miles, I once again traveled down memory lane to 1966. Back to the time of my very first trip when I made my decision to fill my daddy's boots to save the ranch. That trip would forever change me and lead me to the start of my own journey through life as a rancher and a truck driver.

It was a bitter, cold morning the following day after my decision. We all gathered in the kitchen for breakfast and Mama had the table set as usual. Her gospel singing was interrupted by us all sitting down, and she asked that someone bless the food. Buck, being the oldest, offered up the prayer and when he was finished, we all started to dig in. Mama mentioned that she had called to check on Daddy and still there was no change in his condition. She said thought she might get a ride to the hospital to visit and confirm the information herself.

After breakfast, she went to get dressed for the trip and the rest of us discussed what I should do next concerning my learning. I slid my plate back I said, "Well, I guess it's time to figure out how to fill those boots."

We all headed down to the barn, and as I climbed into that old 1958 B-Model Mack, it hit me: I had never driven a truck with this many gears, let alone a two-stick shifter with a hauling trailer. But it was time for me to step up and get these loads where they need to go without hesitation.

Each ranch hand agreed to give me a crash course in their knowledge of the truck even though they had never been off the ranch with it. I told them I really hated to be doing this. And Tiny spoke up and said, "I know, Bobby Ray. I hate it too, boy. But with yer daddy be'n in the hospital and all, we need ya. Ya are the only one who can save us at this point. But don't worry. Buck, RJ, Scooter, and me, we got you, buddy. And remember yer daddy would be so proud of ya right now. Let's get started and, get ya ready for the big road."

I only nodded in agreement with a huge lump in my throat. I then looked around and thought to myself, *Daddy, I need ya! Please be with me through this!* I began to cry a little, sorry that I had not tried to learn back when he offered.

Just then, Buck, being as rough as they come, interrupted and said, "Dry them tears, boy. Time to cowboy up and be a man. Let's get started."

Buck climbed the step and began pointing out the gauges and explaining what they meant. Then it was time to start the truck. He instructed me to push in the clutch and make sure both shifters were free to move when wiggled. When I turned the key, nothing happened. I said that the battery must be dead. They all laughed and told me that I had to push the start button, which Buck figured I knew about and had failed to mention. With the clutch in, I pushed the button. With a few deep, whining sounds and clanking noises, black smoke filled the air and the ole girl fired right up. She idled rough until she was warm and then settled down to her old self.

Buck said, "Now, boy, my part is done. I will let these younger cow pokes take over. I have work to do."

From there, each of the men took their turns in the jump seat for instructions. After several lessons, from shifting into the different gears, to turning and backing, and how to judge my distance to a loading shoot. I felt I was ready to head out on my own although I was truly overwhelmed with the quantity of new information. They then decided to go over the map to get me familiar with the stops I would make for the pickups, deliveries, fuel, and even sleep. That itself was a nightmare to me, and I thought more of my old man and how he ever managed to remember everything.

As we went over the map, they showed me how to write down my route and tape it to the visor, and every time I switched highways or roads, I was to take it off the visor. When I was exhausted from my training and felt I had it down pat, we called it a day at the same time Mama was ringing the supper bell, so we headed to the house.

That evening after supper, we all sat in the den. Mama was telling us of Daddy's condition and how there was no change, and how she was talking to him and telling him about what I was doing and how he would be so proud of me.

"I told him that we loved him," she said, "and we can't wait for him to get home."

Then everyone started telling their own memories with Daddy. I stood by the fire, stirring the embers and recalling my own memories of Daddy. I was in deep thought when Slim asked Mama if he could get Daddy's old Gibson guitar out and play a little.

"I thank that is a great idea," she said.

When he pulled it out of the case he found an envelope with my name on it. Handing it to me he said, "Read it, Bobby Ray."

Instead, I laid it on the mantle, and I stared at the fire. As he began to play, I remembered resonating from that old guitar Daddy loved so much, I recalled the times he had asked me to learn the business. I stood there, more memories came to mind, from the time he taught me to ride a bike, to pitching the baseball around, helping me with my homework on his third-grade education, and working on the cars and trucks.

Especially ole Blossom. How he was nervous teaching me how to drive! Not to mention the manhood talk about the birds and the bees. I guess the most important thing of all is that after he had worked hard on the ranch all day and was so tired that he could hardly eat super, he always made time for the Lord and his family.

I came out of my trance as Mama began to sing a very special song that she had written years ago called, "Jesus is the Answer," a sure sign that she was ready for whatever lay ahead of us. I took the envelope off the mantle and found that the letter inside contained the most inspiring message I've ever read.

It began with, *"My dearest son…"*

Those words alone brought tears to my eyes as I continued.

> *"…Things sure have not been the same without you here. Your mama and I have missed you every day. We want you to be happy and follow your dreams. We are proud of the little boy that we have raised, and we can see what a fine young man you have become.*
>
> *This Gibson, as you know, your mama got it for me a few years back when I went off to the Army to fight in the war. You know how I love to play it, however, as much as I enjoy it, I am afraid it doesn't get much attention these days. Your mama and I talked about it, and we would like you to have it and carry it wherever life leads you. Maybe one day you can get your brother to teach you how to play. Please share it with him. He was our first born and it should go to him, but I think you will need it right now in this trying time. Each time you hold it, you can think about us and all the memories on the ranch.*
>
> > *Merry Christmas, Son!*
> > *Love, Daddy."*

I stood speechless, feeling the love he had poured into this simple note. I felt everyone looking at me, waiting to hear what it said. I considered the mention of my "trying time," almost as if he knew his time was nearing the end. As I stared at the fire, I simply said, "I love you, Daddy, but I need you now more than ever, more than this old guitar." With the tears streaming down my face, I laid the letter back on the mantle and went to my room. There, I crawled into my bed and cried myself to sleep.

The next morning as the rooster made the horrible noise he could (and earlier than usual), I was awakened abruptly. I looked at the clock: 3:45. I said, with a smile on my face, "Yes, Daddy! I'm up." This had to be Daddy's way of letting me know he was watching over me, even though he was hours away in a hospital. I remembered the preacher saying one time that to be absent from the body is to be present with the Lord. So, knowing that my daddy was in good hands, I knew he would put in a good word for me. I jumped up with this new outlook, knowing Daddy had my back.

I got dressed and met the others at the table, but I was too anxious to eat. Instead, I went over the stops with them as they ate. After everyone was satisfied and seemed as excited and nervous as I was, we got up to head to the barn.

They shuffled out the door before I did. I took a few extra minutes putting on my boots and preparing myself for the huge task at hand. I had stepped out the back door and started down the steps when Mama called for me to wait. She met me on the back porch with a large green lunch pail and an old green thermos full of coffee. With tears in her eyes she said, "Here, I packed ya some food for the haul. It ain't much, just yer daddy's usual. Just a couple of biscuits with cold, fried taters, a bowl of pintos, a slice of leftover cornbread, and some stalk onions from last night's supper. Yer daddy always loved them. He said it would stick to his ribs and hold him over till he stopped for the night. There is also a couple of bananas, an apple, and two of my homemade fried peach pies."

She knew I didn't even drink coffee, but she was used to packing the pail and filling the thermos for Daddy. I didn't say anything about it; but I took her offering, hugged her, and said, "Thank ya, Mama. I love ya so much."

She kissed my cheek, grabbed my hand, and said, "Here is twenty dollars from my cookie jar; take it for pocket money. And here is yer daddy's truck stop punch card for a hot meal and a shower. He has an account at several places. You will need it by the time you reach Rose's truck stop over in Amarillo, Texas. That's where yer daddy always stopped and rested and called me." Again, with tears in her eyes and a trembling voice she said, "Be careful, Son! I love ya! Yer daddy would be so proud of you right now. I wish he were here to see ya off on yer first haul."

Trying to hold my own tears back I managed to say, "Thanks, Mama! Don't worry 'bout me. I will be alright! I have Jesus and Daddy watch'n over me. I will call you when I make it to my first stop and check-in on thangs."

Mama hugged me again and then turned and hurried back in the house so I wouldn't witness her emotional breakdown.

I stepped off the porch and headed to the barn with tears in my eyes and a smile on my face because I knew with Jesus and Daddy watching over me and Mama praying, everything would be all right. I made my way to the truck where they had already started it and it had warmed up and settled down to a purr. I put my overnight bag on the passenger side and the pail and thermos in the middle so I could reach them when I needed to. I went to the driver's side, and with everybody there to see me off, I climbed in the seat.

I said, "Thank y'all for sticking around for Mama and Daddy in these try'n times even though ya didn't have to. You could have gone to work somewhere else, but ya hung in there. That is the reason Daddy treats y'all like family and I know he loves ever' one of ya. I will do my best to come through for ya guys. But I will need yer prayers, and Mama will need yer help more than ever. Now, with this load almost two days late, I gotta get my butt in gear and 'hammer down' as Daddy would say."

Everyone moved back and I shut the door. I sat there for a few minutes going over my learning from yesterday and planning my next move. Finally, I grabbed the shifter and tried to put it in gear. The truck grinded with a loud and fierce sound. I shouted, "Why won't this thang go in gear?!" I knew they were all watching and could hear me as I tried again and had the same result. I yelled out this time louder, "Why won't this damn thing go in gear?!"

Dinky, seeing that I was getting mad, came running over and opened the door. She hugged me and said, "Honey, calm down. Ya got this, just thank for a minute." She gave me a kiss on the cheek and added, "Try push'n the clutch and try put'n it in gear."

At that point, I remembered what I was doing wrong, and with less grinding it slipped right in gear. Dinky stepped down and shut the door and I felt like a fool. Thinking I was ready, I let out on the clutch and that old Mack jumped and bucked like that mad bull and then died. Things were not going as well as they did during my teaching lessons. I went through the steps again and tried to get it moving. I did the same thing again and I shouted, "I hate this shit already!"

But I was bound and determined to succeed. I tried several more times and still no success. Slim came over from the milking shed and stood on the step. I rolled down the window.

He said, "Bud, slow yerself down. I know ya are flustered. You got this, and I am gonna help. Climb over and I will show ya a few tricks."

I climbed over in the jump seat, and he took control of the Mack. He showed me a few tricks as we drove up and down the dirt road. Just like Daddy, he made it look so easy. He showed me things like letting the clutch out slowly until it catches and then release it. Starting off in a different gear, depending on the weight. And how to float the gears, as they call it, when you don't use the clutch, you just use the rpms or the sound of the engine as guide. He never once looked at the gauges. He even showed me how to put my arm through the steering wheel so I could use both hands to shift the double shifters at the same time.

We stopped at the barn where he got out, and with his instructions, I climbed back into the driver's seat and was ready to continue. With the clutch in and the right gear selected, I used my new knowledge. The truck started rolling instead of jerking me all over the place.

"Woohoo!" I yelled. I was rolling. However, as I made my way down the dirt road to the main road, I grinded the rest of the gears. I didn't mind; I was happy. I was on my way, though I was sure they were all laughing at my efforts. It didn't matter, I was happy with myself and didn't care. I laughed as I hit the paved road at what the cows must be thinking in the back, sure they were tired of being jerked and slung about.

I was into my trip about thirty mins when I slowly got the hang of it. Not perfect by no means but getting by. After leaving the small town of Orin, Wyoming, I realized I had eight hours or so to my first stop in

Wagon Mound, New Mexico, where I would rest for the night. I was driving along and thinking of my past few days, and I started to cry. I figured I would see if the old AM radio worked. As I played with the knob, I found a country station that was filled with static, but I could make out the tunes. I settled into a groove and sang along with the ones I knew, and I fiddled with the knob to chase the stations along the way. My efforts eventually came to an end as I was getting further away, and the static took over. I just turned it off. As I drove, I started to wonder how Daddy was doing and thinking that it would be several more hours until I could call Mama and find out the answer to the question in my mind. I stared out the windshield at the road and as I was instructed, I did my best to keep the white line in the center of the hood. As I stared at it, I couldn't help but notice Daddy's worn-out Bible laying on the cracked dashboard. As the deciding factor of the line being in the center, it struck me as a sign that God would guide my way.

As I crossed into New Mexico, an unexpected snow had begun covering the road. I was unprepared for this as I was not experienced enough to operate this rig in the snow. I started to feel the coldness from the outside filling the cab and I began to get cold myself. I turned on the heater, which was not working as it should in this old heap, and the snow built up on the windshield. The condensation fog began to take over the inside and was covering my view of the road. I turned on the defrosters and they began to melt what they could, with the help of the wipers, but eventually could not keep up. I felt around in the truck as far as I could reach and found a handkerchief, not knowing what was on it. I used it anyhow and as I wiped the windshield to get a clearer view, the white line only peeked periodically through the snow.

As I made my way, I remembered Daddy telling me years ago when he was teaching me to drive that if I couldn't see the road, look for the white line where it meets the asphalt. I did as he instructed but eventually the white line was nowhere to be found. I was getting nervous, and I clinched the steering wheel so tightly that my knuckles were white. I tightened my whole body when other truckers with more experience would pass me as if I was sitting still. They quickly let me know that I was in their way by blasting their horns. I thought to myself, *I know I am driving a little slow but there was no need in that nonsense!*

I drove a little while longer and with my best efforts to keep her on the road, I was met with failure when I slid off the road and ended up in a ditch. I sat there shaking from the ordeal. For a while, I thought I was going to be there all night, but then a fancy big rig slowly came to a stop in front of me.

A man appeared at the back of his trailer carrying a long chain. I climbed out and met him. He introduced himself as Mountain Man and asked why I was driving Cowboy's rig. I explained that he was my daddy and told I him of the accident and the situation of the ranch. He said he was sorry and hooked the chain up between our trucks. Then he told me how to put it in "granny low" and let out on the clutch when he started to pull. As the chain got tight and I felt the tug, I let out on the pedal, and I started to move. Then just like that, his rig pulled me out with ease, and I was once again on the snow-covered road.

We met between the trucks, and he unhooked the chain. I thanked him as he said, "Hey, partner, that's what us real truck drivers do. We help each other out here on the road as we all need to get back home safely to our families."

With a handshake, we parted ways, and in a flash, he was in his truck, fading out of sight in the snow. I continued my journey once more and I prayed for better weather, hoping this day would come to an end soon.

Because I focused so hard on the road, time flew by without me noticing and before I knew it, the truck stop sign I sought appeared through the snow. When I guided the old truck up to the pump to get my fuel, I noticed everyone looking strangely at me. I didn't know if it was because of the condition of this old rig or the fact that they realized I was much too young to be driving. It wasn't until I went in to pay that the cashier came around the counter and hugged me.

"I am so sorry about your daddy!" she said. "We just found out about his accident from Mountain Man. All of us here knew your daddy well; he was such a good man. He always talked about his family and missed you all when he was out hauling." I told her thanks and that he always said he met some good people out here. I tried to pay for my fuel, and she said, "Put your money away. It isn't any good here. Whatever you need you just get it."

I thanked her again and walked out, marveling at what happened. I fired up the truck and pulled over to the truck lot. I needed to find a spot to begin the task of backing in. It took me several tries, and after about 10 minutes, I finally got it. Everyone must have figured out that I was a rookie driver, but I was proud of myself for not needing help. As I set the brakes, I let out a sigh of relief and thanked the Lord.

When I calmed down from the frustration of my backing job. I climbed out wearing my winter coat and went to search for a pay phone to call home. Within a couple of rings, Mama answered. By the sound of her voice, I could tell something was wrong and I was afraid to say a word. She said hello again, and this time, I said, "Hey, Mama, it's me, Bobby Ray. I made it to my first stop."

With a sigh of relief she said, "Good, son. I am so glad to hear that." Then she began to cry, and with a fragile voice muffled by tears she said, "Son, yer daddy didn't make it. The hospital called about two hours after ya left and let us know that he passed away. I sure wished ya didn't have to go. But ya stepped up and did what needed to be done and yer daddy would have understood. I just knew some'n like this was going to happen."

I stood there in the freezing snow taking the news in and tears flowed down my cheeks. What was a moment of silence seemed to last an eternity.

I mustered the courage to fight back my emotions and said, "Oh, Mama! I am so sorry I wasn't there. I love ya and I need to turn this rig around and come home. Not'n is more important right now than to be with ya and the rest of the family."

There was a pause and then her tone changed. "No, son! We are depend'n on ya right now and yer daddy would want ya to carry on. Ya must deliver that load and make the rest of the haul because there is others depend'n on ya be'n there."

I wasn't in agreement, but I obeyed. I said, "Okay, Mama, I will do whatever ya thank is best."

"That's our best option right now," she said. Then she told me that my brother had arrived, and my sister was on her way. She told me not to worry, that she also had the ranch hands to help take care of everything on her end.

"I know ya are making yer daddy proud, and he will be watch'n over you from heaven. Get some rest and be careful, and know I love ya."

With a broken heart and my stomach feeling empty, I cried all the way back to the truck. I climbed in the seat and sat there a spell, upset and wanting to go home. I figured it best that I eat something, so I grabbed the dinner bucket and opened it up. I ate one of the biscuits and drank two cups of black coffee to wash it down. I had another to go with my pies. I pulled the carpet covered bed board from behind the seat along with the nap sack and made my bed across the seats. As I lay there with my mind in disarray over the death of my daddy, I figured I would eat something else to stop my wondering mind. I fumbled through the bucket and found Mama had put two packs of Daddy's Lucky Strike cigarettes, likely as a habit of doing it for so many years. I figured, what the heck? Why not? My dad always said that he smoked to ease his mind. I opened one of the packs and grabbed his old zippo lighter and lit one to see if it would do the same for me. At first it made me choke and cough and left a bad taste in my mouth along with making me a bit queasy and lightheaded. But with every puff, the effects eased off. It was becoming more enjoyable as I was getting used to it, and in fact it was helping me. I continued for a while and smoked several, and also had another cup of coffee.

I was feeling better. I tried again to lay down. The truck was running but the heat was working hard to keep up with the falling temperature outside. I was shivering as I climbed into the knapsack, but I was slowly getting warm. I lay there as thoughts continued to cross my mind.

I thought of how my last feeling for him was anger for waking me up so early, and then how I resented him for leaving me and me not getting to say I was sorry. I didn't get to even say how much I loved him. I thought of how good of a Daddy he was to us. Even though he was stern in his ways, he loved us unconditionally. What was bothering me most was the fact that I wouldn't make it home in time for his funeral. I would never see my daddy again. These thoughts continued through several more cigarettes until I eventually cried myself to sleep.

In the morning, I checked the oil and water and kicked the tires in preparation to get on the road. I soon was headed to Winslow, Arizona, and then to finish the haul that would take me from there to Amarillo, Texas, on to Oklahoma City, Oklahoma, then finally make my way back through Iron Mountain.

I was hoping and praying the rest of the trip would go smoothly since the snow had let up and the sun was shining bright. I made it on to the delivery in Winslow, and after talking to them about what had happened, they told me not to worry about being late. I thanked them and took to the road enroute for Amarillo. I reached my overnight stay in between and got some rest.

The next day, I was bound for Texas. As I was on my way, the weather changed for the worse and it was snowing once again. Before long, my thoughts of having an uneventful trip quickly diminished as I felt myself sliding off the road and waiting for someone to come rescue me. After about an hour, my rescuer showed up and pulled me out and I was on my way again. This would end up happening two more times until I finally reached my destination.

Once there, I was loaded pretty darn quick and was able to get to Rose's Truck Stop for the night. I fueled, and after I parked, I went in to get a much-needed hot shower and a hot meal. I showed the cashier my card and she directed me to the shower saying she was sorry about my daddy's accident. *News travels fast,* I thought. She asked how he was doing and I told her that he had passed away. She started crying and said she loved him he was always so kind. I laughed inside as I thought to myself, *Are we talking about the same man?* I knew my daddy had a demeaner on the road that we rarely saw.

I finished my shower and ate dinner. Afterwards I found a phone and called home. This time my brother answered and gave me the rundown on things on the ranch. My sister had made it home from Paris, and she and Mama went to the funeral home to finish the arrangements. He wanted me home, but I told him that I regretted it and that I would be home as soon as I could. He understood and we hung up. I went to the truck to warm up and get some sleep.

The following morning, I was up early, rolling before the sun came up. The roads were clear, and I made it through to Oklahoma City without delay. I unloaded and loaded there, so it took the better part of the day, and I bedded down for another early start towards Wyoming.

When I woke up the next morning, I was so sore from the make-shift bed that I could hardly move. After a bit of stretching, some coffee and my newfound joy of cigarettes, I was ready. I rolled on as fast as that old Mack would go until I reached Iron Mountain where I would deliver my final load. They were closed, so I had to wait until morning to unload.

I settled down on the board for a night's sleep, but all I could think about was getting home. The harsh reality set in that I was not there for Daddy's funeral, and I was not there for Mama. Also, I was missing Christmas with my family, which I knew would be hard for us all. Instead, I was out here running this damn haul to save the ranch so Mama wouldn't have to worry for a bit. I was so upset that I covered my head hoping morning would come fast so I could make my way home and be done with all this. I wanted to get back to school and playing football.

Before I knew it, I was awakened when a worker knocked on the window letting me know they were ready for me to unload. It didn't take them long once I was parked. When they finished, I was on my way, and I was happy to be heading home.

It seemed like it was taking forever even though it was only a two-hour trip. I was mentally and physically exhausted and more than ready for it to be over. Here it was the day after Daddy's funeral and the day after Christmas. I shamelessly thought that I was glad because I didn't know if I could handle Daddy not being there for the holiday.

I made a quick stop to grab a cup of coffee (plus one to go) and a pack of cigarettes and was on my way again. As I traveled through Orin and on the home stretch, I tried to prepare myself for the reality of Daddy not being there to meet me and tell me how proud he is of me.

My eyes filled with tears as I turned down the dirt road to the barn. As I drew near, my family ran in my direction to welcome me home. Mama was crying as I stopped the truck, and she met me with open arms, told me she was happy I made it home and how proud she was of me. My brother and sister hugged my neck, too. The rest waited for their time and then greeted me with grateful smiles, high fives, and handshakes from the men, while the women gave me hugs and kissed my cheek.

I told Mama it sure was good to be home. She asked how it was, and I said all right, under the circumstances (I didn't want to tell her the whole truth).

"I hate that I missed Daddy's funeral," I told her.

She said, "I'm sorry for that but like I said before, yer daddy would be so proud of ya for take'n care of yer family; to keep what he has

65

worked so hard to build up."

As the excitement wore off and the sadness of Daddy's passing started to hit me more than ever, Mama asked if I was hungry.

I said, "Shoot yeah, I am. Ya know I can always eat, especially if it's yer home cook'n."

"Well, I'm about to go in yonder and cook some lunch," she replied. "Why don't ya come in and get settled in to rest." I said I would after I grabbed my stuff from the truck.

While unloading my belongings, Slim and Tiny were returning from mending fences. They jumped off the horses and welcomed me home. They told me congratulations and asked how it went. I explained what had happened and made it known that I didn't care none about drive'n the big girl through a snowstorm.

They just kinda laughed and Slim said, "Yer daddy would be so proud of ya."

I said, "That's what I keep hear'n. I just wish I could have been two places at once."

Tiny said, "Buddy, I know it. I hate thangs panned out the way they did fer ya. Sometimes we don't understand GOD'S plan. We are taught not to question him, and we have to trust we've done what he wanted us to do."

I agreed and asked how things had been going with the ranch. "I mean, how is Mama really do'n?" I asked

"She has her good days and her bad days," Slim said. "But she's try'n to hold it together and be strong. She says we will get through this by the grace of God."

The other ranch hands had joined us for the walk up to the house. While we walked, Duke asked, "Did ya get friendly with any of those pretty ladies out yonder on the road?"

I laughed and said, "Heck, naw! That was the furthest thang from my mind." He said maybe next time, and they all laughed.

Scooter punched Duke in the arm and said, "That's another five bucks ya owe me. Pay up!" He exclaims to him, that's the last time as he shoves the money into Scooter's shirt pocket.

Approaching the house, I told them to tell Mama I had something to do and that I would be there in a little bit. I jumped in the pickup truck and headed to the family cemetery. I lit a cigarette when I knew I was far enough out of sight so that no one would know of my new habit. Walking up to the gravesite, I had a lump in my throat and my stomach was in knots.

"Hey, Daddy," I said. "This is not how I imagined greet'n ya when I first let out of here. I know we didn't always see eye to eye on things. I sure wish I had one more time to sit and talk to ya and let ya know how much I love and appreciate all ya have done for me and the family. After run'n this haul, I understand ya a lot better now. I miss ya so much."

I hit my knees and started praying over the mound of fresh dirt and flowers that held my daddy's empty shell of a body and I started to weep. As the tears fell on the flowers, I looked to heaven and began to ask God and Daddy what I was supposed to do now that he was gone. I was torn between what I wanted to do and what I needed to be done. I kneeled there for some time telling Daddy about the journey. When I was ready to leave, I told him that I heard mama ringing the dinner bell and I didn't wanna be late and get in trouble with her.

My walk down memory lane was interrupted when I realized that it wasn't Mama ringing the bell. Instead, it was the sound of the smokey bear behind me and his voice on the CB screaming at me "to pull into the scales" (or chicken coop, as we refer to it). He had snuck in behind me as I crossed the California State Line.

Smokey pulled me in for a quick inspection of my logs and truck. He kept me longer than I wanted him to, and it made me later than I wanted to be. With evidence that I had been crying, he asked if I was okay. I just said, "Yes, memories, ya know."

I guess he felt sorry for me because he said, "Go on get out of here but, watch your weight and speed."

By that time, Short Cake had caught up and passed me. I left the scales and quickly built up my speed. I passed her back, and she shouted over the CB, "Hey! Super trucker, what is yer hurry?"

I grabbed the mic and told her that since I got held up, I was gonna stop at the T/A Truck Stop just ahead in Colfax for the night. We were only an hour out from our destination, and I asked her if she wanted to stop. She said yes but mentioned that I was to buy her supper. I agreed.

At the stop, we grabbed some fuel and found two parking spots together. Cash was excited to see me as I walked over and opened her driver's door like a gentleman to help her out. Cash hopped out and I rubbed his head. He looked up at me with those big brown eyes as if to say, "thanks for saving me from that yelping ankle-biter."

We walked in the Truck Stop and pulled up a seat to finish our chat from the picnic table. I knew suspicion was building in her mind as to what had happened to me, so I finally told her. She scolded me for what I had done and that I should be ashamed of myself for acting like that. She and Jalynn had become friends over the years. When she would go out with me and we were loading and heading the same way, Jalynn would ride with her for some girl-time.

After supper, we walked back to our trucks. Short Cake hugged me and said, "I know ya can fix this, Bobby Ray."

I said, "I know, but I can't get 'er to even talk to me right now."

"She will," Short Cake exclaimed. "Just give 'er some time to thank. You, done right by come'n out here for a little while."

We said good night and I climbed up in the cab to what you would think was a half-starved Cash. He was demanding the tray in my hand knowing it was his. After he scarfed it down, he got out and took his sweet time to do his business as he sniffed all over GOD'S green acres before adding his contribution to nature. When he climbed back in, I gathered my stuff and went back in to get a shower. When I returned to the truck, Cash was asleep, I lit a cigarette and laid there on the little space he had left for me.

I looked at my phone, no calls. Being persistent and patient, I tried just the number once. When there was no answer, I figured I should go to sleep and rest for tomorrow's search for the end of the long white line. I put out my cigarette and faded off to sleep.

5

THE DECISION

Sacramento, CA – Yuma, AZ

THE FOLLOWING DAY, HOURS BEFORE ANYONE WOULD BE up and about, I started my day after getting only a few hours of sleep. I went in and filled my thermos and grabbed a cup of coffee to go. As I made my way out to my truck, Cash had already jumped out and was focusing on his usual morning task. I sipped on my coffee and smoked a couple of cigarettes to wait. When he was satisfied, he joined me back at the truck as I was opening the hood to check things out.

As I did my walkaround, he sniffed along with me like he knew what he was looking for, supervising to make sure I was doing what I was supposed to. When I was finished, I closed the hood and started her up. We were ready to roll. Cash took his place on the bed since it was still dark out and he couldn't see out the window.

As I hit the road, I could see the silhouette of the desert mountain range highlighted by a moon that was full and bright. We were on the last leg of our delivery, and soon the moon disappeared, and the sun took its place in my rear view, now revealing more of the mountain tops.

I thought to myself that God really knew what he was doing when he made the sight that lay before my eyes.

We arrived at our destination a mite early and luckily, we were able to get unloaded and get a reload headed to death row over in Yuma, Arizona. With everything buttoned up, we were ready to hammer down.

We hit the highway and while tracing the eastward mountains, now in my view and the sun shining in my eyes, I would glance at the road and a glimpse of a car or truck would get my attention. For a long stretch there weren't many out. I lit a smoke and settled in for the trip.

Once again, my past caught up to me as I was thinking of Jalynn, Mama, and Daddy, and my mind drifted back to my youth. I began to recall the period after my first road trip, many years ago and millions of miles back.

It was early morning on New Year's Day, 1967, as I recall, a week after we said our last goodbyes to Daddy and laid him to rest. I was talking with Mama over coffee, I told her that I thought it best that I give up my scholarship and take the rest of the year off to help keep the ranch going so she wouldn't lose it. Things had been running pretty good for us this past week. I had just gotten back from the Blake Ranch haul, this time with less interruptions and a little more confidence.

I explained my plan: I would continue to haul the livestock loads, and that I should be able to do even more than Daddy since I didn't have a whole family to take care of. If the others took care of the ranch in my absence, we would be in good shape and probably more profitable.

"After all, I'm become'n a natural at truck drive'n. It must be in my blood," I exclaimed.

She quickly said, "No, son! You will go back to school and continue yer education and make some'n of yerself. We'll be fine, and we'll eventually find a driver fer the haul'n."

"But Mama!" I said.

She said, "Don't *but me,* mister. I'm still yer mama and now, I'm the boss round here."

I left the table angry and went to the barn. Slim was in there and without realizing what I was doing, I lit a smoke.

"Holy crap, Bobby Ray!" he said. "When did ya start smoke'n?"

I said, "Well, after y'all put me in that truck and sent me roll'n down the road, I had to figure out some way to calm my nerves. I was so scared, and Mama had accidentally packed them in my dinner bucket. I figured I would give 'em a try. Don't you dare tell Mama or I'll kick the mess out of ya."

He laughed, knowing there was no way I could ever go toe-to-toe with him without getting my butt handed to me. I told him of my plan and how Mama had refused my idea. He was shocked that she wanted me to go back to school instead of hanging around here to help. I asked him to talk to her and see what answer she gave him. He said he would and that he would keep my smoking a secret.

We continued ranching as usual for the next couple of days and it was nearing my time to head back to Tennessee. I was in the barn and Duke came in and told me that Mama wanted to see me up at the house. When I walked in, she was crying. I asked her why and she said the bank sent a foreclosure on the ranch. She had gone to pay it after the funeral from the money I made from the haul. She told me that they said it was a day late and that they had to proceed with the process of selling it to pay what was owed. I was furious. I told her that I would go down there with Duke and Slim and see what we could do. She said, okay, but she didn't think there was anything we could do at this point.

I stormed out, went down to the barn, and grabbed Duke and Slim. "Come on!" I told them. "We're go'n down to the bank. They're try'n to foreclose on the ranch again!"

After a long conversation with the bank manager, telling him what a piece of shit he was for treating Mama the way he did after all she had been through with Daddy passing, and the fact that he had no compassion or backbone, and with a few idle treats of a good ass whooping, he changed his attitude and agreed to take the money. However, the balance had to be caught up by the end of the month. I agreed, knowing that if Mama would let me stay home and drive, we could do it. We returned to the ranch to discuss it with her. After we pleaded our case, Mama agreed, but she made me promise that I would return to school in the fall.

From there, I made arrangements with the university. They understood my situation, and although it took some doing, we made a deal. Instead of me losing my scholarship, I would have to start all over. That was fine with me.

I called Bubba and told him the news. He understood as well. I told him to take care of my truck, and he said that he would. I went to work finding loads that I could haul quickly to get the revenue we needed as fast as possible. There were a few here and there to help at first but then it seemed to slow to a crawl. I went out a little further as there were more loads, but I hated to since the old Mack was slow, and it had some issues.

I took it to Chapman's so Mr. B could look over it and fix what he could to ensure I would get back home. I didn't venture out too far, just a few trips outside my normal hauls. I was doing good, and the money was coming in, and we were able to make the deadline on the mortgage. I kept running for a while, only coming home as I was passing through to check on things at the ranch. I was now certain that trucking was in my blood; I was becoming a natural as time went by but was still a rookie by the standards of the other truckers I met along the way. They called me *baby trucker* or *greenhorn,* letting me know of their disapproval of me being out here with them.

It was the beginning of spring, and one weekend I was supposed to come home for a week or two to plant crops. I made it almost to Iron Mountain, Wyoming, when the engine began overheating. Before I could get to a safe place to pull off the road, it started knocking and steam was going everywhere. It died as I was pulling over.

I didn't know what to do so I smoked to pass the time and let the engine cool down enough to inspect the situation. Then I opened the hood; coolant and oil were everywhere. I knew then that I was stranded. I waited an hour for someone to stop and give me a lift into town, but I reckon everyone was in too big of a hurry. Finally, I grabbed my bag and started walking the ten miles or so to town where I found a payphone to call home.

Mama answered and I told her what happened. She said she would call Mr. B at Chapman's to see what he thought. I waited for my allotted time to call her back, and he told her that it would be the next morning before he could come that far and tow me in.

I found a motel, got me a room, and cleaned myself up. I grabbed some supper and afterwards, I settled in and watched the *Andy Griffith Show, I Love Lucy,* and *Bonanza*. I must have fallen asleep during *Iron Side* because the next thing I knew, the sun was shining through the window.

I grabbed breakfast and coffee at the café while I waited for my tow truck to arrive. It was some time before Mr. B made it to my motel where I was waiting outside. I climbed in and we headed down the road to get the Mack. Once there, he did a quick overview and informed me that it was done for. I told him to take it to the house instead of his shop and from there, we would figure something out.

We arrived home and when we were putting it under the lean-to off the side of the barn, Mama came out to discuss it with him. He told her what he told me, and she started to cry.

Mr. B put his arm around her and said, "Honey, don't worry yer pretty little head over this. We will see what we can do." She calmed down and nodded as he climbed in his wrecker and drove off.

Mama and I stood around looking at it and talking about what to do. Since I was off the road for a while, we would concentrate on the planting and figure the truck situation out later.

It took a few weeks to work the fields for the hay and the crops. We were even able to do some fixing on the barns and the house, along with mending some fences. With everything in good shape, we were sitting in the den one evening discussing our next move. Mama was worried about what we were going to do. I told her that I was getting tired of driving Daddy's old truck anyway. I was thinking we could get an upgraded truck to keep up with the times.

"Yer Daddy loved that truck," she said.

I said, "I know, Mama, but even with a new engine, the other parts on the truck are bound to go out some time or another. Then we would be back in the same situation."

She agreed, but with worry, said, "How can we afford a new truck?" I told her I would do some looking round and I would figure it out.

After a week, I found one in a nearby county and even though she didn't know anything about trucks, I described it to her. It was a used dark green 1964 Freightliner WFT cab over with a 10-speed transmission, and it had a 5-foot by 2-foot sleeper, which meant I wouldn't have to sleep on the seats anymore. I mentioned that it even had an 8-track player. Mama asked if I thought the ranch had the money in the bank for it. I told 'er it would be tight at first, but that I could make it back in no time and we would still come out ahead. I told 'er the dealer only wanted $12,000 fer it. I thought we could do it and she agreed, adding, "I just hope you are right."

The next day we went and picked it up. The salesman even let me pick out three new 8-track tapes. I grabbed Johnny Cash, Johnny Merle Haggard, and George Jones. I did, however, end up buying Glen Campbell and Loretta Lynn. I figured those would do me for a while.

By May of that year, I hit the road once again. With the truck running better and faster than the old Mack, I was hauling more and more. By summer, I had earned enough money to get a flatbed trailer, a box trailer, and a coal bucket, so I could haul other stuff when the livestock slowed down. I hauled steel out of Pittsburgh, Pennsylvania, and coal out of West Virginia.

I recall thinking that us ranchers got plenty dirty in our jobs, but those steel and coal miners had it rough. They would come out of the mills and the mines covered in rust dust, and the miners would emerge from under the ground and were covered in coal dust so badly that you could barely see their faces. Steel and coal are two of the most important things that keep America growing and thriving, keeping millions employed. They also keep us drivers busy, along with the cattle hauling.

I was staying as busy as I could to build up the ranch and put money back in the bank. After about six months, I was getting the hang of it and my driving skills were getting better. The ranch had climbed out of the hole and was making good profits. I was doing well and making friends with other drivers and load brokers, which was a plus because they would give me good loads. I made sure I got home every now and then to give Mama the C.O.D. money that I had put back, keeping some for myself for running, pocket money, and of course, tank jar savings.

I ran as hard as I could up until July and then I returned home for a break to oversee the branding of the new calves we were able to buy.

When I arrived, my sister Jackie Lee had returned from overseas after attending school in Paris, France. That night, we caught up on each other's business since I had not seen her since Christmas. We discussed things going on with the ranch and how the hauling side was going. I told her I was really making a name for myself and the ranch. She told me she wanted to find a good business job as soon as she could. I suggested she help Mama with that side of the ranch because Mama was so overwhelmed. Unsure of her future employment plans, she agreed to think about it.

The next day the whole ranch was up early for the branding process. Mama filled the house with the smell of a good home cooked meal. After we ate, it was time to head to the corral and get started. Slim already had a good fire going for the branding irons and a pot of coffee brewing. While standing around the fire drinking coffee and discussing the job ahead, out of habit, I pulled my cigarettes out and lit one. Wouldn't ya know it, Mama had finished her kitchen cleaning and had snuck up on the crowd of us and busted me. She swatted me on the seat of my britches and said, "I thought I taught ya better than to smoke!"

I said, "Yes, ma'am, I'm sorry, Mama. I should have known better. I guess I am take'n after my daddy."

Mama smiled. "I guess ya are. Now let's see if ya can work like him." Then she scolded the others for not telling her about my habit, because she figured they all knew of me doing it. Then she took Daddy's place and said prayer for a safe day. We got busy, and just after dark that evening, we were finished. With everything put away, we went to the house and cleaned up for a good hot supper.

After the long hard day and after we ate, we all were so tired that we went on to bed. I could hear Mama praying before she went to bed, and I heard her tell my daddy that he would be so proud of me. Knowing that she thought I was doing a good job and that he would approve meant the world to me. I lay there smiling and eventually slipped off to sleep.

The next few days I rested before I went back over the road. The night before I was to leave out, a few of us were sitting in the den talking about the plans that would take place while I was out. I told them that I was thinking about increasing the distance of my loads as it would be more money for the ranch, and we could save up for the winter months. Mama was a bit set back at first as to my safety. After I assured her that I would take it slow and get as many loads as I could, she was a bit more settled on the idea. Jackie Lee mentioned that if we could afford a decent paycheck for her, she would be willing to learn the process of bookkeeping from Mama and hopefully take over it. I knew she needed a good job, and this would work out for us all. Plus, I had seen her and Slim together over the past week and I had the gumption that she had the fancies for him. Mama liked her idea and said they would come up with a salary that would suit. Once we were all in agreement, I made a few calls about some loads and then I retired to bed for my early morning start.

As I awoke early the next day, I smelled bacon and freshly made biscuits before the usual time. When I made my way downstairs to the kitchen, Mama was there finishing up some gravy.

"I didn't want ya leave'n out without eat'n a good breakfast," she said. I sat down, grabbed a biscuit and dipped it in my gravy. Mama said, "I know ya ain't gonna take a bite without blessing it."

I said, "Mama, ya made it with love, what more do I need?"

She said, "Ya still need to thank God fer it."

Not to get a whooping, I bowed my hand and said, "Lord, thank ya fer this food and thank ya especially fer my mama, amen."

As I ate, we talked of my load plans for the next week. I could see the worry in her eyes. I slid my plate back and told her not to worry. That, I was a big boy now. She said, that's what mama's do, regardless.

I finished my coffee, and she surprisingly set a pack of cigarettes on the table. "Go ahead and smoke one. Yer daddy always did. He would say, 'nuttin' like a good smoke after a good meal.'"

I smoked a couple and had another cup of coffee before it was time for me to head out and fire up my truck. As I was walking out, she put her arms around me and kissed me goodbye.

"I love ya, Bobby Ray," she said. "Please be careful and stay outta trouble."

"I will, Mama, and I love ya, too," I said as I stepped off the last step and into the yard.

As I walked through the morning fog to my truck, I noticed a set of footprints that had been made in the dew-covered grass that led the way to my driver's door meaning someone had been in my truck. I opened the door and sitting on the floorboard was Daddy's green dinner bucket packed with goodies for my trip. I thanked the Lord for my mama and did a walk-around to check all was in order. Then I climbed into the cab and started the engine, listening since it had been a few days sitting quiet. Once I was satisfied, I headed out the haul road to begin my new journey.

I ventured further in all directions, going farther and farther each time. I made it east of the Mississippi River and then found myself out on the East Coast running between the big cities. I made friends and connections along the way, which helped a lot with keeping me busy. I thought of my daddy a lot, and the heartache of his passing grew less and less as time passed.

My skills were improving as the cities have some tight places and more traffic. I figured I would be a real truck driver before too long. I was on a roll and things were going great for the ranch and for myself. Mama and Jackie Lee were doing a great job keeping things going and the ranch hands kept the ranch going. I had put back a good amount of money and sent the rest back home to Mama. Time passed without me realizing it and one night when I called, Mama asked me when I was coming home. She reminded me that I had to go back to school. I had been running so hard that in my mind, I had put school far behind me. I wasn't ready to return, but I didn't want to upset her. I told her I was a couple of days out from home and heading that way.

It was a couple of days, like I had told Mama it would be, and I was heading down the haul road to put the truck away when I saw Slim and Jackie Lee walking from the house to meet me. They were holding hands as I expected from their actions the last time that I was home. I parked the rig, shut her down and hopped out.

"I knew sump'n was up with ya two," I said, and they only smiled and welcomed me home. I asked them, "How thangs go'n?"

Slim said things were great and that he had hired a couple of new hands. I mentioned that I really didn't care to return to school, and Sis said that wis all Mama talked about, how I had promised and everything. I asked them if she had mentioned how she would feel if I didn't return. Sis said she was on the fence about it.

"I'll talk to 'er," I exclaimed as I grabbed my bags and headed to the house.

Mama welcomed me with open arms. "I really thought ya wouldn't come home and go back to school."

I just said, "Well, let me get a shower and rest a bit and we will talk about it."

I returned downstairs from a good nap and all cleaned up. Mama asked if I was hungry and said she would make me a sandwich. I agreed and sat down at the table and waited for her to do so. Things were quiet at first as I ate. I think we were both dreading the conversation even though we both knew what the outcome would be. She started by asking how I had been doing with the hauls. I responded by saying that things were going good, and my truck was running like a top. That I had plenty of people out there getting me loads, so much so that I could hardly get unloaded without having another one lined up.

She said, "That's good business. Yer daddy would always plan several loads back-to-back."

I agreed. She then asked if I liked it. I said that I did, and that truck driving was in my blood and that I thought things were working out for the best. Then she asked me the question that was really on her mind.

With a sigh she asked, "Do ya want to go back to school or continue drive'n?"

I took a deep breath and looked at her with tears in her eyes and said, "Well, Mama, I'll be honest with ya. I will probably regret not go'n back to school. However, I do enjoy truck'n. I feel so free out there on the open road. I feel it was meant to be my destiny."

She said, "Well, ya are a man now, and ya can make up yer own mind. I want ya to know that I love ya and I will support ya either way, even though I wish ya would go back to school. But it is yer life's decision to make."

I had finished my sandwich, and I got up and walked around the table to give her a big hug. "I love ya, too, Mama," I said and then walked out for a smoke.

The next two days I took the time to go over the ranch and inspect operations myself. I was relieved things were all in good condition and I could focus on the hauling since it was time nearing time to do the winter livestock hauling for the locals. I was getting loads left and right and I had to sock my money away in my secret hiding place; the one Dad had shown me years ago. Put it in a peanut butter jar and attach it to the fuel cap, and then drop it in the fuel tank. He said, "Ya can't trust everyone out there on the road, son. This ensures ya have money in case of emergencies."

So, I put all my extra cash in the fuel jar. The rest I would wire home every few days and call to see how things were going, and to see if I needed to make my way back home.

A month of running and I was going through Illinois heading home. I was close to crossing the state line when out of nowhere here came this smokey bear who blue-lighted me to pull over. I slowed down and drove until I was able to get off the road. The smokey got out his scales and weighed the truck and trailer. After the inspection was over, he came back and told me I was overweight and asked if I knew it? I was being honest when I said I didn't. I guess he thought I was being a smartass or telling him a lie because immediately he got a chip on his shoulder. He called for backup and asked to see my trip sheets, manifest, and license. I did as he requested. I guess because I had everything in order it upset him, and he stormed back to the other police cars that had pulled up. After a few minutes they returned and demanded I get out As I did, they put me in handcuffs and put me in the back of one of the cars. I didn't understand why. Then they opened every door on my truck and started tearing everything out and tossing it onto the ground.

After about an hour, they took me out of the car and removed the cuffs and said, "Okay. You owe us one hundred dollars and you will be free to go."

I said, "What the heck?"

He said, "Shut up, boy, or I'll run you in and you can do thirty days." I walked to my truck and pulled the jar from the tank and handed them what they asked for.

It took me a couple of hours to put everything back in order. The sun was setting when I finished so I decided to go to the nearest truck stop to get a shower and eat. Afterwards I settled back in my truck thinking I should head back home before the winter ranch season. I had several loads to haul before I could, so it took two weeks to finally head that way. When I made it home, I took a few days to relax. After that, it would be time to do the usual winter hauls.

From there, everything was going well and continued that way for almost two years with me calling Mama every chance I could and going home every month or so to check in. That was, until I was on a haul that had me crossing Rocky Top, Tennessee, heading south on I-75.

As I crossed the mountain, there was something in the middle of the road and I was too heavy and going too fast to avoid it completely. I was able to veer to the shoulder to miss it with my steer tires and I braced myself for the outcome from the other tires in its path. That's when I heard several loud pops from my drive tire and trailer tires. I slowed as safely and quickly as possible and eventually stopped on the side of the road to inspect the damage.

The object got all my tires except the outside ones on the right side and the inside ones on the left side. I couldn't stay there on the side of the road, and I knew I'd ruin my wheels if I moved any farther. I decided to limp it to the next exit to search for a phone. Luckily there was a tire shop called Farm Boy's Tire Repair.

I slowly rolled across the lot and stopped at the garage where I was met by the feller that owned the place. He introduced himself as Lug Nut (later I found out his name was Nelson). He pulled me into the bay and within minutes, he had my truck and trailer jacked up on one side to remove the tires. Man! He was the fastest tire changer I had ever seen. He handled the large impact wrench like a pro and had it singing like Charlie Daniels on a fiddle.

As it turned out, his whole family worked there to make it a successful business. His wife Gail was the bookkeeper, and his sons Bill and Jack helped him with the small stuff. His friend who helped him out would roll the new tires in and the old ones out. Not sure what his real name was but they all called him Santa Claus, for obvious reasons. However, Lug Nut alone worked his magic and took the tires off and slung them around like it was nothing, mounting the new ones with ease.

I got to know them while I was there, and they were a real down-to-earth family. When he finished with my truck tires, I was road-ready once again. It was close to supper time, and he invited me to his house to eat. We went next door where his wife Gail had fixed a spread for us. I ate till I was about to pop. Afterwards, we sat around talking and the boys insisted on showing me around the farm. They were proud of their chickens, an old donkey, and a black angus bull. The oldest boy, Bill, was interested in any trucking story I would tell him. After a couple to please his mind, Jack, the littlest one and I ended up playing with his toy dump truck and cars. He would build a mound of dirt with the truck and jump the cars and say, *Yee-haw!*

80

After a while, the Lug Nut pulled me away for some adult conversation and a sip of shine as Gail called the boys in for a bath and bed. When I figured it was time for me to leave, I thanked Gail for the home cooked meal and gave Lug Nut a few words of praise for his performance on a job well done. I said goodbye, climbed in my rig, and drove off down the road.

With the 1969 winter cattle haul coming up in a couple of months, I figured I would stay out until then. I returned home before Thanksgiving to help prepare and make sure we were ready. When I arrived, I found that Slim and Jackie Lee had gotten married. Also, Slim was now running the ranch instead of Mama, which kind of upset me because no one had informed me and that was not the plan that we had discussed. RJ had been moved up to lead ranch hand under Buck's supervision, and Tiny had passed away. He and his little family had lived on the ranch for a very long time. Even though he was not family by blood, he was still family. Mama gave him and his family a plot in the family cemetery as she and Daddy did for all the ranch hands that wanted it.

Daddy had hired folks from all walks of life and was known to give people a second chance in life despite their past. He once said, "If ya work for me, then ya are family." We celebrated births, birthdays, weddings, anniversaries, mourned the deaths and celebrated the holidays together. Even though the ranch was running with the changes, things didn't seem to be as the past years. I sensed something just wasn't right. Mama wasn't acting right, and my sister and Slim would whisper about things when I was around. I questioned what was going on and was reassured there was nothing to worry about. Still unsure of what the problem might be, I went ahead with the haul. After a busy few weeks of running cattle, I stayed around the ranch a bit to make sure everything was okay. After my break I headed back out for another long haul.

It was now February 1970, and I had only been running a few weeks. I called home to check on Mama and the ranch. Mama informed me that everything was all right, but I had received a letter from the United States Government and that I needed to come home. I was able to shuffle things around, but I eventually headed home.

When I got there, it was dusky dark, and I noticed that there was no light on in the house. I parked and went to the barns, then to the bunk house, and then the house. There was no one around. I jumped into the pickup and drove down to the diner where RJ's wife worked. They told me she was with RJ and the rest of the family at the hospital with Mama.

When I got there, the waiting room was full of family and friends. I was met by Slim and my sister who informed me that mama had had a heart attack. They said they had wanted to tell me she was having troubles when I was home, but Mama made them promise not to in case I got too worried. They continued that the doctor said she would be okay after a small procedure to open her arteries, although she would need lots of rest.

I went in to see her and she was pale white and looked as frail as I had ever seen her with tubes and wires going everywhere. She could see that I was worried and being the Mama's boy that I was, I started to cry. She couldn't talk she just moved her lips, and I read that she was telling me not to worry, that she would be okay. I left so she could rest. We went home when the visiting hours were over and discussed our plan to take care of her after she came home.

The next day she was to be transferred to Cheyenne, to the big city hospital for her surgery. We got up early and drove down to be there when she went in. After a few hours, the doctor told us she was out of surgery, and everything went well. She stayed there a week and then was able to come home.

When we finally had Mama home and in her own bed, she said that I should open the letter from the government. I told her to relax, that I had plenty of time to read it and that she was more important. I hugged her and gave her a kiss on the cheek, and I turned away with tears in my eyes. As I walked out, I pleaded with God to heal her, and I let it be known that I didn't want to lose her because she was all I had left since He had already called Daddy home.

I was deep in my thoughts of my youth when I felt a burning in my hand which startled me from my daydream. The cigarette I had been smoking had burned down to my knuckles. I then realized all these memories had me bawling like a baby. Even in all my manhood when I think back, I still care for my family so therefore, I cry.

Rolling into Yuma, Arizona, I regained my composure before reaching the cattle auction barn for my delivery. I didn't want anyone to know how sensitive of a man I am so, I pulled in, dried my tears, and washed my face before I exited my truck. I made my delivery and then drove over to the truck stop on the outskirts of town. Since I didn't pick up my new load until the next day, I found a parking spot and decided to try Jalynn, to see if she would at least answer my call.

To my surprise, she answered.

I quickly said, "I love ya, Jalynn"

Click...

The phone went silent.

Being very patient and satisfied that she answered, I grabbed some food for Cash and myself. After we ate, we walked around so he could do his business before we bedded down. We climbed back in the truck and as we settled in, I prayed everything would eventually work out. I looked at Cash and rubbed his head and told him we needed to get some rest for tomorrow's venture down the long white line, and then I rolled over and closed my eyes.

6

CALLED TO DUTY

Yuma, AZ – Las Cruces, NM

BRIGHT AND EARLY THE NEXT MORNING, THREE HOURS before my alarm was to go off, I woke with a nightmare from my Army days, panicked and soaked with sweat. I lay there for some time and gathered my wits before I went in for a shower and breakfast. In the mirror, I looked at the scars left behind from those days and others from accidents and incidence over the course of my life. Thinking back at the time and place where I got them, the one that is hurting me the most is the one in my heart at this moment. I got my fuel, pre-tripped my truck, and filled my mug with coffee and a thermos full to go. Once again, my pal and I were ready to hit the road running the white line.

Cash and I made it to the shipper, were loaded, and we headed down the road with a load of livestock, headed to Las Cruces for the last stop for these cows. As we traveled along Interstate 10, I noticed a car on the side of the road. As I slowed, I noticed a woman on the passenger side with her head in her hands. I pulled my rig up behind her car and put my flashers on to warn others.

I got out of my truck to see what was wrong. She gave me a hug,

84

said thank you, and then stated franticly that she had a flat and didn't know how to change it.

I put my arm around her and said, "Don't worry, honey. I am here to help ya."

The tears stopped and she began telling me that she was heading to Ft. Hood, Texas, to see her husband who had been deployed overseas for over a year. She had been staying with her mother in Sandiago, California, while he was away. She said she must have gotten something in it the day before when she was traveling, but it wasn't flat when she left the motel that morning. I told her I was a veteran myself and that I was there to help her get back on her way so she could be there for his homecoming.

I immediately went to work and took her things that she had packed for her trip from the trunk and retrieved her car's spare tire and jack. As I was jacking it up, I told her that there was coffee and water in my truck if she wanted to help herself. She said thank you and disappeared inside my cab.

Within a few minutes, she returned with the cup from the top of my thermos and said, "This coffee is so good, thank you so much." She started asking about my army time and my trucking career. She noticed the many pictures of my family that were hanging up, showcased by the interior red glow of my cab lights. She said, "You have a beautiful family. You must miss them an awful lot while you are out here driving all over the United States."

I said, "Yes, ma'am, I do miss my family, and it is a hard life out here on this road providing fer them. In fact, so many people don't realize what we go through and the things we miss while we are out here supplying America with the thangs it needs to survive. Just like that of our military men and women, our jobs are always taken for granted by so many. Yer husband can attest to that."

She then thanked me for my service and especially, for stopping to help her. She had prayed for someone to stop, frightened by the cars and trucks that passed her so fast that it caused her car to shake something fierce. As I tightened her spare tire and jacked it back down, she said that my truck was a huge machine and that she had never seen inside of one before. She thought it looked like an apartment in there.

I nodded and told her that it was my home away from home, and that I had missed so much of my family's growing while living there.

When I was done putting everything back in the trunk of her car, she gave me a kiss on the cheek and thanked me again. She handed me my thermos cup and I gave her fifty dollars.

I said, "You have yerselves a night out on me. Be careful and stop and have that other tire fixed as soon as you can."

She said she would, slipped into her car, and pulled onto the road. I climbed up into my truck and sat there for a few minutes before I put her into gear and got underway.

I continued toward my destination feeling good about my deed. I watched the mountain range go by with the sun peeking up just beyond them, giving them a majestic outline. With Cash asleep in the jump seat, we rolled on. In the quiet, my mind turned toward my Army days, years ago, as I left home for military duty.

I remember it as if it was yesterday. It was a couple of days after we were all rested from the hospital stay and Mama had begun to get up and move around, with our help of course. One day while she was passing the fireplace mantle, she noticed the letter that she had told me to open. I had put it out of my mind for now, figuring it was an advertisement for war bonds. She immediately demanded someone get me from my chores and tell me to come right away. I was worried when informed of her wishes and ran to the house. We sat in the den.

Mama handed the letter to me and said, "I thought I told ya to open this the other day. Now open it and see what it says."

I did as she requested, and as I read it out loud, my heart fell to the floor. I had been drafted into the Army to fight in the Vietnam War! Stunned, I stared into space, my thoughts going to my brother who was wounded while at war. Finally, I asked what I should do. Had anyone else gotten letters?

Slim, who was there for the news, said that they all had gotten them, but due to various reasons, they were denied enlistment. Mama informed me as she held my hand that, she thought since I was her baby and the last to carry on the family name, I didn't have to go. But being the mama that she was, she gave me that look of approval if I chose to go. I told her that I thought I should go and fight since it was my patriotic duty to do so.

A tear rolled down her cheek as if she knew I would probably not return as many who have gone to fight did not return home alive. She said, "Yer daddy would be proud of ya for go'n and do'n yer duty as a man, just as he and yer brother had done."

"I know, Mama." I assured her I would do everything in my power to come home safely and she could throw me a big coming home party when I did.

That put her mind at ease as she fought to put a smile on her face. I knew she was tired. I kissed her cheek and wiped the tear off her face, all the while fighting back my own tears. I told her to rest as I put her in bed. I tucked the cover around her and adjusted her pillow. I closed the door behind me and stood outside quietly as I let my emotions go and the tears started rolling like running water. I prayed for God to give us rest and peace over our current situations.

The next day, I drove to the recruiting station in Chyenne, Wyoming, to check in and let them know I was accepting the draft, even though I was the last to carry the family name. They set everything up; I took a test, got a quick physical, and they swore me in. Just like that, I was enlisted. The Army Recruiter said they would contact me as soon as it was time for me to leave for basic combat training. It would only be a week or so that I should have everything in order.

I went home and packed my things. I took my old truck over to Bear Dogs so he could keep it road ready until I return. At the ranch, I discussed things with all the ranch hands, and they assured me that they would look after everything and would see that Mama was taken care of. I called a friend to see if he had anyone that could take on the ranch haul for me while I was gone. He said he was strapped for help, but he would keep an ear out for anybody that could.

As I hung up the phone, Big Mike who Slim had hired a few months earlier (and was just a few years younger than me) knocked on the office door and said, "Hey, boss, if ya need me to run the route and run a few loads to keep us go'n, I am up to the task. I know a little bit about truck'n since my dad has done it, but I will need a little refresher."

I shook his hand and thanked him for stepping up. I told him I would tell Mama to give him a bonus and ten percent of the loads, along with his regular wages, and he was grateful for that gesture. We went and got my truck from Chapman's, and over the next few days, I showed him everything I knew. I was grateful that he was a fast learner and quickly had it down pat. We hauled a couple of short loads to get him some road time. After that, we focused on getting the ranch in shape.

Finally, on a Friday, we were all standing around the barn, Jackie Lee came running saying, the recruiter called and said that I needed to be there Monday morning before six a.m. Mama said we needed to have a going away party the next day. With that, we called it a day to prepare for the party.

Saturday night, our yard was filled with cars and trucks from all the neighbors that came to see me off. There were several jugs of moonshine and sweet tea, and so much food. Mama was even able to come outside and sit with us for a bit, even though she was mad that we didn't let her cook for the event because the whole town pitched in.

The next day we sat around with my leaving on everyone's mind. I called my brother Peanut who gave me some pointers of what I was to expect and told me to not let them get in my head. He said he was proud of me and that I should be proud of myself. After we hung up, we all talked, and Mama cried most of the day. I could tell something was wrong and that she was holding something from me. I wanted to ask her, but I knew she would say it was nothing. I figured she was worried about me and she didn't want me to know how much. She would smile with tears in her eyes and say that she loved me.

Finally, it was time to go to bed so we could get up early for my departure. I didn't sleep well that night as I thought of my future and what lay ahead. It was the morning of March 5, 1970, and what a sad morning it was. I stood with Mama crying on the front porch.

She said with tears in her eyes in her frail, trembling voice, "Son, do yer best and come back home to me. Do what they tell ya to and keep yer head down." With her next words, sent the awaiting tears down my cheeks. "Yer Daddy would be so proud of ya."

With tears still flowing, I turned away and headed towards Slim's truck. We drove away with Mama and Jackie Lee waving. Slim drove me to the recruiting station to meet the bus that would take me off for what I thought would be the worst eight weeks of my life.

Along the way, I said, "Slim, I know y'all kept Mama's illness from me because she made you promise not to tell. Is she hide'n some'n else she didn't want me to know?"

Slim dropped the bomb on me that tore my heart in two. He said, "I think they shoulda told ya, but Bobby Ray, yer mama has breast cancer. She swore everyone to secrecy because she didn't want ya to worry with ya go'n away fer the war, and because ya had to keep yer mind straight fer what was to come."

"I knew it. I could tell some'n was up with 'er," I said and then I yelled at him for not tell'n me sooner, because I would not have enlisted. I would have stayed home to care for her.

He said he was sorry.

I said, "Man, I hate ya right now because it is too late fer me to change my mind!" But I understood him obeying my mama. Even though I knew he had no control over it I made him promise to take care of her and not let her die before I returned home. He tearfully agreed, knowing the possible outcome. Afterwards, I turned out the window and pondered on things as we drove the rest of the way in silence.

We arrived at the recruiting station about thirty minutes early and we sat in the truck talking. He reassured me that things would be alright while I was gone and not to worry.

"Thanks, Slim. I'm glad that I can trust ya with the ranch and to take care of Mama."

When the time came for me to go, I shook his hand and said so long. I took my bag to check in and waited with the rest of the fellas that enlisted. Once our name was called, we were to board the bus and wait for it to be fully loaded. They called us in alphabetical order, so I was soon called to get on and found my seat. As I sat down and settled in, a fella sat next to me. As he sat down, he said, "Hey, buddy, how ya doing? My name is Jim Bo, Jim Bo Painter, they call me Rebel. I guess we are gonna be neighbors for this here trip."

Not being in the mood for idle chat, I said, "Guess so. My name is Bobby Ray James, they call me BR. Listen, buddy, I ain't try'n to be rude or noth'n, but I got a lot on my mind that I need to sort out."

He said, "No problem. Just know I'm here if ya need to talk since we will be buddies for the next eight weeks."

I agreed and turned towards the window.

The bus ride was long as thoughts ran through my mind of what Mama was going through and what I was about to endure. I must have dozed off because I slept through the night and awoke as we reached our basic training destination of Ft. Leonard, Missouri. We were told to sit quietly as the bus driver got off to check in. Unsure of what was to come, we all waited in anticipation.

After a few minutes, a soldier boarded the bus and said, "Welcome to reception. Here you will get haircuts, shots, uniforms, and your equipment. Please wait patiently and someone will be with you in a few minutes."

I thought to myself, *this ain't too bad!*

But what happened next was shocking. A huge man climbed aboard the bus and asked if we had a nice trip. With a few of the fellas answering him with *yes*, in the blink of an eye, the man's demeaner changed as he put on his drill instructor's hat and started yelling at us. I wasn't no chicken or coward but the man that got on that bus scared the living daylights out of me. He then let us know right away that for the next eight weeks he was our Daddy, Mama, Brother, Sister, but a friend he was not!

He kept yelling at us that we had fifteen seconds to "get off his damn bus and grab our bags and get in formation." His watch must have been broken because when he started counting, he missed five through ten seconds on his countdown. We were out and running around like chickens with our heads cut off. There was four more of them same men waiting for us off the bus, screaming at us to get into formation. After just a few minutes, we were getting into some kind of group, and it wasn't to their satisfaction.

"All of you S.O.B.'s get down and start doing pushups until I tell you to stop!" the big Drill Seargeant said.

We were doing our best to do as he said, but after a dozen or so, most of us were collapsing on the ground. This made him mad, and he cussed us for being weak and having no backbone. He called us "yellowbelly pieces of shit." He figured we would be fit to do something else and he said, "Start crawling your damn asses around the building on your fat bellies to get rid of your yellow bellies and don't look up! Keep your nose to the ground and your asses down. I had better see pecker tracks in the dirt from each of you!"

We managed that task like he said and when we returned, still cursing, and yelling at us for not doing it fast enough, he still wasn't satisfied. He instructed us to start running around the building until he got tired. He kept making comments like your parents wasted a good time making you, he said we were the product of poor judgement between two stupid people, and that we should have been wasted in a rubber, and that we would never make it in his army. After what seemed forever, I guess finally he was tired, even though he wasn't near as sweaty or dirty as we were. He said, "Now get in line for your haircuts, your uniforms and equipment."

We were a little faster doing this, even though we were all worn out by then. We were sweaty when we got our buzz haircut, and the trimmed hairs itched my neck as if I had chicken pox. Also, I received the most shots I ever had at one time.

Once we were done there, the physical abuse started all over again and my whole body was hurting, especially my arms and ass, where I got the shots. The abuse lasted most of the day.

We ate lunch and supper outside because we were so dirty that they wouldn't let us in the building. Even then, they only allowed us time enough to take a few bites and then we were back at it.

Finally, it was time to go to our housing and get a five-minute shower, which was cold but welcome. Then when we were in our boxers and t-shirts. One of the drill instructors showed us how to organize our equipment in the lockers and properly make our beds.

"There will be an inspection at five a.m.," he told us. "Be ready, shaved, in uniform with your boots shined." Then it was lights-out. As I lay there, I heard some crying in the darkness. This routine would continue the entire time we were there.

The next eight weeks were hell. We were sleep deprived and put through the ringer with physical training, hand-to-hand combat, and such. Then came the bivouac where we were practically up for three days and had a ten-mile ruck march back to the base.

After that, though, came the fun stuff. Weapons qualifications, I could do with ease since I grew up shooting deer, rabbits, and squirrels. As I expected, I passed that part with a breeze.

The next week, the one before graduation, we as soldiers were now brothers having gotten to know each other better. We knew we'd probably be separated in the weeks to come as we go off to the Airborne and Air Assault School. We gave each other nicknames before we separated and my battle buddy was "Rebel," from Conyers, GA that had moved to Chyenne a couple of years before. "Damn Yankee" was from Michigan. "Tex," yep, you guessed it, had the cowboy hat and all. "Ski" was from Colorado and "Donkey," from Alabama. "Cookie" was from Kentucky. And since I always had gas from the C- rations, they started calling me "Turbo" instead of BR.

With the final day dawning, we were headed into the unknown with the harsh reality that some of us may not return home. I had three weeks of Airborne Jump School and a week of Air Assault School still to attend, as did most of us. We went first to Ft. Benning, Georgia, and then to Ft. Campbell, Kentucky.

After graduation, it was time to get wheels up for our destinations. Besides chit-chat or whispering here and there, I do not think any of us talked during the long flight, each of us in deep thought regarding what lay ahead.

We landed in Vietnam, and with a short briefing, we were promptly loaded on a helicopter, with our belongings in hand, enroute to various forward operating bases (FOBs) on the fighting line. That's where we would really experience the hell of war. As we approached our FOB, we were flown by a field that looked like a huge American flag. But as we got closer, I realized it was a bunch of single American flags draped over the bodies of the soldiers that had died.

We barely had time to settle into our tents when we would join our platoon and at once, start roaming the jungle. It was so hot and humid that my uniform was soaking wet and sticking to my body. The mosquitoes were as big as bumble bees and constantly looking for blood.

Within what seemed to be minutes we were in a firefight with the enemy, to whom they referred to as "Charlie." There were bullets flying all around and even by my head. I could hear them as they zipped by and hit a tree or other obstruction in its path. I was very afraid. Then it happened as I knew it eventually would but was unprepared for it. As if in slow motion, I watched as a bullet tore through my buddy Tex's upper torso, piercing his heart. In an instant, he was dead. Then another brother fell to the ground; they were being dropped like flies. Then there was a grenade. I watched as one soldier jumped on it to save the rest of us and was blown to pieces. That one hit home as it reminded me of my Daddy and the bull. We were all firing back; I shivered at the realization that I was taking lives, and I didn't know how many. That would come to haunt me the rest of my life. Within a brief time, it was over, and we continued our way through the jungle, unsure if we had killed them all or they ran away (I learned later that they had tunnels underground that they would retreat into).

That's the way it went on most patrols. Twenty or thirty of us would go out, and few would return. One day on patrol, Cookie, Gravedigger, Vampire, and the rest of us were temporarily assigned to a different platoon patrolling an area that was supposed to be friendly. Out of nowhere, the familiar sounds of small arms fire filled the air. We were in an ambush! Most of the squad were killed except us and two other soldiers that were wounded. We took cover quickly and held the enemy off until we could radio for help. We took turns dressing the wounds of the others and soon reinforcements arrived. Cookie and I didn't get away unscathed as he took a round in the shoulder, and I took one in the side. The medics arrived and Medivac carried us to the nearest field hospital. One of the soldiers, Private Moore ("Ski") had major internal bleeding and died along the way. It was a sad moment as I watched him take his last breath. I bowed my head and said a prayer, thankful my injuries were not fatal.

Time passed, and as we recovered from our injuries, we sat in the recreational room talking to each other. The soldier that had survived, Sgt. Tim Proof, came over and thanked us for the job we had done to keep him alive. He said seriously and kind of jokingly that if it had it not been for us acting so quickly, he would have fallen off the deep end, because he thought he was a goner that day. With that comment, we nicknamed him "Off the Deep End," or "Odie" for short.

I went outside with him for fresh air and while talking, I learned he grew up not far from me back in the States. We even knew some of the same people.

Back in the recreation room conversing with the rest of the crew, our 1st Sgt came in, talking trash to us about what we did wrong. We didn't know we did anything wrong at all. There was a CSM (Command Sergeant Major) standing by a short distance away who overheard this and decided to step in. He called 1ˢᵗ Sgt Hicks outside for a chat. As we watched out the window, we could hear every word. It was getting heated. I guess 1ˢᵗ Sgt Hicks didn't like being called out, because he took a swing at CSM Rampsburg, and well, what ensued was what I would call a good old ass whooping. He finally finished Hicks off and left with him lying on the ground. He straightened his uniform and then came inside where he introduced himself as CSM Rampsburg. He notified all of us that we were now assigned to his unit and were all promoted to Corporals, which suited us just fine. He said it was a Chemical Company called the "Dragon Unit" that was new in the base camp. He instructed us that when Medical released us, we were to report to him, ASAP.

After three weeks in the infirmary, we were released. After a semi-decent shower and clean shave, we dressed in a fresh uniform and reported to CSM Rampsburg. He informed us of our new assignment as forward lookouts, which meant spending lots of time in a fox hole.

We were granted 48 hours to move our stuff to our new living quarters and relax a little. So, we decided to go to the USO concert featuring Bob Hope and others. We had a blast. The USO helped us get our minds off the war at hand. Even if it was only for a couple of hours, it was refreshing. We returned to the USO as often as we could.

That night after a USO Concert, the squad decided to have a few drinks at the NCO Club. We were now Corporals and were considered NCOs, but at the bottom of the totem pole. We were having a good time, relaxing and throwing back a few beers. Well, I guess the higher-ranking NCOs didn't like that idea and kept making sly remarks about if we were old enough to even be drinking or if we needed a nipple to go on our bottles.

We were just trying to mind our own business while listening to this young lady sing. Her name was Sally. She was from the Airforce attachment, and she came to the base and performed occasionally for the USO. The USO concert took her spot for the week, so she settled for a slot at the club. After her set, she came down to sit with us younger soldiers that were more her age, which upset the older NCO's. She sat on Cookie's lap, evidently setting a date and discussing their future for the next couple of months.

We were all talking and joking around, and one of the older NCOs came up and was backed up by two or maybe three more. He picked up my beer and spit in it. That was all it took for Rebel to start swinging. His boney fists were fast and on target to the guy's face. Cookie picked Sally up and set her to the side out of harm's way, and it was on. Rebel and Cookie started slugging our new enemies and their numbers were growing steadily. We joined in because we always had each other's backs. With arms swinging, we were all over the club, busting bottles, breaking chairs, and tipping tables. Even though we were lower enlisted, we showed them what us six eager soldiers were made of. We busted heads and noses and a few ribs, and by the time the last one fell, the MP's arrived and took us all in. But not before Cookie got a hug from his new girlfriend.

We spent a night in the stockade and were all given an Article-15, along with extra duty on top of our already busy schedule. We were booked solid for the next 30 days. But, hell, if you asked any of us, we would tell you the same thing, the respect and popularity we gained from that scrabble was well worth it.

The day of our first duty assignment, 1st Sgt Hammer gave us our briefing and we met our new platoon sergeant, SFC (Sargeant First Class) Mayfield, and platoon leader, 1st Lieutenant Ross, both of whom informed us that our earlier actions were not going to be tolerated. We were then directed to our lookout point where we would rotate two at a time every eight hours for forty-eight hours, with two days off, and do it again.

The next few weeks were uneventful as things seemed to be relaxing from the war point of view. We didn't even understand what a Chemical Company Smoke / Recon did until one morning, there was a noise we had never heard before and a fog begun to roll in on us. We didn't know what to do so we put on our protective masks. The smoke was so heavy, and the masks were substandard, that we could taste the oil. We thought we were goners, and I started hammering on the metal warning device to let others know of a gas attack.

Then the bullets started racing through the air once again. We returned fire not knowing if we were hitting anything or not. Then in a flash, the CSM Rampsburg appeared out of nowhere like a ninja in our fox hole and said quit firing. The infantry had things under control, then he laughed at us for wearing our masks. He said, "Don't you just love the taste and smell of fog oil?" He then took us over and showed us the machine that was making all the noise. It was a machine mounted on the back of a trailer and pulled by a jeep. He said that its purpose was to heat up and burn the special oil called Fog oil and create a blanket of smoke to conceal our location. In theory the enemy can't hit what they can't see or see movement of troops over the battlefield.

"Welcome to smoke/ recon, Dragon Soldiers!" he yelled with a loud voice. To my surprise, all the soldiers around us responded with "Dragon Strong!"

After the smoke cleared, he commended us for doing a good job as to what the standard operating procedure was. And that he was sorry he forgot to discuss the mission of the unit. He then asked if either one of us had any mechanical know-how. I told him I used to fix stuff back on the ranch. He said he had a task for me. The task was for me to come up with a decontamination system for decontaminating soldiers and equipment. After a day or two, I showed him how I had changed his equipment to manage such a task.

"How did you do that?" he asked me.

I replied with a smile, "I red-neck-ta-fied it, CSM!"

He then brought me to our Commanding officer, Colonel Whinston, who was impressed with what I had done and commended me on the invention. They walked away and talked for a few minutes. After that, I was released from my fox hole duties and was put with the mechanics. I liked that even better as all I had to do as a newly promoted Sgt was to make sure everyone knew what they were supposed to be doing. Which I did very well.

The last 8 months of my 2 years enlistment went by without a hitch. I dated a couple of cute nurses from the medical unit and spent lots of time at the USO or the MWR (moral welfare and recreation) tent. With my time in Vietnam coming to an end. I would begin my Reserve Duty. It was now time for me to go home. With transfer papers in hand, I hopped the first flight out of that hell hole and headed straight home.

Once I was back in the good ole U.S.A., it took two weeks for me to process out of the Army. I received more shots and more briefings and was told where to report to when I got back home and when. I received my final paycheck and got a bus to Chyenne, Wyoming. At the bus station, I called home and Jackie Lee answered. I asked to speak to Mama, and she said that she wasn't there. I told her to tell her that I loved her, and I was heading home. Slim jumped on the phone and asked when I would be coming in and he said he would be there to meet me and give me a ride home.

I boarded the bus, and the same as before, it was a long ride as I thought of what things were like back home. I was too excited to sleep. I was really looking forward to seeing my mama and giving her hugs and kisses and telling her how much I love her and how I missed her.

As we came into the Orin, Wyoming city limits, the excitement began to grow stronger, and before I knew it, we were pulling into the bus station. When the bus stopped, I quickly grabbed my bags and headed to the passenger pickup area.

As promised, Slim met me at the bus station, as I ran over to put my stuff in the truck. He got out and with a solemn hug and a handshake he welcomed me home. I knew something was up because he had never hugged me before. I abruptly asked if everything was alright with him. He never said a word as we climbed in the truck and headed home. I figured maybe he and Jackie Lee had been in a tiff or something. However, it was when he passed the driveway to the ranch and then turned up the road that led to the family cemetery, that a lump gathered in my throat and a knot filled my stomach.

I started crying in an instant and shouted, "Nooooo! Not Mama! Slim, ya promised me!" Then I shouted at God and asked him why he took her before I got home.

We pulled up to the entrance where my sister was waiting.

With tears in his eyes, Slim said, "Bobby Ray, I did all that I could, but I made a promise that ya knew I couldn't keep if the Lord wanted her."

I jumped out of the truck. My sister tried to hug me and I brushed her away. She said, "I wish ya could have been here Bobby Ray."

I made my way over to the granite headstone. I was at a loss for words until I focused on her name and the date, which was only four months prior to this day. I just cried out, "Why, Lord?"

The tears flowed and I was only able to mumble the words, "I am home, Mama, I love ya and I am sorry I wasn't here to take care of ya or to say goodbye."

With the tears still flowing, I stared at the ground and thought how precious she was and recalled memories of her love. How she would doctor our cuts and scrapes, help with our homework, as much as she knew how with her seventh-grade education. Still, she was a wise woman who worked hard to make sure we had clean clothes to wear and would even do some of our chores so we could play. Most of all, how she would pray, which we could hear her through the wall. She would always pray, "Lord, please save my children and watch out for them and keep them safe."

Oh, how I wish I could hear her pray again and hear her sing. It always made me happy to hear her sing gospel music and her praying for us at night set my heart at peace. I will not get to hear either ever again. Nor will I be able to hug her or kiss her cheeks.

I was sad and angry that no one had let me know. But, as angry as I was, I could hear her in my mind saying, *"It's okay, son. Forgive them. The Lord called me home to be with your daddy."* That was her letting me know how much she loved me, even though she told me constantly. I remembered her always saying that GOD, Daddy, and herself would always love us, and even in death, we would meet again, if I accepted Jesus as my Lord and Savior, kept the faith and his commandments, and abided by GOD'S golden rule.

I pulled out my pocketknife and walked over to her favorite rose bush. I cut three of the prettiest ones I could find and placed them on the headstone. I told her once more that I loved her and Daddy.

I walked away with tears in my eyes and went to the truck. I decided to go for a drive, leaving Slim and Jackie Lee to return to the ranch. I drove to Daddy's favorite fishing pond on the back forty acres and just sat there pondering on my life-changing events.

Lost in those memories, I hadn't realized I was drifting out of my lane. I heard the rumble strips under my steer tires and quickly jerked the wheel, nearly sideswiping a car on my left. I got centered and back in my lane and continued on my way, reaching my destination just before dusk.

After a quick check of the truck and Cash returning from his relief, it was time for dinner. After we ate, I figured I would try to reach Jalynn, this time by pay phone. I figured she wouldn't recognize the number and answer. We made our way to the phone booth and stood in line. Cash waited outside while I made my call, although he let it be known that he wanted to talk to his Mama by pawing at the booth and making a moaning howl. I know he misses her as much as I do.

Jalynn answered and said hello. I said in a low, unbelieving voice, "I love ya, Jalynn!"

"Ya used to," she replied and hung up.

Cash and I returned to the truck and went to sleep so we could get unloaded and reloaded the next day to head down the long white line.

7

THE RETURN HOME

Las Cruces, NM – Houston, TX

THE NEXT DAY, AFTER GETTING FUEL AND COFFEE, CASH and I made our way to the feed lot (death row) and got unloaded. We collected our pay, and I gave it to Cash. He knew exactly what to do. He would bury it like he would a bone. There were times that I would find extra money he had hidden in the truck, and it was always welcome!

Once we were loaded, Cash and I headed east, towards Texas. I could tell he was getting restless from the few days we were out, after all, we were getting too old for this road life.

Rolling through Texas, I kept thinking of Jalynn and what she said before hanging up last night. I guess I had gotten lost in thought because before I knew it, we were passing a couple of buses of soldiers heading to Ft. Hood, Texas, either beginning their duty as new soldiers or returning from their assignments to their awaiting loved ones. I laid on my train horns to show my appreciation and respect for their service.

I was on the long stretch of Interstate 10, eastbound from El Paso, Texas, to San Antonio, Texas. As I passed a few more buses of soldiers, I did the same thing again. I prayed for their safety and prayed that they would have a better experience than I did. Wasn't long before I got lost in my thoughts again, as the view from my eyes faded to memories of my return home from war.

After my return home in July 1971, finding out that Mama had passed away hit me hard. I had wanted so much to hold her and let her know I kept my promise. However, God took her home and I had to accept that. I left the cemetery and went for a drive to try and clear my head. I did some thinking and more praying.

I figured with all that I had just been handed, I needed to get it off my mind, so I drove to The Chatter Box, which was a little bar on the outskirts of town. There were some old friends hanging out there, which happened to be all our ranch hands, among others. As walked in, I was greeted with open arms. They started yelling things such as, *"Yee haw! Look what the cat drug in! Look who it is! Little Bobby Ray is home from the war!"* I got hugs and handshakes, and kisses on the cheeks from the women. A couple even kissed me on the lips, which confused me; they were my ranch hands and my friends, and I didn't think they thought of me that way. Maybe I did some growing up while I was over there and they noticed, or maybe they were just drunk.

I figured I would try and catch up and ordered a couple of beers to ease my mind. I tried to pay for my drinks and Bucky told me to put my money away, that it was no good there. My drinks were on him and the rest of the crew. I joined them where they sat beside the pool tables.

They each told me how sorry they were that I wasn't there for Mama's passing and how she missed me. That she prayed for me all the time that I would come home safe, and that God would ease my pain. I think she knew that she would not be there when I did come home. They said she started getting worse a few months after I left, and she turned everything over to my sister and Slim. We talked about the condition of the ranch and how they had run things into the ground. We got caught up on each other's lives as we played pool and drank one picture of beer after another. As we were getting ready to leave, Fancy gave me "more than just a friendly kiss" on my lips. It was a mite juicier than before, and it tasted like Jack Daniels with a hint of Coke. I was taken aback as it was a surprise to me. She said if I needed to talk, she would be there.

101

She grabbed my butt and got a big handful saying, "Mmmm… Bobby Ray." Then she turned and walked away. And with that, we all loaded up to head off on our separate ways.

I returned to the ranch, following the ones that were living in the bunk house, not knowing what was going to happen to the ranch now that both of my parents were gone. By this time, it was evening, and my sister had made dinner. After we ate, I went into the den and Slim started to say something that I knew would probably upset me.

I put him in his place right quick-like and said, "Not now Slim. I need some time to process thangs and I am not ready to talk about it."

I did, however, make it known that the others had filled me in on the goings on at the ranch and that I wasn't too happy about it. I said we would talk in the morning, and I retired to my bedroom for some much-needed sleep.

As I lay there trying to clear my head, I heard footsteps outside of my room. I figured it was my sister going to bed. But with the rattle and turning of the doorknob, the door opened. I saw a female silhouette in the darkness and in seconds, I felt the body of a woman slip under the covers. I knew who it must be after the events at the bar. Plus, the smell of whiskey on her breath gave her away.

I asked, "What are ya do'n, Fancy?"

She said she felt so sorry for me. After all, I had just returned home from a horrible war only to find out Mama had passed away. "Ya must be sad, and I thought ya might need some comfort, snuggles, and anythang else that ya might need. I am here to help."

She started to kiss me like she had before. I had never felt this before, and even though I was now twenty-three, I had never been with a woman. But even though my parents were gone, out of respect for their memory, I politely told her they would not approve of what was happening. She understood and got a little sad as she said she was sorry. She started crying and climbed out of my bed to leave. I grabbed her by the arm and asked her if it was okay, we could just lay there and talk for a while to help ease my mind. So, she snuggled up next to me and we talked for a better part of the night about Mama and Daddy and my Army days, she told me about things that had happened while I was away, and about things going on in town. I was starting to doze off to sleep as I felt her give me one last light kiss on my forehead. And then

I fell asleep.

The next morning at about the time Daddy would usually open my door, I opened my eyes in anticipation of his entering. But in an instant, I became sad because I knew he would not be coming. The sorrow grew when I could not smell the scent of bacon filling the house. I knew that Mama would not be in the kitchen fixing breakfast and to tell me good morning and that she loved me as I came down the stairs.

I rolled over to wake Fancy, but she wasn't there. I got clean clothes out of my bag and changed and went downstairs to breakfast. Just as I thought, there was none. My mother had always cooked breakfast every morning for everyone. My sister, however, did not. I just grabbed a cup of black coffee and made it known by slamming the cabinets that I was not happy at the situation. I then made my way to the porch to see the sun rise in the morning fog and admire God's handiwork.

I sat in silence rocking in Daddy's old rocking chair. I recalled how in the mornings, he and Mama would sit there finishing up their coffee as we were all coming out from the mudroom, headed to school. As the sun met the clouds in the sky and brought light to the day, I heard the crew down at the barn talking and laughing. I could see the light from the usual fire, and I knew there would be some better coffee brewing over it.

Figuring I would go see what was going on, I decided to walk to the barn. As I approached, I was met by Slim, RJ, and Goat, a new hand on the ranch. I knew Goat from town but had never really met him. His real name was Tim Blaine. He moved here from Tennessee and had lived there a while now. He had a small band called "The Last Train Robbery Band." They played in the local bars and events in town from time to time. Goat, reaching his hand out, said, "Thanks, Bobby Ray, for yer service. I am glad to finally meet ya. I have heard so much about ya. I am glad ya are home."

I obliged him by shaking his hand.

Slim then said, "We need to talk about the situation here on the ranch." We went into the barn office and sat down. He then started by saying, "Now, don't be mad, but there is some'n ya should know. We had to sell yer truck and the big John Deere tractor and its extra attachments to keep the ranch going, and that money is about to run out if we don't do some'n soon. We just haven't had the business we had when you were here."

I instantly went into a rage. I asked Slim what the hell they had been doing while I was gone. He said, "Well, yer sister…"

I knew right away we had a problem. I called him a S.O.B. and told him that after all that my mama and daddy had done for him, he had gone and disrespected them by do'n what my no-good sister told him to do. I said, "Yer an asshole, and ya don't have a decent bone in yer body. If y'all weren't married, I would fire you right here and now. But I'll tell ya what I will do…" I jumped over the desk and started punching him and slinging him all over the place. "I ain't that little boy I used to be. Ya are gonna remember this for a long time!"

The other ranch hands heard the commotion and came running as I had almost beaten him senseless. They pulled me off him and told me that it wasn't worth it. I said probably not but it needed to be done. By then, someone had gotten my sister from the house. She came in fussing at me, and I told her to shut the hell up or I would give her a proper ass whooping like Daddy would have. I was not sure that I wouldn't anyway. I was so furious I had to get away for a while.

I took a walk to the cemetery to have a heart-to-heart with Mama and Daddy. I asked them what I should do since they drove the ranch into the ground, and it seemed there was no coming back. I sat there for most part of the day talking to them and waiting for their advice. As I lay beside their graves with the sun shining on my face, I could swear I heard Mama say, *"I love ya. Pray about it, son! And be forgive'n as God has forgiven ya. Remember, God works in mysterious ways. Trust in him to guide ya."* Then, with a small breeze, I heard Daddy's voice say, *"Son! I am proud of the man ya have grown to be. I love ya and I know ya have it in ya to fix this. Ya are a good rancher and a better truck driver than I ever was. Ya have learned so much. Now trust in yer ranch family, treat them right, and they will stick by yer side. Now go and do what ya do best."*

With tears in my eyes, I told them that I would do my best and try to get things back on track the way they should be.

I walked back to the house at dusk and went into the den where my sister and Slim were sitting. Trying to be as calm and civil as I could and stand tall as Daddy would have, I said, "Be'n that I have only been gone eighteen months, and the fact that I made sure that the ranch had enough money in the bank to cover everythang, all ya had to do was make the yearly run to the auction and the slaughterhouse, which Big Mike was to do for me. We had plenty of livestock to raise and sell as well as the money we would have gotten from the local hauls. I found out that ya did not make any of those as promised and the other ranchers had to get outside drivers to run them. Ya sold off most of the livestock and have not planted any crops this year. Instead, after I left and Mama passed months after, it seems ya didn't care about do'n anythang else on the ranch. Ya just wanted the money to do yer own thang, and in fact, it came out that ya wanted to sell the ranch and move on. Well, I am here to tell ya that will not ever happen."

I did not pause to let either of them say a thing.

I continued, "They said y'all barely had enough money to buy feed, let alone pay them for working. They said that you had stopped growing hay for the stock, and Lord only knows what else ya have done. They are work'n here for the simple fact that Mama and Daddy treated them like family, and they care about the ranch, and will hang in there. But they must eat and support themselves and their families. They need to be paid immediately."

Then I asked them how much money was in the bank. They said they didn't really know, they had not been keeping up with the books, that I would have to go down to the bank and find out. That made me even more angry and told them I hated them and that I would deal with them later. I walked out to cool off.

I resented them both for all they had done and as I left, I walked towards the lower barn where we had put Daddy's old Mack truck. As I approached, and with all my emotions on my sleeve, I saw Daddy's truck sitting there with that faded American flag in the rear window. I lost it right there and sat down beside the old truck and let my emotions out. I was questioning God as to why this had happened to me. Why he took the ones I loved and cared about. I must have sat there for a good while because when I looked around, everyone was gone.

I regained my composure and went into the barn. I found a few nails and a hammer and grabbed a long 2'x4' and a piece of rope. I took that old flag from the truck, I nailed that board to the side of the barn, and I raised Old Glory high in the air. Then I saluted her with the pride and respect of a soldier. With that, I had gained my newfound attitude and the plan that I was going to put into place filled my head. With new vigor, I went to the house. I told my sister and Slim to get out if they wanted to sell the ranch. I said I would buy her out and run it myself. I said that I wanted them out in two days.

I went to the barn and gathered the hands to discuss my plan. Then I asked them how much money they needed to get by with until we could build up again. Would stick it out with me? They all said they would and gave me a number that would suffice until things were better. The next day I went to the bank and withdrew most of the funds, leaving my sister and Slim just enough for a hotel and food. I paid the ranch hands and went looking for a truck to do the hauling. I didn't have any luck at first so I decided to wait a few days and see if one came up.

After a few nights with Slim and my sister in that hotel, I felt sorry for them, remembering what Mama said about forgiving. It was decided that I would buy her out. They would live there until I got enough money to do so. Then they could build a house on the 10-acre lot deeded to her by Mama and daddy. Until then, I would need their help so I could get back to trucking. I told them that I would be in control of the money and that I would pay them the same as the ranch hands. We all agreed.

The next day, I went to see if I could get me a new-used truck. I stopped by Mr. B's to see if he had one or knew of one for sale. Luckily, he said he saw one over in another town about sixty miles away. Said it looked like it might need some work, but it wouldn't hurt to check it out. I didn't waste any time since they go quick in these parts. I jumped in the truck and he hopped in the passenger seat saying he'd like to get out of the shop for a while. With that we were off.

Along the way, he said, "I am sorry about ya lose'n yer mama. She was a good woman. I hated to see your truck go. They sold it dirt cheap, too."

We arrived at the field where the truck sat and the owner came out to meet us. He fired it up so we could hear it run. Mr. B raised the hood to check it out for himself. After he did his inspection and was satisfied mechanically, I looked inside. With my overall approval, I asked how much he wanted for it. He quoted me a price above what I was wanting to spend.

"Man, I would like to have it," I said. "In fact, I need it, but that is way more than I have right now. I will have to see if I can find some'n a little more in my price range."

Mr. B. said, "Bobby Ray, maybe with ya just get'n back from Vietnam, the bank could do some'n fer ya."

I knew what he was trying to do, and it worked. Lucky for me, the fella was a Korean War Veteran, and he let me get the truck for less than what I had on me. He said I could use the rest to get the repairs done.

It was an older model, a 1965 Kenworth that had been wrecked, but Mr. B. said he could have it fixed in no time and would cut me a deal on his repairs. It was midnight blue with a sleeper, and an AM/FM radio with a cassette player. I had never seen one of those in a truck.

With the paperwork done, I climbed into the truck and Mr. B. followed me in my truck. I stopped for fuel and a wash job that it desperately needed. Then I headed back to the shop where Mr. B. told his guys to pull it in and get started. I asked him how much it would be.

"Bobby Ray," he said, "yer mama and daddy were good to the missus and I when we first started this here truck stop, so I tell ya what, the labor is free and the parts and material we can trade fer a beef to put in my freezer. How does that suit ya?"

I said, "Thank ya, and I will have the crew go ahead and take care of the best one we got to the processers."

We shook hands and I drove back to the ranch to let them know of the chore for Mr. B. and the deal that I had made for the old truck. I told them, "With any luck, we will be in good shape befer too long." All the ranch hands said with excitement that they were glad that I was back and had control of everything.

The next day, Mr. B. called to inform me he was waiting on a part, and that the truck should be up and running in no time flat. Within a few days, he had it fixed and told me to come pick it up. Goat rode with me and once he saw it, he said, "Wow, Bobby Ray, you are in the big time now!"

I said, "Yeah, I can't wait to see how she does, hammer'n down the road!"

Goat followed me home and I packed my bag. I called some of my old contacts to see if I could get a couple of loads. Luckily, I got 3 back-to-back. I went to the truck stop for coffee, cigarettes, and some snacks. They told me about a new thing that they were calling a "logbook" to keep track of my driving hours. I said it would take some get'n used to.

While the diesel attendant was topping off my tanks and cleaning my windows and mirrors, Old Bonehead, a trucking buddy of my Daddy's, showed me how to fill out the logbook. He told me to keep one for the Department of Transportation (DOT) and one for pay purposes. He said I needed to hide the one for pay so they wouldn't find it; it was illegal to run two books now that the DOT was now governing our driving hours.

After that, I was on my way to the Blake Ranch to pick up his cows headed to death row. I knew I would enjoy a delightful home cooked meal by Mrs. Blake after we finished the loadout.

When I met Mr. Blake at his barn, he rode with me to the corral. He, like all the rest, welcomed me home and told me he was sorry about Mama and the ranch. I told him that things will be different from now on and he patted me on the back.

His ranch hands met us and like clockwork, performed their duties to load me in a timely manner. Still, with all the planning, there is always stuff that can go wrong. In this case, it happened in a huge way as we loaded a couple of cows.

Mr. Rowan, an old friend of Mr. Blake's came up in his beat-up pickup and as he reached the corral and shut the clunker off, it backfired and sent the remaining herd into a stampede. The animals were running frantically everywhere, following one another as they always do. They trampled the corral fence and were running all over the ranch, scattered, and running literally for their lives, as if they knew what their future held. Blake's ranch hands mounted horses and with lassos in hand, went after the strays. There were so many that I jumped back into my truck for safety, the vision of Daddy filling my mind. It took about two and a half hours to contain the herd, get them rounded up, and fix the broken fence.

After the livestock was loaded and they closed the trailer, Mrs. Blake started ringing the dinner bell. That sound always brought a smile to my face, and I knew I would be fed good. I enjoyed dessert and she always had the best cakes and pies and insisted that you take leftovers.

After dinner and with a full belly, I climbed in my truck and headed towards Oklahoma City to unload, then reload, to make my way to Georgia, with my delivery there and my next load coming out of Atlanta. There I was to meet up with my brother Sherman in Fairmount for a visit. After all, it had been years since I had seen him. Mr. Blake said that if I drive through the night, I might just make it. I hit the highway, put the wind to my back, and the white line in the center of my hood and I put the pedal to the floor.

I turned on the CB radio and in an instant the chatter started coming through the speaker. I grabbed the mic and a few drivers answered me back. I told them that I had just returned from the war and they thanked me for my service, welcoming me back out on the road. They did their best to catch me up on the trucking business. We kept talking for as long as the distance between us grew and we were all out of range of each other's radio. I thought, how cool was this? The CB was just like the military radios I had used but built for truckers. There was even special lingo that they taught me during our conversations. Afterwards, I drove through the night with anticipation of seeing my brother.

I was so busy recalling the times, I didn't realize I had driven as long as I did, and I found myself on the outskirts of Houston. The city is bumper to bumper traffic at 7 am. It took a while, but I finally made it through the city, and I was close to my destination that didn't deliver until morning. I found the closest truck stop, fueled up, and drove through the parking lot until found a spot. After I got parked, I called Jalynn again to see if things were different. I didn't get an answer, so I called Amberleigh. When she answered, she said Jalynn had gone on a date. This news made me furious. How could she do such a thing?

I did not make a fuss, though. I told her to tell her I called even though I knew she wouldn't care. I now know how she felt when she learned of my affairs with other women. I called for Cash who'd been out making his rounds, looking for anyone that would pet or feed him a snack. When he showed up, I made sure he was settled in the truck, and I went in for a shower and food.

On my way back to the truck, I stopped by the picnic tables and had a cigarette and tried to call her again. This time, there was no answer. I left a message of plea on the answering machine. I went back to the truck and after Cash had his food, we were off to bed.

109

Sometime after we were asleep, there was a loud noise and my truck shook from side to side. I awoke and instantly knew what might have happened. I opened the curtain to catch whoever backed into me before they drove off as if it was nothing. I still don't understand with all the chicken lights on ole Reba how anyone could not see her. I immediately opened the door to let Cash investigate while I got dressed and jumped out to confront the driver. Cash was good at protecting what was his. I had trained him to sit in front of any truck that was in a wreck with us and not move until I told him to. He is a smart dog, ornery but smart.

When I got out, the driver of the other truck was assessing the damage he had done to my truck. He was Middle Eastern and appeared truly shaken by the event. I asked him what he was thinking. He said he thought he had it, but he was not good at doing blindside backing. I could tell he was nervous as he introduced himself as Hamdi Tark. I told him to move his truck to finish assessing my damage. I saw that he just bent my bumper and slightly cracked my fender. I reassured him it would be okay, and after we exchanged insurance information, I helped him finish backing in. Since I could be a little late, I asked him if he wanted me to teach him the correct way to do a blind side back. He excitedly accepted, and it was set for the next morning. I climbed back in my truck and went to sleep.

The next morning, as the parking lot was emptying out and drivers were on their way, he met me by my truck, and we got started on the practice. It only took him a few times to get the idea and he was so proud of himself. He thanked me for spending my time to teach him the skill. Afterwards, he invited me to join him and a few other Middle Eastern men after their prayer for some breakfast and I accepted. He showed me where they would be in a small out of sight location since they were not very popular for coming over here to work. But he said they were just hard-working men chasing their dream of becoming American citizens and bringing their families over here for a better life.

As I approached the spot where they were eating, I noticed they did not have very much food, and they were eating with their hands. The elder of the group invited me to sit and eat. I thought to myself that there was not enough for all of us as they offered me what they had.

I whispered to Hamdi that there was not enough to go around, and he said, "My brother, we all share what we have and only eat what we need to. We eat to live, not live to eat. So, there will be plenty to go around."

And with that, he handed me a piece of bread and a small dish of chicken and rice. Some of the men only had rice and some kind of soup. As we ate, each one told me their story and I shared mine. And after we were done, I was astounded, as there was still food left and everyone was satisfied. I started to leave, and they saw me off with well wishes, and called me their brother.

I thanked them and said, "Goodbye, until we meet again, my brothers. Be safe and keep the rubber side down."

I made my way back to the truck and headed out, feeling good about myself and my new brothers. I unloaded and got my next load, and headed down the highway, chasing the white line all the way.

8

LIFE LESSONS

Houston, TX -Texarkana- Memphis, TN

THE FOLLOWING DAY, AND WITH JUST A SHORT HAUL FOR the day, I knew it would be an easy one. We made good timing to our destination without a hitch. After we had unloaded at the auction and grabbed a load going to a private rancher, we were heading down the road again. I noticed Cash was getting restless, and I knew he needed a break from riding. I did too, so I told him that we were going to stop at Edwards' Truck Stop. There, he could see Mrs. Edwards who would spoil him as she always done when we stayed there. He looked at me like he understood what I was saying. In excitement, he started acting as if we were already there.

I said, "Calm down, partner, we have a few more hours to go, and one more night in the sleeper." So, with a disgusted huff, he lay down on the bunk to sleep and pass the time.

I made my way into the Texarkana area where we would stay for the night. We'd make a quick unload the next morning and have a few days to rest before the loadout heading to Memphis.

The next morning after we unloaded, we were ready for our break. We eased up the road and pulled into Edwards' Truck Stop. I hollered back to Cash that we were there. He jumped in the passenger seat, looking out the window with excitement, waiting for me to stop so he could go see them.

This place was just a mom-and-pop truck stop that we had known of from years back and they knew us well. After I got my fuel, I went inside to eat. Cash had already made his way in and was making his rounds, happy 'cause he was allowed in. Everyone loved him, and he loved the attention and the treats.

Mrs. Edwards greeted me at the door and said, "Look who it is, Daddy. Bobby Ray has come to visit us." She asked how I was and how things were going at the ranch. She asked how Jalynn and the kids were. I told her about some of what I had done, but I kept the bad stuff to myself so she wouldn't think less of me.

She said, "Ya poor thang. I hope everything works out fer ya, son." She then instructed me to a back booth and said, "Sit here darling. Are ya hungry?"

I placed my order and told them we were there for a 2-day break. Mr. Edwards asked where I was heading to next, and I told him I was headed over to Memphis and then on into Georgia to visit with my big brother Peanut. Considering that we were going to be there and the fact that they lived next door, Mr. and Mrs. Edwards invited us to stay with them and get out of the truck for a bit.

Knowing their response, I said, "I don't want to put ya out none."

Mrs. Edwards said, "Hush that nonsense. Ya are welcome in my house anytime."

Mr. Edwards said, "Bobby Ray, if ya ain't busy tomorrow, I am go'n fish'n. Come with me and you can clear your mind."

I was happy to oblige. I said, "You bet. I don't get to go fish'n much, and I am sure Cash would love to go for a swim."

They told me to go to the house and make myself at home and they would be there in a bit for supper. I paid my bill and went to the truck to get my bags and take out the garbage so it wouldn't sit in there while I was visiting. When I was finished, I tried to call Jalynn to let her know where I was, and to tell her that the Edwards had asked about her. I still didn't get no answer.

I went on to the house and put my things in the guest room. I just lay across the bed thinking of how my life had been turned upside down and how stupid I was to throw everything away for a drink of alcohol. I dozed off for some time until I was woken up by Mrs. Edwards calling me to supper.

We gathered around the table holding hands while Mr. Edwards blessed the food. He said, "Too bad ya won't be here for church on Sunday. I got a good message I am gonna preach on. I think ya would get a bless'n from it. It kinda hits home for ya." I told him I wish I could since I had not been to church in some time.

After supper, we sat around playing cards until it was time to go to bed. I said good night and went into the bedroom where Cash waited. With our fishing trip early the next day, we went right off to sleep.

The next morning, after a quick biscuit and gravy plate that Mrs. Edwards brought for us, we made our way to the pond. The fog was laying heavy on the water and there were ripples in the water from the fish coming up to get whatever they could to eat. There were even a couple of good splashes from fish jumping out of the water. We readied our poles, and with our lines in the water, it was now a waiting game. We talked and fished, and Cash had him a nice swim which kept us from catching anything but allowed us to catch up on times gone by.

When Cash was done swimming, he caught a glimpse of some ducks and began to chase them around the pond until they escaped by hitting the water and quickly paddling away. After a while, I spilled the whole truth to Mr. Edwards about what I had done. He said, "I thought there was more to it than you told us before. Son, I have to say ya messed up, but if ya love her, ya need to do all ya can to get her trust back and treat her like a woman deserves to be treated. Remember, money isn't everythang, but family is."

After spending the day with him and having a good hot meal, I was ready for bed. Cash and I headed to the guest room. I was about to enter when Mrs. Edwards said, "Honey, Mr. Edwards told me of yer and sweet Jalynn's troubles. I am so sorry, but yer love is strong, and ya will get through this. Ya just need get down on your knees and pray about it. Give all yer troubles to God. He will take it from there." Those words sent my tears flowing as I agreed, and she gave me a hug. She said, "I didn't mean to make ya cry. I hope I didn't say anythang to upset ya."

I said, "No, ma'am, not at all. Just the opposite, really. I felt my mama's presence when ya said, 'just pray about it.' Mama said that, too, and it has always had an impact on me. I sure do miss 'er."

She said, "Oh, ya poor dear boy. Bless yer heart. Yer mama is with ya always. Now ya just go get ya some rest, everythang will work out."

Cash had already made his spot on the bed, again leaving me with very little room to stretch out. I climbed into the bed and shoved him over. Then I threw my arm over him and hugged him tightly.

"Partner, I am glad I have ya," I told him. "Ya have helped me get through some tough times in the past and I know ya will be by me through this."

He huffed as if I was disturbing him, and I fell asleep.

The next day when I woke up, Cash had left the bed. I got dressed and walked over to the truck stop where I figured he had gone with Mrs. Edwards to get a meal before we headed out. After I ate my breakfast, we said our goodbyes, reloaded at the local feed lot, and headed towards Memphis, Tennessee. I guess I was just excited to get back on the road after our break because I didn't pay attention to my fuel gauge until my light came on. I guess someone who was low on fuel noticed that I had fueled up and slept away from the truck. Someone had stolen my fuel. I thought to myself, *what is this world coming to?*

I barely made it to the next stop to fuel back up, and while worrying over it, I started thinking of all the things that God has brought me through since I have been out here chasing this white line. My mind started wondering again and I was taken back to the early fall of 1971 and my first signs of trouble after returning home after the war.

It was a trying time, and I was once again on my way down this lonesome road. I unloaded in Oklahoma City and went to the truck stop for a break. While I was out walking one evening to stretch my legs, I met this girl. She asked me if I wanted company for the night. I said, no, that I was okay and that I had early start in the morning. She just said, "Okay, honey," and walked away. I thought, *"Could she be one of those lot lizards or prostitutes that I been hearing about?'*

She didn't look like either; in fact, she was very pretty. I returned to my truck where I smoked a cigarette while finishing up my logbooks and paperwork for the day. I began to settle in, and I had just taken my boots off when there was a knock on my door. I looked out to find this pretty woman looking up at me wearing a black mini dress and high heels.

I rolled down the window and said, "What can I do fer ya, little lady?"

She said, "Hey there, trucker, my name is Tracy. Do you need any company for the night?"

Not knowing any better, I said I didn't know. She said that she needed a friend and that she would take care of me. I thought to myself, *it would be nice to have some company for a change.* I knew deep down that it was wrong, that God wouldn't approve, but I agreed. Without hesitation, she climbed into the truck.

In the truck, she took off her shoes, and for some reason, gave a thumbs up out the window. She threw her purse into the passenger seat. With me standing in between the seats, she jumps up and throws her arms around me with such force that we both landed on my bunk. She asked my name. I wasn't sure I should tell her my real name, so I told her it was John.

She said, "Well, John, what would you like me to do?" I was so nervous that I was shaking. She said, "Are you okay, darlin?"

I explained to her that I had never been with a woman before.

She said, "Oh, honey, this is going to be fun. I am going to take good care of you." She kissed me and grabbed me and said, "Let's just see what you are working with." Then she smiled and told me that I was a real country boy and must have eaten my spinach growing up. She kissed me more and began hugging me, and then things got heated. One thing led to another, and within minutes, she changed me into a true man.

I thought, *"Wow! This is what I have been missing all these years!*

Once she was finished and dressed, we settled in the front seats to enjoy a smoke. She then grabbed my hand and said, "Hey, driver, I really had fun, but you owe me $50 bucks." She never said anything about money before she climbed in the truck. I told her I didn't have it and she motioned out the window. Within a minute, a guy came over to my truck, opened the door, dragged me out, and proceeded to give me a beating that I was not going to forget, none too soon.

Driving the next day, I felt every bruise and broken rib that fella gave me. I vowed to not to do that ever again, and if I did, I would ask how much first to make sure she was not a lot lizard!

I hammered down for many months, just returning home when I needed a week or so off. Then I would hit the road again, all business until the summer of 1972.

After I had put down a good many miles, I was rolling through Nashville, Tennessee, where I saw a sign for a concert featuring Red Sovine. I decided to stay and go to the event. I parked at the T/A downtown and got a taxi to the concert. What a show it was! He sang "Giddy up Go," "Phantom 309," and many more trucker favorites. Don Williams opened, and they both gave one heck of a concert. After the show, I returned to the truck stop to grab a few winks before I headed out the next day.

I rolled hard over the next few months and things were going good for a chance. The ranch was out of debt and in good shape for the winter haul. Over the next few months, I was back to my old groove, stopping at roadside juke joints to catch a show, have a drink (or two), and be on my way.

By November that year, I had seen many country music singers across the United States in every little county fair or roadside bar that I could. Such singers as Mearle Haggard, Willie Nelson, Johnny Cash, Dolly Parton, Loretta Lynn, George Jones, Kris Kristofferson, and Kenny Rogers. Really too many to mention them all. I even saw Elvis Presley. I was hooked and I was living the dream. I even got a chance to attend "The Outlaws of County Music" concert, which included Willie Nelson, Waylon Jennings, Jessi Colter, and Tompall Glaser. A few months later, I saw The Highwaymen, which featured Willie, Waylon, Johnny, and Kris.

I learned lots of stuff over the next couple of months. I even had girlfriends in several states. I remember this one girl I dated a few times when I would go through Bakersfield, California. She was a hoot. She got me drinking hard liquor and smoking pot. She always gave me a good time and sent me off with a few joints to keep me rolling. I was good to go everywhere I went.

The beginning of 1973 seemed as if it would be a good year. That was until one night in March, I was in New Mexico with a load heading to Amarillo, Texas. I could take my time getting it there, so I stopped at a rest stop (or pickle park, as we refer to it). While I was out of my truck one night, I was checking for a sound I had heard earlier coming from my trailer. I made to the rear of the trailer in the dark of the night when a fella came up behind me and grabbed me around the neck. I suddenly felt this sharp pain in my side and was pushed to the ground. I lay there for a moment dazed before I realized that I had been stabbed and was being robbed. He grabbed my wallet and took out the little bit of cash I had in it and then ran off. I made my way to where someone could see me and yelled for help and then I collapsed beside my steer tire.

When I awoke, I was in the Emergency Room being stitched up. They said I was lucky that he had not gotten any of my organs and that someone was able to hear my cry for help. They finished stitching me up and then put a bandage around my stomach. Afterwards, I was discharged. I asked the nurse if she could call me a taxi and she said she would, that I should wait out front.

While I was waiting for a taxi to take me to my truck, I was talking to a fella who said his name was Chris Le Doux. He was waiting for someone who would give him a ride towards Texas. He said he had taken a hard blow after he was slung off the horse. That his friends had to leave to make it to the next rodeo.

I said, "Are you a cowboy or something?"

He said, "Yeah, something like that."

I said, "Well, don't sound like they were good friends."

I offered to give him a ride as I was heading in the same direction. What else did I have to lose? When we reached my truck, he paid the taxi driver, and as we were walking to my truck, he said, "What are you going to do without money?"

I unscrewed my fuel cap and grabbed a piece of fishing line. That sorry, no-good bastard didn't get *all* my money. I hauled out my peanut butter jar with my savings in it. I said, "My daddy taught me this."

With that, we climbed in and were on our way.

We drove through the night and talked about everything under the sun. He told me he was a champion bareback bronc rider on the rodeo circuit for many years and that he was also a songwriter and singer. He said he was hoping to retire soon and just do his music. He noticed my guitar in the back and asked if he could play it. I told him that it was a

118

family heirloom, and I didn't know but a few chords. He asked again if he could play it and I told him to go ahead. He grabbed it and began to play. He thumbed it for a while and then he saw my University of Tennessee t-shirt hanging in the back. With a grin, he played "Rocky Top". He then sang me three of the songs he wrote, "Cadillac Cowboy," "This Cowboy's Hat," and "Silence on the Line". He played for some time longer and then fell asleep on my bunk. I drove through the night and on into the morning.

I was exhausted by the time we reached Amarillo, Texas. I pulled into the truck stop just before the Cadillac Ranch. I hollered back to the bunk and told him we were in Texas. He gathered his belongings, we said our goodbyes and went our separate ways. I thought, *"What a heck of a nice guy."*

I drove to the grazing lot to rest the cows until I could get unloaded. I dropped my trailer and bobtailed to the nearby truck stop and found a spot to park. I tidied up the inside of my truck and grabbed a shower, some supper, and did my laundry. I spent the rest of that day and the next resting in my truck and taking the pain pills they had given me at the hospital. I was feeling pretty good by the next evening. I went into the truck stop and got another shower. I grabbed a bite to eat and decided I would just go ahead and stay one more night and unload the next morning and get a reload out.

The next morning, I picked up my trailer which the men had already loaded. I paid my dues for their service and gave them a tip for loading me up so I could just hook up and go. I made my way to the death row lot and unloaded and reloaded, heading towards Tennessee.

I drove all the way through to Nashville, Tennessee. After unloading, I found a load heading to Macon, Georgia. It was late that evening when I finally got loaded, so I decided to bed down for the night.

The next day I decided I would go to the Grand Ole Opry and see who was playing. Jerry Lee Lewis was the headliner, and he brought the house down with an amazing show. After the show I went back to my truck to rest for the trip to Georgia.

The next evening, instead of going all the way to Knoxville and then down, I figured I would venture over and give Monteagle a try. Monteagle Mountain is on Interstate 24, between Nashville and

Chattanooga. I had never driven over it before now, but I had heard how dangerous it was.

The upside wasn't bad as I topped the crest. It could be bad going down, so I dropped my gears and eased down the other side. It was an ass pucker of a decline. I thought a couple of times that it was going to run away from me, but I kept her steady. I could see the traces where trucks had lost it and cleared a path through the trees, and there was some debris from others that had failed to hold it back.

I crossed the Georgia line, and since it had been years since I had seen my big brother Peanut, I decided to stop by his truck stop that sits at the intersection of Hwy 53 and Hwy 411, in the small town of Fairmount, Georgia.

I loved this small town. It had no red lights, a little game room, and a burger joint called the Tasty Freeze. They had the best hamburgers and shakes, besides my brother's place. Peanut's Truck Stop was the place to be on the weekend. His wife Cassandra (Dimples) and he started this place after he was wounded in the war. They moved here to be closer to her family. It was one of the best stops for truckers. They offered good home cooked meals and a hot, clean shower. Good thing he paid attention to Mama's cooking instructions. I got there a mite early so I grabbed a few winks until I knew he would be there.

It was almost noon when I woke up. I was starving so I figured I would get in there and get my fill. I walked in and as usual, Peanut was in his favorite place sitting at the piano. I got close to him and said, "What's a driver got to do to get fed around this place?"

He turned and kept playing with a smile on his face. He was a master of the piano and self-taught, at that. They call him the piano man; everyone loves to hear him play. Once he was done, he got up and met me with a hug.

"Aren't ya a sight, bubba! Why didn't ya call and tell me ya were stop'n by?"

I said, "I wanted to surprise ya! And the look on yer face, told me I succeeded."

He said, "Good to see ya, little brother." Then he yelled back to the kitchen, "Dimples! Ya better drop a double order of okree in the fryer. And while yer at it, fix a triple bacon cheeseburger with jalapeños and no mayo! Make it quick, we have a hungry trucker out here."

Dimples walked out wiping the sweat from her forehead and said, "I had to come out and see who ordered the Bobby Ray Special. Low and behold, it's the man himself."

I said, "Wow, did ya name a special after me?"

She said, "Dang right, we did, and it's a big hit. I sure am glad ya made it over this way to see us."

I said, "I feel special now, eat'n a special named after me."

She gave me a hug and said, "Have yer food out in a jiffy. You two catch up."

I said, "No hurry."

She yelled back over her shoulder, "I know ya are a James, and when it comes to food, it can't come fast enough!"

My brother said, "She ain't wrong!" He then asked me how I liked trucking life. "Not how I pictured yer life panning out."

I said, "Family first, bubba, ya know that. Plans change; sometimes fer the better and other times not. I have got to keep our family ranch go'n. Jackie Lee and Slim almost lost it again. It is our legacy that Daddy built, and I gotta do what I can to keep it run'n." Peanut nodded and I said, "Ya know yuns could always come back home and run the books for me. Dimples could do what she does best and cook fer the crew. Sis tries but, Lord, bless 'er heart, she can't cook like Mama used to or Dimples does."

He said, "Well, brother, ya sound just like Daddy. I can't say I haven't pondered on it. But truth be told, we are happy right where we are with our little business."

I said, "I understand, ya have got to do what's best for ya both. As for me, I am dig'n this life on the road. Seeing the country, meet'n some nice people from all walks of life. Now that's not say'n I don't have my share of troubles, but it sure keeps thangs interest'n. Ya know, I have a good crew back at the ranch and I know they can handle it. If I can keep Jackie Lee and Slim out of the money, that is."

He said, "I will try to talk to Jackie about it. I am still the oldest and I will tell her how it is."

Dimples brought my food out and we talked as I was trying devourer this monster of a burger. Although we talked about our lives, neither of us brought up the war stuff, as we fight those battles inside of us. We just kept it uplifting and enjoyable for the short visit.

While I was eating, with grease all over my lips, a pretty lady walked in, went to the counter, and ordered a salad.

"Be right with you, hun," Dimples said.

I looked at Peanut and said, "See, I told ya, brother. I am about to meet me a sweet little lady right now.

Peanut shook his head. "I see that my little brother has finally become a man."

"Just live'n life; enjoying the finer things in it," I said. "Whether she is nice or trouble, I don't know, but I am soon to find out."

He said, "Funny you should say that…" He called her over. "Joy, this is my little brother, Bobby Ray. He's a truck driver, and he also runs our family ranch back in Wyom'n."

I was embarrassed to look up with this mess on my face. I quickly wiped it off and stood up to say, "Glad to meet ya, Joy. Care to join us? We are all family here." Then I said, "Ya from around here, darli'n?"

"I'm from over in Adairsville," she said, "but this place is worth the drive on pay day."

I agreed and said, "Well, I'm glad the road led ya here while I'm here." She asked me what I was do'n later, and I said, "Just hang'n in my truck."

She handed me a flyer showing that there was a double feature at the Twin Bridges Drive-In for "truck driver appreciation." They were showing *Smokey and the Bandit,* starring Burt Reynolds as the Bandit and Jerry Reed as The Snow Man, as well as and *Convoy,* starring Kris Kristofferson as The Rubber Duck. There would also be two special singers to perform a few hit songs.

Joy smiled at me and asked, "Would ya like to take me to the show? They have bobtail park'n especially fer it."

I said, "Sure, honey, I would love to..."

Dimples rolled her eyes and said, "Be nice, Bobby Ray."

I just winked at her and said, "Yes, ma'am." Then I told her that I needed to get my truck washed and cleaned up first.

We finished eating and walked out to my truck. I disconnected from the trailer, and we drove over to the truck wash. In no time flat, she was clean and shining. We put ice and beer into my cooler and grabbed a few snacks. I told Peanut I would square up with him in the morning, but he said, "It's on me. Go and have yerself a good time, ya deserve it."

So, we hit the road for the drive-in.

We pulled in and to my surprise, in the back, there were fifteen or so bobtail rigs in a row. Truckers were on their CB's spreading the word. There were chairs on the lawn and coolers all over the ground. We were accustomed to sharing, so I pitched in my cooler of ice-cold beer.

It wasn't long before the emcee came over the speakers and announced the singers on the stage. Low and behold, it was the one-and-only Jerry Reed, and Kris Kristofferson, and C.W. McCall doing the theme song from the movie *Convoy*. Man! They really put on a great show! We had a good ole time that night. Especially when the performers came and hung out with us drivers.

After the show, as suggested by the owner, we stayed at the drive-in since we had been drinking. We settled in the bunk and talked for a while, then our conversations were replaced by kissing. One thing led to another, and before I knew it, we were both enjoying each other's company. Afterwards, we fell asleep in each other's arms.

The next morning, as the sun was making its way through my bunk curtains, we were awakened to the sounds of truck horns signaling that they were leaving. We got up and went over to the concession stand where the owner had set up some breakfast and coffee for the truck drivers before they headed out. Once we had our coffee and were more awake, we climbed back in the truck and drove to Peanut's where I asked Joy if she would like to join me for breakfast.

She said, "No, I'm just go'n to head on home, but thanks for everythang. I had so much fun."

We said our goodbyes and as she climbed out of my rig, I said, "I hope to see ya again sometime on my way passing through."

She handed me a piece of paper with her number on it and then blew me a kiss. "Sure thang."

I went in to grab breakfast, shower, and to say goodbye to Peanut and Dimples.

Peanut was already behind the counter, serving up biscuits and gravy. He said, "Must have been a good one since I just seen Joy climb out of yer rig."

With a big smile I said, "Yes, indeed, it was. And let me tell ya, she is full of joy." Then I said, "The show was great. I wish ya could have

123

come and seen it. We got to hang out with Jerry Reed, Kris Kristofferson, and C. W. McCall.

Peanut said, "I am glad ya had a good time."

I ate my share of gravy biscuits and grabbed a quick shower. I thanked my brother and Dimples and told them I would see them next time. Then, I got in my truck and I, too, was on my way.

The next few months went by without a hitch. I was hauling everything I could get my hands on if it kept me rolling down the white line so I could settle with my sister. The road suited me well. However, I did miss my college friends, and I will probably always wonder how my life would have turned out if I had gone back. I thought of those days often. My friends and teammates. And my old girlfriend.

I was glad to finally catch up with Bubba after he had graduated from the university of Tennessee and was finally able to bring my old truck Blossom back. He took really good care of her and told me that he hated that he hadn't gotten her to me before then. He said school was hard and after his freshman year, he had to buckle down and get on track. I had told him while he was on the ranch that I hated to leave school and the team. He had said, "Don't be sorry. Ya did the right thang. Yer Mama and Daddy raised ya right."

Bubba told me that he had gotten a job with *Sports Illustrated* as a writer. I was envious of him, but my life had been chosen for me. He commented that the others had gotten good jobs and had moved to various states. We agreed before he left that we would have our own reunion someday. After that time went on and we both had our lives full, we grew distant and only got in a quick call now and then.

I was so busy hauling cattle and other freight that I barely had time to stop in and check on the ranch. That is, until I rolled through Texas one night in June 1973. I had the hammer down and was in my own little world so didn't see the state trooper in the shadows. Before I knew it, he had me blue-lighted.

When he was writing me a speeding ticket, I must have been acting strangely. He told me to step out so he could search my truck. At that moment, I remembered the baggie of pot my girlfriend had left behind. I just knew I was busted, and I was going to be going to jail.

When it was all said and done, I was sentenced to one year and one day in Federal prison. It was in prison where I learned to play the guitar.

I did my time, kept myself clean, and was released after only nine months. But I couldn't go across state lines for three more months. So, I went home.

I worked on the ranch and hauled local loads to get by. We were still okay on the ranch since I had saved a great deal of money.

Or so I thought.

While I was imprisoned, the bottom fell out of the cattle business and costs had gone through the roof. I had to go and take out a loan and use my truck as collateral, unlike my daddy who could just borrow money just on his name and reputation. I figured it was enough to see us through for a while.

I was lucky enough to get a job driving for a local dump truck outfit which kept us from going under again. After my forced "vacation," I needed to get on the road again and make some good money.

So, I did.

I was clean and doing well financially, but I felt something inside building up and I could not explain it. Was it the pressure of the ranch needing to succeed? Was it the passing of Mama and Daddy? Or was it my memories of the war?

The answers to these questions I could not find.

This brought me to the first time I decided to stop and get me a bottle of whisky. In the beginning, it helped take off the edge, just a nip or two. Then I was drinking more and more to keep my mind off my past. And then one thing led to another.

In California in August 1974, I stopped for the night, and that is when my life started being turned upside down.

I met this girl at a little bar outside of Fresno. She said she wanted to spend the night with me in my truck. I asked her if she was a lot lizard, and how much it would cost me. She said she wasn't, and that it wouldn't cost me anything. She just wanted a good time. I agreed and we went out to the truck.

We were drinking and smoking pot and she asked if I wanted something to make the party even better. I was curious so I asked her how much it would cost. She said it wouldn't cost anything, except the cost of the powder. She disappeared for a few minutes and came back. Then she introduced me to what she called cocaine. At first, it burnt my nose, but soon enough, I got used to it. The stuff was exactly what I needed, and we partied all night until I passed out. When I awoke the next morning, I had a huge headache, and I noticed she was gone. After getting myself together, I realized she had robbed me of all my money and even the valuables from my truck. I thought, *"Well, she was right; it didn't cost me a thing, it cost me everything."*

I grabbed the peanut butter jar from my tank, fully regretting my decisions of the previous evening.

I continued with the money I had and made a couple more runs until I was able to get my finances back on track, start putting money in the jar again, and wiring the rest to the bank.

After that, I ran hard for about two years, going home every month to check on the ranch. I'd stay a week or two to make sure my sister was doing right by me, then I would hit the road again. I was happy that I had done so well, and for the fact that the ranch was doing great, and everything was running like clockwork.

Then everything changed in the summer of '76.

I was taking a week off in Clear Water, Florida, and I met this cute waitress named Mandy Clark at this little seafood restaurant. We hit it off right away and ended up going out several times that week. She was four years younger and tried to keep me on my toes. Every time I went through there after that week, we would go out. Finally, things started getting serious and I asked her if she wanted to go out, over the road with me. She was excited, and after getting her stuff together, she took some vacation time, and we went on a little road trip. We were on the road for a week. We were in Georgia and heading to Florida to take her back. I pulled over on the side of the road and set my brakes.

Looking over at her, I said, "Mandy, ya know I have never felt like this with any woman before. I am in love with ya and I believe ya love me. So, what do ya say we just go ahead and get hitched?"

She was so excited, and said, "Yes, I would love that!"

We rolled through Ringold, Georgia, and stopped to see the minister. We were married after just six months of dating on and off. She continued with me over the road for a while, and we had a wonderful time. We went to the ranch a couple of times, and she really loved it there. Shortly after our last visit, she said she was tired of being on the road. She asked if we could get off the road for a while and said that she didn't like that life anymore. I agreed since we were newlyweds, and I wanted her to be happy. We settled on the ranch, and I took a local job running horses for a nearby ranch, while attending our ranch and doing the usual runs to the auctions, ranches, and feed lots. After a few months, I couldn't take it anymore. I felt penned up and we were arguing a lot. I spent most of my time at home in the barn hitting the mason jar, sinking into a depressed state again. I needed the open road. One day, I told her that I had decided to go back out, and we had a huge argument. Two days later, I packed my stuff; I needed the open road to keep me happy.

After that, I was running hard and hardly ever home, leaving her alone on the ranch. I guess the love wasn't there after all, because she started going out to the local bars, doing who-knows-what with anybody that would pay her attention. When I came home, she broke down and told me of her doings.

That was it for me. I told her to get out and go back to Florida, because I didn't want her on the ranch anymore. She pleaded and said she was sorry, but I wasn't having any of her gibberish. She cheated on me, and that was it for us. I told my sister to make sure she left, and I hit the road. In just two short months, I received notice that we were divorced.

In May of 1977, I was once more enjoying the freedom of being single and living life up on the open road. Driving, dating, drinking, smoking, sniffing cocaine, taking speed, and any other pills I could get my hands on. The more I was rolling and tending to my addictions, the happier I was.

One night in this little truck stop in north Georgia, I was introduced to something that would change my life forever. This driver they call Nighttime Freddie gave me a long black pill, said it was called a "west coast turnaround." Along with that, he handed me some toothpicks and said, "These will do the trick, too, buddy."

I felt I needed something new, so I swallowed that pill with my last sup of Colorado Cool-Aid (a can of Coors). I left there and headed up I-75, then I-40, over towards Nashville, Tennessee, when it hit me. The next thing I knew, it was the next day, and I was almost to Amarillo before I knew it.

After that, I was up until I reached Barstow. A 3-day trip in 2- days. I was hooked. I had to have more to keep it going and keep me rolling.

127

I was unstoppable and uncatchable, until I topped a hill one morning going 80 miles per hour through Arizona. Wouldn't you know it, on the other side was an Evel Knievel cop (motorcycle cop) taking pictures of folks as they topped the hill. He took my picture with his little machine doing 80 in a double nickel (55), which cost me most of my hidden savings and 30 days in jail.

While there, I met a little feller about 13 years old that the sheriff was trying to teach a lesson. They brought him in because he was getting too hard for his mom to handle, misbehaving at home and fighting with the other kids. Heck, he even tried to pick a fight with me. He was wiry but he had the heart of a warrior. I heard them call him Martin, so, I tried to start a conversation with him on his terms.

I said, "Martin, whatcha in fer, little buddy."

"Fighting," he said.

I asked, "Why ya like to fight?"

"I'm practicing being a professional wrestler."

"Do the other kids know this?" I asked and chuckled a little bit. This made him mad, and he took a swing at me to show me he could whoop me.

He said, "I am the 'Boogeyman,' and I will put a hurting on you!"

I figured I would try to settle him down and I asked him what his favorite wrestlers were. He mentioned a few that I knew, such as Dusty Rhodes, The Andersons, Andre the Giant, Executioner #1, and Bobo Brazil. I admit, he had a good build for what he wanted to do but was too young at this point.

He was there with me for two days, going in and out of the cell for counseling, only to return madder than a hornet, cussing and throwing a temper tantrum. I guess that the imprisonment of that little man and the attempts from the sheriff and the deputies weren't working because they called in reinforcements from the local juvenile boy's camp. A huge man whose shoulders barely fit through the door arrived, and he must have been seven foot tall because he had to duck to get into the cell.

Once inside, he started screaming at Martin, and quickly made the boy cry, even though he was in his mind tough as nails. Against the little boy's wishes, this man picked him up by the seat of his britches and carried him away, with the boy trying his best to escape his grip. I can only guess where they took him to learn his lesson.

128

Once my time was up, I was released from jail. My truck had been damaged by the tow truck when they towed it in, and I didn't have money left to pay for it. I had to figure something out. I inquired with the owner, and he said he had an old Peterbilt in the back that needed a water pump and radiator. Said he would be glad to trade me with a little money on my end for the repairs. I agreed and grabbed my emergency money from the fuel tank.

It was a 1970 black Peterbilt 352 Cabover with silver and red pinstripes. I transferred my stuff and got a hotel to relax after my unpleasant stay at the local jail. After the repairs were made, I was ready to hit the white line running.

I climbed up in my new truck and with the large pipes, I was blowing black smoke and roaring as I headed out of town. I passed the boys' camp and there my little friend was with the rest of the troubled youth from the state. That huge man was out too, there towering over them, and they were obeying every order. I put the hammer down and headed towards my ranch. I needed a break, and I figured a month off would do the trick. After those life lessons were learned, I slowed everything down for a while and simply enjoyed life on the open road.

Suddenly, I was brought back from my stroll down memory lane with the horns of other trucks passing by, letting me know they were coming by, since I had my CB turned down low and didn't hear them hollering for me. Miles and time had gone by as I recalled the past. I rolled into Memphis and pulled into the Petro to settle in for the night with a can of sardines and crackers for dinner, and Cash had a can of Alpo. My depression was setting in, and Cash knew it. He just snuggled up next to me to let me know he was there. I didn't want to interact with anyone, and I didn't want to get out of the truck unless I had to. I lay there listening to the radio and a familiar voice came through the speakers. It was the cowboy that I had given a ride back in '73. He had become a famous singer/songwriter, and he was singing "Whatcha Gonna do with a Cowboy" as a duet with Garth Brooks. That set me thinking; I figured I would give Jalynn a call.

129

I climbed in the front seat to have a smoke and call, but I was rejected with Amberleigh telling me she still was not ready to talk. I left her the same message: "Tell 'er I love 'er, and I am sorry."

I hung up and called my kids to see if they had any insight into their mama's plans, and to see if she had said anything. Jr. said that he had been busy with things as he was getting new shipments for the bar and western store, but she did come by his house to see the grandbabies. She hasn't offered any information on her plans. Faith and Lacey had gone and seen her two days ago, and they said she was doing better. They said that they could tell through her conversation that she was still in love with me. That eased my heart some knowing there was a glimmer of hope. I told them I would see them in a few weeks, and we said our loves, and goodbyes, and hung up.

I climbed back into the bunk where Cash and I had another snack of beef jerky and Vienna sausages. With a full belly, I said my prayers and went to sleep to rest for the next day's adventures down the long white line.

9

THE ADDICTION

Memphis, TN – Tallahassee, FL

AS DAWN AWOKE THE TRUCK STOP, AND FEELING BETTER from the news the kids told me last night, I decided to go inside for a big plate of biscuits and gravy, plus a slice of country ham for Cash. Plus, I wanted to freshen up before my delivery. As I entered, I was immediately greeted by this pretty little waitress with a body fit for a model and the voice of an angel. I smiled and said, "Good morn'n, darlin," as I always said to the waitresses.

She smiled said, "Good morning!" as if she had had a lot of coffee. However, it was still sultry.

She led me to a corner booth, and being a man, I watched her walk away with her tight jeans trying their best to keep up with her wiggle. As I sat in the booth, I told her I would have the biscuits and gravy and a coffee, and I wanted to get four slices of country ham to-go. She scribbled down my order and then went to another table to fetch me a clean ashtray. It wasn't but moment before as she returned with my coffee which she sat in front of me and said that my food would be out in a jiffy. Although it was still early the morning, the tone of her voice changed in a flirty unexpected tone, as she said again in that sultry voice, "If you need anything at all, and I mean *anything,* just ask and it's yours."

I simply replied, "Thank ya, darlin. I am good for now."

Her smile faded and she walked away. After a few sips of coffee, she returned with my food. This time as she started to leave, she turned around and winked at me, patting her behind to show she was offering more than what was on the menu.

Back in my younger years, I would have taken her up on her very tempting offer. But I politely declined, telling her that I was married, and I had to eat and be on my way. Before leaving, I did, however, give her some advice. I told her that she was very a pretty young lady who had her whole life ahead of her, that she did not need to get involved with one of us truck drivers because it is stressful life. That he would be gone for weeks at a time, she would always wonder where he was, what he was doing, if he was being faithful, if he was alright, and when he would be home.

"Everythang is so uncertain deal'n with a truck driver, include'n the money," I told her. "You won't be happy be'n second to a driver's rig. To a trucker, his rig is his first love, regardless of what you offer him. If he he's not drive'n, he'll be either be clean'n and shine'n or fix'n on it."

She said with a halfhearted smile that she just wanted to get out of that little town and see the rest of the country and hopefully find love one day.

I told her that she had the rest of her life to find true love and she would be better off not chasing after just any old truck driver. I told her she would know *the one* when he comes along.

I picked up my cowboy hat from the seat beside me and laid down a twenty-dollar tip to thank her for the service. I walked out, and before I knew it, she came running out and gave me a hug and thanked me for the money and the advice.

I made my way out to my rig with my thermos supply of coffee. I gave Cash his meat and it was gone in a flash, without him savoring any of it. He licked the ham juice from his lips and looked at me as if to say he wanted more.

"Cash, ole boy," I said, "ya need to slow down. I am in no shape to be lift'n you in and out of this truck when ya get too fat to do it yerself."

He just huffed at me in disagreement and jumped on the bed. I poured me a cup of coffee and made my way over to my destination.

After I made my delivery, I found a reload from a nearby farm and headed for Tallahassee, Florida. Somewhere between Memphis and Nashville, I started thinking about that little gal back at the truck stop…

It reminded me of the night in October 1978, when I stopped to see Mearle Haggard at a honkytonk in Midland, Texas. Walking in, I noticed several beautiful women I could see myself taking back to the truck. I was in dire need of some female company. I strolled up to the bar and ordered a tall cold beer and a shot of old Jack. The bartender scraped the head off my draft and poured me a double shot of Jack Daniels whisky and set both in front of me.

I asked, "How much, my friend?"

He said it was already taken care of by the lady at the end of the bar. He pointed to this cute lady sitting there in a jet-black T-shirt busting at the seams, with an image on the front glowing under the lights of the bar. It read, "Truckers like it Loud, Hammering Down with the Lights On."

Tipping my cowboy hat, which once belonged to my daddy, and smiling at her, I made my way over to thank her proper for her kindness. I put my arm around her and said, "My name is Bobby Ray. What is yer name, sweetheart?"

She said, "You can call me Caroline, and yes I am sweet."

Smiling, she asked if I was from around these parts. I told her I was just passing through in my big rig to pick up a load of livestock tomorrow. I said I was tired and needed a break. I saw the sign for the show and, since I loved to listen Mearl Haggard, I just had to stop to catch the show.

She said with her cute smile, "Good. I just came here to have a good time and maybe show some cowboy a good time. Since you are a trucker, that is a bonus for me." She put her hand in my back pocket, moved in closer, and whispered, "Would you like to have a good time with me tonight?"

How was I supposed to say no to this beautiful lady's request? I squeezed her tight around the waist with one arm and tipped my daddy's old Stetson hat saying, "Yes, ma'am, I thank I would."

With my answer, she grabbed her beer from the bar and said, "Let's dance." She grabbed my big gold and silver belt buckle (which once belonged to my daddy as well) and led me to the dance floor.

We danced most of the night and drank our fair share of booze. Merle really put on a good show as always; we would stop every now and then to rest and just listen to him sing. I requested "Mama's Hungry Eyes," which is by far my favorite song of his.

After Ole Hagg was done playing his set for the night, I grabbed a six-pack to go and asked her if she would like to continue our party in my rig. She gave me a big Texas smile and with a big Texas, "YEE-HAA!" said, "Lead the way, cowboy."

She hooked her finger through my belt loop, and we made our way through the bar and out to my truck in the parking lot.

She said, "Is that your truck lit up like a Christmas tree." I said it was and she said, "It is so pretty!" as we climbed inside. Once there, she quickly made herself at home in my home on wheels. She took her off boots and shed her T-shirt. Underneath was a tank top that barely held what she was blessed with. Grabbing her purse, she asked if I wanted to do a line of nose candy.

"What's that?" I asked.

She said, "Cocaine, dummy! But this is not ordinary stuff. It has something in it with a little extra kick."

With some hesitation I said, "Okay, I guess so, but just a little." I have done cocaine before but never done *this* stuff. To my surprise, I did more than what seemed to be a little bit. Within a few minutes of my first snort, I began to feel the rush of the powder. It was unlike the "west coast turnarounds" I was used to taking. It was like an overload of caffeine, and not having a care in the world. As if I had gained some kind of superpower. I felt more alive than I ever have.

After our little treat, we lay back on my bunk and started fooling around. Regretfully, I don't remember much after her asking me if I was ready for her to show me the good time that she promised. I really don't recall anything after that, as the drugs took over my mind and it seemed like I was somewhere out in space.

The next day I awoke alone. All I could think was I hope she enjoyed the night because I could hardly remember a thing. I had a pounding headache and was exhausted from the little bit of sleep I had gotten. My nose was burning and there was a little trace of blood under it that I noticed in my bunk mirror. I didn't know what to do with myself after that. I climbed into the driver's seat with what little energy I had, and made my way to the local truck stop, figuring a hot shower would perk me up.

I went and cleaned myself up in a hot shower and then grabbed a quick biscuit. Then I went over to the feed lot to get a load headed to Florida. While they were loading me, I got to talking to the owner, Eldrid Denny, about the night before.

He said, "Boy, stay away from that stuff. It will get ya in trouble or even kill ya. I have known ya for a long time and yer father and mother even longer. They are probably roll'n in their graves at what ya are out here do'n. Ya need to find ya a good woman and settle down and run yer family ranch. Not stay out here chase'n the line, try'n to get with every piece of tail ya can."

I just nodded my head even though I felt that I knew what I was doing and could quit anytime I wanted. The fact is, I was happy doing what I was doing.

His help finally finished loading me up and I got my paperwork. As I climbed up in my truck, I bid them farewell. Within a few minutes, I had the hammer down and was on my way. Life was good, and the money was great, as I was chasing this long white line.

However, unbeknownst to me, my life was about to change.

As I recall it was in late December 1978, I was down near Miami, Florida, shortly after the night with that young lady. I was worn out and since Daddy had passed in December, I hated that time of year anyhow. I grew depressed and I felt I needed some more of the stuff to get things off my mind. I had just pulled into the truck stop and figured I would ask around until I found some.

I approached a shady-looking dive bar and figured it would be the place if any. I asked this ole fella that was coming out and where I might get some, and he pointed me in the direction of a girl that could hook me up with whatever I needed. After a quick and secret meeting, I had what I had come for.

I walked back to my truck with my baggy hid under my hat. Once there, I found myself unsure and nervous, because I was by myself and didn't know how I would react. Since I was needing to get going to make my run on time, I decided to take a west coast turn around to wire me up until I got a chance to experiment with my stash. Once I was feeling the pill take effect, I was ready to put the hammer down.

I drove straight through and delivered my load in Denver, Colorado. I was empty and found the nearest truck stop for a break that I desperately needed. After a hot shower and a bite to eat, I settled in my bunk for some sleep. I slept for the better part of the day and into the night. I awoke in a sweat, on edge from a nightmare about the war. I lay there trying to get it off my mind. I smoked a few cigarettes, and they did not calm my mind one bit. I grabbed the purple Crown Royal bag from the glove box where I put my stash. I put it in a line and with a straw and a snort, up my nose it went. Again, within a few minutes, I was back where I was with her that night feeling my superpowers.

I was feeling good and the more I did, the more I needed it. I was putting down more miles than I could ever have imagined, doing good for myself and the ranch. Or so I thought. I ran for almost a year with only a couple of stops by the ranch and then only when I needed a break.

By the end of summer of 1979, I found myself running out on the west coast. I was coming through Bakersfield, California, and it just so happened that Red Sovine was doing a roadside bar show. I had to catch it as he was one of my favorites. He sang all his usual trucking songs, plus he did a couple of numbers he had just recorded called, "Teddy Bear," and "Phantom 309," which were by far real tearjerkers. It was a good show.

I had been up all day driving, but I needed rest, so I lay down. I guess the excitement from the night had me restless, so I reached for my bag and got me a good snort of my magical powder. Once again, I was ready to roll!

I spent two weeks on the west coast, running like crazy day and night, until one day, overjudging my courage on the Ole Grapevine in California. I found myself over speed and smoked my brakes into a fire on the trailer. By the time I saw it, it was too late. I tried to slow down, but I was out of control and ended up in the ravine at the bottom with my truck on its side. I was in a confused and dazed state of mind, but I felt immense pain and could see that my clothes were becoming soaked with blood. Plus, I couldn't feel my legs. The smell of the burning rubber, black smoke, the feel of the warm blood ran across my face, and the pain in my body was the last thing I remember.

When I came to, I was in the ICU. There were doctors and nurses all around to inform me that I had been in a horrible accident and that I had been in a coma for almost two months. They said my sister had come to visit several times and that she wanted to know when I finally opened my eyes. I told them to call her, because I was too ashamed of myself to talk to her. They said they would and when I was ready, they would bring me a phone. I asked them how bad it was, and they said when I came in, I was barely alive. However, since then my body had had the time to heal somewhat. They said however, I still needed more hospitalization time to completely heal. I was there for another 6 weeks doing physical therapy. After that, I was transferred to another rehab facility for 6 more weeks.

During that time, I had two great nurses. Danielle Ellis came in on Mondays, Wednesdays, and Fridays, and Taylor Springdale would come on Tuesdays and Thursdays. They helped me get through my physical rehab, always encouraging and smiling no matter how mad I got when I couldn't perform the tasks that they asked me to do. We would get to talking during our hour and a half session and I would tell them bits and pieces of my life's story. Then they would tell me theirs and we became close friends as time went on.

Danielle would talk about her little man Miller who was in love with baseball and was such a talented player. In fact, he was an all-around sports fanatic. She said he even played basketball and was going to give football a go when it was time for tryouts. She told me he loved watching wrestling and named off some of the ones he liked. One of his favorites were Goldberg and Cain (which I found out later as I was passing back through that little town where I spent my thirty days as a guest at the local jail but this time as a visitor. That the giant of man that ran the boys farm was Goldberg himself and wrestled only on the weekends as a semi-retired wrestler). I told her that I had met Goldberg once in this small town. She took my picture one day and showed it to him, and now he calls me Goldberg. She told me that he asks about me all the time. She even mentioned how much he loved boiled peanuts and could probably live on them, as well as hot wings and boiled crab legs. I said I could, too. She talked about how he was a brave little man that had ridden all the roller coasters at their nearby amusement park except the biggest, but he was slowly getting up the courage. I gave her some money one day and told her to take him to the amusement park to ride the biggest coaster. I told her to tell him to be a warrior and conquer that big ride.

The way Danielle spoke of her son was very uplifting, especially after learning she was a single mother working full time and she always managed to be there for him to support him and not miss a moment. I told her she was the brave and courageous one and a great mama to her amazing little man.

Then there was Taylor. She would tell me about her husband Dakota who was a talented and upcoming bull rider. He was gone all the time all over the country to rodeos, and she did her best to get by while he was away. She was lonely from time to time, and she loved talking at work because she was the only one besides her son which she was raising mostly alone with Dakota was gone so much. Her son Caine was in his terrible twos and was the light of her life. She said he made her day even though he was a mess when it came to getting into stuff.

During my many days of therapy, I got to know her son Caine through her eyes. She told me that he was her little cowboy. He was clearly the center of her world and her drive. She showed me a picture of him. He had the bluest of blue eyes and was so ridiculously cute with an ornery grin. She said he was growing so fast and kept her busy. She said that when he woke up, he wouldn't cry. He'd just grab his ball and say, "ball, play." He had a bad habit of saying, "dang it," which I thought was cute. She was a good Christian woman and didn't want him to pick up bad language and habits. He loved playing catch, and he was adamant that you do right (or his way, as she called it). He loved monster trucks and knew all of them by name. She said it was hard to keep up with his mischief, but I told her to enjoy those moments; that he would grow up fast and she would miss those days.

When she had first mentioned Dakota and the fact that he was a bull rider, I was immediately taken back and felt a pounding pain in my chest as I was reminded of that horrible day in my youth when my daddy had the run in with our bull and how my life was changed in an instant. And took off in a new direction. I was so scared for her and the most horrible outcome she might face one day. I kept my feelings to myself so as not to upset her and put that fear in her. Although I figured she already had that fear held deep inside of her but didn't let it show. I told her that she herself was a great mama to him and that she was a very strong woman.

After another two months, and a couple more surgeries, I was able to walk on my own, but still had issues with the feeling in my feet. I had most of the use of my arms and all my internal injuries had finally healed. I was ready to leave the hospital. We said our goodbyes and I told them that I really appreciated their help and that I was sorry for the way I had acted in the beginning.

I finally got the nerve up and called my sister and told her where I was going. To my surprise, she was very worried about me, and said that the ranch was doing good, and that she couldn't wait until I was able to come home. I was then released to the county jail where I was to serve a six-month sentence for DUI.

There, I met more interesting people from all walks of life. They taught me things such as how to play poker, craps, and quarters, for extra money or necessities I might need. I didn't win often since I wasn't very good at those games. I even got a few jailhouse tattoos. My last three months, I was put on the chain gang to work along the roadways, and other odd jobs around the county. I was glad because I had nothing and needed the money since I was losing at our gambling activities. It paid only $5 a day and except for the necessities, I saved what I could. I rolled my savings up and emptied the tobacco out of a few cigarettes from a pack and stuck the money inside with a small amount of tobacco in the end. No one ever knew the difference. I had my special one marked so that I would know not to smoke it or give it away.

While I was working on the roadside, the big rigs would come by, and I wished I was out there running and chasing that never-ending white line. But it gave me something to look forward to.

When all was said and done, I was released, this time to an addiction rehab facility. Against my will I accepted my punishment and went for 2 more months. Not only did they help with some of my physical ability restrictions but with my addictions as well.

There, I had the pleasure of meeting two more of the most knowledgeable and friendliest nurses. They made my stay a little more pleasurable. Especially Nichole Webb, who was a firm believer in God. She helped me with my physical therapy, and she talked a lot about God.

She sang songs while we did therapy, which reminded me of my days when Mama and Daddy would take me to church. I knew a few from my childhood days and sang along from time to time.

Nichole was pushy and even bossy when it came to getting me to do my therapy, but her singing helped me get along. She told me on our first session that she had three girls. Ashley, the oldest, Grace, in the middle, and Moriah, the baby. She mentioned that they all loved to sing. After I was there for a while, I wanted to hear them, and she started bringing them by after church. These little girls would melt my heart when they sang gospel songs outside my room. They weren't allowed to come in, they had to stand out in the hall, and it would echo throughout the hospital. Their favorite was "Even If". But I loved it when they sang "Amazing Grace" and "So Much to Thank Him For." She would talk about how they loved to dance, and how they loved summertime, and going to their aunt and uncle's house in Tennessee, where they got their favorite homemade vanilla ice cream with sprinkles on top.

We talked about the Bible often and she told me all about her husband Niles, who was a construction worker of some sort. But her girls were the subject most of the time. She said that they said to let me know that they would pray for me. I remember one day when they were done singing and were getting ready to leave, the oldest, Ashley, snuck her head in the door and said, "I love you. I hope you get out of here soon." It touched my heart that she had compassion for someone she didn't even know. I thought to myself, now that is God's work.

During my stay, it was Marie Strickland that helped me most with my addiction issues as she talked about her and her husband Wayne (Doo, or Big D, as she calls him). She told me of their own addictions, all that they went through, how they overcame it, and even spent time in jail over it. She talked about recovery options and programs. She told me about how she got into helping with addiction recovery as a coping method to help her as well. She said that they have a busy schedule between the two of them because she works at the hospital and helps with counseling at the local women's shelter as well. Her husband was an industrial mechanic and is also in a soft ball league with other recovering addicts to help him cope.

She talked about her five children and how they are what kept them going. Her oldest son Floyd was a senior in high school and has gotten a scholarship to play football for the University of Georgia. They have twin girls, Kay-Kay and Annie, who were thirteen but thought they were twenty-five. She said they grow up so fast and think they know everything.

She told me that her baby girl Ann is a smart little girl with dolly curls who likes to be the center of attention. I guess she talks about me when she goes home because her little girl drew a picture of me as a stick figure and my truck and sent it by her to give to me. It said, "I hop yu git betur luv ann." I knew what she meant and told her to place it in my windowsill for me to look at.

She said her little boy Tony (or Co-Co, as they call him), is into everything as is starting to walk and explore.

She mentioned that they all like to go watch the dirt track races on Saturday nights and on Sunday, they all go to church. She told me to keep the faith and remember my steps from the program, and if I ever needed to talk, she would listen. I thanked her for caring and sharing her life with me, that her story gave me hope knowing I can get better.

My time with them was coming to an end and I hated to leave not knowing what my future held. Before I was released, Nichole said her girls wanted to meet me and I agreed. They met me in the lobby, and each gave me a hug, and told me that they loved me. I waited there in the lobby as did the two deputies that were around the corner so the girls couldn't see them to take me on to my next punishment. At my request, they did not cuff me until the girls left. I didn't want them to witness the police officers loading me cuffed, in the squad car to take me to my next place of healing.

While I waited, I called home to tell my sister what was happening. Jackie Lee told me that she was glad to hear from me and that she was excited that I was doing better than I was when she saw me lying lifeless in the hospital.

From there, I was sentenced to six more weeks in sort of a rehab house on a farm that was run by this lady, Jean Childers and her family, which happened to be a friend of Marie's. She was a wonderful woman and made sure I was set with everything that I need for my stay. She said she loved taking care of people and showing them what they are capable of after they have had a rough go at life. I was taken good care of. I had tasty food and every comfort I wasn't used to for the last nine months or so. Jean made me some homemade dressing that tasted just like my mama's, and her meatloaf was the same. She cooked other things such as fried salmon patties, fried taters, pintos, corn bread, homemade biscuits and gravy. I was quickly gaining strength, and my weight was quickly on the rise. I was enjoying my time, and it didn't seem like a sentence at all.

The greatest joy was getting out and helping her husband Chuck fix stuff around the homeplace. He was a regular handy man. We built things out of pallets and old wood for them to sell at the local flea market to help with the cost of running the place. We would work and talk about hunting and fishing, and we even got the guns out for target practice a time or two. I also enjoyed working in the garden with her wonderful kids and getting to know them. There were five in all, and each were unique in their own way.

Lamar, the oldest at the age of twenty, stayed at home and worked for them. He was into girls and going mudding. On the weekend he would come in with his truck covered in mud and they would spray him off with the garden hose before he could come into the house. He was a hard worker and very mechanically inclined and made sure everything on the farm ran properly.

Andrew was fifteen and was just learning to drive. We would go 'round and 'round in the field practicing all that was required for him to pass the driving exam. He had a little girlfriend and when she would come over, they would sit in the truck and pretend they were on a date.

Then there was Charlie who was just a little younger and hardly came out of his room except to eat and work on the farm. He was not the least bit interested in really learning to drive. He and Luke, the middle boy who was thirteen and a whiz at his video game, "The Atari 6400". They would play games for hours on end and sometimes, they would let me try.

Luke was also in the Boy Scouts. While Andrew was into girls, he would ask me questions about them, and I told him that I was not the one to help him out in that category. I did, however, help Chuck and Luke out on a weekend camping trip with the Boy Scouts.

Then there was Hope, the youngest at eleven and the only girl. She looked just like her Mama. She would teach me how to do crafts and paint as best as I could with my bum hand. She would say, "You can do it, Bobby Ray. Just concentrate and let your head talk to your hand." She would even pitch in on fixing things around the house. She loved softball and we would go out and play pitch and practice hitting.

While I was there, we even went with Marie to watch the dirt races. All these things helped me tremendously and reminded me of the joys of life. It helped me remember my forgotten days as a child growing up on the ranch, before my search for the end of the long white line began.

As my time on the farm was nearing an end, I was gearing up for my release back into the real world. I was finally able to call home again to let them know that I was coming home, and my time was almost up at the farm.

After a few more days, the time for me to leave had come. We stood there with tears in our eyes because the strangers now had become family. We said our goodbyes and I climbed into the taxi that would take me to the bus station, which would take me on my long ride back to the ranch.

Along the way we would stop for breaks, and as we got closer to the ranch, my nerves were racing. I needed something to calm them down. It had been months since I had had a cigarette and on our last stop, I bought a pack and a lighter. My first one was terrible as it was in my younger years. I had prayed many times that God would take the craving away and I thought it was gone, but the vise they had on me was just too strong. I had a couple more while we were stopped, and it seemed to do the trick, even though I knew it was all in my head.

In September of '79, after almost a year of me being gone, I was finally home. It took a little time to get my mind straight by working the ranch for a while with the hands. This helped me clear my head as we would herd the cows and mend the fences. Outside work, we would hone our shooting skills, talk about women (when they weren't around), trucks, and guns. We had a good camaraderie between us.

After a while though, I grew restless and needing something more. With my addiction behind me and a clear head, the bills were starting to pile up. I talked it over with Slim and asked if he thought any of the guys would like to make extra money by running the usual hauls. After talking with them, he said RJ was the only one who was interested in taking on the task. With him doing so, I decided to finance a truck for him and one for myself and hit the road once again. After some deliberation, I settled on a used Freightliner. It was a black 1972 cabover. It had some slight issues, but it was cheap enough that I could afford it. After getting it serviced and set up for travel, I once again was ready to hit the road in search of new beginnings.

I was so far in my past that I had forgotten to stop and get fuel, but when my fuel buzzer went off, it brought me out of my thoughts. I had just crossed the Florida line. I stopped and got my fuel and a snack for Cash and myself.

I continued my journey until I reached a truck stop outside of Tallahassee, and since I was a day early, I decided to park for the night. After a quick check on old Reba and a bathroom break for Cash and myself, I fed him his usual two cans of Alpo. Even though I knew he wanted something more from the restaurant, I told him he would have to wait until I went in and had my dinner.

I leaned back in the seat and lit a cigarette and decided I would call Jalynn. It rang a few times and then it was answered. The voice on the other end sent chills through my heart as I heard Jalynn finally say hello.

I said, "Hey, beautiful, it's me." She hung up. I tried to call her back, but there was no answer.

I went in and ate supper and got Cash a snack as promised. We had settled down to sleep when my mind started running wild. I had to try again. I said to myself, *I ain't giving up on her. She is the best thang that has ever happened to me.*

I called her again and when she answered, I heard breathing on the other end with a crying sniffle. I knew it was her. I heard only silence, then she hung up. I tried again, but I kept getting a busy signal. I guess she took the phone off the hook to keep me from calling. I went back to thinking about her. I cried a little and then went to sleep with Jalynn on my mind, thinking how I missed her so much with me being out here chasing this white line.

10
New Beginnings

Tallahassee, FL – Maimi, FL

THE NEXT DAY CAME QUICKLY. IT WAS 3AM AND ONE HOUR before delivery. I managed to get myself together in time to get fuel, have a cup of coffee, fill my thermos, and grab some snacks before heading over to the sale barn, where I would spend most of the day.

I reached the sale barn just as the sun was coming up. There were so many trucks that I had to park way in the back and wait until they needed me to unload. I noticed a group of people standing around in a circle, screaming and yelling. I knew immediately that there was a bare-knuckle match going on where folks would bet on the match in hopes of winning. The winner would get his cut of it and go on about his business with bragging rights. We used to have them all the time while we waited. I admit, I have been in my fair share of them, and won and lost some. I remembered Daddy would always say, *"No matter how big and bad ya thank ya are, there is always someone else bigger and better than ya."*

I figured I would wait in my truck for my turn to unload. It was soon my time, and I unloaded and thought if I stayed around, I would get a reload from someone who purchased some of the livestock.

At this particular livestock sale there was a rodeo expedition to follow, showcasing a few of the sport's greatest champions. There were bull riders such as Lane Frost, Tuff Hedeman, Big Nuke. He was a fine and talented upcoming Champion Bulldogger, as well as a talented singer, and was to perform a few songs after the show. There was also a young man named Ryder (Sticky) who was only fifteen and the son of the rodeo and stockyard owner. He was quickly making a name for himself in bull riding. He was last year's junior champion and was also showing his skills in saddle bronc riding and tie down calf roping.

I waited to see if I would get a reload and to catch the show afterwards. While I was waiting, there was a rancher who had a long horse trailer. He must have left his trailer gate unlocked, and with no sign of him, the horses decided to make a run for it. Within seconds, twelve horses were loose and running wild through the stockyard. I thought to myself, *this is going to be bad*, but without hesitation, the cowboys jumped into action and did what they did best, and quickly avoided a stampede. Everyone pitched in to help, because that is what us country folks are raised to do. I remember this young teenage girl that came out of nowhere and started rounding up with the fellers. Man, she could ride like a pro. She handled that horse and rope like some of the best men I know.

After about fifteen minutes, they were rounded up and in a corral. I had gone over to see if I could lend a hand and met a young lady about fourteen years old. I asked her name, and she said Rhiannon Savage. I told her she was a great rider, and she said her daddy, Clayton, taught her how to ride, and trained her to be a barrel racer. She told me that he was a bronc buster and bull rider, and that they were both rodeo champions. She said they were going to have a show later in the day so I hung around to see the show, although I knew it would bring back memories of Daddy.

Finally, it was time for the show. Her daddy was as good of a bronc buster that I had ever seen. And when it came time to do her performance, she was great. It made me think of my own girls and how they used to love to ride.

The show lasted for about an hour and afterward, she caught me and introduced her daddy. While we were talking, Big Nuke walked up along with Ryder, and we all got to talking. I commended them on their performances. Ryder said he was planning on going pro when he got old enough and wanted to be just like Chris LeDoux and Casey Tibbs. Big Nuke said he wanted to be like his hero Bill Pickett, who introduced bulldogging to the rodeo. I told them that I enjoyed the show and the music and that I hoped to see them again sometime soon. I started making my way back to the truck lot, in hopes that I would get a load out of there petty quickly.

I waited outside of my truck, smoking and having myself a bottle of ice cold of Coca-Cola, watching Cash run around and play. The rancher that we helped earlier that day came up and said his latch was broken and asked if I would haul what he buys to Miami. Said he would pay cash. Needing the money, I agreed.

After the sale, we loaded up a couple of bulls and ten cows, and I was on my way. As I hit the interstate, the sun was setting, and traffic was building. I decided to stop at the Loves and get some rest, let the vacationers settle down before continuing. I figured a few hours in the sleeper would do it and I would be on my way. However, I lay there thinking about my life, tossing and turning the whole time. When I couldn't take the restlessness anymore, I went in and got my daddy's thermos filled with coffee and a cup to go. I also got a carton of cigarettes and Cash a bag of beef jerky for not getting into any trouble at the stock sale. Then I was ready to roll once again. I was tired but there was no use in laying around if I couldn't sleep. After all, I was just going to Miami. As I went down the highway with the sun setting beyond the horizon, I started thinking once again about Jalynn and how we met.

It was January 1980, when I left the ranch with a purpose; my outlook on life had changed. I was running mainly the mid-west so I could be close to the ranch if I was needed. One day during July, something inside me told me I needed to head East. I found me a load and eventually, I made my way over to the east side of the country and found myself rolling down the Eastern Seaboard in search of the unknown.

I was coming out of Maryland when I decided to take I-68, a new interstate that was supposed to be a short cut to West Virginia. It wasn't too bad, and I was making good time. There were huge hills up and

147

down, but I was cruising right along. That was until I was crossed into West Virginia and passed a place just before Morgantown, West Virgina, known as Coopers Rock. I started down and I guess I had a momentary flashback of the Grapevine Hill accident. I was a bit scared and hesitant to say the least. Although it was not as steep, I kept my foot on the brakes, which I knew better. When I saw the smoke begin to roll out from my tires, I knew that I was in danger of catching fire. I needed to let off the brakes, if I had any left, and try to cool them down. Instinctively, I put on my flashers and put the hammer down to cool my brakes. I started yanking on my air horns to warn others of my intent so they would know to get out of the way. I was going so fast that my whole truck was shaking.

This continued until I reached the bottom of the grade and there was a sign warning of a big curve. I figured I would probably roll it over as I came into it and that would be the end of me for sure. Luckily, as I approached, there were no cars around and I moved over to the left hammer lane in an attempt to make it as straight as possible. Sure enough, as I held on tight to the steering wheel and hoped for the best, I hugged the inside as much as I could. As I came out of the curve, I traveled back into the right lane, and with my speed, I ended up moving on over to the shoulder and rode it out until my rig started slowing down on its own. I downshifted to help her out and when I came to a stop, I set my brakes to keep it from rolling, instead of just putting it in gear and shutting it down, which I knew was a mistake. My brakes could seize and probably catch on fire from the heat. With a racing heart and emptiness in my stomach, I jumped out, grateful to have escaped death once more. All I could think about was my life and all my mistakes throughout the years. It is true what they say about life flashing before your eyes.

I inspected my truck and trailer. Just as I suspected, they were seized up and still smoking; I knew I wasn't going anywhere without a tow truck. I kept my fire extinguisher handy in case a fire broke out and climbed into the truck. I sat there reflecting for about an hour or so, and a gentleman stopped to see if I needed help. I told him I could use some and he said he could take me to a repair shop to see if they could help. As we walked back to his van, he said his name was Ralphie. He introduced me to his friends, Kochie, Smitty, and Rudy. He said they were with the local Army Reserve unit and were heading for their weekend duty. They took me to the nearest truck repair shop to see about getting towed and repaired.

When the tow truck returned with my rig, they informed me of the damage and said it would take at least a week for repairs. They suggested a little hotel there in Morgantown, West Virginia. I grabbed a taxi and made my way over and got me a room for the week.

I settled into my room, and I took a shower before lying down for some TV. There was a trucking marathon showing *Breaker-Breaker*, starring Chuck Norris, *Black Dog*, starring Patrick Swayze, and *Over the Top,* starring Sylvester Stallone. From time to time, I was in and out of sleep, and after a while, I gave in and went to sleep. When I woke up, it was suppertime, so I decided to go find me something to eat. I stopped by the front desk to ask for recommendations.

That's when I saw her behind the counter.

A beautiful woman, short in stature, with long, wavy strawberry blonde hair, the bluest of eyes, and a radiant smile. She asked if there was something that she could do for me. I do not believe I had been so nervous in my entire life. I could feel my face begin to flush and my stomach was doing flips. I opened my mouth, but all I could do was stutter gibberish. Finally, I said, "My name is Bobby Ray, from room 300." Then I blurted out that I she was the most beautiful woman my eyes had ever seen.

"Thank ya," she said. "My name is Jalynn, from the front desk." Giggling with an obviously witty sense of humor, she asked, "How can I help ya today, Bobby Ray?"

I told her that I was looking for a good place to eat close by, if she could recommend one. She gave me a list of restaurants and then circled her favorites. I chose the closest of her picks so I could walk to it. I said only "thank ya, darlin," so to not embarrass myself more, and I walked out to begin my walk to the restaurant.

On the way, I thought to myself how beautiful she was and how I wish I would one day end up with a woman like that. But I knew deep down that a woman like her would never fall in love with a man like me. I was just a poor ole truck driver and not very handsome at all.

Thinking to myself, *I'm too rugged, I have these scars on my face, and I have this limp from my stupid mistakes.*

149

At the diner, I sat in the very rear of the place, facing the door. A waitress took my order and before she could return with it, a fella with a somewhat a familiar face came over and asked, "Aren't you Sergeant James.?"

"Yes," I said, "but that was a long time ago. I'm a civilian now."

He said, "It's me, Private Joe Cook. Do you remember me? You guys called me Cookie."

I told him I remembered him, and he said he and his wife Julia owned the place. He said the meal was on him, as my friend. I thanked him and he asked what I was doing in this part of the country. I told him I was still a truck driver and told him what had happened earlier. He said only, "Yep, happens all the time."

We talked briefly about our Army days before his wife Julia brought my food out. She pulled him away to let me eat. I will have to say, it was pretty good food.

After I ate, I said goodbye and told them I would be back since it was close to the hotel. On my walk back to the hotel, I smoked a couple of cigarettes to satisfy me after my supper and to calm me for my next encounter with Jalynn.

When I went to the desk, she was gone, so I went up to watch TV. It was Friday night so I figured I would catch my favorite shows, *BJ and the Bear, The Fall Guy* and of course *The Dukes of Hazzard*. As I sat there watching the shows and having a few beers, I still couldn't get her out of my mind. Her hair, her smile, her sweet voice… I could imagine her in my life, and what a good life it would be back on the ranch. She would love it. We would get married and have kids and be a happy family.

I must have fallen asleep thinking about her because the static from the station signing off woke me and I still had her in my thoughts. I tried to go back to sleep but was unsuccessful. I got dressed and went for a walk, figuring it would help clear my head so I could sleep. I smoked a few cigarettes and continued thinking about her. I stopped by the front desk to inquire about her and Clementine, the girl at the front desk, said that she was her friend, and that she had mentioned me to her and thought that I was a real nice guy. She was hesitant to give me any details, but seeing I wasn't leaving without knowing something about her, she gave me a few insights into her likes and dislikes. She also mentioned that she was into collecting angels. I thought to myself, "*My angel like angels huh how funny is that.*"

My chat with Clementine gave me hope of a chance to get to know her better. I went to my room on a new mission to get to know Jalynn. Before I fell asleep, I prayed to God that he would bless me with this beautiful angel, and if it was meant to be, that she would accept my offer of going out with me.

The next morning, I went out for breakfast and there she was. I stopped for a little small talk to get a feeling of how she reacted since I knew Clementine would have told her about our conversation. Then I went out and found the Waffle House, that was a little further than Cookie's Diner. As I was eating, I figured I would ask her out on a date.

While walking back, I wracked my brain on what I would say to her. As I returned, I gathered my courage and prepared myself for the rejection, because even though she was on my mind, she was out of my league.

Upon reaching the counter and seeing her standing there smiling at me, I felt a lump in my throat. I took a deep breath and swallowed hard. I said, "Hey, Jalynn. I was wonder'n if ya might like to join me for supper tonight. It would give me someone to talk to other than the waitresses." To my surprise she said yes, but we would have to go to her house first. I agreed and she said she got off at 5 p.m. With excitement I went to my room and nervously awaited that time. It seemed like the longest six hours in history. I took a shower and put on my cologne, and then sprayed it around the room to disguise my smoking habit. Afterwards, I sat on the bed watching TV. As time was nearing and as a sign of faith, I got down on my knees and prayed, thanking God for answering my prayers.

When the time arrived, I made my way down to the entrance where we met up and she let me know she lived forty-five minutes away, across the Pennsylvania state line, in a small town called Holbrook. She mentioned that there wasn't much there but a country store, a school, a church, and bus shop. I said that it was okay because I was so used to traveling long distances. The time passed by quickly as we chatted about different things. Talking with her was easy and comfortable and I wasn't as nervous as before. We laughed, we sang along to songs on the radio, and I had this feeling come over me where I just knew we were soulmates. I wanted to kiss her so bad that I imagined how it would be to feel her lips on mine.

We finally arrived at her house and went inside. She introduced me to her parents. Her mama, Mrs. Holbrook, was in the kitchen cooking dinner. The aroma of chicken and homemade biscuits reminded me of my mama. Her daddy, Mr. Holbrook, was sitting in the living room watching the Pittsburgh Steelers play on TV.

We made small talk as I waited for Jalynn to freshen up. He told me the history of the little town and how it was named after his ancestors, who had settled there over a hundred years ago.

Her parents asked if we could stay for dinner and Jalynn showed up and said, "Sorry, Mom and Pop, we already have plans."

Seeing her out of her uniform and all dressed up, I was at a loss for words. How was it possible for her to look more beautiful than I already thought she was? I will never forget what she was wearing, a floral burgundy and pink top, white corduroy pants, and pink and tan cowgirl boots. I thought to myself, *be still my beating heart!*

Her friends Lindsay, Jo, and Lee arrived at the house with a quick introduction. We jumped into Lindsay's car and headed back towards Morgantown. Along the way, she pointed out the village of Rogersville. It was a small community of homes with two churches, a funeral home, and a convenient store. Then we passed by a rough-around-the-edges village by the name of Bucktown. It consisted of a coal mine, a junk yard, and what she referred to as a bad news bar, which included a little restaurant and a no-tell motel.

We then entered the city of Waynesburg. She and her friends said that it was the closest city and was where they would travel for groceries and gas. It had to be one of the smallest cities on the map, they said. She talked about this area and growing up appreciating it, the only downfall being having to travel so far to a decent place to work.

We then hit the interstate headed southbound, back towards Morgantown. That is when her friends began interrogating me. Let me just say, they held nothing back. I admit I was a little intimidated, but I did not mind answering their questions. I had to respect that they were looking out for their best friend. I seemed to have passed their test.

We finally arrived at the nightlife establishment. We ordered some appetizers and some drinks, making small talk as we ate, then headed to the dance floor. The next song that played was one I had never heard by Willie Nelson but had heard by the Everly Brothers. It was called "Let it be Me." I fell in love with this version, as if it was done just for Jalynn and me. I took Jalynn by the hand, and I put the other on her lower back. I held her tight, and I never wanted to let her go. With our fingers touching, I could feel our hearts beating simultaneously, as if it was one strong heartbeat. I leaned in and thanked her for accepting my invitation, and that I prayed that God seen fit for us to be together.

I gave her a long, gentle kiss as we danced. The softness of her lips touched mine and I felt a pleasant jolt rivet throughout my body. It was as if she had sent a warmth to the coldest parts of my heart, a feeling I had never felt with any other girl before. I knew then that this girl was the one.

We danced the night away as if we were the only two in that bar. The night came to an end way to soon, and her friends drove us back to the hotel, where I was to get out so they could head back to their little town. I had feelings for Jalynn and my heart was overloaded with her presence. I didn't want the night to end. I found it hard to say goodnight, I could not let go of her hand.

She exited the car with me to say goodbye. She told me that she enjoyed the date and mentioned that if I was still there the following weekend, that we could do it again. We embraced in a romantic hug; she had her arms around my neck, and without thinking, I slipped my hands in her back pockets, holding her butt while pulling her body into mine.

After a few more of those gentle kisses, she said stuttering, "I, I, I… gotta go."

I knew by her voice that it was her passion and quest for love that was on the rise.

She said, "I have tomorrow and the next day off, but I am busy tomorrow. I will try to come see ya the next day and we can sit in the lobby and talk."

The rest of the night, all I could think about was her touch and the passionate kisses we shared. Her voice was so soft and tender, I wanted to know more, I wanted to know everything about her. Most of all, I wanted to make her my wife and spend the rest of my life making her as happy as she had already made me.

The next day, I awoke with Jalynn still on my mind. It was nearly killing me knowing it was her day off and I would not get to see or talk to her all day. I spent most of the day in my room. I did manage to take a walk down by the Monongahela River, still very deep in thought about Jalynn and the great night out that we had the evening before.

I headed back to my room as I was getting ready for my favorite shows to come on. I decided to order some pizza. It soon arrived and as I was eating, *BJ and the Bear* was coming on. As it was about to end, I heard a knock at the door. I answered and there stood Jalynn with a bottle of wine in her hand. She asked if I would like some company and I responded yes, of course I would like that. We sat down with some wine that we had just poured into the hotel's plastic cups. We were just fixing to get comfortable leaning up against the headboard and I leaned in to steal me a kiss. My intentions were interrupted by *The Dukes of Hazzard* theme song, and she quickly perked up.

"This is my favorite show," she said. "My family and I watch it together as often as we can." I told her it was my favorite, too. We sat there watching and cuddling, with me wanting to kiss her so bad. Then out of nowhere, she said, "I wish that Roscoe would leave them Duke boys alone!" As if it were real life. I found that to be cute.

After the show was over, I turned the television off, and we sat on the bed talking about everything. I started massaging her neck and she said it felt good. I continued to her shoulders, and she asked if I would massage her back. I said yes and she stretched out on the bed. I slid my hands up under her shirt and started from her pants line and made my way up. When I reached her bra, with two fingers I undid it.

She said, "Oh, ya must be experienced."

I said, "No, just a little trick my brother told me about."

She said, "Don't ya be go'n and explore'n other parts."

I told her I would never dream of it, but it was indeed on my mind. She said as I continued that my hands were like magic, and she could get used to this kind of spoiling all the time. While I worked my magic she asked about my family and then she told me about hers. I told her the story of how I came to be a truck driver, I even shared some about my Vietnam days. She told me about how she had always dreamed of traveling and getting to see different parts of the country.

She had been there for a couple of hours and had not offered up one kiss, so I took the matter into my own hands. I blurted out, "Jalynn, I really need to kiss yer beautiful lips again. I can't wait much longer."

She said, "Well, cowboy, if ya want it, ya will have to come and get it."

That was my cue. I leaned in and wrapped my arms around her and held her tight as we kissed. This time it was with more passion than she had given the night before. She let her tongue gently part my lips and it started dancing with mine as they explored every inch of our mouths. This lasted for some time until our jaws needed a break.

When we broke our embrace, I said, "Wow, Jalynn, ya are a wonderful kisser."

She said, "Mister, ya ain't bad yerself, but that is all ya get for now. I am a proper gal, and I feel if we keep on, thangs will get too intense for us to stop before we go too fer."

I said, "My mama and daddy raised me to respect women. I understand completely." And we just cuddled on the bed. We talked for the better part of the night and eventually fell asleep in each other's arms. I had set an alarm for her as she had to go to work downstairs in the early morning.

The next day, I spent a lot of my time in the lobby so I could see her, and we could talk, which for the next few days seemed to be a normal routine for me. We came to know a lot about each other.

One day she was busy, but she was able to pass by on her way to take some towels to a customer. As she passed where I was sitting, she slipped me a note asking if I wanted to go to one of her favorite places with her after work. I gave her a wink.

Just before her shift ended, I was outside pacing back and forth in the parking lot, anxiously smoking one cigarette after another. She came out, sneaked up behind me and caught me.

"I was wonder'n if ya had an unpleasant habit," she said giggling.

We made our way to her car, and I asked about this favorite place she was taking me to. It just so happened to be the same place, Coopers Rock, close by where my truck had broken down. She said it was her favorite place because it was so peaceful, not to mention beautiful. She talked about the incredible sunsets that overlooked the mountains and river. I could not wait to see it with her.

She also said she would go there often to pray and feel close to God.

She said that she had gone there before our date and asked God for someone that would love her and treat her the way a woman is supposed to be treated. I then thought to myself how my mama would just love this girl.

We drove up the steep hill on the interstate to the exit at the top and drove back through the woods and there we parked. We then hiked to her favorite spot and spread out a blanket to prepare for the sunset. She was certainly right; the view was incredible, it quickly became my favorite place, too.

I held her in my arms as she sat in between my legs. I told her I had wished that our time together did not have to ever come to an end, that being with her was so nice and that it felt so right. I was over the moon excited to hear her say that she felt the same way. As the sun began to set, she turned to look up at me and we shared yet another kiss, this time being the longest and most passionate one of all so far.

She then abruptly pulled from my arms mumbling the words again that I will never forget. "I, I, I... gotta go!"

I knew exactly what was going on and being a gentleman about it, we quickly packed up and headed to the car. We drove back and she dropped me off at the hotel. We said our goodbyes and she said she would see me tomorrow. Jalynn drove away, leaving me a little confused, wondering if I did or said something wrong.

The next day, I got a call from Kochie saying that my truck was repaired and could pick it up anytime. I asked if there was any way they could run it up to me. He said sure that the garage owner was a good friend of his and he would make him since I didn't have a way to get down to it. I told him he could find the payment for the bill in my fuel tank, and I would see him in a bit. I gathered my belongings and made my way down to the front desk to check out. Jalynn was standing there in front of the elevator. It was her day off and I was expecting her to stop by, thinking we could spend the day together, and I told her my truck was repaired. I did not want to leave without saying goodbye.

She caught me off guard as I immediately noticed she had cut her long, wavy, strawberry blonde hair, one of the things I loved about her most before getting to know her.

She said, "I am glad I caught ya, we need to talk." She then said to me, "Bobby Ray, I have been do'n some think'n and pray'n. In this short time that we have spent together, I cannot seem to thank of anythang else besides us, and the time we have spent together this week. I do not want to say goodbye to ya. I want ya to stay."

I told her I would love to stay but that I needed to get back on the road, that I had the ranch to take care of. She started to cry, and I put my arms around her. I then asked, "Would ya consider come'n over the road with me?"

She responded by saying, "I have prayed fer the Lord to show me the way and all signs point to ya. So, it is certain that I will follow ya anywhere if that is what ya would want."

I was jumping for joy inside. I lifted her feet off the ground, kissing her as I spun her around and around. The small crowd in the lobby went from staring to clapping. It was just like a happy ending in the movies. As I lowered her back onto her feet, she told me she had prepared for this being a possibility and had packed a few bags. She was all smiles as she turned to Clementine and said, "Tell Mr. Bill, I quit."

She told her that she would send her mom and dad after her car. We went out to retrieve her bags from the trunk of her car and by then, they were pulling my truck and trailer into the parking lot.

She said, "Is that yours? It is so sexy!"

I said, "Not as sexy as you are."

When the fella pulled the air brakes and got out, I thanked him, and they left. I got Jalynn's bags and tossed them into the truck. I gave her a boost into the passenger seat, and as she settled into her new spot, and I climbed into the driver's seat I told her it was a new beginning for both of us. She leaned over and kissed me and then she said what I had been waiting for all this time.

She said, "I love ya, Bobby Ray."

I told her I loved her too and we hit the road and headed south. We stopped by the nearest truck stop to get fuel, coffee, and her some snacks, and anything else she might need, and we pulled back on the big road. We put the wind to the rear and began our journey.

I was used to running alone and using whatever I had with a lid to use the bathroom or getting out to squirt the dirt or check my tire water as we say. I didn't expect she would have to go every hour. I told her she was going to have to get bucket broke, and she asked me what that meant. I told her she had to potty in a bucket, and she disagreed with a

157

disgusted look on her face. I said if I am going to make time and money, we can't stop every hour. She informed me that she would not be peeing in a bucket. I told her how long we had to go before we were to stop. So, after a while of not stopping, she reluctantly gave in and decided she had better do something. So, to the sleeper she went with a lot of complaints about how gross it was and that I should stop. The more she complained, the more I swerved my rig between the lines and laughed. But within a few minutes, she was bucket broke.

Later that night after we had eaten dinner and returned to the truck to get some sleep, I apologized for making her use the bucket. I told her that my actions were mean, and I would try to stop when I could from now on. She hugged me and said she loved me and knew I was doing it on purpose. Then she climbed into the bunk, and I slid in next to her and we snuggled up.

She whispered, "Bobby Ray, will ya love me forever."

I said, "Yes, my love, I will."

Then we finally got to know each other. What a wonderful feeling to know that she was mine forever.

The next morning, we awoke and grabbed a bite of breakfast and coffee and were on our way once again. We went on for a couple of days, stopping only when we had to. Jalynn said she couldn't take it anymore and asked if we could get a hotel. I said we had some time to spare, and we could take a weekend off.

We found a little motel and she was so happy to finally have a nice hot shower. When she was finished, she came out in a long white nightgown. I told her she looked like an angel, and I was glad she was my angel.

We spent the weekend snuggling, talking, and loving each other. Monday, we headed out, bright and early, to get our next load and to see the country. We enjoyed each other's company. It felt good to finally know that I had found my true love, and I thanked God for sending her to me.

Afterwards, I took her home to the ranch to meet everybody. I remember her face as we drove up the long driveway towards the house. She said, "Oh, honey, this is so beautiful."

Once we were parked at the barn and everyone was around as usual to greet me, they were taken aback to see I had brought yet another woman home since the last one didn't pan out so well. After everyone had met her, some of them knew right away that we were really in love and gave me their approval. We went to the house and rested for a while, and after dinner, I took her for a horseback ride to the cemetery and showed her the rest of the ranch. We came to the best view of the ranch next to the cemetery and we put down a blanket under the biggest oak tree on the land. After a bit I took out my pocketknife and carved our initials in the oak tree under my grandparents and my parents. I cut a rose from the rose bush and gave it to her, and I kissed her and told her I loved her. We lay there for a while so she could see the sun set over the mountains. A song came over the radio then, it was, "I Need More of You," by the Bellamy Brothers. I told her that this was how I felt about her. We had a long, romantic kiss and we lay back to watch the sun set, wrapped in each other's arms.

We stayed for a few days and then we were off again for another trip. We were as happy as could be running the white line together.

As usual on my memory journey, I lost all track of time and soon I found myself in southern Florida. I rolled into Miami and made my way to the address I was given. There was the biggest farmhouse I had ever seen. It didn't even look like a farm with the greenest grass cut perfectly. The fences were even and in a straight line.

I met the rancher by the barn, and we unloaded. He gave me the payment he promised, and I made my way to the nearest truck stop. I figured Cash and I needed a break for a couple of days. We ate good and I talked to him about my plans to take him to the beach for some much-needed fresh air. He got excited as if he knew exactly what I was talking about.

As we were about to climb into the truck, he started howling and grabbed me by the pants leg and pulled me back.

I said, "Boy, what is wrong with ya?"

He jumped up into the truck and grabbed Jalynn's scarf that hung from my visor. He brought it to me and was acting crazy.

I said, "Do ya want me to call yer mama?" Cash jumped down and headed to the phone booth and waited for me. I said, "Come on, boy, we don't need to go to the phone booth anymore. I have a phone right here."

I pulled it out of my pocket and called Jalynn to see if she would talk to him. She answered and I said very quickly before she could hang up, "Cash wants to talk to ya."

She agreed so I held the receiver over his ear as he was standing with his front paws on the steps. He listened close and was moaning to her every word as if he understood and made a barking, whining sound as if to say, "I love you." Then he was done. I took the phone and said, "I love ya, too," but she hung up.

Cash and I climbed back into the truck. We snuggled up to each other and were off to sleep, to rest up for our next adventure running this long white line.

Ryder Carothers at 8 yrs. old. A little cowboy daydreaming about his future. Ryder has since grown into a fine young man. He has lived his whole life as a cowboy. The dream of all little boys. He has been tied to cow trucking his whole life. He is co-owner with his dad teaching him the ropes as the owner of Carothers Rodeo Company based in Howe Valley KY. Now at the age of 14 he has been riding bulls now for over 2 yrs. He has proved himself and won the title of Kentucky's 2023 Reserve Champion Jr. Bull Rider. He was able to do this despite the fact that he had to sit out half of the season because of a broken femur. Ryder has recently added Saddle Bronc and Tie Down Calf Roping to his career. He intends on going Pro when he turns 18 yrs. old. He also intends on following in his dad's footsteps and climb up in a big rig to do himself some stock hauling as soon as he is able.

11
FAMILY LIFE

Miami, FL- Daytona Beach, FL

EARLY THE NEXT MORNING, WAY BEFORE DAWN, I WENT to the truck wash and had my truck and trailer cleaned up, inside and out, since the trailer was a mess from my last haul. They quickly had her shining like a new penny. I returned to the truck stop for fuel and a top off my thermos, and I sat there wondering what I should do next.

In the end, I decided we would drive to Daytona Beach to see if we could catch the sunrise and get a little beach time before it got crowded. We left heading north on I-95 and there was no one out at that time of morning. The four-hour trip went by very quickly as I thought more about how to fix what I had broken. I did a lot of praying, although it felt as if my prayers were not being heard.

Once we rolled into Daytona, I made my way to the beach to see if there was a place where I could park my rig. After I found a nice spot, Cash and I went out for our morning adventure.

We found a place where we could relax away from the crowd that would soon be filling the beach. I was enjoying my cup of coffee and Cash was running in the sand, chasing seagulls, knowing he couldn't catch them, and swimming out as far as he could before I called him back. As I watched the sun start to break the water, and the ripple of waves crashed on the shore, I felt this calm over me. I remembered how

161

Jalynn and I would sit on the back porch with our coffee every morning I was home and watch the sunrise. Jalynn would say, "I love this time of the day with ya. It lets me know that God is still watching over us, and he has given us a chance to be better than we were yesterday."

My memories revved up again, this time about how our little family got started.

It was July1980, and after we had been on the road for almost six months and had only been home a couple of times, Jalynn said to me one morning, "Honey, I have to tell ya some'n."

I said okay, figuring she had to go to the bathroom and knew I hated to stop. It was probably something she just couldn't do in a bucket, or it was time for her monthly woman issue. She told me that she needed to get off the road for a while.

I said, "Okay, darlin, we can take a couple of days off next week."

She said, "No, ya are not hear'n me. I need to get off the road fer, oh, let's say about seven months. I'm pregnant."

I said, "What? How? When? Are ya kidding me?" I was so surprised. I said, "Are ya sure?"

She said yes, she was over a month late.

I said, "Ya mean I'm go'n to be a daddy?"

"Are ya mad?" she asked.

I told her, "Hell, no! I'm excited! This is great news!" I pulled over on the side of the road and I took her in my arms. I hugged her tight and said, "I love ya, Jalynn. Ya have made me the happiest man once again."

She pulled back slightly and said, "I have been afraid of how ya would react because ya love truck'n and ya said that ya never wanted to stop."

I told her that I was very happy, and that she could always talk to me about anything. Just because I loved trucking, we were in this thing together, and that we would get through it just fine.

I pulled back on the road, and since I was hauling a load that didn't really have to be in no hurry, we decided to take a break and celebrate the news. We found this little truck stop with a bed and breakfast next to it and got us a room so she could relax. I called my sister and informed her of the news. She was just as excited as we were and said that she would go up to the cemetery and tell Mama and Daddy. I told her of our plans to return to the ranch and that I would take a local driving gig. So, with some good planning and without hesitation, we headed home. We stopped every night to stay in a motel for Jalynn to rest which meant it took us about a week and a half to make it home.

We returned to the ranch where we made immediate plans to get married at our family church. Jalynn's family and her friends were able to come out to join us for the celebration, which tickled her to death. When I picked up her parents from the airport and we headed back, I could tell that they were disappointed in the whole matter. I could feel them staring me down from the back seat. They didn't say too much. They just kept asking how much further until we reached this so-called ranch. I said it was not much longer and when we got there, they could rest up. Goat had ridden with me to keep me company and to run interference if needed. He did his job to set them straight on my so-called ranch, guessing they thought it was just a small house on a couple of acres.

When we were crossing the old iron bridge that was the divider between The Blake's Ranch and ours, he pointed out that the property line followed the creek for about three miles and was just over that same distance the other way.

He said, "On these 3000 acres, we have two ponds, or lakes, four barns, a couple-acre garden and several acres of hay fields. Keep in mind we have one thousand head of cattle and twenty-five horses."

We turned down the driveway and drove the mile back to the house.

Mrs. Holbrook suddenly changed her tune about the ranch and said, "Wow, Bobby Ray, that is a beautiful house!

I agreed and said it did need some work, but it was over one hundred years old, and that that my pawpaw had built it when he married my granny. Mr. Holbrook was in agreement with his wife and accepting of my spread of land and everything we had there.

We made it to the house and my wife came out to meet them and to show them around, which I was glad about because I desperately needed a cigarette and a few swigs of 'shine to ease my mind. I made up an excuse that Goat and I needed to take care of something, and we both ran off to the barn to satisfy our thirst.

After everyone had settled in, the ladies fixed supper. After we ate and the ladies had gone into the den to immediately get started on the rushed wedding plans, I asked Mr. Holbrook if he wanted to go out and relax with the rest of us. He agreed and as we sat there, we talked about Jalynn's future with me and trucking. He said that he wanted his daughter taken care of and that she didn't need somebody that was going to be gone all the time. I promised to take good care of his daughter and never hurt her or leave her because I loved her probably just as much as he did. We sat there and talked with the rest of her friend's husbands and the ranch hands while we enjoyed some 'shine, warming by the bonfire.

The rest of the week went by quickly, and then the wedding day came. I remember it like it was yesterday. With all our family and friends there I was nervous but doing okay. That was until I saw Jalynn in her beautiful white wedding gown that Mrs. Holbrook had made for her, and her hair was flowing with long strawberry-blond curls again. She had the most amazing glow about her, like an angel.

After the wedding was over, we went on our honeymoon to Clearwater, Florida. I had taken her there once during our time on the road. It had been the first time she had ever seen the Gulf Coast. Clearwater instantly became her new favorite place. We stayed there for a week and then returned to the ranch.

We were doing fine. I was able to take out a VA loan from the bank to buy my sister's part of the ranch, as well as make necessary repairs and cosmetic updates. As Slim and my sister were preparing to move, it was time for me to get to work. I worked long hard days on the ranch and worked in the house at night, getting it where it needed to be. I wanted to make our ranch look and run more efficiently. We had enough funds left after we took care of everything that we were able to prepare a nursery for our little one on the way. Everything was complete and working as it should for Goat, RJ, Tiny, and the rest of the crew. I figured that it was safe to get back in a truck and bring in more money.

I got the local gig hauling hot rock (asphalt), dirt, and gravel for some extra money to build revenue for the winter. I was home with Jalynn every night, and we were getting anxious awaiting the birth of our first born. Well, I was, anyway. Jalynn was miserable. She had morning sickness all the time, more than usual, as I was told. She was gaining the expected weight, and her feet were swollen all the time. Her friends would pitch in and fix the meals and clean the house when she was unable to get out of bed. I felt sorry for my angel because she was going through so many changes. She said one day that she was ugly and unattractive, that I would leave her for another woman.

I stopped her in her tracks, and I said, "Baby, I know yer hormones are out of whack and ya just feel awful, but ya are my wife and my angel that God seen fit fer me to have, and ya are still beautiful." I promised her that there would never be a woman that could ever take her place. I hugged her tightly and said, "I love ya more than my life itself."

In mid-November of that year, and as the time approached for our baby to arrive, our emotions were running wild and we started arguing. As things were getting tight with money for bills and for the money to pay the ranch hands, some of them quit. As new to-be parents, we didn't know what we were going to do. We had begun to have these little arguments, and instead of facing the facts, I would go off to the barn and take a few sips from my jug.

One day things got out of hand when we got a letter from the bank letting us know that we were two months behind on the mortgage, and it was the final notice before they would foreclose on us. To my surprise, Jalynn said she thought it best I go back over the road. She said with the help of the hands that were left, she thought she could manage the bookkeeping while they took care of the ranch, and RJ could run the local hauls. With it being decided, I gave my two weeks' notice at work and prepared my truck for the trip.

After I got it serviced and loaded, I was ready for the long haul. I called Mr. Blake to see if he had any livestock to haul. He said he did, and I told him I would be there the next morning. I kissed Jalynn goodbye and climbed into the cab. I reassured her I would be back in two weeks. She reconfirmed that she would be okay. RJ and Goat would be around if she needed them. I told the men to take care of her while I was gone and as we shook hands, they happily agreed to the task, knowing I was going out to earn their paychecks.

I climbed into the seat of my truck and before shutting the door, Jalynn climbed up on the sidestep for one last hug. She said, "I love ya, Bobby Ray. Please be careful." And then she gave me a real long goodbye kiss, and everyone was hoop'n and holler'n as she stepped back down. I shut the door and told them to stop it with a smile on my face. Laughing, I fired the old truck up and headed towards the highway.

The first thirty minutes or so, I was doing fine. However, as I pulled my rig up onto the highway, out of nowhere, a 4-wheeler car came across the lane and nearly ran me in the ditch. It was so quick that I didn't have a chance to downshift. I stalled out right there in the middle of the roadway. With my nerves in a rage, I started it back up and pulled it to the shoulder.

After a few moments, I regained my composure and put it back in gear to continue to The Blake's Ranch. I hadn't been to the ranch in a couple of years and when I pulled onto the road and headed towards the barn, I noticed some changes. There was what seemed to be a dirt trail around the pastures, as if a car had been driving around the edges. Maybe Mr. Blake got his grandkids a go-cart or three-wheeler. As I reached the corral, I seen Mr. Blake sitting on a motorized buggy, not on horseback, or propped upon the fence with a cup of coffee. That is when I noticed something different about him; he only had one leg. Out of curiosity, I asked what happened. He said that he had had a tractor accident, it rolled over and crushed his leg, injuring it so badly that they had to take it off.

"I'm sorry about that," I said.

He jokingly replied, "Don't be. I save money buy'n only one boot."

As I was getting ready to leave, another truck made his way to the corral. As the driver stepped out, I noticed a familiar face. It was my old army buddy Odie. He had gotten him a truck and was hauling cattle. I stayed until he got his trailer loaded, and by that time, Mrs. Blake was ringing my favorite bell. She always had enough food for visitors and never let anyone leave hungry. She insisted on seconds and a to-go plate, with no room for argument.

After supper, Mr. Blake, myself, and Odie went outside for a smoke by the fire pit. Mr. Blake asked if we wanted to stay for the night and head out in the morning. We were stuffed to the gills, so we agreed. With that, he pulled a plug out of the ground, reached in the hole, and pulled out a mason jar.

"Here, fellers, take ya a swig of this," he said. "We learned this trick from a feller down at the golf course. He gave us one of those fancy contraptions to pull the plug of dirt and grass out of the ground. My granddaughter, Missy, made this last week. She took our family recipe and put her own twist on it, and boy, is it smooth going down."

It sure was good and cold from being in the ground and Mr. Blake was right; this 'shine was so smooth going down.

"Around here, they call her Moonshine Missy," Mr. Blake said. "And 'er 'shine is right up there with the very best."

And told us that she was also going to start making whisky. She had different flavors, which appealed to the women. I commented on how good it was and he called her over from her hidden spot in the barn. She was not the young lady I remember from my past visits. She was now a beautiful woman, with long blond hair flowing from underneath her cowboy hat. She wore cowboy boots, cut-off over-all bibs, and a very tight tube top stretched to its limits around what the good Lord blessed her with. I thought my buddy Odie was going to fall out of his chair as she came running at her grandpa's request.

Missy gave Odie and I a big hug and gave me a big kiss. "Hey, Bobby Ray, I sure have missed ya, honey. How have ya been?"

I told her I was fine and gave it no thought, but for Odie was now in love with someone he could never have. She thanked us for the compliment on her 'shine and returned to the barn to watch her still. As she was walking back, she deliberately swayed her hips, which caused her butt cheeks to shake, drawing attention to the fact that her shorts were cut off way too much.

As she was walking, the thought entered my mind of how the good Lord had blessed her in that area as well. If Jalynn knew my thoughts, she would kill me, but I thought to myself, *I may be married but I am still a man.*

Mr. Blake said, "Ya boys mind yer raise'n and keep yer hands to yerselves. Missy is off limits."

We talked for a while about livestock and our military experiences, and of course, about women and trucks. We were sipping from the jar all along and it wasn't long before we felt the effects of Missy's good brew. When we decided to go to the trucks and bed down, Mr. Blake insisted we take a jar with us. We accepted, and again, he reached over and pulled the plugs of grass from the ground to get four more jars. We took our 'shine and said good night, and we both climbed into our trucks before the liquor hit us and we wouldn't be able to walk. I crawled in my bunk and before I knew it, I was out.

The next morning before the rooster could even crow, I woke up to the aroma of fried bacon and sausage and Mrs. Blake's cooking. I climbed in the driver's seat and looked over; Odie was there having a smoke. I told him we were gonna get fat if we stayed around there too long, so knowing she would tan our hides the next time around, we decided to leave before she caught us. We snuck down the gravel road towards the highway, and hit the big road headed east.

The sun was coming up and blinding us with its glow, and we decided to stop and get fuel and take a quick break to give it a chance to get above our visors. We talked about Missy; Odie said she was a cowboy's dream.

"Yeah, I grew up with 'er," I said. "She's kinda wild but is as sweet as a Georgia peach." Then I commented that she had filled out quite nicely.

We had some coffee and a few aspirin to ease the effects of her 'shine and to wake us up. After our break was over, we hit the big road again and hammered down. The sun was up higher in the sky, and it was getting hot outside.

After we had driven an hour or, we talked on the CB to pass the time. Odie hollered at me to check out "this fine seat cover" (a beautiful woman in a car) coming up fast, about to come around us in a T-top Camaro.

He said, "Oh, man, she's built to any man's imagination and only wear'n a bikini top and a skimpy pair of cut-off blue jean shorts."

In an instant, he was honking on the horn to show his approval as she passed. With in a few moments, she was passing me, and I took notice. I waved out my window and honked my train horns in agreement with Odie. She was really moving, and we were hard on the pedal to catch her. She blew us a kiss and waved, but what she did next sent my head spinning. She slowed down just enough so I could see her undo the strings from her top and sling it back at me. The wind caught it, and wouldn't you know it, it flew right at me and got wrapped around my driver's mirror. She sped off, leaving us with our imaginations of what that tiny bit of fabric had covered. I took her top off from my mirror and tossed it in the back. For what seemed to be a hundred miles of running together and trying to catch up on our past, we tried our best to catch up with her. After that, our CB conversation was interrupted constantly by the chatter of this gal passing other trucks and giving them similar thrills.

Finally, we rolled into Kansas City, Missouri, where we were to pull off and release the cattle to the rest pastures, to give them a break from the confines of the trailer. We each had our own corral where we backed in and dropped our trailers. The crew there would unload and reload them in the morning.

Once we were bobtail, we pulled into a truck stop for the night. We ate dinner and grabbed a shower to clean up. We got out our chairs and were sitting beside our trucks when we noticed a crowd of drivers forming up for a challenge of bareknuckle fighting.

Odie said, "Hey, Sarge, why don't ya get in on that fight? I am sure ya would win a match or two."

I was hesitant at first, but then I agreed because I could use the extra money if I won.

It came my turn, and I was taken aback when the fella hit me square in the face and I saw stars. In an instant, my army training came to memory, and I whooped that poor boy until he finally gave up. I was handed my winnings, and I put my name back in for another round. In the end, I won three fights and lost two.

I received my winnings and Odie, and I returned to our trucks. I was in some pain from the fighting, so I grabbed my bottle of pain pills left over from my accident that I had, for some reason, hidden. I popped a couple and chased them down with cold coffee.

We said good night. Odie climbed into his truck, and I grabbed my stuff to go back in for a shower to wash off the sweat and blood that had dried on my body. Afterwards, back at my truck, I counted my loot. I made $400 for my efforts. I pulled my jar from the fuel tank and added that to the rest of my savings. Since there were people around, I figured I better put it in my side box so that no one could get it if they had seen me pull it out. I wiped the fuel off so it wouldn't smell up my truck, and locked everything up, and I took a walk.

I found the pay phone and called to see how Jalynn was doing. Of course, I did not tell her of my fighting matches. We talked for a few minutes and then I went to my truck to get some sleep. The next morning, we ate breakfast, and it came time for us to leave. Heading back over to the rest lot to get our trailers hooked up, hoping they were done loading. Before we hooked up, I paid for the both of us for their services and then we reconnected to the trailers, and we took off.

We hit the road and hammered down towards Tennessee, talking on the CB from time to time. Every now and then, he would mention Missy. I kept telling him she was out of his league, that he needed to find himself a good woman that would settle him down a bit.

We came into Chattanooga on I-24 where we split and went our separate ways. I headed south to Atlanta, and he went north to Knoxville.

I decided to go see my big brother since I was going to be in Georgia. I pulled into the truck stop and parked. I went inside and there sat my brother with "Ole Bone Head," an old trucker friend of ours. We chatted for a while, and I ordered my supper. I then went to the pay phone to check on Jalynn since it was just two weeks before I had to be home for Christmas. Goat said RJ and his wife Ashlynn had taken her to the ER because she had gone into labor a month early. I hung up and called the hospital.

"Bobby Ray," she said over the phone, "ya are just in time. Ya are the daddy of a baby girl. I named 'er Lacey Jo after my grandmother."

I told her that it sounded perfect to me and that I couldn't wait to meet and hold our little Lacey Jo. I asked Jalynn how she was feeling, and she said she was tired. I told her I wished I could have been there. She was understanding, as always, of the road life and said it was alright. I told her how proud I was, and I made a promise that as soon as I got everything back to where it needed to be financially, I would return home and pick up where I left off on the local runs. We would raise Lacey Jo and be a happy family once again. She mentioned that she could get a job down at the diner with Ashlynn to help out. I disagreed and said she should stay home and raise our little girl. Finally, I told her to get some rest, and I would be there in a week or so.

"I love you," I told her. "And give a kiss to my baby girl."

After I hung up, I was so excited that I went in and told the whole truck stop of the news. My brother offered a celebratory beer. I said I had something better in the truck and that he should follow me. We walked out to my truck, I reached under the passenger seat, and I brought out the jar of 'shine.

My brother said, "Bubba, I don't drink anymore because I got saved, and now, I am live'n a new life."

I said, "Aww, come on. One little sip won't hurt. After all, we are celebrate'n my little girl."

He said okay and took a sip from the jar. I took what would be about two shots in one swig and we headed back inside.

He sat down at the piano and started to play. My brother is one of the best self-taught piano players I have ever known. Dimples set my dinner on the bar, and as I ate, he continued to play. He played "Free Bird" and "Tuesday's Gone," because he knew I would appreciate them.

Then he told me to listen, and he played his version of an old gospel song, "How Great Thou Art." Then he played "Amazing Grace." Then to my amazement, he sang this song called "Thanks to Calvary," which really hit home for me. I shed a tear and quickly wiped it away so no one would catch me crying.

When he finished, he turned around and gave a smirk, knowing he was one of the best, but he was modest about it.

"What do ya think of that little brother?" he asked.

I responded, "Ya are the piano man!"

After I ate my dinner, we said goodbye since I would be leaving early. He hugged my neck and said, "I love ya, Bubba."

I said, "I love ya, too." And I returned to my truck. As I was laying in my bunk, all I could think about was my little baby girl, and I thanked God for the addition to my family. I thought about how I missed the birth of my first-born little angel by chasing the white line.

The next day as the sun continued its climb into the sky, I was getting ready to hit the road. I was in a hurry and didn't check everything properly. I started to pull on the interstate and my truck sputtered and died. I checked around to see what the problem was and in doing so, I realized that whoever was beside me last night had stolen my fuel and took off before I woke up. Luckily, I had taken the money jar from my tank. I walked back to my brother's place. He got three five-gallon cans of fuel and took me back, Once it was in there, I fired it up and he followed me back to his truck stop where I filled the tanks and gave him $300.00. He said keep the change, which was just under half of the whole cost, which I knew would help him and Dimples out. I gave him another hug and climbed into the cab. I was once more on my way, in search of the end of the long white line. Sadly, I didn't know that would be the last time I would see my big brother. I was notified a year later in December of 1982, that he died of a massive heart attack. I had been in California and was unable to make it back to attend his funeral.

The morning must have gotten away from me as I was in deep thought and was interrupted by Cash licking my face. I guess he was bored chasing the seagulls and wanted my attention. I found a stick and we played fetch for a bit. Then went to the hotel to get a room for the night, and to watch TV and eat lunch. We watched a few shows and had our bellies full. Our activities got the best of us, up in age and all, and the road had taken its toll. We fell fast asleep.

I woke in a panic thinking I had overslept. It was only 3 o'clock, so I called to check on the next day's load only to find out it had been cancelled. But there was a load of hogs going past Knoxville, Tennessee that would pick up the next morning. I told them to book it for me and I would be there to load it before sunup.

Cash and I lay there for a while. I tried to call Jalynn again because I was feeling depressed. Bad thoughts were going through my mind, and she was my rock and my counselor, and she could always get me back on track. She didn't answer and so I grabbed Cash and held him tight.

I confided in him once more and said, "Buddy, I figure our life will never be the same. I guess Jalynn has made up 'er mind to give up on me since it seems I can't change my ways. I guess it best to give up on myself, too."

I contemplated suicide, ways I could end everyone's suffering. I could take my pistol and shoot myself, drive my truck real fast and let go of the wheel, or I could take a bunch of pills and go to sleep. But as I lay there with Cash snuggled up by my side, feeling his heartbeat and his body rise and fall with each breath under my arm, I recalled my time in rehab with those three blonde angels singing, "So Much to Thank Him For." I began to cry and I asked God for help.

As I prayed, I felt hands on my shoulders as if someone was praying

172

with me. At that moment, I knew it was God, his presence, that I felt so strongly. It was a calming peace in my heart and in my mind and those thoughts of ending it all faded from my mind.

I got up and wiped my tears. I took Cash out to do his business and smoked a couple of cigarettes while he took his sweet time. After that we returned to the room and drifted off to sleep with ease.

The morning was sure to be much brighter with my faithful dog and the knowledge that God did not give up on me. He had renewed faith and hope in my heart and showed me that with him, all things are possible.

12
TROUBLED WATERS

Daytona, FL – Knoxville, TN

THE ALARM SOUNDED AND IT SEEMED AS IF I HAD JUST gone to sleep. With tired eyes I managed to make a pot of coffee in the little pot the hotel provided. I took Cash for his morning routine, and I enjoyed my coffee and cigarettes back-to-back. I packed our belongings, and Cash toted his favorite stuffed toy as we made our way across the desolate and quiet parking lot. After a quick onceover of my truck, we climbed inside. With the turn of the key and a press of the start button, this monster of chrome and steel roared to life, filling the air with black smoke. I flipped my many light toggle switches to "on" until the headlights, running lights, and chicken lights brought the parking lot to life. We waited for the air tanks to build to pressure so the brakes would release, and then we were ready to roll.

We headed to the T/A for fuel and a better cup of coffee. I asked if they had any leftovers for Cash, which they did, and when I set them before him, he scarfed them up as if he was starving.

We made our way through town easily with no traffic and as we pulled into the parking lot of the hog feed lot, Cash jumped into the back, I think because it made him sad to know the fate of the hogs, and he wanted no part in it. Once I was loaded, we set out heading north towards Georgia and into Tennessee.

174

As we crossed the Georgia line, the sun was rising, and traffic grew heavier on I-75 north. Through the city of Valdosta, we had to slow our speed as I had it wide open to make good time due to our new load's time frame. Once we made it through town, I put the hammer down again to make time as I knew I would be creeping through Atlanta.

As I was rolling, I slipped off daydreaming of my past once again, as thoughts of how life was back on the ranch when I returned home to start our new family.

We were doing alright for a while. Things on the ranch were going slow as the economy was changing, and the bigger ranches were taking over the industry. We still had a few good hands like Goat, Bucky, Sissy, RJ, and Bug. Of course, Slim was there to oversee things, but they were getting tired of working for little or nothing as we fought to keep the ranch going. The rest had gone over to work for a bigger ranch outfit. Jalynn took care of Lacey Jo, and I was running the white line, and we were just able to make ends meet.

In February 1982, I was finding out that it was costing me more being on the road, with the cost of food and fuel combined with the revenue that had taken a plunge. I did what I could, and only ate one hot meal a week. The rest of the days it was either sardines and crackers or Vienna sausages. Most days, I lived on coffee and cigarettes. Life was hard and I began to slip into depression. The nightmares were more frequent and interrupted the few hours of sleep I was able to get.

After almost a year of running the roads, one day I was parked at the truck stop and needed something to take the edge off. I bought me a fifth of whisky, and without realizing it, I finished it off in no time flat. My mind was wandering and as many times before, I figured that suicide would be the best solution. I grabbed my .44 from the seat pocket and sat there crying, trying to get up the nerve to put it to my head and pull the trigger. Sitting in my bunk, I was shaking like a leaf with sweat pouring from my body. I held the pistol to my head a minute and thought, *this is the end.*

I prayed that God would take care of Jalynn and Lacey Jo. While I

175

said those words out loud, it sparked feeling in me, and God spoke to me. He said, *"My son, there is no burden on earth that you can't bear if you would only accept me as your personal savior, and I will give you rest."*

I had never really heard him speak to me before. His voice was like a whisper in the wind, but at the same time, it was so loud that it made my heart pound in my chest. I didn't know what to do, so I answered back, and asked, "God, is that really you? Can you give me the answers I need to go on?"

In my amazement I heard him again.

He said, *"Lay your burdens down, and pick up your cross, and follow me, for I will never leave you, nor forsake you."*

All these things I was hearing him say I remembered hearing the preacher say in church when Mama and Daddy would take us as kids.

I cried out, "Lord, please forgive me and save me. I don't want to go down my old paths again. I love my family, and I want to be home with them."

When I said those words, a peace came over me like I had never known. I knew right then that I had been saved by his blood. I shouted, "Thank ya, Lord Jesus, for saving my soul!" I made a promise to him that I would never touch another drink or drug for as long as I lived.

With my new life as a born-again Christian, I dried my eyes and knew that I needed to call Jalynn. She had started going to church after we were married and had given her heart to Jesus. It was just after midnight when I jumped out of my truck and went to the pay phone to call her. I had forgotten my change, so I had to call her collect. I was so excited, that I even told the operator my news, and that I was calling my wife to tell her. I couldn't believe it that when I told her, she shouted and said, "Praise the Lord!"

 The phone rang a couple of times and with a tired voice, Jalynn answered and accepted my call. She immediately asked if I was alright and questioned if I had been in a wreck.

I said, "No, baby, I have good news. I have been saved! Jesus saved my soul! I was in my truck with bad thoughts, and I started praying, and he spoke to me. I gave my heart to him. I am a new man!"

Jalynn said, "Praise God! Thank you, Lord! I am so proud of ya, Bobby Ray. I love ya so much."

I said, "I love ya, too, Jalynn, and I promise I will never touch a drop of booze or drugs ever again for as long as I live. I love ya and Lacey Jo so much and I miss ya both. Can you believe it, after all these years my mama's prayers are finally answered."

She said, "Yes, I am sure yer mama is shouting the news all over heaven."

I told her that I was going to start heading home and we could work together to make a better go at things. She agreed and we said goodbye so she could get some sleep although I was too excited to sleep right away. I went to my truck and cleaned it up, and then I laid down for a few minutes and dozed off.

The next week couldn't pass quickly enough as I wanted to get home to my wife and baby girl. When I made it back, they were waiting in the yard as I pulled my truck down the driveway. I stopped by this old mulberry tree and just looked at them. Lacey Joe was now learning how to walk but was still unsure of herself as she fell there, in the yard. I smiled and kinda laughed, however, I was also sad because I had missed her taking her first steps as well as her first birthday. I thanked God for blessing me with such a beautiful family.

I continued to the barn where I parked and jumped out to go hug them. Lacey Jo was a little scared at first since it had been a while since she had seen me. I tried to hug her, and she clung to Jalynn's neck and wouldn't turn to see me. That hurt my heart so bad that I teared up.

Jalynn said, "Don't worry, honey, she is just shy."

Though I knew that I had been gone so long that she had forgotten what I looked like. I didn't blame her; she was just a baby and couldn't help it. We went into the house for me to settle in. I reached my recliner and that was it for me, I was out.

I awoke to find that Lacey Jo with her babydoll in her arms hitting me on the leg, trying to get me awake. She handed her doll to me for us to play. I felt good about that, knowing that she had remembered who I was. She climbed into my lap and gave me a kiss, and the words that came out of her mouth made my heart jump with joy.

"Da-da lub…"

I hollered at Jalynn and told her what she had said, and she told me that she had been teaching her and she had been saying daddy for some time now. I said, "Well, honey, I ain't miss'n out on nutt'n else. I am home now, and we are gonna be a happy family, no matter what comes our way."

The next day, I went to the quarry and got my old job back. They even gave me a little bump in pay. I thanked them and thought, *this is God's plan.*

I worked days there and, in the evening, I would help take care of things on the ranch. On the weekends, I would do a couple of close hauls for extra money. Things went well for a while, but then things started taking its toll on me.

With the economy changing, I was finding it hard to keep up with it. The more money I made, the more I had to put out to keep us from sinking. I was working day and night with very little sleep. The stress had begun troubling our marriage. We were s becoming distant and were arguing more and more. It had also attacked my Christianity; I quickly forgot my promise to God. I started back drinking here and there to ease my mind.

First, it was just a few beers, but after a while, it was so much that it didn't work anymore, and I was hitting the whisky bottle. The more I drank, the more I wanted, and then it was all I wanted. I didn't want to be around anyone, and I would become angry at the littlest things. Jalynn and I would get into arguments and fights. Lacey would run to her room crying, and this continued for a while.

Then, one day when I had drunk a little too much and had taken all that I could, I started yelling hurtful things at Jalynn and was hitting walls in my rage. I kicked the front screen door open and threw an empty bottle of whisky at my truck. It shattered into pieces, and it scared her. Jalynn started crying and picked up Lacey Jo, who was crying as well.

She said, "Bobby Ray, I am not gonna stand fer this kind of abuse. I do not deserve to be treated this way. I did not do anythang wrong fer ya to attack me in this manner. Ya promised God and me that ya would never drink again. Ya have broken yer promise to us both. Ya need to stop. Ya need to get some help."

She took Lacey Jo and went to stay with Amberleigh for a while. I was alone and didn't know what to do without her, so I kept drinking. I eventually quit my job driving the truck and just piddled around the ranch. After about three months, I was drinking very heavily and always had my flask or a bottle with me.

178

One day, Goat was working nearby and came to me as I was stumbling through the stables, talking out of my head to the horses.

He said, "Bobby Ray, I thank yer drink'n has gotten the better of ya and ya are act'n like a fool. Ya have lost yer wife and daughter and if ya don't stop, ya will lose everythang ya have worked so hard fer all these years."

Well, that made me angry due to my condition and I yelled at him and said I am the boss around here ain't nobody gonna tell me what to do. I took a swing at him, and to my surprise, he didn't take it lightly. He swung back and landed his fist right across my face.

We started fighting as he wrestled me to the ground, all the while saying, "Ya might be the boss, but I am yer friend, yer family. Ya need to straighten up before ya hurt yerself and others who care about ya." He finally got me into a position where I could not move or escape, and he said, "I love ya, man. Ya are my brother, don't do this to yerself or yer family."

In that moment, I was reminded that there are people that do care about me. I stopped dead in my tracks and started to cry. He held me there for a while and I finally said he was right. He threw my arms around his neck, and he hollered for Doc to come over. He and Doc carried me to the side of the barn and threw me in the horse trough. They dunked me a few times and then they gave me a cold cowboy shower with the water hose. Once I was sober enough for their liking (I think they were enjoying the punishment a bit too, since I had been such an ass to them all), they helped me into the house and made me a pot of coffee. After a while, I was sobered up, and the reality of everything that I had done hit me. I began to cry again and asked them if they would care to take me over to Amberleigh's house to talk with Jalynn.

At Amberleigh's house, Jalynn and Lacey Jo were outside on the swing set. As I walked up to where they were, Amberleigh came out of the house and headed towards me.

"Bobby Ray," she said, "ya need to leave."

Goat quickly put her in her place saying, "Shut up, Amberleigh. This is between them. Ya need to just mind yer own damn business and let them alone."

I asked her if we could talk for a few and to my surprise, she agreed. The guys watched Lacey Jo as Jalynn and I went for a walk. She said she had taken a job to pay her way for stay'n with Amberleigh and she had just gotten off work and was tired. I told her that I was sorry for my drinking and my behavior.

I said, "Can ya find it in yer heart to forgive this foolish cowboy?"

She said, "I love ya, Bobby Ray. I will forgive ya if ya can stop drink'n and promise to never—and I mean *never*—drink again. If ya do, we are done. I mean it. Can ya promise me that? I do not want Lacey Jo to ever see ya in that condition or act'n that way again. If ya really love us, then ya will change."

I promised her and God that I would stop drinking and that if she would help me get straightened up, I would not ever be that man again. She agreed but informed me that she wouldn't come home until I proved I could change. I completely understood. She said she would come over every day to see how I was after she got off work. I said I would love that and asked if she could bring Lacey Jo from time to time and she agreed.

After we left, I told Goat and Doc that I loved 'em, and that they would have to help me through this thing. They agreed, but said if I didn't clean up my act, they would whoop my ass good.

After about a week of her coming around to do her usual checkup, I told her that I had found a job hauling chickens and it was decent pay. She said that was great and she was proud of me, which made me feel good. She said maybe we could go on a sort of a date the next day, which I happily agreed to.

After she left, I started cleaning the house so she would see that I was trying. I even jumped on the John Deere and mowed the grass. That always gave me time to think, and I enjoyed it. I thought about us and planned my next move to get her to come back home. I was tired afterwards and just took a shower and went to bed.

The next morning, I had a new feeling that everything was going to be okay. I piddled around the house to ease my excitement of our date. It was nearing the time that she was supposed to be there, and I figured I had better go clean myself up. That night as we had planned, she showed up to the house as I was getting ready. I was taken by surprise as she came into the house unannounced and came into the bathroom where I was standing in my boxers trimming my facial hair. I noticed her in the mirror looking at me. She was still the most beautiful woman

I had ever seen. She was wearing a white sundress with her long strawberry blonde curls waving down her back. She even had on her cowgirl boots and hat. She knew that always drove me crazy. I knew she did it on purpose. I was so lost in my thoughts that she startled me by smacking me on the ass.

She said, "I have missed this side of ya."

I said, "Well, maybe l if I continue to better myself, ya will come back home, and it can all be yers for the take'n."

Walking into our bedroom, she said, "Maybe so, just keep do'n right and we will see."

After I was dressed, we headed out to eat at the local steakhouse and people were looking, because like I said before, it was a small town, and everybody knew everybody. Before our food arrived, I could tell she was kind of embarrassed and blushing at the stares we were getting. I asked if she wanted to get our food and go back home to the house where we could escape the stares and the whispered comments.

She said, "Please, if ya don't mind."

So, we got our food to go, away from the gossipers.

Driving to the house, she slid over next to me and put her hand on my leg as she always did. She took my hand and placed my arm around her neck and snuggled up close. She whispered, "I love ya, mister. I hope ya realize that."

I turned and kissed her on her forehead and said, "I love ya, too, babydoll, and I know everything will work out, because it was God who joined us together in the first place."

She snuggled up tighter for the rest of the ride.

We arrived at the house, and I held my door open so she could slide out of the driver's side. When she did, her boot slipped off the side and she started to fall. I grabbed her and helped her up. I hugged her tight for several minutes, just embracing her love, and she lifted her head and gave me a kiss on the lips. We walked up on the porch, and I opened the door and welcomed her in.

She said, "What a gentleman ya are."

I just told her that I had prayed and waited so long for us to be back together and to have my family back.

We sat at the table eating and talked about us, figuring out how we could manage things. I suggested we go into the den where I could build a fire, and we could relax.

Jalynn turned on the radio and I walked into the room to hear a song that I loved playing. "Close Enough to Perfect" by Alabama. I grabbed her hand and pulled her in close and we danced like we used to. I leaned in and whispered that I love this song, but in my eyes, she was perfect to me. She started to cry about the time the song ended, and I asked why.

"I miss be'n yer wife," she said. "And you hold'n me every night."

I said, "Why don't ya just come back home? I have changed; I seen the error of my ways. Please, honey, I cannot live without ya any longer."

She agreed and as we stood there holding each other, it happened. Jalynn laid one of her most passionate kisses on me, and it seemed like it lasted forever.

When we parted lips, she said, "Why don't ya take yer wife to bed and make love to 'er?"

Without hesitation, I swept her off her feet and carried her to our bedroom. I laid her on the bed, and we made love like we had not done in forever. In fact, we did so several times that night. Once we were worn out, we laid there and talked and snuggled until the sun came up.

After that night, our love was renewed, and we spent the daylight hours talking about important changes that needed to be made. Then we drove over to Amberleigh's and loaded up their belongings, and I brought my family home.

After a couple of months, I was in the stables working when Jalynn came to me. She had a certain glow about her, and she grabbed me by the hand. With a blank look on her face, she said, "Bobby Ray, we need to talk."

Expecting the worst from the way she had said it, I stopped what I was doing and hugged her tight. "What is it, honey?"

She said, "We're gonna have another baby."

I was so happy, I picked her up by the waist and swung her around. "I love ya Jalynn," I said holding her tight.

"I know ya do, Bobby Ray, but this means we are gonna need extra income, which we don't have since ya are just run'n local."

"I will find a second job and let the others handle thangs around here," I said reassuring her that we would be okay.

Within a couple of days, I had a second job driving at night for the local methane gas drilling company that had moved to town. It would allow me to keep hauling our cattle when needed and haul chickens as well. It would be enough to get us where we needed to be financially to take care of our family, the ranch, and the ranch hands. It did for a while, but I could feel myself slipping into depression as the days went by. I thought I could work through it, but within a few months of working with the rig crew, I wasn't as happy about it as had been. I found myself wanting the open road. I knew Jalynn would not agree to it, so I kept it to myself. Still, it was driving me crazy.

Slowly and in secret I started to drink whisky again to take the edge off. I had it under control, or so I thought, until I had a particularly rough day where nothing seemed to go right. I had awakened from a bad dream and that set the mood for the rest of the day. I had a flat on my pickup truck and had to get Goat to run me to work. Traffic was slow due to construction, and by the end of the day, I had had enough. I grabbed a bottle from the liquor store before Goat came back to get me. I drank five shots and within minutes, I was feeling good again.

I tried to hide it with breath mints as I waited for my ride. That is when I noticed my truck pulling in; they had fixed my tire. I was worried that since they had to move my seat to get my jack out, that the bottle that I had hidden had been found. I was trying to find the words to say to Goat so he wouldn't tell Jalynn, but then I saw it was Jalynn picking me, not Goat. I was caught and my heart sank.

Jalynn slid over and asked if I would drive. I declined and said I was tired, so she got us on the road. Then she began to question me. I could tell by her tone that she knew; whoever found my stashed bottle must have told her.

"I have some'ng I want to ask ya," she said. "And I want ya to be honest, because yer answer will determine the outcome of this conversation. Have ya been drinking again?"

Not wanting to argue or make her furious with me, I lied. "No, honey, I have not."

She reached under my truck seat and pulled out a half empty bottle. "Then ya need to explain this."

She held it in front of my face, and I knew things were going south. I said, "I can't help it, Jalynn. I'm unhappy do'n the same thang day in and day out. I need a change."

183

She told me that she was not going back to Amberleigh's and that I needed to get out, because I made her and God a promise that I would never drink again. Then she started quoting scriptures about promises. She said would not tolerate it or watch me become the hateful man I was when I drank. I argued my case about more money and freedom from being a long-haul driver, but she didn't want to hear it.

We argued all the way back to the ranch. She was crying when we pulled into the driveway, and she said the best thing for me to do is get in my truck and leave. I switched places with her and peeled out of the driveway, slinging gravel everywhere, and I headed to the bar. There I found a few fellow drinkers that agreed with me and others that didn't. The more I drank, the more I convinced myself that they did not understand my heavy burdens because they hadn't walked in my shoes. So, I grabbed a bottle of booze to-go, jumped in my pickup, and took off down the road.

The next morning, I woke up in my big truck not remembering how I got there. I went into the house to try to smooth things over with Jalynn, but her mind was made up. She started yelling at me to get out and search for the "end of the long white line," or whatever it was that I was in search of. I asked her what she was going to do and how she was going to run the ranch. She said that she had called her parents, and they were heading out to help. She said she didn't need me to run things. I knew they were probably angry as hell with me by now, too, so as not to complicate things even more, and because I loved her, I grabbed a packed a small bag, and I left.

Outside, I climbed in my big truck and took off. I was angry at myself for what I had done, and with a heavy heart, I headed to the truck stop to see if anyone had a load that I could get. I knew I should not leave her alone, that I should have fought for her love and got myself sober so I could be the husband and the daddy I needed to be.

Later, as I was heading down the road to pick up a load I found, I thought about how she used to ride with me, and the memories poured back.

Once when I returned home for a break, Jalynn asked if she could come out with me. I knew if I said no, I would never hear the end of it, so I said, "Sure, honey, I would love that."

With excitement, she gave me a quick hug and a kiss and went to pack her bag for the early morning start.

I got us a few loads to get us started. We would go on a sightseeing tour while enjoying our time together. The first load would take us through the Colorado Rocky Mountains, and then over to Washington, and down the Pacific Coast. Since she had never been that far west, I thought it would be exciting for her to see.

We left out at the crack of dawn, and being that early, she went straight to the bunk to finish her sleep. I went and got loaded and we hit the big road heading south to Colorado Springs. By that time, she was waking up and told me to stop so she could use the bathroom. I thought to myself, *here we go again! This is going to be a long trip.*

Luckily, we were not in a big hurry, so I obliged. I fueled while she went in the store and then I parked and joined her for breakfast.

Afterwards, we loaded up and headed west through the Rockies. As we hit the big mountains, I guess she had forgotten what it was like and on one of the many downgrades, the jake brakes bellowed long and deep to slow me down.

Jalynn let out a gasp and said, "Oh, Lord, that scared me."

I laughed and said, "You better get used to that; we still have a way to go yet."

She said, "Maybe I should just get in the bunk."

Which she did, but still looked out at the scenery as we rolled along and hid when we hit a steep downgrade. I was laughing inside, but I must admit, it was wonderful having my angel ride along with me.

When we were out of the big hills and she felt safe, she would climb back in her seat where we would have some great conversations. When we would bed down to sleep, it felt great to wrap her in my arms and feel the comfort of what I missed all the times of being out here alone.

We made it to the West Coast and then headed down through Washington and Oregon, and then on to California, where we would take a weekend off to enjoy a small vacation on the beach. I remember this so well because I never told her about the Old Grape Vine.

We passed the signs for Bakersfield, and she got so excited, saying, "Hey! That is where Merle Haggard and Buck Owens are from!"

She talked about that for miles and was taken by surprise when we started down the long stretch. She didn't have time to jump into the back, so she sat there with her face as white as a ghost, with a death grip on the arm rests. Once we were back on level ground, she hit my arm and scolded me for not warning her. I couldn't hold back my laughter, which made her even madder. I told her afterwards I was sorry, but that I wanted her to experience it just once in her life. She told me to never do that again and that although she was scared, she did enjoy the view.

We made it to Los Angeles where I dropped my trailer, and we bobtailed to a hotel on the beach. She was excited at the sight of the ocean and thanked me for stopping.

That weekend, we had a blast as we went shopping and played on the beach. At night, we would walk on the beach as the sun was setting. Then we would retire to our room and snuggle all night like we used to when I was off the road. In the morning, I would make coffee and wake my beautiful angel from her peaceful slumber with a kiss and say I love you. When our weekend was over, we hit the road headed east on Interstate 10, towards Texas, and then we were to head home.

When we finally reached the ranch, she was so glad to get out of the truck. I had to laugh again when she said, "Don't ever take me across Texas, it takes forever."

"Now you know how I feel when I get home," I told her.

I rested for a few days before I headed out again. Though I enjoyed Jalynn riding with me, I enjoyed running alone so I could stop when I wanted to. I was able to enjoy the freedom of the road when she was not around, I could do no wrong out here chasing the long white line.

When I came out of my daydream, I didn't realize I had already come through Atlanta and Chattanooga to find myself at the Knoxville/Nashville split. Making my way towards Knoxville, I noticed a few changes that were not there in my earlier travels through the city. More truck stops and shopping malls, and before I knew it, I was hitting a new set of DOT scales. They pulled me in to be weighed, and after that, pulled me to the side to check my paperwork and logs. That's when I was nailed.

Due to all my life happenings and my daydreaming, I forgot to catch up my logs and I was hit with a hefty fine. However, they let me make the corrections and did not hold me there on an OOS (out of service) violation since it was just this one trip that my logs lacked updating. Plus, I was honest about not logging anything. I politely told them I appreciated it and thanked them, and that I was going to make my way to the nearest truck stop and rest since I was out of driving hours for the day.

As I made my way to the Petro, I noticed that one of the officers had followed me to make sure I stopped like I said I was going to. I drove around and found a spot to park for the night.

Cash and I went to call Jalynn from the payphone in the drivers' lounge and get some food. Jalynn didn't answer and the food was not that good.

I walked to stretch my legs and Cash roamed parking lot as usual. My recollections of the day weighed heavily on my mind, and I couldn't imagine what Jalynn was feeling. I had done her so wrong so many times and yet she always managed to forgive me. Each time she did, I would promise her and God that I would not do those things ever again. But each time, I ended up breaking my promises. I thought to myself she would never find it in her heart to forgive me and love me again and I couldn't blame her one bit if she didn't.

I found myself back in my truck and before I opened the door, I got down on one knee and prayed for the Lord's forgiveness. I asked him to ease Jalynn's pain from my broken promises and for the way I treated her.

After I finished, I was in hopes that he had heard my prayer. I called for Cash, and he came running, so we climbed into the truck. I was so tired from all the driving that I had been doing and wasn't used to it, and with all that was going on with my family, and thoughts in my head, I had not really gotten a good night's sleep in over a week. I figured I would try again so we climbed into the bunk to try and get some sleep for our early morning delivery.

13

LIFE BEFORE THE WHITE LINE

Knoxville, TN

AFTER CLIMBING INTO BED, I TOSSED AND TURNED TRYING to find that perfect spot that I had worn out over the years. It was early yet, and the sun had not gone down, and I just wasn't that tired. As I was unsuccessful in my attempt to sleep, I decided to venture into the truck stop and see what was going on. I talked with a few drivers and then grabbed a couple of snacks and a cold drink. The drivers told me about this show that was being held over at the fairgrounds featuring a singer who was also a truck driver and had several albums out. Assuming the DOT had forgotten about me, I decided to disconnect my trailer and drive over there to get my mind off things.

The singer was a fella by the name of Tony Justice, and he sang good ole truck driving songs, some that I knew and some he had written himself. Man, they were great songs, some upbeat and some pulled at my heart strings, considering my past and current situations. He was truly a great performer and songwriter, and the fact that he was also a truck driver meant that he knew his material well and lived life on the road. He had his truck off to the side of the stage and boy, was she a beauty. A gold Peterbilt 379 that he called Purgatory.

After the show, he did a meet-and-greet and let me tell you, I am glad I got to meet this fella. I will never forget him. He was down-to-earth and poured his heart and soul into his music. I met some more truck drivers, and we soon became friends.

Billy Stoneking was another stock hauler and had several trucks running on the roads. He and his wife were from Pennsylvania and were in a long nose Pete. He said had been driving since he was 18 years old.

There was John and Kim Jaikes from Pennsylvania, as well, also husband and wife, and both drove trucks. His was a purple Kenworth and hers was a purple Pete. She told me about how they would switch lanes going down the highway and that is how they danced when rolling down the road. I thought that was an awesome story that they could tell their grandkids someday.

After the show, I returned to my truck where Cash was anxiously waiting. We drove back to the truck stop, and I reconnected to my trailer and went in the store to get a cold drink. As soon as I got back to my truck and I opened the door, there was Cash with his tongue hanging out in anticipation to see if I had brought him anything from my trip into the store. I had gotten him a few beef sticks for a snack after that bad meal we had. We ate our snacks and laid back down. I tried to go to sleep but heartburn had set in, and I gave up and went back to pondering my life.

I was currently in the "The Volunteer State," the same city where I was to start my new life and career away from the ranch as a VOLS quarterback, all dressed in orange and white. What would my life have been like if it had not been changed on that unforgettable day? The day I ended up spending my life chasing the white line.

I started thinking back to when I was in grade school. I remembered how Daddy and I would listen to the broadcast of the football games. When we finally got a TV, we would watch them together when he was home off the road and not working on the ranch, which wasn't that often.

While watching the games with him one day I said, "Daddy, that's what I wanna do. I wanna play football."

My mama signed me up for the local little league team. I loved playing the sport from the beginning. The others picked on me because

I didn't know any of the rules, but once I learned them, everything else came naturally. The more I played, the better I got. The ranch hands would take turns throwing the ball with me when they had free time. Daddy was gone a lot, but when he was home, he loved throwing the pig skin around. We would run plays until I was a pro at each one and he even built me what they called a sled. It was metal and had a dummy-like pad covered in burlap that I would practice hitting to knock down my opponent. He would hit me while wearing some homemade pads so I would get used to being tackled. He hung an old tire up for me to throw the ball through the center of, and as time went on, he narrowed the hole for me to hone my skills. All the practice helped because I was becoming unstoppable, throwing touchdown passes, one after another.

I played football through middle school and on into high school. People were starting to take notice. Especially the girls, who I would chase when I had time between the ranch, football, and school. In the summer when I wasn't busy with all that was going on, after my chores, I would spend time with Missy, Mr. Blake's granddaughter, who was a couple of years younger than I was. We would go fishing and swimming, and on a couple of occasions, we went skinny dipping. We did fool around; however we had a good friendship, and I didn't give it much thought.

I eventually had a steady girlfriend. Jess and I started dating my freshman year. We never got serious or did anything our parents wouldn't approve of. We were young and just coming into our teenage years. Things changed in our sophomore year when we started kissing here and there.

When it was time for me to learn to drive, Daddy taught me how to do it in the pastures first. Then on the haul road, and eventually out on the main road. When I got my learners permit, the first car he bought me was a '57 Chevy, and it was a good fixer upper.

Before I could fix her up, I was out driving on an old dirt road and I wanted to see how fast she would go, figuring Daddy wouldn't find out. I was too inexperienced to be doing such, and it got out of control. I ended up hitting a telephone pole. The crash totaled the car and put me in the hospital for a few weeks with a broken leg and arm. I thought my dreams of playing football were over. But after surgery, in no time at all I was back to playing.

190

At home, I was grounded for a good while until things settled down. Then Daddy bought my old 1960 Ford pickup. It was orange and it needed some work, so I worked on the ranch for the money for parts and such. When Daddy was home, he would help me tinker with it, and he even repainted it. I remember him teaching me what I needed to know about the mechanics of it for when I was able to go out on my own, driving.

Sometimes, Jesse would come over and I would drive her around the ranch. One day while we were out, we parked to take a break, and we started hugging and kissing. Out of nowhere, feelings came over me that I had never felt before. I told her something was wrong. I was sweating and my mind was in a whirlwind. I didn't know what was happening to my body.

She said, "Bobby Ray, you're such a goober! That's normal. I learned all about fool'n around from my cousin. She's eighteen and lives in the city and knows a lot about things."

Jess began to explain things to me and afterwards, I thought of what Mama and Daddy would think. But most importantly, I wondered what God would think. I went to church with Mama and Daddy, and even though I was not saved at the time, I still believed in God. Mama would say when I was acting up during the service that God was always watching us. I knew in my heart that he was watching me with Jess, and I knew he wouldn't approve of what we did. I told her we could not do that anymore and that she could not tell anyone ever. She agreed and we drove back to the house, and she went home.

I drove straight past Daddy, who was outside of the barn, and I went straight to the house. I snuck in hoping Mama was too busy to notice that I had returned, and I quickly went to my room and prayed that God would forgive me for my actions.

We never did anything like that again. Jess decided that she wanted to know more and broke up with me to go out with other guys on her quest. After that, I just focused on football and my grades.

During my high school years, the team won the State Championship three years in a row, and we were undefeated for two of those years. Football was my life, and I was living the dream. On the last day of school of my junior year, the coach caught me on my way out to my pickup and asked me if I had given a thought about what I was going to do after I graduated.

I said, "I am gonna play football, coach," not fully understanding what he meant.

He said, "You need to figure out what career path you want to take, because football isn't everything."

I just responded, "It is to me! I am gonna play fer the Pittsburgh Steelers."

He said that I needed to be realistic and not depend on football as my career.

I said to the coach, "All I wanna do is play ball."

He said, "Just think about it, Bobby Ray!"

I agreed and went on my way.

That summer I practiced and worked on the ranch. I had talked to Mama about what he had said, and she agreed. She said, "Ya are a good football player, and ya should get a proper education, but ya know yer daddy intends on ya work'n on the ranch and eventually run'n it for him."

I tried to talk to him about it all the time, but he wouldn't listen to anything I had to say about it. He would just say, "Don't disappoint me, boy. Ya need to learn this ranch because it will all be yers someday."

The summer ended and it was nearing time to start my senior year. When school started, the coach, not really agreeing with my answer from our conversation, had talked to the counselors. They agreed with him and signed me up for a journalism and broadcasting class.

One assignment my teacher Ms. Jones had us write for the class was a third-person interview with ourselves. It was to cover our career and accomplishments. At first, I had a hard time thinking about what kind of career I wanted for my future, because football and the ranch was all I knew. In my mind, I was one of the best high school quarterbacks ever and I wanted nothing to do with the ranch life. I had lived it long enough.

As I sat in my room that night with my pencil in hand on a blank sheet of paper, I thought of my future career. I wrote the word "football." It was the only thing I could come up with, because I could not make the ranch my career. While writing about what I liked about it, I jotted down my favorite teams and players. I picked my favorite player, Charley Johnson, who played for the St. Louis Cardinals. I then put myself in his place and I asked myself questions about what it was like to play for the NFL and how much he got paid. I imagined that our answers to that would be the same: "I don't do it for the money. I do it for the love of the game, and for America." I wrote how it was to play in all those big cities and in front of all the crowds. After all, we live in a small town, and I had at the time, never been out of the state.

The day finally came when I had to get in front of the class and read it as if I was doing the interview. I was so nervous, as I didn't want to complete the assignment, and Ms. Jones said if I didn't, it would reflect on my grade. I knew if I didn't do well, my daddy would not let me play the sport I loved. So, I gathered my courage and went to the front of the room where I stood quietly for a few moments and then I began my interview. Ms. Jones approached me after class and praised me for a job well done.

She asked if I had ever considered a career in sports journalism. I told her I hadn't given it much thought. She said I should, because she thoughts that I was a natural at it as I was with football, and the fact that I knew the ins and outs of the sport. "Plus," she said, "you could probably get a scholarship and go to college and play football and get your education too."

That sounded great because I knew my parents couldn't afford to send me since they sent my sister to Paris to attend college. They were depending on me to work on the ranch after high school.

After class, I went home and told Mama and Daddy what she said. I told them that I thought that was exactly what I wanted to do. Mama said what she would always say in any decision-making process, "Pray about it, son. God will show ya the way. And know that whatever ya decide to do, yer daddy and I will support ya in yer decision."

We started football practice earlier than usual that year to prepare us for the biggest year of high school. We were on fire during the season, winning every game under those Friday night lights. We breezed into the playoffs. We knew that there had been college scouts looking at us during the year, but there were rumors that college recruiters were coming to our small town to witness our talents. This made the headlines in all the newspapers, as it was to be our final game, which just happened to be the state championship game.

The day arrived and we were all so nervous as we prepared to face our competition. As the night unfolded, life as I knew it had never felt so good. We were playing our hearts out. When it was all said and done, we had won our fourth state championship.

After the final buzzer, it seemed that the whole town rushed the field to congratulate us on the win. That's when I noticed the coach and two other men coming towards me. It was loud, but I did catch how they introduced themselves. One was from the University of West Virginia and the other from the University of Tennessee. As we talked, I was still excited as we headed to the locker room, and I left my Mama and Daddy to talk to the two men.

The celebration continued in the locker room as we were all pumped up. We had showers and returned to the field to meet the press. They were asking all kinds of questions to the senior players as if we knew all the answers. The main question that was on their minds was what college we were going to sign with. I still had no idea. I needed time to think, so afterwards, I sat down with each of the men along with my parents to discuss the details. They each offered me everything I could ever want, and both agreed to give me time to think on my decision.

I never dreamed this could be possible and after I thought about it a little bit, I put it to rest for a while as I had to get back to the task of finishing school and graduating. I was, in fact, set on going to college. That was until an Army recruiter came to the school one day to talk to us about a career in the U. S. Army. After listening to what the gentleman had to say and pondering on it for a while, I was torn between becoming a sportswriter and joining the Army.

After talking it over with Mama and telling her about my struggle to decide, she said, "I would usually tell ya to pray about it—and I hope ya still do—but I pray you don't choose the Army."

The discussion had upset her as she had dealt with Daddy and my brother going away years ago to fight in the war. She tried not to let it show but I could see the tears building in her eyes. I decided to drop it for now and talk it over with Daddy when he returned from being on the road, even though I already knew his thoughts on the whole matter. I finished my chores for the night and went to my room and never discussed it with her again. And she never asked.

The last month of my senior year came. It was a typical Saturday as Daddy woke me at the first crack of dawn in his usual way, by opening the door, and in his commanding, voice saying, "Get up, boy, yer waste'n daylight."

Today was the day, and it was time for me to make one of the most important decisions of my life. I wanted it to be the right decision, so I went off to think about it for a while after working the ranch and doing my chores. I went to my favorite place on the ranch where the river split from our place and flowed towards town. As I sat, I must have drifted in my thoughts and had fallen asleep. When I awoke, the sun was meeting the mountains, and I knew it would be dark soon. I headed back and when I reached the house, there were people waiting for me. The coach, the two other men, and the Army recruiter. They were also accompanied by half the town, and I went inside with them wanting me tell them my final answer. Mama and Daddy behaved as they usually did, despite the growing crowd and reporters outside. Ironically, my father was watching football and my mother reading the Bible.

I simply walked over and said, "Mama and Daddy, I want to be a Volunteer. Not for the Army, but for Tennessee."

My mama jumped up and said *hallelujah*, as her prayer was answered. She hugged my neck as she was crying and said she had never been prouder of me. I glanced over at my daddy and could see a tear in the corner of his eye. He was a man of few words when it came to stuff like this.

He got up from his chair and as he walked by, he patted me on the shoulder and said, "Way to go, son."

Deep down inside I knew he was hurt because he was dead set on me staying on the ranch.

Daddy went out onto the porch and asked the Tennessee Recruiter to come in. He told him if he didn't stand behind his word on what he was offering me that they would have words. The fellow knew what Daddy meant and said, "Yes, sir."

After I was done signing all the papers, Mama let everyone else in. The other two men congratulated me and left. Everyone else hugged me and shook my hand. After the excitement was over and it was all quiet, all I could think about was I was finally going to play college football!

After graduation, I worked all summer on the ranch, which made me appreciate the fact that I had chosen to go to college and not stay around there. Daddy paid me what he could, and I saved every dime for my transition. It wasn't long before summer came to an end and it was time for me to leave the ranch in search of what the future held in Knoxville, Tennessee. I admit I was a little nervous, as this would be the first time I would be away from home for an extended period.

I spent a few days packing my clothes and things I thought I might need and put them in the back of my truck which I covered with a tarp to protect it from the weather. I told everyone bye that was on the ranch. They wished me the best and shook my hand and the ladies gave me a peck on the cheek and said be careful. Before jumping into my packed pickup truck, my mama hugged my neck and told me that she loved me and to be careful. Daddy wasn't there to say farewell. He had left out the day before on his way to Colorado in his cattle hauler. I was used to it, and it was second nature to my family and I for him to be on the road during family events.

Suddenly, Mama said, "Hold on, son." She ran inside and a minute later, came running out with a thermos of coffee and a bagged lunch. She said, "Take this, son. It will help ya stay awake on yer trip."

I didn't want to hurt her feelings, so I accepted it with a smile. I would just pour it out somewhere down the road. I fired up my truck and left her crying on the front steps. I looked in my rearview mirror as I drove away and seen her sit down on the step and put her head in her hands. I knew she was praying for me as usual. I waved my last goodbye to everyone as I drove down the driveway past the barns and I headed towards the interstate. Passing through town there were signs up wishing me luck, and some folks came to wave bye as they knew I would have to pass through as I left.

It took me two and a half days before making it into the city of Knoxville. I took my time and stopped when I needed to, or if I saw a scenery that caught my eye and pulled over to take a picture with the camera that the ranch hands had given me as a going away present. I was in awe at all the beauty as I went from state to state. I thought what an amazing country we live in. God really painted a beautiful picture when he made her.

When I finally arrived, I checked in with the dorm's RA to get my assigned room. I proceeded to my designated room. My roommate was already there and unpacked.

196

I said, "hey, man, name's Bobby Ray." He stood up and all I could think to myself was, *I sure hope we get along!* He was tall and big, a little mean-looking, too.

He said, "Hey, name's Johnny Stone. I'm from over round Memphis way, but everyone calls me Bubba. Ya a ball player, too?"

I said I was. He asked if I liked to party. I hesitated, because truthfully, I had never done any partying back home. I knew my dad would have my hide. So, I just said, "sometimes."

He said, "BR, (that's what he called me, and it stuck) we're in college now. We will party all the time."

I simply said, "Cool!" We became friends very quickly. This was a guy I wanted to have my back for sure.

Bubba helped me carry my belongings up to my room. I quickly unpacked and Bubba said, "Let's go find some grub."

I was glad because I was starving. We walked down the streets of Knoxville and there were pretty girls everywhere we turned. Bubba could hardly contain himself. He was whistling and hollering at them all. I was hiding my embarrassment. I did not want to give this brute any reason not to like me.

We met up with some other members of the team at the local diner. We all seemed to hit it off quite well. They invited us to a party that night at their frat house. Bubba was tickled since we were freshmen. He was whooping and hollering the whole way back to our dorm. I could see already what a party animal this guy was going to be.

As we were getting ready for the party, Bubba said, "I sure hope to get me some tail tonight."

I was wondering if he had even been alone with a girl before. I just smiled and shook my head. We took off down the street, me hoping this all didn't go sideways, as we had our first football practice the next morning. I knew this was not going to be my thing but didn't want to be the outcast. As soon as we arrived, we were handed a cup of beer from the keg that I later found was in the bathtub filled with ice. I was in a different world for sure. I took my first sip. I did not much care for the taste but continued to take small sips until I somehow acquired the taste. It didn't take long for me to start feeling the effects. I had never had alcohol before and everything else that night was a blur.

The next morning, my alarm went off and I awoke with a bad

headache. I guess this was my first hangover. I forced myself out of bed and made my way to the cupboard for my Goodie Powders. I then got dressed and headed to the field.

My first practice was rough. I told myself, *no more drinking! Especially when you have conditioning practice the next day!*

Classes soon began and I was starting to miss home. I called to talk to Mama and see how things were going back home on the ranch. She told me everyone was missing me, and things were not the same without me there, but she was proud of me for following my dreams. She said she missed me, and she loved me, and I said the same. Then we said goodbye and I hung up the phone.

I went back up to my room to study. Bubba must have gone off to yet another party. I assumed he had a good time because he didn't come home that night. Instead, he came busting into our room and hollering, "Whoo-wee, Bobby Ray, you sure missed a good'n last night! The girls were on point and this ole dog went a hunt'n!" This behavior went on every weekend while I sat in my room and studied when I wasn't practicing.

Soon, it was time for our first game. I knew being a freshman I wouldn't get much play time this year, especially since our seasoned players were so good. I was standing by as a third-string quarterback since there were a few of us on the team. I figured it would most likely be that way for me for now.

After several weeks of this, I was really feeling homesick. Things weren't going the way I had expected but tried not to let it show. One tough night, I managed to avoid Bubba by taking a walk. He would tease me and want me to go partying. So, I headed uptown on foot to Gay Street to check it out. I saw a lit-up marquee with big flashing letters that read, "Tennessee." It was the Tennessee Theatre, and it just so happened that they were showing a cowboy movie. I thought it may help me feel closer to home, so I walked up to the ticket booth.

I saw a cute girl sitting there and her name tag read, Becky.

I said, "One please, Miss Becky!"

She said, "Seventy-five cents."

I handed her my coins, and she asked if I was from around there. I told her no, I was from Wyoming, and only there attending college. She said she was also not from there and that she was also attending college.

She said she was a small-town girl, from Cartersville, Georgia. We hit it off very well. It was time for the movie to start so I headed inside and took a seat. About halfway through, she came in and sat beside me with a bag of popcorn and offered me some.

After the movie, I asked if she would want to go grab a burger. She said, "that would be rad." I didn't know what she really meant by that. I thought that must be the way they talk in her small town.

We walked up the street to the campus diner and went inside and ordered our food. We ate and enjoyed each other's company. I even opened up a bit and told her a little about how I was missing home. She told me that she also sometimes missed home, but that city life was growing on her. She didn't live on campus. A few of her friends went in together and rented a house instead. We finished eating and Becky invited me to come with her and hangout. She said she hated going to the house alone, that her roommates had gone to a party, and that she was not much of a partier. Another thing we had in common.

When we got to her place, she poured us a glass of sweet tea and put on a record. It was a type I wasn't used to that she called rock-n-roll, and the band was called The Rolling Stones. I told her that I had only listened to Country music up until then. She laughed, I guess because I only knew one kind of music.

We sat there talking about our hometowns and I was thinking, *she really gets who I am.* Hours passed quickly, and I told her that I should head back to the dorm, that I had an early class the next day.

She sighed and said, "Okay, I reckon if ya gotta."

I stood up to leave and when I did, she caught me off guard by standing on her toes to peck on the cheek. I impulsively put my hand on the back of her neck and gave her a bigger kiss, smack dab on her lips.

She blurted out, "I'm a virgin!"

I chuckled, which made her upset, and then told her that I was, too. I don't think she believed me, but she asked if I could stay and cuddle. And that is what we did, although, I would not have minded if it were a little more. I woke up to the alarm she had set for me and left out as she was still sleeping. On the way back to the dorm, I was thinking how I really needed that and how much I really wanted to see her again.

I stopped by my room to change my clothes, put on some deodorant, and grab my books. Bubba had just woken up from a night of his

199

mischief and before I made it to the door, he said, "You dog! Ya got some last night!"

I had to be cool, so I just quickly said while rushing out the door, "I ain't tellin'!"

Bubba threw his pillow as I closed the door, and I headed to class.

I spent the next couple of months juggling class, sitting on the sidelines, and when I wasn't in class or at a game, I was hanging out with Becky. Nothing ever happened between her and I, we were just best buds.

Before long, it was time for Christmas break. After our final game, as we were leaving the field to head to our cars, a few of us that were friends were discussing our plans. When it came to me, Bubba asked if I was staying on campus to party with him, and I told him I decided to go home and see my family over the holidays. Little did I know my college life and future in football would soon be over.

I was jarred out of my trance regarding my high school and college days as the sound of a truck backing in next to me and setting his brakes disturbed my thoughts, I snuggled up next to Cash and told him I loved him, and again, he made a sound as if I was bothering his sleep. I pulled the covers over us and in minutes we were both off to sleep for tomorrow's run.

14

THE TEMPTATION

Knoxville, TN - Savannah, GA

THE NEXT MORNING, AFTER BREAKFAST AND COFFEE AND we got our fuel, we hit the road, headed to the slaughterhouse to unload. Cash stayed in the back while we were there and when they were finished, they paid me, and we were on our way to our next load.

We had to go to the other side of Knoxville to get loaded. It took a while to load us up and while they were doing so, Cash and I walked around looking at the horses in the barn. Cash saw some ducks that he thought he just *had* to have and away he went. I tried to call him back, but he was on a mission, one that would take him right through a huge mud puddle. He returned covered with mud and soaking wet. I scolded him and I knew he hated to get a bath, but there was no way he was getting in my truck in his condition. He gave me his sad puppy dog eyes as usual, but it had to be done.

I took him over to the water hose and washed him off. I then told him to shake it off and go lay in the sun and dry off. He moped off to find his sunny spot.

It took about another hour to finish with us, and then Cash and I were ready to hit the road. We hit interstate 40 and headed through the Smoky Mountains of the Cherokee National Forest. We were just over the North Carolina line when the thoughts overtook me of how I was really missing Jalynn and Lacey Jo. I thought of what could have been and how I messed it up with my drinking. That's when I remembered Marie from rehab telling me that I had to follow the steps she taught while I was there, and that if I ever needed anything, to give her a call.

I stopped at a truck stop once I got through The Gorge. I took out her number that I had kept all these years and hoped she would answer and remember me. As the phone rang and was picked up, I recognized her voice as she said hello.

"Marie," I said, "this is Bobby Ray, the truck driver. Do ya remember me?"

She said, "Sure, I do. How have ya been?" I told her what had happened, and she scolded me for not following the steps and going back to my addiction. She said, "Bobby Ray, I know ya are a strong man physically, but yer mind needs to be strong as well. I know ya have the willpower to beat yer addictions."

She went through the steps with me and then we prayed. Afterwards, she said she would get a prayer line started for me. After talking to her for a while I felt a little better about the situation.

I told her thank you, she said, "You've got this," and we hung up.

I went through the steps again and tried to figure out where I had messed up. There were several instances where I failed. How could I fix my life? As these thoughts ran through my head, I started thinking, not only of Jalynn, but of my kids and what I had done to them in breaking my promise. While I drove, I drifted back to April of 1983, when Raymond Nathaniel was born.

Jalynn had just kicked me out of the house, and I was out on the road for a few months. I had tried to get her to talk to me, but she never wanted to, as she was still heartbroken. I kept on until one day, her dad answered the phone and told me that the best thing I could do was to stay out of her life. Her parents had talked her into filing for a divorce. I would lose her and everything if she went through with it. I would go out of my mind. The ranch was just a material thing that I could live without, my wife and my kids, however, I could not.

One night I called some of my ranch hands and pleaded with them to try and get her alone and convince her to talk to me. I told them I had to apologize and plead with her to let me come home. I called a few days later to check on Lacey Jo, also I had my hopes that my plan had worked. To my complete surprise, agreed to talk with me. She was however quick to let me know she was in no place to forgive me for what I had done. She agreed to meet me to discuss our future and my place in it. I told her it would take me awhile to make it back around, but I would be there as quickly as I could. She reiterated that she was only willing to talk. I was grateful for that much, at least it was a start.

I started making my way across the U. S. to make my amends. It was taking longer than I expected as broke down in Chicago, Illinois. I had to get a hotel for a few days for the repairs, so I grabbed some food and settled in for the night.

After I ate, I called to let her know of my situation and to check on Lacey Jo. Bug, one of the lady ranch hands, answered the phone, which surprised me. She said that RJ had rushed Jalynn to the hospital because she had gone into labor. Jalynn's mom and dad had followed them, and RJ's wife Ashlynn was to meet them there after she got off work.

I hung up with her and called the diner to speak with Ashlynn. She told me that Jalynn had been in earlier and confided in her that she really did love me and didn't want to go through with the divorce, but her mom and dad was pushing her to do it. She wanted me to come home and get some help so we could be a family again.

I told Ashlynn that I was coming home in a few days and was willing to do whatever it took to get her back. Ashlynn and RJ had agreed to watch Lacey Jo, and when I got there, she would keep her a couple of days so Jalynn and I could talk.

I called the hospital after we hung up and they said Jalynn was resting. They informed me that she was having complications and that they had to stop the labor. I worried about her and the baby, and I asked the nurse if I could talk to RJ. When he got on the phone, I told him that I would be there within a week, and I thanked him for agreeing to take care of Lacey Jo while Jalynn was in the hospital. He said, "No problem, brother, that's what we do, we take care of each other."

It took me just over a week to get home, and by the time I arrived, my wife was home, and I was a daddy again. This time to a baby boy. I was so excited to see her and my son, to hold them and give them both love.

We had picked out a boy and a girl name for whichever was to be born. If it had been a girl, we were going to name her Joyce Ann, and if it was a boy, we would name him Raymond Nathaniel, and call him Ray or Jr. We settled on Ray, and I was glad she kept the name we picked out together.

Once the excitement had worn off from me meeting my new son and reconnecting with Jalynn, the rest of the folks left for the night, and we finally had a chance to talk. She told me that I had hurt her more than I would ever know. That it would take a while for her to forgive me, and that I had to earn her trust back since I had lied. She said I needed to get help for myself and stop drinking. I happily agreed to that, and she said I was to also get a steady job where I would be home every night to help her raise our young'uns.

Jalynn then said that since I was back home, I would need to either stay in my truck or get a motel, because she was not ready to let me move back in.

I agreed and said I would get a room, since I would just be there for a few days at a time. I discussed with her that I couldn't come off the road just yet, but I would slowly work towards it, and we could be a family once again.

We spent a lot of time together when her parents weren't hovering over us, listening to every word we said and offering their disapproval of me being there and her for even considering working things out. It starting to get to me but luckily, my visit was short. I was only home for about a week before I had to hit the road again. Over the next few weeks, I called as often as I could when I found a pay phone to check on Jalynn, Lacey Jo, and Little Ray.

It was eight weeks before things settled down and I had enough money that I could afford to take off again. When I got home, my wife was in tears. She said she hated me for being out there on the road all the time. I told her that it wouldn't be much longer now before I could be home for good. She was upset at my decision to go back out over the road, and we had an argument. She said she wanted to go back to Pennsylvania to live with her mama and daddy. That made me furious since I was trying so hard to get us on track financially.

I told her to just give me a few weeks and I would come off the road. I told her not to overreact and think about what she was saying. I said that if she needed to go visit for a while and see her old friends, that it was fine.

Jalynn thought for a bit and settled down. She said that she would love that, and we hugged. I gave her a kiss and told her I loved her. She said she loved me, too, and we quickly laid the argument to rest.

Over the next few days, we ironed things out before I headed out on the road once again. This time, I was only supposed to be gone for two weeks while she was out visiting with her folks. My two weeks turned into three weeks, and then a month. She was so furious, and I kept telling her that it would all be worth it in the end. From that time, on it set a precedence for me of going out for a month and only coming home for a couple of days and going again. Each time was the same as we would be fine and happy, and then before I left, we would end up arguing and I would storm out the door and head to my truck. I tried to stay in touch and routed myself by the house from time to time if the load allowed. This went on for almost a year.

One day in September of 1984, I called home one night and Jalynn answered the phone crying. When I asked her what was wrong, she said she was pregnant again. I reassured her that things would be okay. In fact, things were getting better financially, and I could start shortening my time on the road. That eased her mind somewhat. Before we hung up, I told her I loved her and that I would be home soon.

With things slowing down, I was home more and more each time. I helped with Lacey Jo and Ray as much as I could while tending to matters on the ranch.

We had arguments from time to time about me being out on the road, and I told her if we were going to make it, I had to keep running like I was. I had already slowed down a good bit and I thought things were improving with us as husband and wife. That was until I got home one night in March to her to find her in a very depressed state of mind. She was in the bed, curled up in a ball, and crying her eyes out. I tried to comfort her. Against all I tried to do, she kept pushing away and trying to argue.

Finally, I had had enough, and my anger got the best of me. I found a bottle I had hidden in the barn from before and started drinking. The more I had, the angrier I got until I stormed back into the house and started throwing her clothes into a bag. I told her if she was that unhappy, that she could just leave, and I would take care of the kids.

I must have scared her because she called for Goat to come to the house, and she asked him to take her to Amberleigh's house.

I didn't remember anything more as I eventually passed out. When I woke up the next day, I yelled her name and didn't get any answer. I went out to the barn and Goat informed me of what I forgot.

I jumped in my truck to drive over there, and as expected, she refused to see me. I started pleading with her to come home and she declined, saying she was leaving me because she was scared and never wanted to see that side of me again. She said the best thing for me to do was to leave before she called the law.

I jumped back in my truck and headed down the road, thinking of my situation and trying to figure out how to get her back. Ironically, as I drove, the song "I told You So" by Randy Travis came on, and as I listened, I knew I had to go crawling back and beg her to come home.

I returned to the ranch and told the guys about the situation. That I was going back out over the road to clear my head, and I would be back. I would send money for their pay, and I offered them a bonus if they would step up and run the ranch for me. They all agreed and deep down I knew that they did that because of my Daddy. The next day, I loaded up and was on my way back to chase the long white line.

Over the next few months, I started drinking more often. I called to check on Lacey Jo and Ray a lot and to see if Jalynn had found it in her heart to forgive me. One day in June 1984, I called and when she answered, I found out that I was a daddy again. It was a girl, and Jalynn said her name was Faith Ann. She said I could keep calling and checking on them, but as of this point, she still did not forgive me and would not talk to me about anything except our kids. So, back on the road and back in the bottle I went. Mile after mile and bottle after bottle.

With the months going by so fast and eventually turning into a year, my phone calls home spread out further and further. I missed so much of my kids growing up and the time went fast by with me slipping further and further in the drinking.

I stopped at a truck stop in Iowa late one night in July of 1985, and found a spot way in the back. As I was walking from my truck to get a shower, I felt something in my back and heard a voice that said, "Don't move, give me your wallet."

I was being robbed. I guess I had enough liquid courage in me that I wasn't about to let him have what I had worked so hard for. I resisted his request and without hesitation, he pulled the trigger. I felt the round pierce my side and as I hit the ground, he grabbed my wallet and headed off between the trucks.

The shot was heard by other drivers, and they came out of their sleepers to see what had happened. They called for an ambulance. I was taken to the hospital where they immediately took me into surgery. They removed the bullet and sewed me up. Afterwards, I was admitted for observation, and I told them to call Jalynn to let her know what had happened, and I explained that that she would not talk to me.

To my surprise, she asked for me. We talked for a minute or so. She said that she had been pondering about us and the kids and that she thought that after I got discharged that I should come back to the ranch. She would meet me there when I got home and that we really needed to talk.

It took me a week for me be well enough to leave. I called and she came over and we talked all night. We confided in one another, we laughed, and we cried all through the night. As the sun came up, she said she had to go because she had to go to work. I asked if she could bring the kids over to see me and she said it would be the next day before she could make it happen.

I spent the whole day after she left helping Slim and the others out on the ranch. I was not used to the hard work and by the time the sun set, and we ate supper, I went straight to bed. The next day, she brought the kids over to see me and she introduced me to my baby girl, Faith. She was as beautiful as I expected, just like her mother. We played all day and even ate dinner together.

After dinner and with hesitation, she said if I promised to never touch a drink again, she would come back home, and we could try and work on our marriage. She said that the kids really needed their daddy.

Not knowing at this point in my life if I could keep that promise, I promised anyway and agreed without hesitation. We hugged each other tight, and she gave me one of her most passionate kisses. So, over the next week, she moved back home, and we were a family once again.

We still had some trust issues and financial issues to work on so we agreed that I would do what I did best, I hit the white line running.

We were good for a while until the loneliness of the road set in. In the summer of 1986, while in Atlanta, Georgia, a gal I knew that worked at the Petro asked if I wanted to go out on a date to see Alabama in concert. I figured I was out here, and Jalynn would never know otherwise. I agreed and we made our way to the concert. They had a new song out; the first time I heard it I loved it. The title was "Roll On," a true trucker's song and it reminded me of my own life.

It was a great concert, and when it was over, we returned to my truck where she asked if she could spend the night. I grabbed her hand and helped her up into my truck. As we were climbing up, I realized it was wrong. But I needed attention, I told myself. Once we were inside, she started rubbing on me and as she did, I was thinking about that song from the concert. It made me think of my family back home and I told her I couldn't go through with it. I explained why, and she understood.

She said, "Since I'm here, we can just snuggle up and sleep."

I agreed but instead of us sleeping together, I grabbed a blanket and climbed in the jump seat and laid my head against the window.

The next morning, she said that she enjoyed me taking her to the show, and I said likewise. After I got my fuel and coffee, I was on my way, with thoughts about the night before.

I was rolling down the interstate when over the CB, I heard a familiar voice. It was Odie. He said, "Turbo, is that you?"

I said, "Yes, where are ya at?"

He said, "I'm on your back door, ole buddy, and fix'n to blow right by ya!"

He passed me only because I let him and then I showed him what power I had and passed him back up. We were rolling along, chatting about where we had been and what we had done, not paying any attention to what was going on. Suddenly, a 4-wheeler cut in between us to exit, and when they did, they were so close that he had no time to slow down to keep from hitting them. With a quick reaction, he turned his wheel. He couldn't avoid hitting the car and the impact blew out his left side steering tire, sending his truck over onto its side. I watched as Odie was thrown out the windshield opening, hit the ground, and tumbled and slid along the shoulder.

I quickly pulled my truck over and ran back to him. I assumed he was dead, but with a check of his pulse, I found he was alive, but badly hurt and unconscious. Blood was everywhere and I could tell his legs and possibly both arms were broken. I couldn't tell where the blood was coming from so, I immobilized his head and assessed his wounds, reluctantly remembering our army training. He was injured far beyond any care I could give him. I checked on the folks in the car. They were good to go, just shaken up. I then ran back to my truck and jumped on the CB. I broke Channel 19 for an emergency and for someone to notify the police and paramedics. I returned to Odie and stayed with him until the ambulance got there. Once he was loaded up, I left.

Later that day, I called his wife to check on him. She told me that he would never be able to drive again and maybe never walk. He had a broken spine along with broken ribs and both legs, and one arm was broken. I told her to keep me informed and that I would call when I could.

I was empty and on my way to pick up another load, but because we were best friends and had history together, I decided to go to the hospital and sit with his wife in the Critical Care Unit. I would go back with her during visiting hours and let him know I was there for him and his family and that I would help in any way I could. After a few days, he showed vast improvement and they moved him to a regular room where we could see him all the time. They set him up for a few surgeries and physical therapy and his wife told me it was okay for me to leave and get back on the road. I told her if she needed me, I would stay, but she said they would be fine. I said I would be back in a few days to check on him. We hugged and said goodbye and I was on my way.

I left Georgia, headed back over Monteagle Mountain to Nashville, thinking about Odie all the way. Once I was unloaded, I got a reload heading to Florida. I did a turn and burn, and back through Atlanta I was headed. On the outskirts of the city, I saw this fella in the rain walking with a guitar on his back. I slowed my rig and stopped to pick him up. This was to be the beginning of me breaking my promise again and was the start of something worse.

He introduced himself as JB Walker and that he sang southern rock (or as he called it, biker music) and that he was headed to interview with a fellow by the name of David Allan Coe, being held at a well-known biker bar called the Iron Horse Saloon in Daytona Beach, Florida. As we rode along, we talked about life, places we had been, and things we had done, good and bad. I told him my story and he offered me friendly advice on life and living. He told me one thing I will always remember: "Live each day like it is your last and roll hard."

We were halfway to our destination, and I asked if he could tune an old guitar of mine. I didn't know how since I was just learning. He asked what kind it was, and I told him it was a1964 Gibson Country and Western that had been in my family for years. I told him the story of how my mother bought it for my dad before he went to fight in the war. How she had saved as much as she could and paid less than one hundred dollars for it, which was a lot back then. My daddy loved that guitar, and I could still hear him play as he and Mama sang gospel hymns.

JB climbed in the back and laid the case on the bunk. I heard him sigh and he said to me, "Brother, this is a beautiful girl ya got here." He picked a few strings and in minutes, he had it sounding right as rain. He played a few songs, and I could tell he was very good, and that he had a future in the music scene. When he was tired, he asked if he could sleep for a while. I said he could make himself at home. As I heard him rustling through my snack box, I knew he was doing just that.

Just before we hit the city, I woke him up. Climbing into the jump seat he said, "Thanks, brother, I needed that."

I found a place in the parking lot big enough to accommodate my rig and trailer. We threw on some cologne and made our way through the crowd and rows of all kinds of motorcycles. As we did, we were getting some awkward stares from the rough looking folks outside. I stopped to admire this one bike and he pulled me away.

"Ya might not want to do that, they are particular about their bikes," he warned.

We crossed the street to the main bar area, and I realized I was in as strange a place as an old country boy and a truck driver could be. I didn't fit. There were motorcycles and rough dudes everywhere, with tattoos all over, and I must admit I was intimidated.

After a few moments, an attractive lady came up to me and asked if that was my rig out there. I replied yes, and she asked if she could see inside. I said yes, but only after JB Walker's show, which also featured a feller named Dustin Lee Benefield.

We had a few beers waiting for the band, and she introduced me to a lot of the people in the bar. I came to find out that even though they were not what I was used to, they were some awesome folks. I started to feel at ease and by the time the show started, I had made some new friends.

The announcer introduced JB and she led me to the stage. We cheered him on, and it seemed the whole bar was loving his music as we were. His set lasted for thirty minutes. Then Dustin did a 30-minute show. I was feeling the effect of my beers and I knew I was wrong for doing so, because I loved Jalynn. But I couldn't help myself.

I had an uneasy feeling in the pit of my stomach, but I went on and asked her if she was ready to look inside my truck. The woman grabbed my hand and led me towards the door in a hurry.

JB and Dustin caught me on the way out and both wished me luck. As I took her out to show her my truck, she said it was sexy and shiny with all the lights. I opened the door and helped her climb inside.

She said, "This is so cozy, would you like to snuggle with me?"

We laid back on the bed and started exploring each other's bodies and things got heated very quickly. I switched off my red bunk lights and the rest is history.

The next morning as we climbed out my rig and faced the lingering partiers from the night before, one girl said, "Looks like JB was not the only big hit last night."

JB and I said goodbye, and as I drove away, I heard him say, "Roll hard, brother!" I later learned that he started his own band called JB Walker and the Cheap Whisky Band. They were extremely popular among the biker scenes.

After that, I started making my way home. Heading back through Nashville, I stopped at the T/A for the weekend. I called Jalynn to check on her and the kids, and the whole time, I was scared and shaking at what I had done. I tried to ignore the fact that I had cheated on my wife and hoped that she would never find out. After we hung up, I called to check on Odie, then I went into the truck stop for supper.

While eating, I started talking to a couple who owned their own trucking company. They called it Diato Trucking short for (Damn I am tired of trucking). He introduced himself as Jason Baxter (The Lunatic) and his wife Angie Baxter as (The Drifter Queen). After we ate, we all headed back to our trucks, we exchanged numbers and went on our way. Little did I know through the years we would become close friends. I then made my way on to the house with the memories of my journey buried in my mind.

I was deep in my thoughts of my horrible past and was abruptly startled as my CB came on. Channel 19 came to life, and I heard another trucker say, "breaker one-nine, how bout you, northbound, you got your ears on?"

I returned and said, "Come on back, driver, I copy ya, old buddy."

He said there was a car on the side of the road. The rain was coming down so hard that I could barely see the asphalt and within a couple of minutes, I saw the flashers of the car distorted by the rain. I moved over as truck drivers do and slowed down to try not to drench them with my passing. As I passed, a man soaking wet was trying to flag me down and I noticed a woman laying across the back seat. She, too, was getting wet. I knew something was wrong, but I was too fast to stop so. I flashed my lights to let him know I saw them, and I hoped he knew I would return by me doing so. I slowed down and hit the next exit and backtracked as quickly as I could to see if I could help. After I made my way back around, I pulled up behind them with my flashers on to warn others to move over and put my headlights on bright so I could see better in the dark and assess their situation. I walked up to see what the problem was.

To my surprise the woman was screaming and the man who was in a panic told me she was in labor. He had rushed home and forgotten to put gas in the tank. They ran out and no one would stop and now the baby was not waiting any longer. I told him to relax that I would help as best as I could. I told him to keep her as calm and that I would be right back, as I was going to use my radio to call for help. I went to my truck and put out the breaker 19 emergency message over the CB. I told them where we were and if any trucker had their ears on, to keep their eyes peeled for a police officer or someone that could help.

Returning to the car and hearing the lady scream and cry even more, it was clear that the baby was coming whether we were ready or not. I took my rain jacket and put it over the door and the top of the car to shield her from the rain and I tried to calm the lady as her husband assured her of my intentions. He held her hand and wiped her head with a water-soaked rag that I had gotten for her from my truck, along with a handful of my clean t-shirts. I asked her if she needed anything and she said in a hurtful cry, "Something for the pain."

I ran back to my truck and grabbed my old mason jar that was now about half empty that I kept for my own emergencies. I returned and made her take a couple of good sips to help ease the pain. I guess her husband needed it too because he finished it off and handed me back an empty jar.

I was nervous as I looked again to assess her condition. I asked her if she was feeling a little bit better and she said she was. I could see the hair on the baby's head, and I knew it would be just a matter of minutes until she would deliver her baby. I prayed a little prayer, and as did, I felt peace and the voice of God say, "I've got you, my son!"

I had delivered calves before, so I figured it was kinda the same process. I took a deep breath and told her to push. I guess God answered my prayer and he was right on time, because as she was relaxing before the next contraction, the rain was coming to an end, and I heard sirens in the distance.

I looked up and said, "Thank ya, Lord."

She was ready to push, and just before the next one, there was a paramedic by my side to take over. I was happy to let him. I told him that I had given her a couple of big sips of moonshine to relax her which he disagreed with, but what was I supposed to do? I had to ease her pain.

I stayed back in the distance during the birth even though they said I was okay to leave. I stayed until the baby boy was born, wrapped up in my shirt, he was crying as they laid him in his mother's arms. Then he stopped crying, and I knew he was safe.

I thanked God for his miracle and as they were being loaded into the ambulance, they both thanked me for stopping and doing what I could. I guessed they noticed my big belt buckle with had BR on it. He asked what the "B" stood for, and I told him Bobby. As they were leaving, the father said they had agreed to name the baby boy Bobby, which made me proud of the deed I had done.

After the excitement, I needed a cigarette. I climbed back in my old truck, and I sat there on the side of the road, in no hurry to move. While thinking of the miracle I had just witnessed, I was saddened and disappointed in myself at the fact that I had not been there by my own wife's side and witnessed my own children's birth. I started to cry as thoughts filled my head of all the things I had missed all these years of being out here. I prayed that one day my family would forgive me and for God to not let me ever get in the shape that I was in.

I gathered my thoughts and was on my way to deliver the load. I was more than glad to get that load delivered and find my next one. Unsuccessful for the next load, I decided to head to the truck stop and search for one the following morning.

Cash and I settled in, and we ate our dinner. After another unsuccessful call to Jalynn, I told Amberleigh where I was and to give Jalynn the message. I returned to my truck, I said my prayers, and Cash and I went off to sleep.

15

PROMISES BROKEN

Savannah, GA– Daytona Beach, FL -Virginia Beach, Va

THE NEXT MORNING, I WAS LYING IN MY BED, HAVING A cigarette and a cup of coffee, and thinking about the night before. God answered my prayers, even though I had broken my promise to him. I was unworthy of even praying for forgiveness. But I knew from reading the bible that he loves us no matter our faults. He is always there to pick up the pieces of our lives and has the power to mend them back together when we shatter them beyond our repair.

Suddenly, there was a knock on my door which got my immediate attention. To my surprise it was the manager of the truck stop. Jalynn had called there since I had let Amberleigh know where I was. I had not heard my phone ring because after all the excitement from the night before I had forgotten to charge it. The manager said she was crying and that she asked if they would find me and have me call her back immediately. She told them to tell me that she was in the emergency room at our local hospital. I walked into the driver's lounge and called the hospital and was directed to her bedside phone. When she answered, she was crying. I was trying to settle her down but because she was so upset, and her voice was distorted by her cries. I couldn't quite make out what she was saying, however, I did understand her when she said the most important words I could ever hear, "I Love Ya!" My heart was filled with joy, and I said, "Oh, baby, I love ya, too!

When she was calm and I could understand her, she asked where I was. I told her I was in Savannah. She told me she had been in a wreck and was in the hospital. She asked if I could make my way back because she would be in there a while and that she needed me. Without hesitating I said yes, but it would take me a few days because I had loads lined up and had to make sure that I took care of them because I had already been paid for them on a contract deal. After we hung up, I started calling my contacts to see if I could shuffle the loads around. They did find me another good paying load that was going to Virginia Beach that would put me on a better route to get home. They said that I could return and complete the contracted loads after I got things situated back at home, but it didn't pick up until Monday. I went and found me a spot at a local truck stop and called to check on Jalynn and to tell what was going on.

She was still in pain, and she told me that her mom was flying out to take care of her. I felt a little easier knowing she would be taken care of before I got home. I told her I loved her, and I would be home as soon as I could, and I told her to hang in there. She understood as she always had even if she knew I was lying or not.

As I climbed back into the truck, I let the fact that it was only Friday night slip my mind. What was I going to do all weekend, confined to my truck? I decided since I was so close to Daytona Beach, I would go see if my old friend JB Walker was still hanging out at the Iron Horse Saloon.

I dropped my trailer and bobtailed down and found a place to park. I made it to the saloon earlier than expected and before they opened. I went over to the Waffle House and grabbed something to eat, and of course something for Cash since he loved their food, especially the chicken and pork chops. I returned to my truck and after he was fed, we relaxed, and I must have dozed off because when I awoke, it was dusk. I decided I would head over to the Iron Horse Saloon and see my old friend. Of course, I would not be having any alcohol to drink since I knew what would happen. However, it was a good atmosphere, and the people and conversations were good over there.

The music was loud as always, and I met some of the unfamiliar staff and bikers. It had been years since I had been there. They had added more bars to the place and a bigger stage. They even had a bar and seats

216

above the original place up in the trees and you could really see the stage from there. When I asked about JB, the bartender told me that he was overseas on a USO tour for the troops and said that he had been doing that for some time now. She pointed to a section of the saloon and said I could buy CDs of his latest recordings along with other bands that had performed there, which I did to support my old friend. I figured since he wasn't there, I would walk across the street to my truck and rest until morning. Then I would head back to my truck.

As I was leaving, I recognized a familiar but aged face by the bar. It was my overnight companion from years ago. As I approached, she also recognized me and instantly came running for a friendly hug and a kiss. We conversed and she of course flirted for a while. She told me that she had settled down for a bit and got married to the man who was the old manager and a legend at this saloon. She asked if I remembered him from before. To my amazement, I did. She said he had passed away the previous year and she was now the bar manager.

I told her the story of my life and what had happened. She offered me advice and overnight companionship. I think hers was fueled by wanting to relive our night of passion that we shared years ago. I apologetically thanked her and told her that I could not take her up on the offer. After about an hour of us catching up on old times and her giving me the latest news around the saloon, I heard the familiar sound of my buddy Dustin Lee. I walked to the stage and stood there while he did his set, offering occasional approval of his songs.

After he was done, I started to head back to the bar and he stopped me and said, "Hey, man, good to see you finally decided to come around."

I told him that I had been too busy to stop in over the years.

We talked for a few and then he said, "Well, old friend, I got to get back up there."

We shook hands and he walked back to the stage.

I returned to my truck and climbed into the sleeper. Cash and I slept all night and most of the day. Once we got up and took care of our business, I went to the Waffle House for coffee.

I climbed back in the truck, and we headed north to Savannah. When we got to the truck stop, I went in to get a shower. When I returned, Cash wasn't in the truck. He had let himself out. I hollered for him, and he did not come, so I went looking for him. After a few minutes, I found him at this rig with a woman and her dog. She said that he came up to her and wanted to play with her dog Misty. I figured as much. He was such a womanizer when it came to lady dogs.

I talked with the woman for a little while for Cash to have some fun running around with his new lady friend. He is such a trooper it does him good to get out and run around with other dogs. I was finally able to pull him away from his newfound friends and we walked back to the truck and were off to bed for the night.

The next day I spent time cleaning and polishing Ole Reba Up while Cash was out roaming in between his naps. I called the hospital several times to check on Jalynn. I felt sorry for her for being in there and me not being there. I was ashamed because I was the reason that I wasn't. I was happy however that she was talking to me finally. Before we hung up each time, she said she loved me, and as I always did, I told her that I was sorry and that I loved her, too.

I made one final call before I went to bed for the night. We talked for some time and then she said in a kind of an upset tone, "I guess ya forgot again as ya have so many times in the past, and I had hoped that ya wouldn't have forgotten this time."

I thought, *"What in the world is she talking about?"* I racked my brain for a minute and then it dawned on me. It was our anniversary. I said I was sorry, and I tried to make excuses for forgetting. There was no excuse. I should have remembered. She said I had forgotten it so many times and that I've also forgotten her birthdays as well as our kids'.

"Not to mention more of the important thangs and days ya have missed be'n out on the road." She reminded me that I wasn't there for none of their births, school plays, sports, graduations, and I even missed their weddings. RJ and Goat had to walk my girls down the aisle in my place when Lacey married Doc and Faith married Hoss. I even missed Ray and Gracie get'n married. I had never heard her swear before, but she said, "Damn it! Bobby Ray, ya even missed the births of our grandbabies!"

I thought about what she said, and it really got me angry at myself. It made me sick to my stomach and seeing myself from her point of view.

I said, "Wow, honey, I never really thought about how much this road has deprived me of in my life with ya and the kids. I am a sorry husband and daddy."

She said, "No, ya are not. We know that ya love us, and it is the life of a truck driver that did it all. Ya were just do'n what ya thought was best to make a living for us. But I will tell ya that you should have called us on those special days. Instead of wait'n until we brought it up when ya would call or return home. We still love ya and we understand that ya have a problem, and we know that ya can fix it."

I agreed with her, and we hung up. I went on to bed, but I laid there most of the night thinking and praying.

The next morning, I headed over to the stockyard to get loaded up. Once I was buttoned up in the back, I headed that rig north towards Virginia Beach. Making my way to the big road, I put the hammer down and was rolling hard.

While I was chasing the line, I was once more in deep thought of my wife, wondering if she was okay, if *we* were okay together. While I was thinking I thanked God that she would even talk to me. The fact that she said she loved me put me on cloud nine.

I recalled from my memory the last time God answered my prayers and forgave me of my sins. A time when I thought things were going great after we had gone through a rough patch on the ranch.

It all started some years back after I had returned home from a two-month run on the road, only stopping by the house for a quick day's rest. I found out that the ranch was not doing as well as I thought. I had been running good freight and making sure to send money home, but I guess it wasn't enough. The economy was hitting bottom, as it had in the past, but Jalynn didn't want me to worry about them or the ranch while I was over the road.

While she was working at the diner, I worked on getting the ranch back where it needed to be. It seemed that my plan would work out for the ranch and my family, but I was wrong. A storm came through and destroyed our feed crop and garden, leaving us with the reality that we wouldn't have anything to feed the cattle once our stockpile was depleted. Nor would we have vegetables to can and put up for the winter. I had to go to the bank and refinance the ranch for the money to pay the hands that had not quit. I had to get hay from an outside source and had to get more cattle, mend the fences that the storm destroyed, and take care of other problems around the place.

Once those things were attended, I had extra money to pay our ranch hands a bonus for sticking around. I even hired a few more hands. Tank and Rocky came to work for me, and I called some that had worked for us before, and they said they would help when they could but weren't going to give up their other jobs and that was ok with me, I just needed the help. During that time, I had mended things with my sister, Jacky, and I asked Slim to come back and help me. He didn't want to, but Jacky talked him into it. I didn't tell Jalynn I had to refinance because I didn't want to stress her out even more.

After three more weeks everything was in place and doing good. Jalynn said that if I came off the road, she would cut her hours back at the diner, and we could all be a family once again. Aware of the ranch's situation and the new loan hanging over my head, I agreed.

Money was tight but things were going well. We ran the ranch for about three and a half years, and I watched my kids grow into young adults. Before long I had them all riding horses like pros. I guess it was in their blood too. Jr. was even learning to drive the tractor and help get hay and feed to the stock. He was even able to drive my truck around the ranch and hook up the trailer and back it into the loading corral. The girls we learning to cook with their mama and when they could sneak off, they were with their daddy at the stables. I was a proud daddy of three wonderful kids.

Before I knew it, Lacey Jo was sixteen and driving herself around. One day I caught her and Doc flirting with one another. I wanted to tell them to cut it out, but I let it slide. The next thing I knew they had started dating. I let it be known I was not happy about this at all. There was a bit of an age gap, and it just didn't sit well. I told them they had to break up and I was about to fire him.

Lacey Jo said, "Daddy, hearts know love, age is only a number. I love him, Daddy. Ya know Doc is a good man. Can ya just be happy er us?"

She was right. After all, this was her life. I gave her a hug as I whispered in her ear, "Okay, baby, but if he hurts ya, he will answer to me!"

When it was time to take the yearly trip to the sale and pick up a new herd, I took Ray along. We hauled a few loads for other ranchers either to their ranches, death row, or to the slaughterhouse before going back and picking up our stock. I took Jr. so he could see how it was done so that one day he might take over for his old man. I showed him things to look out for when choosing stock and introduced him to the right people to know when conducting business.

On the way home one night I let him drive even though he was only 14 years old, and boy was he nervous. I told him I was right beside him and that he knew how to handle the rig. Within minutes he was shifting and driving like he had been trucking for years. I took the chance to show him how to slip gears and never even use the clutch. He liked that a whole lot better.

We returned to the ranch with our herd and put them out to pasture. Jr. said, "Thanks fer take'n me with ya, Daddy. I enjoyed our time together."

I gave him a huge bear hug and told him I loved him, and I was proud of him. I said one day he could do it by himself and I would retire to my recliner.

He laughed and said, "Daddy, ya ain't never gonna quit ranch'n. Ya love it too much."

I threw my gloves at him and said, "Ya got that right, boy."

As I was putting stuff away and he had gone to park the rig, Faith Ann came running as she usually did for her fair share of love from her daddy. I picked her up and swung her in the air as she hugged my neck tight.

She gave me a kiss on the cheek saying, "Daddy, I love ya so much and I miss ya when ya are gone. Mama is mad at ya fer miss'n Sissy's graduation."

I had totally let it slip my mind as I had been out with my boy having a good time. We made our way up to the house where Jalynn was fixing dinner. I kissed and hugged her tight and told her that I loved her so much and how great of a job Jr. had done and I even let him drive. She scolded me and told me that her son was not gonna be a truck driver.

I just smiled and said as I walked away, "It's in his blood."

To my surprise none of them said anything about the graduation. I thought, *"What the heck, what are they up to?"*

As I entered the den, Lacey and Doc were sitting a little closer than I approved of, and I let them know very quickly. Lacey jumped up and ran into the kitchen with her mama.

Doc floored me then when he said, "Mr. James, I love Lacey. I would like to ask yer permission to take her hand in marriage."

My heart sank deep in my stomach from his request. Jalynn came into the doorway and waited for my response. When I said no, she said, "Honey, they're in love, and ya know he is good to her."

After some arguing and deliberating, they talked me into accepting and agreeing they could get married. It broke my heart. I was gonna lose my little girl.

While we were sitting at the table eating and discussing their future, I told Doc that it would take some time, but I would have them a house built on the ten acres that I had set aside for each of the kids. He asked if it was alright with me that he had been saving his money and would purchase a new mobile home and put it on the land. I thought, *"Now there is a young man with a good head on his shoulders."*

I respected him more at that point. However, as I sat there staring and my bowl of buttermilk and cornbread and onion, I thought, *"Well, now I have a wedding to pay for along with everything else.*

I knew that I had to do what had to be done to keep up with it. I pondered it a while and one night while we were lying in bed I turned to Jalynn and told her that I needed to go back over the road. She got upset and asked why. I said I wanted to make sure we had enough money to set Lacey Jo and Doc up for a good go of things. She thought for a while and agreed with me, although I still didn't tell her about the loan.

With it settled I went back out and started running the white line in hopes that everything would work out for the better. I only had six months to make a go at it before the wedding. I rolled hard for those months and the plan worked, and I was heading home for the wedding.

I was in Toledo, Ohio, when my truck started to overheat and suddenly, steam and coolant was going everywhere. I pulled over to check it out and found that my radiator had a huge crack in it. I had to get towed to a diesel shop and after their inspection, they told me it would be a few days before they could get a new one in and have me rolling. I was so upset. I found a motel and called home to let them know of the situation. Jalynn was so mad at me that she started yelling and blaming me for everything. I told her that we could change the wedding, and she said, "It is in two days, and we have family and friends that have come a long way!"

I told her I was sorry, that I didn't plan for this to happen. She said, "Well, since ya chose to run the road, I guess it is your fault." She said that Goat or RJ would give her away.

"And ya can just stay there by yerself and thank about what a mess ya have created," she said. "Oh, and by the way, ya will just have to figure out how ya are gonna apologize to our daughter. She will never forgive ya fer this. It is her special day, and she expects ya to be here." And then she hung up.

I ended up being down for a week and the wedding went as planned without me being there. I was upset and so was Lacey Jo. I tried to call her and apologize but she would not talk to me nor would her mama. I was finally rolling again and headed home. When I got there neither one of them would even have anything to do with me. I figured with some time they would get over it. Eventually they came around and everything was smoothed out but not forgotten as they were quick to throw it up in my face.

Just after a few months of them being married Doc came across a good deal on a bigger plot of land and a house. He moved my baby girl off the ranch to live their own life. He still worked for me. While I was working in the barn one day Lacey Jo came in with her mama and when I turned around, I saw the same glow that Jalynn had had on her face from years ago. She smiled and hugged my neck and said, "Daddy, ya are gonna be a pawpaw."

Over the next few months, Jalynn and I showed Lacey how to keep up with the books so she would have a job, since they were about to become parents themselves. We were all excited. I stayed home for a while. With the hands at the ranch and Slim there to run things, and the ladies looking after the books, we were in good shape. Then I returned to the road once more.

The ranch was running like clockwork over the next few years as we were a happy family even though I was gone a lot. Jalynn would go out with me from time to time as she had done in the past. She always said that it was her vacation away from the ranch, but I knew it was her way of keeping me out of trouble. When she was around, I could do nothing wrong. She kept me on the straight and narrow. However, she could only last a week or so then we had to head back home. She loved to see the country and experience the mountains, but she never liked coming down the steep grades and she would always climb in the back to hide her fear. Plus, she complained about the ride being too rough and the bunk was too hard.

She always said, "I don't see why ya like this life so much."

I would always reply, "It is in my blood, baby."

We were doing well for ourselves, and except for a few health problems and minor issues we were prospering. My kids grew up. Ray graduated and married his high school sweetheart Gracie. He got his CDL's and was running the local runs. Faith Ann graduated and married Hoss and they moved off the ranch and gave us eight more grandkids between the three of them.

We were doing fine until the vet checked the herd just before we were to go to market and said that most of them had a disease and could not be sold. He said it was best that we kill them all to get rid of it to keep it from spreading to the rest of the head. We isolated them and Ray and a few of the others dug a huge hole over in the far back of the ranch in the unused pasture where we could kill and bury them to save the rest of the heard. I hated shooting them with several of them being my prize stud bulls.

This hit the ranch hard as we were fixing to go to the auction. I was depending on the money to repay the loan from refinancing the ranch which I had kept a secret from everyone all this time. I was paying it with the petty cash that I would save for it and pay when I came home. However, this time the loss was too great as the market had fallen way too low and I had to break the news to Jalynn. She was furious with me for doing what I did and lying about it and not telling her. She said she would go talk to the bank and ask her parents for the money and I told her not to as they already hated me as it was. I told her I would let some of the help go and cut back on other things and go out for longer runs and come home when I could and earn the money myself. We argued and I said I would do what I had to do to save the ranch. I kept a few of the hands and sold some equipment and sold off the rest of the herd.

Because the ranch was headed for foreclosure and against Jalynn's wishes, I hit the road for a three-month trip. I had been out for a month, running hard, when I had the notion that I needed a drink or two of whisky to ease my mind. Since I needed a break anyway, I stopped at a roadside bar to have a drink. It ended up being a binge and I had trouble getting started that Monday. I even headed off in the wrong direction and then ended up on a two-lane road while trying to get turned around. It was a chore, but once I made it, I was back on the road.

Rolling steady for two more days, the urge to drink hit me again. This time it was three days before I was able to drive again.

I rolled down the road for a month until I reached the edge of a small town in Arizona where I found a little bar. After a few cold beers, I was feeling good, and I got me a bottle of whisky. I went to the truck to drink, and I got to remembering that I still had a stash of cocaine tucked away from years back. I grabbed the little bag from my secret hiding place and I had me a couple of lines. After a few minutes, I was feeling great, but the mixture of cocaine and whisky hit me hard, and it was lights.

I do not remember anything after that until the next morning when the local yokel sheriff knocked on my door and woke me up. He could smell the whisky and even though I wasn't drunk, he took me in and impounded my rig. I had to call home and break the news to Jalynn that I had broken my promise and the fact that I thought I could hide it. She was not too forgiving of my actions. She yelled at me and then said she was done with me and for me not to even worry about coming home, because I was no longer welcome.

I sat for a week in that small city-jail cell until I was released. I walked to the T/A since my rig was still impounded.

That evening, I sat on the curb outside the entrance with my head in my hands, trying to figure my life out. That is when I heard a voice from behind me say, "Hey, son, what's yer trouble?"

I said, "Nuthin' ya can help with."

He said, "How about a good ear to listen to ya? Get'n thangs off yer chest can help more than ya thank."

I lifted my head with tears rolling down my cheeks to see a slender older man in his 50's with grey, thinning hair and glasses. He sat down

225

beside me and asked my name.

"Bobby Ray," I said in a muffled voice.

He said, "My name is H.M. Stell. They call me Murphy." He took out a small metal can of Bruton snuff and poured his cheek full. "I tell ya, son, aint not'n better than Jesus, a good woman, and a good dip of snuff."

We sat in silence for a few moments and then I began my story.

"Ya see, buddy, back some years ago, just after my first daughter was born, my wife and I were emotional wrecks, and I got drunk and made her so scared of me that she left for what seemed to be an eternity but was only about 6 months. She eventually forgave me, and we worked things out, and she came back home. But only after I had promised to never drink again. It was okay until the finances started catch'n up with us and I had to go back out over the road. While I was out run'n the road, I got lonely and ended up cheat'n on her a couple of times. I was drink'n and do'n drugs, too. I even spent time in jails and prison for all the stuff I done. I think I was do'n it to keep my mind off my life."

Murphy nodded and listened on.

"And just a few days ago I stopped at the bar just outside the city limits to have a drink. One thing led to another, and I took a bottle to my truck and found a little cocaine that I had hidden years before. The next thing I knew I was woken up by the sheriff and he hauled me in and impounded my rig. The thing that hit me the most is that I had to call my wife and tell her. She told me not to bother coming home. So now here I sit with my life torn to pieces."

Murphy said, "How about let's take a walk. I got some'n I want you to see."

We wandered around the parking lot for a while until we came to his rig. He said, "This is my truck."

It looked to be a clunker of an old International Transtar Eagle. It was faded with rust patches here and there. I thought, *"What the heck is so special about this truck?"* Then he opened the hood. The engine was as clean as a whistle. Then he started the old truck, and it purred like a lion. He showed me the interior and it was just as clean as the engine.

"Ya see, driver," he said, "it ain't what is on the outside that counts. It is what is inside that matters the most. You need to look at your inward self and fix that first. Then everythang else would work out in time."

He didn't seem to have much of an education, but he quoted all of chapter four from 2 Corinthians by heart. He said he and his wife Bertha Mae were Christians, born-again children of God.

"And God puts his children where he wants them. That means he has led me to ya because he seen that another one of his children was in need. Do you believe in God? Are you saved?"

I said yes, I believed and was saved. But I was not where I needed to be with God. He said that Jesus said that he would never leave nor forsake us. All I had to do was reach out and take hold of his hand and let him back into my heart. We walked to the rear of his bobtail truck where he showed me a huge, faded painting of a white dove outline that had a purple cross in the middle and under it. I read the word "forgiven."

"Ya see, when ya get out of God's will, all ya have to do is call on his holy name and ask for forgiveness and ya will be forgiven," Murphy said. He quoted more Scriptures from the Bible to cover that part as we walked around to the other side of his truck. He opened the door and introduced me to his wife Bertha Mae who was sitting in the passenger seat reading her Bible by the dome light. She was just as nice as he was. She said she went with him everywhere.

We stood there and talked for a while, and he asked if I would go with him to meet a friend, and I agreed. We made our way back to the store and to my surprise, we headed into the Truckers' Chapel.

After a moment, a minister came out and they got to talking like they were old friends. As they talked, I could hear music in the background. I don't remember exactly what happened next, but I remember this song playing that mentioned going from the bottle to the cross. As I listened my heart began to break, and tears were rolling down my cheeks again. Another song started playing and I listened to the words. "Don't turn away" is said, and after it was over, the pressure of my situation broke me down. The conviction I was under hit me hard as it felt like I was sweating, and my heart was beating out of my chest.

Murphy heard my sobbing and turned and asked if he could pray with me. I didn't respond; I just hit the altar with him and his friend right there beside me, each with a hand on my shoulders. I poured my heart out and pleaded for Jesus to save my soul and help me through my situation. After what seemed to be an eternity, I felt yet another hand on

227

my shoulder that was not of either of the other two men that had knelt with me to pray. At that moment, I felt a peace like I had never known come over me. In my heart, I knew then that God had heard my prayers. I was once again forgiven and renewed in my faith in Christ, and everything would be all right. I thought to myself, *I wish my mama was here so I could tell her the news and let her know her prayers were answered.* But she was probably dancing all over heaven, shouting and praising God and spreading the news.

When we left there, I was a brand-new man, and I told Murphy I was sorry I didn't get to meet his friend. He said that the man I was talking to was just the minister of the chapel, that as I knelt there at the altar, I had indeed met his friend as I prayed and gave my life to him.

As he was about to leave, he reached in his pocket and handed me some money. "Here, son, get ya something to eat and tomorrow go get yer truck out and head home to yer family."

I thanked him and we hugged and shook hands, and he was on his way. He disappeared into the darkness of the night fog like an angel.

I had to call Jalynn and tell her what happened. She was happy to hear the news but said it would take more than just my words to prove that I had changed. I said I will do whatever it takes. I slept in the chapel that night as I had nowhere to go. The next day I went downtown and got my truck and headed home, as Murphy had instructed me. That is where I would stay put for years to come; being a husband and a daddy to our kids was to be my new life.

By the time I came back to reality, I was rolling across the Virginia state line, and it was already dark with fog was rolling in. The snow was coming down pretty good and had already covered the road when I just happened to see the faint flashers of a car. I thought they were going slow because of the weather, but as I got closer to investigate, I seen that they were on the side of the road and the hood was up. I eased my rig over in front of them and got out to see if they were okay.

It was an elderly couple and their engine had overheated. I grabbed my flashlight so I could see if I could offer any help. While looking at the situation with my light, I seen that the heater hose had busted. Since I kept spare parts and junk in my truck, I grabbed two clamps and a small piece of pipe, two jugs of coolant, and spliced the hose. Within minutes, I had them all fixed up. He asked how much he owed me and said nothing. He thanked me and went on our way to the big city, and I found the mechanic shop next to the truck stop. I made sure the couple was okay when I left them at the mechanic's and told him there were several hotels around.

I left and found my own parking spot next door at the T/A and called to let Jalynn know where I was. I could tell she was still upset but excited at the same time. I told her that I would be home in a few days that everything was going to be okay. I knew she liked for me reassure her. I told her I was going to eat and go to bed.

"I love ya, babydoll," I said.

"I love ya, too, Cowboy," she replied.

We hung up and I lit a cigarette and sat there for a few. Trucks had begun to get off the road to get out of the weather. I went in to wash up and grab supper for Cash and myself.

Cash and I ate our supper and went to the sleeper to get some rest. We were tired from the days running and we could not deliver until the next morning. I was lying there and there was a knock on my door. I thought it was a lot lizard at first, but the trucking industry had worked hard to get rid of that kind of nonsense, including human trafficking. I heard the knock again and heard the voice of that frail old man say, "Driver, are ya asleep?"

I hollered and told him to hang on. I put on my pants and hopped up front into the driver's seat and rolled down the window. He said that he just wanted me to know that he appreciated everything I had done for them, and he wouldn't take no for an answer when he handed me some money. He said they had gotten a room for the night and would be out of the weather and warm because of my kindness. I took the folded bills and laid it on the dashboard. I thanked him and reached out and shook his hand, and he turned and walked away. I had me another smoke and as I sat there, I unfolded the money and counted five one-dollar bills. I asked God to bless that lil' old couple and get them to wherever they were traveling safely.

16
THE NEW LIFE

Virginia Beach, VA – Chicago, IL- Billings, OK – Fargo, OK

EARLY THE NEXT MORNING, I WALKED OVER TO THE T/A and had breakfast. After I fed Cash his usual T/A meal of two pork chops and a piece of chicken, I called Jalynn to see how she was feeling. When she answered, she was crying and said that she was scared that I would go back to my old ways. I assured her that I would not and that with her love and support and a few changes I would not hurt her ever again. That we would figure it out together when I got home.

She calmed down a bit and said, "Bobby Ray, I have loved ya since that night in the hotel when we were snuggle'n, and ya had yer arms around me. I was thinking to myself that this is what I wanted. A strong man that could handle anything, yet with gentle hands that would hold me when I was scared and a heart that would love me through it all. I really miss the man I fell in love with. I want to feel that way again."

I started crying and I said, "I do, too, babydoll. I know we can have that feel'n again once I get back home. Ya will see. We just have to pray and trust God and get back in church."

She agreed and we talked about what else we needed to do when I got there. After a few minutes the doctor came in and she had to get off the phone. I told her I would let her go for now but not forever. We hung up and I had a good feeling.

After I had gotten my fuel and coffee, I made my way to the delivery. After I delivered to the livestock auction, I was waiting around until the auction was over to see if there was anybody that would need a load hauled out. I sat there for a better part of the day just watching the event. Once it was over, I walked back to my truck and put my for-hire sign in front of my truck for advertisement. About 30 minutes went by and I was approached by this fella in a fancy suit. He asked me which way I would like to go. I told him I was trying to head west so I could get some home time. He said he would pay extra if I was willing to go up to Chicago and deliver and then reload and head to Ft. Collins, Colorado, with two other stops in between. I agreed to the deal with the rancher to take his purchases to his farm on the outskirts of Chicago. He paid me right there on the spot and immediately after our conversation I pulled into the loading shoot and got loaded. Once everything was taken care of, Cash and I headed west out of the city.

Once I hit the big road, I put it to the floor so I could make good time. I was feeling good knowing that Jalynn would welcome me with open arms, and I would not leave her anymore. While traveling the almost straight road with the sun in front of me, I thought to myself how I wish my life had taken a straight line instead of all over the place.

As I drove, my mind wondered back over my past. I thought about how over the span of the last few years things were great, until my health caught up with me, and one day while I was home and working out on the ranch, Turbo Jr, along with the other ranch hands, were out mending fences. It was getting late and everyone stayed to help. It was hot and I wasn't feeling so great anyway. I was sweating more than usual and there was a slight twinge in my ribs and a pain starting to shoot down my left arm. I was worn out, but I kept going because it had to be done.

While we were working, I was getting more and more exhausted and I felt something hit me in my chest. I yelled for Ray as I fell to my knees in pain and then I passed out. When I came to myself, I was being loaded into the back of my truck and I could see Faith and Jalynn were crying. I passed back out and then when I awoke again, I was in the ICU.

231

Jalynn was there holding my hand and there were wires all over me. I was out of it and when I tried to talk, I realized that I couldn't speak because there was a tube in my mouth and down my throat. When I squeezed Jalynn's hand, she screamed in excitement. Immediately the doctors came rushing in to see what the commotion was about. They checked me out and then once they seemed to be satisfied, they informed me that I had had a massive heart attack and that I would need surgery to repair my heart. This led to a double bypass to fix the problem. My stay in the hospital lasted about two weeks and then I was headed home for eight weeks of what would be a painful recovery.

Once I was home, the hard reality set in and I had to face the fact that my life as I knew it was over. I had to quit driving a truck altogether, which I knew would put us under financial pressure and cause a hardship and would put tension between Jalynn and me. I had to start a strict diet of no salt; man, was I miserable.

We didn't know what we were going to do. Turbo Jr. said he could take over and do the hauls since he had his CDL's and worked for a local company. He took over for a few years and I just worked around the ranch as much as I could. We were still just barely getting by. We had cut everything back to the bare minimum, even the help. We were slowly going under and sinking deep in debt.

Just when I thought things couldn't get any worse, we received a call one night from a policeman from a hospital down in Albuquerque, New Mexico. He informed us that our son had been in an accident. He said that a man had ran a red light and hit him head-on as he was turning. It had been hit with such force that it had slung him out the driver's side door and he was hurt pretty bad and was in the ICU.

We immediately drove over and picked Gracie up and we headed down to the hospital. When we got there, they had him hooked up to every machine possible. The doctor told us that he had a broken back, a broken leg, and several broken ribs, along with internal injuries. He was in a medically induced coma so he would not feel the pain. They told us that his brain was swollen and it would be hard to tell if there was any major damage until the swelling went down and they could wake him. They had him in traction for his leg and back.

We got a hotel room where we could sleep in between visiting hours. When we would go in and visit, we would talk to him to let him know that we were there just in case he could hear us.

The accident put him in the hospital for a while. One day while we were out eating Gracie called to check on him and they said that they had taken him out of his coma and that he was awake. She started to cry, and Jalynn asked her if he was okay. She said he was and they both shouted hallelujahs. I thanked God for the miracle. We went straight over to the hospital, and he was sure happy to see us even though he was now feeling the pain. With them running several tests on his brain, they said there was no major damage, and that with surgeries they thought he would make somewhat of a full recovery.

After several back and leg surgeries he was on his way to recovery. He had healed enough to do therapy to help him walk again. After a few weeks of that he was ready to be released to be in our local doctor's care. We headed home where we rested in the comfort of our own house. He and Gracie stayed with us until he was able to do things on his own. He could manage but, due to a head injury, he was left partially blind and would never be able to drive a truck again, which devastated him, since he wanted to follow in my footsteps and didn't want to disappoint me. I told him that I was not worried about that, and I was most definitely not disappointed in him. I was just glad he was alive.

We had to get RJ to do our loads for us for a while. As the ranch was slowly going under, it seemed that there was no way to keep it going for much longer. We sold as much stuff as we had to get by until there was nothing left except the house and land. We had to let everyone go and we gave the deeds to ones who lived on the ranch or in the cases for the ones who had passed away and their families still lived in the houses that daddy had built for them. So that they wouldn't have to move and to thank them for their many years of service.

After Ray was well, he and Gracie were able to go back to living their own life. Left alone to ourselves and with the inevitable hanging over our heads, Jalynn and I decided that it would be best to sell the farm and move on with our life without the stress and responsibilities. We put the ranch on the market, and it wasn't very long until we were getting offers. We needed to make sure that we had enough to pay the bank off and have enough to live on until I would be able to fully retire.

One day this fella from New York came by in his fancy suit and inquired about it and told us that he wanted to buy it and move his big ranch operation west. I told him that I would only sell it if he promised to keep it as a ranch in honor of my daddy. We shook hands on it, and afterwards, I knew it was wrong because he had a light handshake. I remembered Daddy saying never trust a man that doesn't have a firm handshake. But we were up against a rock and a hard place and had no other options. He had the bank draw up the papers and, in a few days, it was sold. He gave us the money that was left over after the bank got what was due them and he gave us three months to find a place and to move out. We looked at several places and nothing suited us.

Then one day, Mrs. C called out of the blue and said that she had heard that we had sold out and mentioned to Jalynn that we should move over their way to Evanston, Wyoming, where they had moved when they sold the truck stop. She said there were several farms for sale that might be a fit for us. She told her that she could work for her at the diner at the new truck stop. We drove over one weekend with Gracie and Ray to take a gander to see what was out there. We settled on this farm just outside Evanston in Bear River, Wyoming. Ray said that he and Gracie could move with us over there because they had specialists that could help him with his disabilities.

Once everything was final, I started packing up. That was hard enough on its own with everything that we had and everything my parents and grandparents had collected over the years, but the hardest thing for me was when I had to take down the ranch name sign that my grandfather had carved over 100 years ago and hung across the entrance.

With us all packed up and headed west, we left Lacey Jo and Faith Ann back in Orin. Eventually they missed seeing us all the time and ended up moving out to be closer to us.

One day, Ray got a letter in the mail that said that his case from the wreck had been settled and that he would get a check for his pain and suffering. He was so excited and asked me what he should do with the money.

I said, "Son, it is yer money and ya should use it wisely. Put it into some'n that would create you some revenue on top of your disability."

It took a while, but he ended up using the insurance money to buy a little bar and grill with a small western store attached on the side and an apartment over the bar. He and Gracie moved out on their new adventure. It was on the outskirts of town but still close to us. He called it "Turbo's Place" after my CB handle and since everyone called him Turbo Jr, it suited.

After that, it was just Jalynn and me. We were doing good for a couple of years until the money from the sale of the ranch ran out and Jalynn's pay checks weren't enough to sustain us. I was working odd jobs when they were available. We needed more money and since the government wouldn't give me disability, I had to take a job hauling horses for a local horse farm just using an old pickup and a horse trailer. I was okay for a while and the pay was decent. Until one day after a routine checkup and mammogram, Jalynn was informed that she had breast cancer. The news was hard to bear, but I told her we would get through it.

Since Mama's passing, things had gotten better with things like this but it didn't help her from feeling scared. They told us that they had made medical advances with breast cancer and told us our options. After weeks of chemotherapy and radiation and with no results they decided it would be best to remove her breasts. This decision was devastating to her. She said she would never be the same. After the operation she cried for several days and then her depression set in. She questioned how I could ever love her again. I told her that God put us together for a reason and no matter what they had to take away, I would always love her and be right by her side. Also, if I still had her in my life, it was a gift from God. I hugged her and held her tight and kissed her forehead as her emotions overcame her and she cried. I told her I loved her and would throughout eternity.

She stayed in the hospital for a couple of weeks and then was able to come home. She had to take more time off from her job at the truck stop. I did what I could until we just couldn't keep up with the bills. We had let alone the hospital bills from her and myself. I worked as much as I could, working overtime and odd jobs. I knew we needed more, and I was getting burnt out. Being a lifelong truck driver, I needed more. I needed a big rig to satisfy my yearning for the open road. That is where I knew the money was at.

Just so happened one day in the spring of 2008, I was at the Waffle House in town and as I walked in, there sat the Baxters in a corner booth. While I was talking to Lunatic, he said they were passing through. He asked me what I was doing there, and I explained the whole situation. I told him I needed to get back out and run the big roads. He said he had a used 1998 Pete 379 that I could use until I got back on my feet. Against all the arguments and pleas from Jalynn and despite my health issues in the past, not to mention the fact that I did not have my Commercial Driver's License anymore, I wanted to go.

We talked for a bit and before he left, I told him I would think on it. I figured, why not? I had nothing else to lose. I had been doing what I was told to do health wise, and on my last visit, I got a clean bill of health. I told Jalynn we didn't really have a choice; we were struggling, and bills were piling up.

Within a day or two she came to me and said, "Honey, I guess ya are right about going back out over the road. Just promise me that you won't stay gone too long at a time and ya will stay outta trouble."

I promised her and so with it settled.

I went down to the DMV and got my CDL's back. I called him a few weeks later and took him up on his offer. I asked if he could have someone bring it over and I would run them back across when I headed out. He agreed and within a few days here came my new ride pulling in the driveway. She was a beauty. Bright orangish copper color, like a fiery redheaded woman. I instantly named her Reba after Reba McEntire, who was as redheaded as they come, and a hit country music singer. I spent a day getting her cleaned up and packed my stuff inside. The fella that brought her out had someone follow him for a ride back which suited me just fine because I didn't know which way my new journey would lead me.

As I climbed up in the cab, my past came back to me. I was at a point in my life where I felt okay health wise. Jalynn still offered up her worries, but I was finally going to be back to doing what I did best and loved. I felt at home in the old truck. A little rusty maybe but at home. They gave me several good back-to-back loads that would give me a chance to make some money fast.

I was running hard and doing great. One night I was on the end of this small town in Iowa and trying to find the white line through the pouring rain when I happened to spot a little German Sheperd pup on the side of the road, hunkered down and shivering. I pulled over and picked him up. I placed him inside the truck and dried him off. I put him in the passenger seat, and he perked up. Johnny Cash was on the radio, so I named him Cash. As he settled into his new home, I pulled back onto the road, and we were rolling once again putting Reba in the wind. Cash and I were inseparable and went all over the United States. I talked to him like a human, and he would give an occasional bark, huff, pant, and even a nod from time to time, as if he understood what I was saying. This went on for years as we searched for the end of that white line.

I eventually worked out a deal with Lunatic and over the next three years, I paid them for the old truck. We were rolling, and the money was getting better since Ole Reba was finally paid for. I was hauling everything they could throw at me, and I was busy. Jalynn seemed happy even though she still didn't like the idea of me being on the road. I would stay out three weeks at a time unless she needed me home for something. After that, I was gone again, in a good groove. With Cash by my side, we were trucking like never before.

But after a while, the economy was going south. The freight prices declined and the market hit a downhill spiral while the cost of fuel climbed higher and higher. I couldn't make ends meet anymore, so I had to figure out what to do, all the money went for food and fuel. I decided to park the truck and take a local hauling job again, and this time I was pulling a tanker.

Cash was a trucking dog, and he went with me as my faithful partner. Things were going okay with me hauling water to and from the drilling rigs. After about two years, things were beginning to slow down in the oil and gas fields and work grew scarce. We were home more than I was working, which led us back to the old truck despite the odds stacked against me.

I finally made it to the other side of Chicago and while waiting to get unloaded, I called Jalynn. I could tell by the sound of her voice that something was wrong. I said hello and I could tell that she was dreading talking to me, probably because she was still upset and disappointed. Then she just hung up.

With that I headed back to the truck and backed to the gate where I got unloaded. Then I headed to the corral to get the other load we had agreed upon. I was getting a load that would take me to Billings, Oklahoma, and then I was to get a load to go from there to Fargo, Oklahoma, and then to on to Ft. Collins, Colorado. Then I would finally be heading home.

After I got loaded, I stopped by the T/A for fuel and coffee, and enough cigarettes to see me through. I was rolling along good and making up time. It was looking like I would get there in time to deliver and bed down and then pick up my other load the next day. Cash hung his head out the window as we rolled along, both of us jamming to trucking songs. I pushed that old rig to its limits as well as myself. We were passing traffic left and right as they wouldn't get out of my way. I was hammered down.

It didn't seem like we had been on the road that long before we had to stop for our break. We were there for just a little while and because I was anxious to get these loads out of the way, I decided to keep running, enjoying life on the white line.

We rolled for a better part of the night when I found a little old truck stop just off the interstate where we parked for the rest of the night, which was only a couple of hours. After our nap, we got our fuel, coffee, and food, and were on our way to Billings. We would be there in just a few hours, but I knew they would be getting close to shutting down for the day, so I hammered down.

To my surprise, when I got there, they said to go ahead and pull in and they would and unload me. While they did, I took that time to call Jalynn. This time I guess she found the words she wanted to say, because she was crying as she told me she understood that I had a heavy load to bear. But that didn't excuse my behavior towards her. She said that she needed that time to think about if she should give up or to keep fighting for our marriage. She then said that she loved me and that she wanted to fight for us, and that whatever demons I was facing, we needed to do it together. She said that she was beginning to get depressed at Amberleigh's house. That she would pack up her stuff and head back home to the ranch and see me when I got home. Before she hung up, I told her I loved her, and she said she loved me, too.

I was filled with joy at the fact that God once again showed up right on time and answered my prayers in full. I asked the fellas there if they would see if the feed lot over in Fargo would stay open long enough for me to get loaded, since I was only just over two hours away. They returned and said yes, if I hurried, but it would cost me $400 to pay the fella's working there. Since I had been paid upfront by the city slicker, I agreed and took off, hammering down the highway.

Once there, they loaded me right away. However, it was late, and I was a little tired. I found the nearest truck stop on the outskirts of Fargo. Cash and I did our business, ate, I said my prayers, and went to bed. I needed a nap, just enough to get us through. That way we could get up early and hit the road and run the long white line home.

17

THE LONG JOURNEY HOME

Fargo, OK- FT. Collins, CO – Evanston, WY (Bear River)

THE NEXT MORNING, WITH JUST THREE HOURS OF SLEEP, I fueled up and we were ready to roll, coffee and cigarettes in hand. I gave Jalynn a quick call to let her know I loved her and that I was on my way. We hit the road, and I kept hearing her sweet voice telling me the news of her coming back home to the farm. It made me jump for joy inside. I was so close to retirement, and we would not have to be apart very much longer.

I headed down the road heading west with happy tears in my eyes. I was thinking of the good news and of what the last couple of weeks had been like and I was glad I was finally coming off the road for good. I was getting too old to be running like this. I was ready to retire and be with my beautiful wife, this time for good.

After a few hours, I stopped for a quick break so Cash could stretch his legs. I sat there in the driver's seat and closed my eyes. While I did, I thought of how Jalynn would react when we embraced. I just wanted to pull her in and hold her tight and tell her in person that I love her. I knew that it would be so romantic, and something that I had longed for the past two weeks. I was going to try my best to make that feeling last forever.

Cash startled me when he opened the door. I quickly opened my eyes and made sure it was him and not someone trying to break into my truck. I gathered myself together and called each of my kids to tell them the news. Faith Ann told me that her mom had called already, and she was as excited as I was. I knew I was not always there for my family throughout the years, but they know I love them, and I know they love me too.

After Faith Ann, I called Ray. He said he was proud of me for realizing I had made a mistake and for making up with his mama. He said he hoped that I would do better and do right by her from now on.

Finally, I called Lacey Jo, and she said she was excited, but she was surprised that her mama had forgiven me. She told me if I did it again, I could forget about seeing her or my grandbabies, the ultimate bargaining chip for me to behave myself. I agreed with her and said that I would be the best husband, daddy, and pawpaw I could be. I told each of them that I loved them and for them to kiss my grandbabies for me.

After I rested for a little while longer, I was ready to roll again. I topped off my fuel tanks and got my thermos full and a cup to go. I made my way back onto the big road and hammered down once again. As I was going down the road, I was thinking of all the stuff that needed to be done to clean up the mess that I had made. There were a lot of important things to discuss. Plus, I was thinking of what it would be like after I retire and spent every minute with the woman I fell in love with. I wanted to go on trips and take her out to wine and dine her like she deserved after all these years for putting up with me. So many thoughts were running wild in my head like a hundred mustang horses. I could not hold my excitement. I rolled down my window and shouted to the heavens, thank you, Lord!

With the hammer down I was making my way one mile at a time. I guess because I was so tired and excited, once I got out of the populated areas, time seemed to slow down to a crawl. I had it on the floor and it still seemed like I was never going to make it. I was questioning my efforts to get home as fast as I could. I was not the young driver that I used to be when I could run and run on little or no sleep at all. I was getting so tired that I was lighting one cigarette after another. I would smoke most of it and then I would go off into my thoughts as I would start to doze off rest burn down until it would burn my finger and send a signal to my brain that I need to wake up.

After a few more hours, or an eternity in my case, I finally made it to Ft. Collins, Colorado. I got unloaded as quickly as they could possibly unload me. It was getting late by the time they finished, and I decided to sleep in the lot instead of going to the truck stop. Figuring that I was already there, and they could reload me in the morning, and I could head back out just after daybreak.

I didn't sleep well at all at all. The thoughts were running through my head from my past life to what would lie ahead of me in my future. I dozed off finally and was awoken up by the sounds of pickups, big rigs, and loud voices. Cash had already gotten out to mingle with the drivers. I got dressed and headed into the office to grab me a cup of coffee. There were already a good many drivers waiting. I made my way through the maze of them to the coffee pot to get me a cup and try to wake up more. There was some idle chat between the drivers. They were catching up on all the latest news. Since I hadn't been to this place before I just got my coffee and went outside for a smoke.

As they were chatting, I heard a familiar voice and thought that it could that be Murphy. But it couldn't be. I had to go and check it out. I walked into the dispatch room next to the office and I noticed a few pictures on the wall that were of a few trucks that I recognized and some familiar faces from my past. I looked in the office and saw that it was in fact Murphy. Then I noticed a plaque hanging on the wall that read *H.M. Stell, Owner.* Wow! He was the owner of this new feed lot. There was a big poster of him with his old truck.

I peeked in the door and said, "Hello, stranger, do ya remember me?"

He said, "How can I ever forget?" He came out and we got to talking and he asked how I was, and I told him the story. He said, God loves ya, brother, and he forgives you. Just remember that."

"I know, I know," I agreed.

I asked him how things were going for him. He said that he had just bought the place, and this was his first large shipment. And even though he was the owner, he was still running cattle. After we talked for a few, he said, "Hey, let's pray." And we knelt right there in the dirt and prayed.

Afterwards we went to join the other drivers. I was shocked as I walked out to the staging area. As I got closer, I could hear them talking, and even though it had been over two weeks, I was still the subject of their conversation.

They said, "Well, look at that. Turbo has come to bless us with his presence."

RJ was standing there with Blue Bird and to my surprise there was Odie, whom I had just seen days before. He said he just had to drive the distance to see all his old friends and to help this old timer out and supervise. We all laughed and joked with him about hauling one in his pickup. Bone Head and Big Mike were also there. And low and behold, there was my old Army buddy, Rebel, whom I had not seen in years. He said that he had been driving, running the Southeast so he could be close to his family. He had heard of this event and wasn't going to miss it. After the jokes subsided, they asked me how things were going with Jalynn. I told them the good news.

After our joyful reunion, Murphy prayed and gave his instructions. After that, I hung around with Murphy and he confided in me. He said that he had faltered in his faith and hit rock bottom. After a wreck, he lost everything and was physically unable to drive for a good while. He was seconds from taking his life when God spoke to him, and he started praying and he rededicated his life to God. He promised if God would heal him, he would dedicate his life to serve him. And he did and he blessed him with this place. He told me that his new handle was "Preacher."

I said, "Preacher, that suits ya. God is so good. He could have easily given up on us, especially when we were ready to give up on ourselves."

"His promise, that he would never leave us has stood true forever and I too have found my way back to him. And I vowed to get it right this time. God has given us so much to be thankful for and I know now more than ever, if I walk with him daily, I will never take his precious gifts for granted again."

Preacher then said to me, "Bobby Ray, it does my heart good to hear ya say that. We both have certainly been through a lot through our years of run'n this old road. God has helped us face our darkest days. The thangs we seen when we were called to war in Vietnam has been a heavy cross to bear all these years."

"I don't know about ya, but those demons were buried down so deep, not that I am make'n excuses for the mistakes that I made in my life since our draft days. God has helped me get to the root of it and I now realize it was his will fer me to endure that time as well as the course of my life to then bring'n me to where it is I am supposed to be, walk'n daily with him."

I said, "Wow, Preacher! Ya are so right, he certainly worked overtime on us."

We both chuckled then gave each other a brotherly hug and a firm pat on the back.

I said, "I love ya, brother!"

He said, "Back at ya, Bobby Ray."

We all got loaded and I rounded up Cash, and then we said our goodbyes. As we climbed back in our trucks, Channel 19 came to life with our conversations continuing until we could no longer hear each other as we hit the big road heading our separate ways.

I was thinking of the brotherhood all of us drivers had. The fact that we all had our own job to do, but if one of us was in trouble, the others were quick to stop what they were doing and help each other out. I had seen this act of selflessness many times over the course of my long driving career.

I was awake and feeling pretty good after my time there even though I didn't get much sleep. I was rolling along, and time began to slow down again. I started confiding in Cash to see what he thought about us going home and of the fact that his mama would be waiting for us. He sat high in the seat and barked loudly to show his excitement. We rolled on for another hundred miles or so and I started to doze off and I figured I had better pull it over. Once I was on the ramp of the closest exit, I crossed my arms and laid my head on the steering wheel. I slept like that for an hour and then I was once again ready to roll.

When I finally got to my delivery at Ft. Collins, they were ready and waiting for me so they could finish and leave. The two big bulls I had in there started giving them fits and did not want to come out of the trailer. They had to wait until they calmed down because no one could get in there with them in case they got out of control. Because of them, they decided to lock my trailer up and let them have over night to calm down. It was now dark, and Cash and I ate a few cans of Vienna sausages to cure our hunger as we laid in the bunk to sleep. Even though I was beyond tired, I slept a little. But because I wanted to get home, it was not restful.

Bright and early the next morning, they showed up to finish unloading and to get me reloaded. The bulls were ready to come off and once they were put out to pasture, they rounded up the other livestock that I was to be loaded with. They took their time getting me loaded and I guessed that they were on overtime.

After I was loaded, I went and got my fuel, coffee, and cigarettes. Then without hesitation, I was heading down the road headed for Evanston, which meant home for us.

Heading down the road towards my destination and getting closer to Jalynn, I started thinking of everything that I have been through in my life and what Jalynn, and I have endured during our marriage, and I started to pray and thank God for carrying us through and thanked him for my family and most of all for saving my soul.

The sun was now on its way below my visor and starting to get covered by dark clouds, and I couldn't see the horizon without squinting. Even though I had been driving for only an hour or so, I had been up most of the day, still tired from my hard running and lack of sleep. I figured I would stop near Orin and take a nap before continuing to the delivery, and once I made it there and got unloaded, I would be on the home stretch a few hours from the house.

I drove on until I reached the old Chapmans truck stop where I got a cup of coffee, and a snack cake, and a snack for Cash. I thought about taking a little nap, but figuring I would be okay to drive the extra six hours so after I got empty, I could be home quicker. I would be over on my logs, but I had not kept up with them since Virginia Beach. I figured I had driven that far before with ease in my early days and there was no sense in wasting ten hours of sleep when in just a few short hours I could be back at home with Jalynn. I told Cash we were just gonna keep rolling until we made it home and he huffed in agreement. We hit the road, and I hammed down, bound and determined to make it home.

As I drove across I-80 west towards home, the sun had disappeared behind dark clouds and with the misting rain, it was somewhat foggy and gloomy. I approached Three Sisters, and as always on days like today when the weather is just right, it looked like the road continued up into the Heavens. I guess my age had caught up with me. I started daydreaming as I always did, thinking I was so close to home and I could not wait to get there and start my new life with Jalynn. I was in a trance from the long stretch of highway and the still gloomy weather. The sounds of horns honking at me brought me back to reality. I realized I was heading into oncoming traffic, going way too fast with hardly any time to react. I turned the wheel too hard to the right and found myself heading for the edge of the road. In an instant, I went airborne. It was like my life was in slow motion and as my world turned sideways and then upside down and sideways again before my rig came crashing down. I could hear the steel crumpling, and the dirt and glass flew everywhere. Some shards hit my face and penetrated my skin. I could smell the coolant and fluids as everything came apart. With another hard hit, I felt something pierce my side. Not knowing what it was and unable to see it, I was in trouble. After what seemed to be a lifetime, my rig slowly came to a stop.

I was fading in and out of consciousness and noticed that Cash had slowly scooted his way to me and laid his head on my chest. I felt as if I was trying to open my eyes but couldn't seem to find the strength. I could faintly hear Cash whimpering. As I held him close, I could feel blood taking over his soft fur and I could tell he was also badly hurt. Even though my eyes were not open I could feel the warmth of light shining and it was getting brighter by the second. An image then appeared in what seemed to be how I would imagine God to look reaching down with enormous yet tender looking hands. Magnetically drawing me in, closer and closer.

I then heard a soft yet stern voice whisper, "I am still here with you, my son."

I felt confusion as my body felt so light as if I were floating while standing on my feet. I felt no pain, just a sensation of pure joy. I was thinking of nothing else other than how I wanted to feel this feeling for all of eternity.

God then said to me, "I have now showed you what is in store for your eternal life. This is what will be one day, my son. However, it is not your time just yet. No more searching for the end of that white line, for I am of all you ever needed to find."

As I was hearing these words, I heard the voice of an angel reading scripture, then I heard that same voice saying, "Bobby Ray, please wake up, I need ya, we all need ya!"

It was my own angel Jalynn, who was at the hospital by my side. I opened my eyes enough to see Jalynn. Cash was patiently waiting beside my bed as if he sensed a change. His head perked up and then he perched his paws on my bedside rails. I could then hear the familiar sound of his dog tags jingle, just as I had every morning when we would wake me.

My eyes still half closed, I slowly reached out hoping it wasn't a dream and that he too was okay. I felt his fur and stroked his head. Then I knew it was for real. My faithful companion was there, it was for real.

Faith was the first to notice my movements. She said, "Daddy?" as Jalynn was thumbing through the Bible to find more scripture.

Jalynn then came to my side and leaned down to kiss me on my forehead saying that she loved me. Even in the shape I was in, she still managed to make my heart flutter. My kids rushed to my side with tears of joy. Cash jumped into the bed to be a part of our joyful reunion. Cash began licking my face and I as I rubbed his head and I whispered to him, "We found it, buddy, we found the end of the long white line."

TRUCKER LINGO, NICKNAMES, & 10-CODES

What follows are lists of fun and informative lists regarding Trucker Lingo, 10-Codes, and City Nicknames.

The source material is photographic so we have enhanced them as well as we could for this printed publication. Enjoy!

Trucker Lingo

Pumpkin – A Schneider truck, because of its orange color.

Radio – A CB radio. Radio check – How's my radio working, transmitting, getting out there.

Rambo – Someone who talks tough on the radio, especially when no one else knows where they are.

Ratchet jaw – Someone who talks a lot on the radio, while keying-up the whole time and not letting anyone else get a chance to talk.

Reading the mail – Not talking; just listening to the radio.

Reefer – Usually refers to refrigerated van trailer, but sometimes just to the reefer unit itself.

Rest-a-ree-a – Rest area.

Road pizza – Roadkill on the side of the road.

Rockin' chair – A truck that's in the middle of two other trucks.

Roger – Yes; affirmative.

Roger beep – An audible beep that sounds when a person has un-keyed the mike and finished his transmission. Used on only a small percentage of radios.

Roller skate – Any small car.

Rooster cruiser – A big, fancy truck; a large, conventional tractor with a lot of lights and chrome.

Runnin' you across – The weigh station is open, and they're weighing trucks, probably in a quick fashion.

Salt shaker – The road maintenance vehicles that dump salt or sand on the highways in the winter.

Sandbagging – To listen to the radio without talking; also "readin' the mail".

Sandbox – An escape ramp, which sometimes uses sand to stop vehicles.

Schneider eggs – The orange cones in construction areas.

Seat cover – Sometimes used to describe drivers or passengers of four-wheelers.

Sesame Street – Channel 19 on the CB, named as such because everyone lives there.

Shaky – California in general, sometimes Los Angeles, and, occasionally, San Francisco.

Shiny side up – Your vehicle hasn't flipped over after a rollover or accident. "Keep the shiny side up" means to have a safe trip.

Shooting you in the back – You're being shot with a radar gun as your vehicle passes a law enforcement vehicle.

Short short – A short amount of time.

Shutdown – Put out of service by the DOT because of some violation.

Sleeper Creeper – A prostitute; same as a lot lizard.

Skateboard – A flatbed, or flatbed trailer.

Skins – Tires.

Smokin' scooter – A law enforcement officer on a motorcycle.

Smokin' the brakes – The trailer brakes are smoking from overuse down a mountain grade.

Smokey or Smokey Bear – A law enforcement officer, usually highway patrol.

Split – A junction, where the road goes in separate directions.

Spy in the sky – A law enforcement aircraft, same as a "bear in the air".

Stagecoach – A tour bus.

Stand on it – Step on it, go faster.

can easily drown out a lesser one.

Key up – Pushing the transmit button on the CB Mike. "Key up for about 20 minutes, and tell me how bad you are".

In my back pocket – Behind you; a place you've passed.

In the big hole – The top gear of the transmission.

K-whopper – A Kenworth tractor, or just KW.

Kojak with a Kodak – Law enforcement using a radar gun.

Landline – A stationary telephone; not a cellular phone (not exactly slang but newer truckers might be confused by it).

Large car – A conventional tractor, often with a big sleeper, lots of chrome and lights, etc.

Left Coast – The West Coast.

Local information – A driver asks for local information when he needs directions in the area he's unfamiliar with.

Local-yokel – A county, city, or small-town officer.

Lollipop – The small reflector or marker poles on the sides of the highway.

Lot lizard – A prostitute that solicits truck-to-truck in a truck stop or rest area.

Lumper – Casual labor that loads or unloads your trailer, often requiring payment in cash.

Mama-bear – Refers to a female law enforcement officer.

Male buffalo – A male prostitute.

Mash your motor – Go fast, step on it. Same as gouge on it and hammer down.

Meat wagon – An ambulance.

Merry merry – Merry Christmas.

Motion lotion – Diesel fuel.

Moving on – Heading down the road.

Mud duck – A weak radio signal.

Negatory – Negative or no.

95th Street – Interstate 95.

On the side – On standby.

Parking lot – An auto transporter, often used when the trailer is empty.

Pay the water bill – Taking a bathroom break.

Pickle park – A rest area frequented by lot lizards (prostitutes).

Pigtail – The electrical connection from the tractor to the trailer. Named for its curliness.

Plain wrapper – An unmarked law enforcement vehicle, usually said with color added as a description: "you've got a plain brown wrapper on your back door".

Plenty of protection – Usually means there's plenty of police in the area, might also be used to tell drivers to go ahead and step on it because there's speeding four-wheelers ahead blocking or covering for them.

Pogo stick – Usually, a metal, flexible support located on the tractor catwalk, that holds up the connections to the trailer.

Power up – Go faster, speed up.

Preeshaydit – Appreciate it.

General mess of crap – A GMC truck

Georgia overdrive – Putting the transmission into neutral on a downgrade, to go extremely fast. Not recommended!

Go-go juice – Diesel fuel.

Good buddy – This used to be the thing to say: "10-4, good buddy". Not anymore, as this is now calling someone a homosexual.

Good neighbor – Usually used when you're showing appreciation to another driver, as in "thank you, good neighbor".

Got my nightgown on – I'm in the sleeper, and ready to go to sleep.

Go to company – When you tell another driver from your company to go to the designated company CB channel. Drivers do this so that they can talk about company business or personal matters without monopolizing channel 19.

Go to the Harley – Turn your CB to channel 1.

Got your ears on? – Are you listening?

Gouge on it – Go fast, put the throttle to the floor, step on it, etc.

Granny lane – The right, slower lane on a multi-lane highway, or the Interstate.

Greasy – Icy, or slippery.

Greasy side up – A vehicle that's flipped over.

Green Stamps – Money.

Grossed out – Your gross vehicle weight is at maximum capacity; commonly 80,000 pounds.

Ground pressure – The weight of your truck, as in "the scale's testing your ground pressure".

Gumball machine – The lights on top of a patrol car.

Hammer down – Go fast, step on it.

Hammer lane – The left, passing lane of traffic.

Hand/Han – What a driver sometimes calls another driver. Stems from the term farmhand, and means helper, or fellow worker.

Handle (CB handle) – The FCC encourages the use of CB handles. CB handles are nicknames that are used to identify the speaker, in place of an actual name. A driver often selects a handle that he feels reflects his personality or describes his way of driving.

Happy happy – Happy new year; "Have a happy happy, driver".

Having "shutter trouble" – Having trouble keeping awake.

Ho Chi Minh Trail – Refers to California Highway 152, known for its abundance of accidents.

Holler – Call me on the radio, as in "give me a holler when you get back".

Home 20 – A driver's home location.

How 'bout – When you're trying to contact other drivers, you can say "how 'bout you, eastbound?".

Hood – A conventional tractor, as opposed to a cab-over.

Hundred dollar lane/High dollar lane – In certain heavily populated areas, trucks will be prohibited from driving in the far left lane, with a heavy fine for violators. This term refers to that prohibited lane.

Jackpot – The same as a gumball machine. A patrol car's lights.

Key down – When you talk over somebody who's trying to transmit. A bigger, more powerful radio driver, come on".

Comic book – The logbook.

Commercial company – A prostitute.

Convoy – A group of trucks traveling together.

Copy – Transmission acknowledged, agreed with, or understood, as in "that's a copy, driver".

Cornflake – Refers to a Consolidated Freightways truck.

County Mountie – County police, often a sheriff's deputy.

Covered wagon – Flatbed type of trailer, with sidewalls, and a tarp.

Crackerhead – A derogatory term; insult.

Crotch rocket – A motorcycle built for speed; not a Harley-Davidson.

Deadhead – Pulling an empty trailer.

Destruction – Road construction.

Diesel car – A semi-tractor.

Diesel cop – A DOT, Commercial Vehicle Enforcement officer.

Donkey – Behind you. "A bear is on your donkey".

Do what? – I didn't hear or understand you.

Double nickel – 55 mph, considered the optimal balance between speed and fuel efficiency.

Doubles – A set of double trailers.

Drawing lines – Completing your logbook

Driver – What drivers call other drivers on the CB, especially if their CB handle is not known.

Driving award – A speeding ticket.

Downstroke – Driving downwards, downhill, on a decline.

Dragon wagon – A tow truck.

Dragonfly – A truck with no power, especially going uphill.

Dry box – An unrefrigerated freight trailer. Also considered a dry van.

18-wheeler – Any tractor-trailer.

85th Street – Interstate 85.

Evil Knievel – A law enforcement officer on a motorcycle.

Eyeball – To see something.

Feeding the bears – Paying a ticket or citation.

Fingerprint – To unload a trailer by yourself.

Flip-flop – Refers to a U-turn, or a return trip.

FM – An AM-FM radio.

42 – Yes, or OK.

Four-letter word – Open; referring to weigh stations being open or closed.

4-wheeler – Any passenger vehicle; cars or pickups.

Freight shaker – A Freightliner truck.

Front door – In front of you.

Full-grown bear – State Trooper, or Highway Patrol.

Garbage hauler – A produce load or produce haulers.

Gear Jammer – A driver who speeds up and slows down with great frequency.

Big R – A Roadway truck.

Big road – Usually refers to the interstate, sometimes any big highway.

Big truck – An 18-wheeler or tractor-trailer. "Come on over, big truck".

Bird dog – A radar detector.

Big word – Closed, when referring to weigh stations. There is often a big sign preceding the weigh station indicating whether the station is open or closed, in bright lights. From a distance, you can't tell what the word says, but you can usually tell whether it's a big word or small word. So, when you hear "the big word is out", you'll know that the weigh station is closed.

Black eye – A headlight out. "Driver going eastbound, you've got a black eye".

Bobtail – Driving the tractor only, without the trailer attached.

Boogie – The top gear (the highest gear) of the transmission.

Boulevard – The Interstate.

Brake check – There is a traffic tie-up ahead, which will require immediate slowing down or stopping. "You've gotta brake check ahead of you, eastbound".

Break – If the radio's busy, saying "break-number" is the proper way to gain access to the channel and begin talking.

Breaking up – Your signal is weak or fading. Brush your teeth and comb your hair – Be on your best driving behavior (usually means a cop is out and about looking for people to give tickets).

Bubba – What you call another driver, often in a kidding way.

Bulldog – A Mack truck.

Bullfrog – An ABF truck.

Bull hauler – A livestock hauler.

Bumper sticker – A vehicle that's tailgating. Sometimes called a "hitchhiker".

Bundled out – Loaded heavy, or to maximum capacity.

Buster Brown – A UPS truck or driver.

Cabbage – A steep mountain grade in Oregon.

Cabover – Abbreviated term for Cab-Over-the Engine (COE) type of tractor (no longer commonly used in the United States).

Cash register – A tollbooth.

Checking ground pressure – The weigh station is open, and they're running trucks across the scales (see "running you across").

Chicken coop – A weigh station, often called just a "coop".

Chicken lights – Extra lights a trucker has on his truck and trailer.

Chicken hauler or truck – A big, fancy truck; a large, conventional tractor with a lot of lights and chrome. Also, one who hauls live chickens.

Comedian – The median strip in between opposite lanes of traffic.

Container – Refers to an overseas container; intermodal transportation.

Come-a-part engine – Cummins engine.

Come back – An invitation for the other driver to talk. Sometimes used when you couldn't hear the last transmission, "comeback, I didn't hear you".

Come on – Telling another driver that you hear him calling you, and to go ahead and talk. "Yeah

All locked up – The weigh station is closed.

Anteater – Kenworth T-600; this truck was so-named because of its sloped hood, and was one of the first trucks with an aerodynamic design. Also known as an aardvark.

Alligator – A piece of tire on the road, usually a recap from a blown tire, which can look like an alligator lying on the road. These alligators are hazards that are to be avoided, if possible. If you run over them, they can "bite you" — bounce back up and do damage to hoses or belts, fuel crossover lines, or to the body of your tractor. They can also bounce up and go towards another vehicle, possibly causing an accident. A baby alligator is a small piece of tire, and alligator bait is several small tire pieces. Sometimes simply called a "gator".

Back door – Something behind you. "There's a bear at your back door".

Back it down – Slow down.

Backed out of it – No longer able to maintain speed, necessitating a need to downshift. When a truck's climbing a steep incline, and for whatever reason, the driver has to let up off of the accelerator, he'll lose whatever momentum he had and have to downshift. "I'm backed out of it now, I'll have to get over into the slow lane."

Back row – The last rows of parking in a truck stop, often a hangout for prostitutes (see "lot lizards").

Bambi – A deer.

Base station or unit – A powerful CB radio set in a stationary location.

Bear – A law enforcement officer at any level, but usually a State Trooper, Highway Patrol.

Bear bait – A speeding vehicle, usually a four-wheeler, which can be used to protect the other speeding vehicles behind it.

Bear bite – A speeding ticket.

Bear den or bear cave – Law enforcement headquarters, station.

Bear in the air – A law enforcement aircraft which can be monitoring the traffic and speeds below.

Bear in the bushes – Law enforcement (at any level) is hiding somewhere, probably with a radar gun aimed at traffic.

Billy Big Rigger – Another term for "supertrucker"; one who brags about himself, or his big, fast, shiny truck.

Bingo cards – These cards held stamps from each state a motor carrier would operate in; these cards are no longer used and have been replaced by the Single State Registration System (SSRS).

Bedbugger – Can refer to a household moving company or the household mover himself.

Swinging – Carrying a load of swinging meat.

Taking pictures – Law enforcement using a radar gun.

10-4 – OK, message received. Some drivers just say "10".

Thermos bottle – A tanker trailer.

Through the woods – Leaving the Interstate to travel secondary roads.

Throwin' iron – To put on snow tire chains.

Too many eggs in the basket – Overweight load or gross weight.

Toothpicks – A load of lumber.

Travel agent – The dispatcher, or sometimes a broker.

Triple digits – Over 100 mph.

VW – A Volvo-White tractor.

Wagon – Some drivers refer to their trailer as a wagon.

Walked on you – Drowned out your transmission by keying up at the same time.

Wally world – Wal-Mart (the store or the distribution center), or a Wal-Mart truck.

West Coast turnarounds – Uppers; speed or benzedrine pills; the idea is that a driver can drive from the East Coast to the West Coast, and back again without having to sleep. Obviously illegal.

Wiggle wagons – A set of double or triple trailers.

Yard – A company terminal, drop a lot, etc.

Yardstick – A mile marker on the highway.

Common 10-Codes

10-35: Confidential information (That's none of your business).

10-36: The correct time is...

10-37: Wrecker needed at... (Some jerk left his car and it needs to be towed).

10-38: Ambulance needed at (Some poor sap needs medical attention).

10-39: Your message delivered (I'm not that type of delivery boy but I did it anyway because I'm a nice person).

10-40: I am not a trucker and am saying 10 followed by a random number.

10-41: Please tune to channel...(I want to speak with you more privately, or possibly "go away")

10-42: Traffic accident at (Some shmuck needs to learn how to drive).

10-43: Traffic tie up at (If I have to wait in traffic for an extended period of time, the least they could do is have something cool to cause it!).

10-44: I have a message for you (Someone else was too impatient to tell you personally).

10-45: All units please report (I am so lonely).

10-46 to 10-49: I am not a trucker and am saying 10 followed by a random number.

10-50: Break channel.

10-51 to 10-59: I am not a trucker and am saying 10 followed by a random number.

10-60: What's the next message number?

10-61: I am not a trucker and am saying 10 followed by a random number.

10-62: Unable to copy, use a phone (Is my CB malfunctioning or is that yours).

10-63: I am not a trucker and am saying 10 followed by a random number.

10-64: I am not a trucker and am saying 10 followed by a random number.

10-65: Awaiting your message or assignment (I'm listening).

10-66: I am not a trucker and am saying 10 followed by a random number.

10-67: All units comply (Obey my orders, chump!).

10-68: I am not a trucker and am saying 10 followed by a random number.

10-69: I am not a trucker and am saying 10 followed by a number that has a sexual connotation, haha I am so funny.

10-70: Fire at... (Hold on those aren't streetlights).

10-71: Continue with the transmission in sequence.

10-72: I am not a trucker and am saying 10 followed by a random number.

10-73: Speed trap at...(them bears are looking for food!).

10-74: I am not a trucker and am saying 10 followed by a random number.

10-75: You are causing interference (Please stop ruining the airwaves for everyone else).

10-76: I am not a trucker and am saying 10 followed by a random number.

10-77: Negative contact.

10-78 to 10-82: I am not a trucker and am saying 10 followed by a random number.

10-84: My telephone number is (Feel free to prank call me when I'm sleeping).

10-85: My home address is (Please rob my house).

10-86 to 10-90: I am not a trucker and am saying 10 followed by a random number.

10-91: Talk closer to the microphone (Have you never used a microphone before).

10-92: Your transmitter is acting up (Did you drive your truck into a lake?).

10-1: Receiving poorly (I can't hear you).

10-2: Receiving well (I can hear you).

10-3: Stop transmitting (Shut up).

10-4: Affirmative/I agree.

10-5: Relay message (Pass it on).

10-6: Busy/Hold on a second.

10-7: Out of Service (either going out of range or no longer using the radio)

10-8 In-Service (Just signed on or came into range)

10-9: Repeat message (Come again?).

10-10: Transmission Completed (Thanks for coming to my TedTalk).

10-11: Talking too rapidly (Take a breath and try again).

10-12: Visitors present (Stop talking about all the lot lizards from last night).

10-13: Weather/road conditions

10-14: I am not a trucker and am saying 10 followed by a random number.

10-15: I am not a trucker and am saying 10 followed by a random number.

10-16: Make pickup (hitching a load).

10-17: Urgent Business (What I'm about to say is important).

10-18: Anything for us (Why should I care)?

10-19: Nothing for you (No).

10-20: Another word for location.

10-21: Call by telephone (This stupid radio isn't working right).

10-22: Report in-person to...

10-23: Stand-by (Pay attention)!

10-24: Completed last assignment (I still haven't been paid yet)!

10-25: Can you contact (I'd like to speak with your manager)?

10-26: Disregard the last statement (I was wrong or intentionally deceiving you).

10-27: I am moving to channel... (like an airport, I am announcing my departure).

10-28: Identify your station.

10-29: Time is up for contact (You are boring me and I don't want to talk to you anymore).

10-30: Does not conform to FCC rules (Do you want a fine?)

10-31: I am not a trucker and am saying 10 followed by a random number.

10-32: I will give you a radio check.

10-33: Emergency traffic (rubberneckers).

10-34: Trouble at this station.

10-93: Check my frequency (Do I sound like I'm underwater).

10-94: Please give me long count (tell me the whole story, I have nothing better to do right now than to listen to you ramble)

10-95: Transmit dead carrier for 5 seconds (will you all shut your lips for 5 seconds? Geez).

10-96 To 10-98: I am not a trucker and am saying 10 followed by a random number.

10-99 Mission completed (Just got paid!)

10-100 Need to go to the bathroom (I should have known getting an extra big Gulp was a bad idea!).

10-101 to 10-199: I am not a trucker and am saying 10 followed by a random number.

10-200: Police needed at... (Somebody is breaking the law).

10-201+: I am not a trucker and am saying 10 followed by a random number.

Now the next time you listen to CB talk, you can breathe a sigh of relief when someone annoying you pulls a 10-27, because you will understand the CB radio codes.

City Nicknames

The Big A – Atlanta, Georgia
Air Capital – Wichita, Kansas
Armadillo – Amarillo, Texas
The Alamo – San Antonio, Texas
The Astrodome – Houston, Texas
The Apple – New York City
Bean Town – Boston, Mass.
Beer City – Milwaukee, Wisconsin
Big D – Dallas, Texas
Big O – Omaha, Nebraska
Bull City – Durham, North Carolina
Bikini – Miami, Florida
Bright Lights – Kansas City, Missouri
Capital City – Raleigh, North Carolina
CB Town – Council Bluffs, Iowa
Charm City – Baltimore, Maryland
Cigar City – Tampa, Florida
Circle City – Indianapolis, Indiana
The Cities – Minneapolis and St. Paul, Mn
Cow Town – Calgary, Alberta
The Dirty – Cleveland, Ohio
The Flag or Flagpole – Flagstaff, Arizona

The Flag or Flagpole – Flagstaff, Arizona
Philly – Philadelphia, Pa
The Gateway – St. Louis, Missouri
Gold City – Goldsboro, North Carolina
Guitar – Nashville, Tennessee
Hog Town – Toronto, Ontario
Hotlanta – Atlanta, Georgia
The Irish – South Bend, Indiana
Lost Wages – Las Vegas, Nevada
Mardi Gras – New Orleans, Louisiana
Mile High – Denver, Colorado
Motor City – Detroit, Michigan
Music City – Nashville, Tennessee
The Nickel – Buffalo, New York
Okie City – Oklahoma City, Oklahoma
The Peg – Winnipeg, Manitoba
Queen City – Charlotte, North Carolina
The Rubber – Akron, Ohio
Sack of Tomatoes – Sacramento, California
Shaky City – Los Angeles, California
Steel City or Town – Pittsburgh, Pa
The Swamp – Montreal, Quebec
Windy City – Chicago, Illinois

ADDITIONAL DEDICATIONS

I also dedicate this book to my parents, James Hubert (Jimmy) Edwards and Barbara Ann (Bobbie) Stell Edwards. Both have gone on to Heaven. I want to thank them for loving me and raising me up in church and for being the best of parents. You always taught me that I could do anything if I put my mind to it and taught me to use my imagination and creativity. I love you and miss you!

To my children, I want you to know that I love each of you. And I say to you do not ever give up on your dreams. Ashtynn Taylor Blake, Kellan Ray Edwards, Hailey-Anah Faith Edwards, and Raven Dunn.

I also want to add a special dedication to my father- and mother-in-law Keith and Regina Blake for their support in this life venture. I love you both!

I would also like to add a very special dedication to my other mother- and father-in-law Joyce (deceased) and Nathan Baker (deceased). Joyce would ask when this book would be published and that she wanted a copy. Unfortunately, the Lord called her home before I could finish it. I know you are in heaven with Mama, Daddy, and Nathan. The first copy I autograph will be for you. I love you.

To the rest of my family and friends, of which, some are in this book by a nickname or by your middle name. I want to thank you for putting up with me. I know there were times I said I would be there but just couldn't make it. Just know it wasn't my fault. It's trucking! I love each one of you.

I want to give a special thanks to Jason Cripps and Angie Cripps for giving me the opportunity to drive for them. And for treating me like family. Also, to Angie for helping me with this book with some editing and suggestions.

I want to thank all my truck driving brothers and sisters who travel the highways and byways of this great nation while enduring the hardships of the road all while keeping America running. Thank you.

A special thanks to my Military Veteran brother and sisters who have served and who are serving presently to keep America free and other countries as well. Thank you from my heart.

And finally, an incredibly special thanks to the Veterans who have made the ultimate sacrifice to protect our freedom and way of life of our great nation.

God Bless the U.S.A.!

Sincerely,
Raymond Edwards

In memory of "Big Mike"
You are missed every day.

Mike Hughes, my wife's mother's brother, a true lifelong truck driver.

THE STORY BEHIND
End of the Long White Line

I was traveling west on Interstate 80 West back in September of 2020. Covid 19 was at an all-time high. There were many deaths worldwide. The economy had taken a big hit. As an owner operator in the trucking industry I, along with my family and the rest of the world, were struggling.

While I was on this lonely stretch of highway known as *Heavens Highway[1],* rolling along and listening to trucking songs, I started praying to God, asking him what I was going to do. My family and I were in trouble with me out here. I was the major provider for us, and my income was decreasing rapidly.

While praying, God spoke to me and said, *"My son, I am here, and I hear your plea for help. The answer is within you. Search your heart and everything will be okay."* He said, *"You are a truck driver, and you know the struggles that every driver has out here on the road. I give you the inspiration of using your imagination along with your knowledge to write these things down and publish a book so that the whole world can know about the things you encounter daily. You do this and I promise I will take care of the rest. And remember, I am with you always."*

After I prayed and knew that inner peace, the song, "Long White Line" by Sturgill Simpson came on. It was God's way of giving me the start of the book.

I was soon finished with my day's trip, and I found a truck stop to take my 34-hour break. I gathered my things and before I could get out of the truck, God started filling my head with the words that were to be the beginning of this book. I just sat on my bunk in my sleeper with pen

---

[1] So named because of its appearance on an overcast day; the cloud cover causes the road to look as if it ascends into heaven.

in hand and started writing. I learned right then when God tells you to do something, he means right then. Don't wait until it is convenient for you. It has not been easy, and it took a few years, but I now give you *End of the Long White Line.*

This book is fiction, written to show the struggles that we as truck drivers and as service members may face or have faced in our careers. Whether it be starting out or learning along the way. From accidents to experiences along the way. As well as missed occasions such as births, birthdays, marriages, and deaths of loved ones.

I would like to mention that this book does not in any way represent who I am or the life I lead or have led in the past.

To my Christian brethren. This is just a book, not my life as a Christian. I know there will be a few of you who will say otherwise. Please have an open mind while reading this. The Bible tells us not to judge one another. I know there will be some who throw stones. However, I want you all to know I prayed about this even before I wrote a single word. I will also pray for those that do. But I hope this will be a blessing to you.

To the truck drivers. I know there will be many that may not agree with some of the content within and that's okay. I thank you, Truck Driver, for taking the time to read it. I hope it will be a blessing.

To the veterans of Vietnam. I apologize for anything that I have written that may not be true to the events that may have been at the time. I and the rest of America owe you the upmost respect and I salute you.

To the rest. I hope you enjoy reading this book as I have enjoyed writing it. I truly hope that it will be a blessing.

Thank you,
Raymond Edwards

ABOUT THE AUTHOR

In his own words…

Howdy, reader. I hope you enjoyed reading my book. Now, if I could take you on another short trip down memory lane and let me tell you about myself.

I was born in Kennesaw, Georgia, to Barbara (Bobby) and Jimmy (James) Edwards. We lived in Cartersville, Georgia. At the age of 5, we moved to Fairmount, Georgia. I was raised there until I was 16 years old, and then we moved to Smyrna, Georgia. There, I attended Campbell High School. Along with my basic studies, I did 4 yrs in the R.O.T.C Program and held the highest rank as Cadet Commandant.

In 1997, I joined the Army Reserves, and shortly after Basic Training and AIT (Advanced Individual Training) as a Light Wheel Vehicle Mechanic, I volunteered for a deployment to Bosnia and Kosovo.

After returning to the States, I realized I wanted more, so, in 1999, I joined the AGR Program (Active Guard Reserve). I was attached to the 300th Chemical Company (CBRN) in Morgantown, West Virginia. While there, my unit was deployed shortly after 9/11.

In 2005, I met my wife Jaimie Lynn Blake in Morgantown, West Virginia. She was from a small town in Pennsylvania called Holbrook.

After we were married, I chose to go back to the Reserve side of the Army and make a career as a Truck Driver. I got my CDL, and I was now chasing the white line.

After driving for a while, I felt I needed more. I had the opportunity to go back on active duty for several more years with my unit to train and conduct missions as a Search and Rescue Team.

After that, I was deployed again in 2010 to Kuwait. There I got involved in the USO (United Services Organization) and volunteered most of my spare time (over 500 hours). After I returned, we moved to Knoxville, Tennessee, where we have resided for 10 years.

But let me back up a smidgen...

After we moved, I had a unique opportunity to go back to work for the USO in Kuwait, and then on to Afghanistan, and continued my reserve duty. I worked there for just over a year and a half.

After my return home, I took back to driving a big rig and have done so for the last 8 years. In 2018, I was honorably discharged from the Army Reserves. With just over 21 years, and with 14 of those being on Active duty.

All my hard work and dedication did however take a toll on me, and I am sad to say that as of August 2024, I became a Disabled American Veteran. I still love the military and support all who serve. I love my country, my family and big trucks. But most of all, I love my God, and I thank him for saving my soul many years ago, and for keeping me safe and guiding through all of these years.

END OF THE LONG WHITE LINE

is soon to be a major motion picture.

Written by Raymond Edwards and Jaimie Edwards
Screenplay by Christopher Hensel and Teri Lynn Hensel
Produced by Jeb Stuart Productions
Directed by Christopher Hensel

Learn more and get involved at
https://www.jebstuartproductions.com/

"We only use private money. We are always looking for angel investors who would love to join our family. Come get involved in Family Faith Based Films! 774-318-1488"

~ Chris Hensel, Jeb Stuart Productions

Made in the USA
Columbia, SC
25 September 2024